OURS
Blood Ties Series

A.K ROSE
ATLAS ROSE

Copyright © 2022 by A.K Rose

All rights reserved.

No part of this book may be reproduced in any form or by any electronic or mechanical means, including information storage and retrieval systems, without written permission from the author, except for the use of brief quotations in a book review.

*This series would be **nothing** without all my wonderful readers. Those who found me through the power of TikTok and reached out on Instagram.*

You know who you are. I cannot thank you enough for all your wonderful support and dedication, you've seriously made this ride a dream come true.

I hope you're ready for lots more where this came from.

Atlas. xx

Warning

The Bloodties Series is part of the Cosa Nostra, mafia world which contains several interconnected series. The tone is **dark**, involves a number of romantic interests for our female main characters and reader discretion is advised.

More information on the content warnings can be found here.

Please be aware of your own triggers and limitations. This is a Mafia/Gang related world and are not heroes or heroines, they are hungry, ruthless and they do bad things to themselves and to others.

If you're okay with this, please read on. I hope you enjoy this darkly rich, forbidden series. I can't wait to bring you *so much more....*

Listen along to the playlist here on Spotify

Warning

Dive into the dark, dangerous Cosa Nostra Institute World here

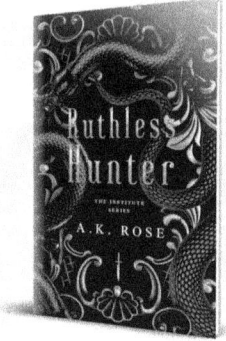

ONE

Tobias

BOOM!

The crack of gunfire ripped through the night. I flinched, lying on the ground, waiting for agony as I stared at the weapon in my father's hands. But it wasn't his gun that had fired. *It was another.* One that glinted in the darkness from between the trees.

Then, through the gloom, someone stepped behind Dad. But he didn't see that. Instead, he stumbled forward, then slowly looked down. Blood bloomed black, sticking his white shirt to his stomach. I couldn't move, pinned by the sight of that stain and my own panic racing through me.

He was going to kill me…He was going to kill me. He was going to—

"I won't go back to them, do you hear me?" Elle spoke as she moved into view. "I won't go back to what they made me do."

Her eyes flared as she looked my way. I waited for the weapon in her hand to follow, for her to take out not one Banks tonight, but two. A panicked glance to my right, at my gun out of reach, and I knew I'd be dead long before I could even move.

But she didn't take aim. Elle fixed her empty stare on me. "Give her up." Her words were barely audible. "She's as good as dead anyway."

Then she slowly lowered her hand and turned, racing back the way she'd come, leaving with nothing more than the snap of a twig in her wake.

Then there was silence...

Smothered by the booming of my heart.

Jesus...

JESUS...

My father released a moan and pressed his hand to his side, trying his best to stanch the flow. I lunged, scrambling to my side, and grabbed that shine of steel. I was past the point of caring for him now as I swung my hand, leveling the sight of my weapon on him. But he didn't move...not even to aim at me.

Do it....

Just fucking DO IT.

My finger trembled as I curled it around the trigger. In my head, I didn't see the few good times we'd ever had. No, I saw him drunk, sitting on the edge of his bed with his shirt buttoned wrong and the stale stench of betrayal wafting in the air while our mother wasted away in the bedroom below.

He'd cheated. *He'd fucking cheated!* I knew that even without Lazarus telling me the truth. That was the moment he changed for me. He wasn't a father. He wasn't even a man...

Then I saw *him*, standing inside the door of our home, his shirt drenched with Nick's blood. He would've let our brother die.

Just let him bleed out like he was *nothing. When he took her from me.*

Ryth.

He'd handed her over.

Gave her to that fucking place.

A wounded sound ripped from the back of my throat. *He'd handed her over to them. Let them—he—let—them...*

I clenched my jaw, willing my finger to curl tighter until I felt that kick. *Doitdoitdoitdoit—*

"Tobias," he called my name, staring at me.

FUCK!

I sucked in hard, panting breaths and lowered my hand. I couldn't do it. Couldn't bring myself to pull the fucking trigger. I was pathetic and useless...hating that I was *his goddamn son.*

His knees trembled, then gave way, sending him crashing to the ground.

I shoved forward, wincing at the agony. But the bullet in my thigh was nothing compared to the stabbing in my chest. One that felt like barbed wire wrapped around my goddamn heart as I grabbed his arm. Squeezing...*squeezing...squeezing.* "Just." I pulled him up against me. "Stay the fuck with me."

"*T!*" Nick roared in the distance. "For Christ's sake. *TOBIAS!*"

I jerked my head toward the sound. Desperation took control, forcing me to call out. *"Over here!"*

Nick's steps were thunderous as he rushed from the trees and relief at the sight of him hit me like a blow. My breath escaped, deflating me in an instant.

I needed him...more than I'd ever realized before.

And from the panic shimmering in Nick's eyes, I realized he needed me just as much. He glanced at the pale-haired guard dead on the ground not far from us, then turned back to me. Sadness. That's all I saw, sadness and fucking regret. I looked away.

"She's gone," Dad groaned. "I'm sorry, Ryth's gone."

I forced the words through clenched teeth. "Like hell she is."

Nick grabbed Dad, fisting his shirt and wrenched him close. "What the fuck do you mean, she's gone?"

I wasn't going to lose her, not again—*not now—not ever*.

"*I'm s-sorry,*" Dad slurred.

"Save your fucking sorry," I snapped as the sound of baying dogs came.

Nick glanced my way, then shoved dad backwards. "We have to get out of here."

"No." That nauseating agony came alive through my thigh as I stumbled for the trees. "Not without her."

"*T!*" Nick barked, stopping me. "You stay here and you're fucking dead, you understand that?"

I stared at that darkness, listening to the sound of their dogs.

"How the fuck can you help her then?"

"She's gone," Dad mumbled. "It's no use—"

"*Shut the fuck up, Dad!*" my brother warned. "Or so help me God, I'll leave you here to die."

Leave him...but not her...

I turned to Nick and inhaled hard. Cold air carved all the way through my chest. I couldn't leave...*not without—*

"Please, T," he pleaded, his eyes glistening in the night. "I can't lose you too."

It was those words that shattered my resolve. I winced, swallowing a moan of agony, and limped back. "Move." I shoved our father forward.

But he stumbled, then fell, leaving Nick to grab him at the last second.

"Help me," my brother demanded, trying to hold his weight.

He was going to kill me...he was going to... "Fuck," I growled, and slid my arm around his other side.

Hate burned inside me as we stumbled along the dugout and back through the trees. Each step we took was one more away from her. But I couldn't do anything about that now. Stem the bleeding. Patch the wound. Get more guns, then come back. I clung to that as we stumbled for the fenceline, finding a section that'd been cut.

"Can you hold him here while I get the car?" Nick yanked, opening the gap as wide as he could.

I heaved dad forward. But our father's movements were weak at best. He collapsed against the ground, his face paling in the moonlight as I shoved him through the gap in the fence to the other side. "You better hurry."

"I will," Nick said, and was gone in an instant, limping as he hurried back toward the crash site and the old Charger that sat sideways in the middle of the road, next to the dark sedan that had crashed into us.

"I'm sorry," my father whispered.

Fuck. You.

"Son."

Son?

I jerked my gaze to the piece of shit, grabbed him by the shirt, and slammed him back against the fence. "Son?" I spat. "*You want to call me that now?*" I stared at him like the stranger he was. "You came to fucking kill me."

His eyes widened. There was a tiny shake of his head, but it was all lies. Spineless...cowardly lies.

You were going to fucking kill me! My heart screamed. The words resounded in my head, until it was swallowed by the icy truth. *He didn't care...he'd never cared, not about me, or about Mom. Or about anyone but himself.*

In the end, I couldn't even look at him. I turned away, watching my brother instead. "Save your fucking sorry for someone who gives a shit."

Nick made it to the car and climbed in.

"Tobias."

I winced at the rasp in my father's voice. I didn't want to listen to his words...didn't want to hear the rasps in his breaths. I closed my eyes, didn't want to see the desperation in his stare. No more...no...goddamn more. But I was trapped in his torture, one where I wanted to let my father go, and at the same time cling tight to the painfully thin thread that still tied us together.

It was only blood that tethered me to this man.

Because it sure as hell wasn't fucking love.

I clenched my fist, keeping my voice low. "Say one more fucking word and I'll leave you to bleed out on your own."

I took a step, desperately wanting to just keep going, to leave my father and his betrayal behind. The Charger squealed as Nick started the engine and nosed the busted muscle car around the debris, heading toward us. He pulled up in front and climbed out, cutting through the headlights as he rounded the front.

Only then did I turn around. I grabbed our father as he looked up at me with those pathetic fucking eyes. "Move," I growled, heaving him to stand.

Nick yanked open the back door, and somehow, we got him inside, leaving him to fall against the seat while we shoved his feet in and slammed the door.

Headlights cut through the trees on the other side of the fence. I hated leaving her…hated leaving them both. But we didn't have a choice. *Goddamn you, Caleb…*

Still, it felt like a knife to my chest as I yanked open the front passenger door and climbed in while Nick slipped behind the wheel.

"Nick," our father whispered from the back seat. "Thank you."

My brother jerked a savage glare over his shoulder and snarled, "Save it."

He met my gaze as he turned back. We both knew our father didn't deserve it, and that sometime in the next few hours he was going to die. The Charger lunged forward as Nick punched the accelerator, heading us down the darkened road that ran alongside the compound then finally back toward the city.

Pain dug in my leg like a damn knife, leaving me to clench my fists and close my eyes. Flashes descended. Fear. Failure. The moment that pale-haired bastard had come for me.

She'll scream, his words resurfaced. *But I like it when she does that.*

I turned my head toward the window, keeping my eyes closed.

But I like it when she does that...

I like it when...

I like it...

"T?" Nick called.

I licked my arid lips. "I'm okay."

I tried to succumb to the darkness, but it wasn't the vacuum of nothingness that waited—*it was Ryth.* The last kiss...the last touch...the last time I'd held her. My heart thundered in kind, beating the memory home until she was all I thought about.

Who the fuck was I kidding?

She was all I *ever* thought about.

Getting her. Keeping her. *Craving her.*

The Charger slowed, then turned before Nick spoke. "We're here."

I opened my eyes, feeling like I'd been down forever, then I blinked and shoved my feet against the floor, driving myself upwards. A look over my shoulder, and I saw the shallow rise and fall of our father's chest. He was still alive. I held on to that, not because I gave a fucking shit about his life. No. I cared about hers.

Nick pulled the Charger into the driveway and killed the engine before climbing out. I followed, rounding the car to get to our father from the other side. He was weaker, barely able to hold his own weight. We carried him up the stairs of the Rossi safehouse and back inside.

"I've got him." I gripped the old man's shoulders, taking his weight. "Call Freddy, he'll know what to do."

Nick just gave a nod and slipped his arm away, dug into his pocket for his phone instead, and lifted it to his ear.

"Tobias..." Dad's whisper was hoarse, drawing me away as Nick started to speak.

But I didn't answer, just fixed my focus on Nick as he stepped closer to the window. My knees trembled as I gripped our father. I couldn't hold him, not all his weight, and I buckled. We both hit the sink and slid down the cupboard, hitting the floor.

Nick glanced our way as he spoke, then hung up the call.

"I called." He came toward us. "He said Laz is at some island off Africa. He's dealing with his own stuff, but he knows a guy who knows a guy."

He looked at dad. "So just hang on for a little longer, okay?"

"You *will* hang on," I warned, turning my gaze to his. Because you need to tell us how to get her out of there."

Our father licked bloodless lips and closed his eyes. "She's in there now. Only a dead man can get her free."

The last words were barely audible, but I still heard them. "What the fuck do you mean, a dead man?"

Silence.

"Dad!" Nick knelt and pulled him up by his shirt. "What the fuck do you mean, a dead man?"

"Dead man..." Dad whispered, and slowly opened his eyes.

"What *fucking dead man?*" I roared, staring into my father's eyes. After all he'd done...*after all he'd done to me?* "No." I forced the word through clenched teeth and drew back my fist.

"T!" Nick roared.

But he didn't know...

He didn't *really* know...

The true extent of what this man was.

TWO

Caleb

You were never meant to fall for her...

My mind was stuck on those words. I stared at the door, listening to the heavy thud of boots as they echoed, coming closer. Fear found me, but it wasn't for me. I tightened my hold on her hand, drawing her behind me. "Stay close, princess."

Ryth pressed against my side as the sound of steps came closer, growing in crescendo until they were deafening. I clenched my fists and shifted my stance, ready to start swinging the moment the door opened.

But it never did.

The sound grew, then passed as the guards raced along the hallway and past the room they kept us in.

"Tobias," she whispered my brother's name. "It's him, I know it is."

She thought he was coming for us.

But she was wrong.

Her fingers slipped between mine as The Priest's sick smile rose in my head. *I don't believe you.* My own desperate voice rose. *Tobias isn't dead...he can't be...do you hear me?* I shook my head. "No."

"No, what?"

I closed my eyes. She didn't know, and there was no way I was going to tell her. *I couldn't tell her.*

Nick's face rose to fill my mind. I could see it now, him kneeling on the ground next to our brother's body as he opened fire...he'd kill everyone he could—and probably been killed himself in the process.

Because of me.

I let her go and stumbled forward, bracing my hand on the wall.

I should never have gone to that goddamn club...should never have tried to kill Killion.

"Caleb?"

I didn't turn my head, I couldn't look at her. Not yet.

"What's wrong?"

I shook my head as the snap of a lock sounded, drawing my gaze to the door. A guard stepped inside, scanned the room, and settled his focus on me. I said nothing, waiting for him to move. The Priest followed, that cocky grin on his split lip not as evident now that he knew he couldn't kill me. He glanced at Ryth, standing behind me. "You're being moved."

I stepped in front of her. "Why?"

"Why is no concern of yours." The Priest's jaw tightened as he narrowed that stare on me. "You won't cause a problem, do you understand?" There was a scowl before he looked at Ryth once more. "She seems calm, Caleb. A little *too calm*." One brow rose as he turned to me. "You still haven't told her, have you?"

I shook my head. "No," I growled. "I won't...because it's a lie."

There was that smirk again, that knowing, *fucking* smirk. "Is it?"

Is it?

"Told me what?" she asked.

A twitch came at the corner of my eye. I fixed my stare on that piece of shit who stood in front of us dressed in a black full shirt and white clerical collar. He was no fucking priest. And no fucking man, for that matter...*he was the goddamn devil. A devil who had all the fucking cards.*

"Denial won't change the truth, Caleb," he murmured. "As a lawyer, you know that better than most."

"Tell me what, Caleb?"

I opened my mouth to speak, to say the words that hung heavy in my heart. The words *he* wanted me to say.

But I couldn't do it...

"I can tell her, if you prefer?" the devil murmured.

"You know, that has gotta hurt." My voice was husky as I stared at his busted-up face. "I bet it does. I bet it hurts like an absolute bitch."

His gaze hardened to a cruel, terrifying glint.

"Tell me what?" Ryth demanded.

Without missing a beat, he spoke. "Your stepbrother is dead." He watched her like a hawk. "Yes, I'm afraid Tobias won't be coming to rescue you, Ryth. No. He won't be coming at all."

Everything moved in slow motion. My knees trembled, but I forced myself to turn and face her. "Ryth," I whispered, my focus on every glint...and every twitch.

"No." She shook her head. *"NO."*

Rage burned, but I swallowed it. "It's going to be okay." I lifted my hand to her face.

But she pulled away, and that hurt more than anything. "No. *Don't you touch me!* That's not true...*that's NOT TRUE. Do you hear me?*" she demanded, her eyes growing wide. "No. Just, no."

"Ryth..."

There was a tremble of her lips as her voice thickened. "No, Caleb," she whispered and tears shimmered in her eyes. She looked at the bastards watching us, and then just...*cracked*.

I lunged as her knees gave way, catching her in time. Her pain was a shotgun blast to my chest as I pulled her against me. Cold, hard rage followed, the kind that'd made me a murderer. But this wasn't about my anger. It was about her.

"We'll get through this..." I grasped her chin and turned her gaze to mine. "You hear me? We *will* get through this."

It didn't matter that she'd only been in our lives mere months. Because it felt like *forever...*

Forever that she'd been in our hearts.

And forever that we'd been in hers.

Tears slipped from her eyes as she turned her head. She saw them and, in an instant...her anguish unleashed. *"You BASTARDS!"* She tore from my arms and lunged across the room.

But The Priest and the guard were already striding out of the room. She hit the door as it closed, her fists slamming against the tempered glass panel. "I'll *kill you!*" she screamed at them. *"Do you hear me? I'LL FUCKING KILL YOU!"*

Her screams resounded as she slammed her fists against the door. *"I'll fucking kill you! I'll kill you...I'll fucking kill you all..."* She stopped beating her fists against the door, and slumped against it instead. *"I'll fucking find you..."*

Brutal, rasping gasps consumed her.

I closed the distance, grabbing her and pulling her into my arms.

"I'll kill them, Caleb," she whimpered without even looking at me.

"I know, princess." I stared through the glass at the empty hall. "I know."

THREE

Nick

Thump!

T unleashed, driving his fist into the side of Dad's face. One look at my brother and I knew there was no stopping him, not anymore. He was a mask of malevolence. A weapon of fists and fury. *No.* He was a fucking *product*. And what they'd created when they gave Ryth to us.

My breath stilled, a burden in my chest. *Our sister...*

"You *will* fucking tell us how to get her out of there!" he screamed. "You hear me? *You WILL fucking tell us!*"

My brother was a man possessed. Dad's head snapped to the side with the blow. T struck again, his time hitting him in the mouth. The result was instant. His lip split open and blood welled down his chin.

"T," I rasped as dad's head lolled backwards.

"You *will* tell me what I want to know!" Tobias roared, wrenching our father forward. *"You will fucking tell me!"*

Dad's eyes fluttered, then opened. He stared at my brother as though he was a stranger. "You..." he whispered, his eyes falling closed again. "Were never meant to fall...*for her.*"

T froze with the words, one hand fisted in Dad's bloody shirt and the other cocked in the air. "What the fuck did you say?"

Silence.

"What the...fuck did you SAY?" my brother raged.

I took a step, drawn by the same savage need. "Tell us what we want to know."

Dad's eyes opened, and for a split second, I saw him, the man I'd loved. The man I'd fucking *defended* over and over and over again. But there was no more defending, not him...or us.

Thugs.

Murderers.

Brothers...

I didn't blame T for shooting him...right now, I wanted to do the same.

"Tell us how to get her out," I demanded.

Dad gave a small chuff, that split on his lip stretching wide. "There is no *out*. Doesn't matter...*she's not worth it.*"

"Worth it?" Tobias' voice was chilling. *'Worth it?"* He drove his fist into our father's face once more. *Crunch.* "WORTH IT! She is WORTH EVERYTHING!"

Dad's head snapped backwards. But I could see the end...saw it all in the way his head snapped backwards...and the glazed film on his eyes.

Crack!

"She's fucking WORTH IT!" *Crack!* T was an animal. *"She's fucking worth it!"* He never stopped, never flinched, just dived into that fucking rage with bloody fists and a savage hunger for blood...

No.

Not blood.

Our sister.

"Dead man..." My father's last words were a hiss.

Still, Tobias wrenched him forward. *"What fucking dead man? Dad...DAD!"*

But he couldn't answer, because he was already gone.

"T." My voice was husky as I stared at his white knuckles smeared with blood. *"T!"*

My brother's gaze was fixed on that empty stare. *"Answer me. What fucking dead man?"* he roared, as though he could will him back to life by his desperation alone.

Maybe T should've thought of that before he pulled the trigger and ended our father's fucking life?

Christ, this was a mess.

But he couldn't...no one could, and outside, the throb of a V8 engine drew my attention.

I pushed up from the floor and headed for the window, pushing the curtain aside as an expensive black Range Rover pulled into the driveway behind the dented Charger. "T," I called, wary.

But the guy didn't climb out and start firing. No, he reached across to the passenger seat instead, and dragged a big bag of some kind with him as he climbed out. The driver's door closed with a thud as he scanned the front of the warehouse, catching the movement as I let the curtain go.

The thud of his boots resounded as I opened the front door and stepped out. He scanned me up and down. "You Nick?"

Freddy's man...

That's who this was.

I exhaled hard and nodded. "Yeah."

He glanced at the open door beside me. "You gonna let me in, or do I have to patch up whoever has been shot out here?"

Shot...shot...he's not. I swallowed hard, unable to move for a second...

And he saw. A scowl came before he softened his tone. "You want to let me in, buddy?"

I scanned the street and stepped aside. "He's inside."

The guy moved like a fighter, thick shoulders bunching as he hauled the bag with him and stepped inside. He didn't even flinch at the body lying in the kitchen. I locked the front door and followed, watching him as he neared Tobias, who still had dad's shirt clenched in his fist.

"He didn't tell us who," my brother said as he slowly lifted his gaze. "He didn't tell us who."

"You want me to have a look?"

Care. Compassion. The kind of carefulness that only came with years of practice echoed from the guy as he reached for my brother's hands and gently pulled them away. "Let me look."

Tobias did, watching with a shell-shocked stare as the guy did his best. He pressed two fingers to my father's neck and waited.

I could've told him it was useless. But what was the fucking point?

What was the point of anything?

They had our sister.

And now our brother.

"I'm sorry." Freddy's guy dropped his hand and shook his head. "He's gone."

Tobias slumped to the floor, his hands resting on the top of his drawn-up knees as he stared at me blankly. "What the fuck do we do now?"

He looked at me as though he hadn't thought it'd come to this. What did he think was going to happen when he took aim and squeezed the trigger?

"There's no easy answer," Freddy's guy answered. "What I can tell you is, he's gone, so I guess you need to think about family."

Tobias glanced his way, frowned, and focused as though he finally realized someone else was here. He glanced at our father's body. "Not about him. About *her*...our stepsister."

"Stepsister?" The guy glanced my way, confused.

But it wasn't just confusion, was it? He was...wary. "They have your stepsister?"

They?

Tobias stared at the guy. "What the fuck do you know?" My brother pushed upward, climbing to his feet. His eyes darkening to that terrifying glint. *"Who the fuck are you, anyway?"*

"DeLuca," he answered. But it wasn't out of fear. He was concerned, but not about us. "Who has your stepsister?"

"The Order," I answered, earning a glare from T. One I met with my own. "Freddy sent him, right? So that means we can trust him."

Trust him to patch a wound maybe, but trust him not to go to the cops? I stared at T. The last thing I wanted was my brother charged with patricide. My heart raced and my mouth went dry. In my head, I saw them when I raced through the trees…T with his gun in his hand and our father bleeding in his arms.

"Trust?" T glared, snapping me back out of my head. "Hasn't the last twenty-four fucking hours told you anything, brother? We can't fucking trust him. We can't fucking trust anyone." He glared at Dad. "Not even blood."

"I'm not with The Order." DeLuca shoved up from the floor.

"Yeah?" T was pissed now, more than he was before. "Who do you work for?"

"Sacred Heart Hospital."

My brother grew furious, stepping closer to the guy. "I said, *who the fuck do you work for?*"

But the guy never backed down. Instead, he withstood my brother's wrath, bloody knuckles and all. *"I work* for Sacred Heart and *no one else.* I'm sorry about your father and your stepsister. I have one of those of my own, so I know how it feels. You want to protect them…you'll do *anything* to protect them, but you can't. Not against men who want her."

He wasn't talking about Ryth here…he was talking about himself.

"Oh yeah?" Tobias was full of rage now.

"She's in her own trouble," DeLuca answered, and looked away. "Which is why I asked."

Those words stopped T cold. He scowled, staring at this *guy who knows a guy in the Mafia*.

I took a step closer. "In trouble how?"

He looked like he was going to answer before he froze, scowled, and looked away. "Not with The Order." He reached into his pocket and pulled out a business card, handing it to me. "Call me if you need anything. Just not the Rossis, okay? I don't need any more problems where they're concerned."

"Problems?" Tobias looked like he was going to push him for answers. "What kind of—"

But then DeLuca looked at Dad. "I can take care of him, if you want...until you're ready."

Take care of him...

What did that mean? Hold the body for ransom while he threatened to go to the cops? Or worse. *I know a guy who knows a guy*, those were Freddy's words. What guy did he know? I needed to find out. I needed...*to protect my family*.

"And what if we're never ready?" My voice was detached as I stared at the guy.

The doctor met my gaze. "Then I can take care of that too."

Who the hell was this guy? He sure as hell wasn't just a goddamn doctor, that was for sure. He had connections, and from the way he flinched when I spoke about Ryth, they were the wrong type of connections. "Okay." I looked at the card, *Lucas DeLuca, Emergency Medicine, Sacred Heart Hospital*. "You can take him."

T stared at me as though I'd grown a second head. I knew what he was thinking, *we can't trust anyone*.

But look where that had gotten us.

If we'd trusted someone when this shit was going down, then maybe we might've had a chance. What chance did we have now?

"Want to give me a hand getting your father into the car?" DeLuca asked Tobias.

T looked like he was about to explode. But then he nodded and without a word, went to work. Tobias grabbed dad under the arms while DeLuca grabbed his feet. They heaved him up. I stepped behind, grabbed the straps of DeLuca's medical bag, and lifted, grunting with the weight. No wonder the guy was fit.

They struggled, shuffling more than walking as I moved ahead, scanning outside the warehouse before I motioned them forward. They had dad down the stairs and stepped sideways toward the back of the Rover. "Want to grab my keys and hit the button for the back door, Nick?" DeLuca winced.

I strode closer, shoved my hand in the pocket he aimed my way, and pressed the button, watching the doors open automatically. Both grunted as they dropped Dad onto a dark tarpaulin with a *thud*.

Hard breaths filled the air. DeLuca brushed his hands against his black jeans and reached for the keys. "Thanks." He glanced at Tobias, who surprisingly didn't look like he wanted to rip the doc's head off anymore. The guy didn't shy away, not from anger...or death.

I almost liked him, if I could trust him, that was. I glanced at the card in my hand.

"I'll be waiting to hear from you," he said, looking my way.

I gave a nod as the doctor climbed into the car and started the engine. We said nothing as he backed out of the driveway and onto the street. Red lights flared bright in the night as the Rover braked, then pulled away...leaving us to stare as it disappeared.

"What the fuck do we do now?" Tobias asked.

"I don't know," I answered, because we'd run out of options... and people to trust. "I just don't know."

FOUR

Ryth

I sat against the wall, staring blankly into nothing. Not thinking. Not feeling. Not *existing*. There was a grating *gnashing* sound which filled my ears, and it took me a while to realize it was me. My jaw ached from the violence of the shudders, cold clung tight. Even under Caleb's thin shirt I was frozen...except for my throat. No, that burned, like I'd swallowed shards of molten glass.

But it wasn't glass, that felt like fire. It was...it was...knowing Tobias was dead...*and it was all my fault.*

All my fault. The words resounded and I couldn't stop them.

All my fault.

All my fault.

I closed my eyes.

All my—

"Ryth," Caleb pleaded, his voice just as husky and raw as mine. "Say something."

He rubbed his hands along my arms, trying his best to draw me back. But I couldn't come back. I was trapped here, locked in Hell, where I wanted to scream and keep screaming and until I could kill the men who'd taken Tobias from me.

Your stepbrother is dead.

Your stepbrother...is dead.

Your stepbrother—

The snap of a lock came before Caleb's hand clenched around mine. But I didn't care. They could bring in anyone they wanted. It didn't matter what they did to me. They couldn't hurt me anymore than they already had.

"Out." The sharp bark came.

Caleb rose in front of me. His raw words pushed into the ache. "Where are you taking us?"

He tried to protect me, tried to comfort me. It should be *me* comforting *him*. After all, it was *his* brother.

Little mouse...

Tobias's voice filled me. I inhaled, reveling in the ache that followed.

Fight.

I flinched with the word and shook my head. I couldn't fight. I was done with *fighting*. Why bother? I only ended up here anyway. In the place my mom had sent me.

"Now," the guard demanded.

"Ryth," Caleb croaked as his fingers brushed my cheek. "We have to go." I opened my eyes, finding that tortured stare. "We have to go, princess."

I slowly shook my head. "I can't...you go. Just go, Caleb."

Anger sliced through the pain. "Like hell I will."

He leaned forward, grabbed me under the arms and heaved me from the floor, pulling me against his bare chest and lifted. I wound my arms around his shoulders and buried my face in his neck, sinking into the heat of his body. His muscles corded. His breath was a rush as he held me tight.

Your stepbrother is dead...

Your stepbrother is...dead.

I closed my eyes under the glare of the hallway lights and wound my legs tightly around him as he carried me from that room. The heavy thud of boots echoed before the click and *thud* of the automatic doors. Locked away. Just like I was before, only this time I didn't have Vivienne.

I thought about her as we turned a corner and headed deeper into this pit of vipers. Did they find her? Did they drag her back to this place? Or was she free?

Free...free of what? There were more versions of this Hell out there. I was sure of that.

"Stop," the guard growled.

I opened my eyes and glanced along the hallway to the other closed doors. But this wing didn't look familiar. I tried to think, but my thoughts were slow and murky, hidden somewhere under the heavy throb at the base of my skull. The guard opened the door and stepped aside, motioning for us to enter a room.

Caleb stepped inside, scanning the room without so much as a snarl of anger. His hold tightened under my ass, drawing me harder against him. I hadn't forgotten that he was living on borrowed time, that any moment he'd be taken from me, just like Tobias.

Right now, we had a better chance at surviving if we complied. The door closed with a *bang* behind us. We both flinched and I lowered my feet to the floor.

"There's warm clothes here." Caleb pulled away, leaving me with that chattering sound in my ears. He crossed the room, sinking into the gloom, and returned. The red light blinked from the corner of the ceiling. I knew without a doubt they were watching our every move.

"I'll take care of you." Caleb reassured as he came back to me. He reached up, grasped his shirt and pushed it off my shoulders. I caught the wince as he stared at the red negligee. The one Killion had ripped from me before he...*before he...*

My teeth gnashed harder.

"Easy now," Caleb urged, moving to stand in front of me.

His dark eyes bored into mine. He knew what he was doing, shielding me with his body as he reached up and slipped the straps of my negligee down. "You shouldn't have to wear this. *None of you* should have to wear this."

He knew...

He knew.

I stared into that dark abyss and saw the truth. Of course he knew. *How many?* I wanted to ask the question. *How many women wearing white, black, and red had he seen?*

But I couldn't hear the truth. The blow of that would be too brutal.

So I let him slide the straps down and move close, covering me with his body instead as he slipped my hands into the fleece sweatshirt and pulled it down.

I found that blinking red light again as he sank to his knees, pushing the negligee low. Cold moved between my thighs as satin and lace fell around my feet until Caleb dropped his head forward, resting it on my stomach. His breath hitched as desperation flowed out of him. The sound of that was more wounding than anything they'd ever done to me. I lifted my hand and ran my fingers through his hair.

The touch so tender...

And more powerful than a bullet.

His hands slid along the backs of my thighs to grip my ass. The kiss was tender on my stomach, then a brush of his lips on my abdomen...electricity coursed through me as he looked down.

"Christ, you feel good," he murmured, lowering his head to kiss the top of my mound, then he stopped. His brow furrowed before he pulled away. I winced at the brush of his hand on my hip. "Does this hurt?" He lifted his gaze.

The muscles of his jaw flexed as I nodded.

He swallowed and turned back, sliding his hand over my thigh. As though he marked me by his touch alone. *Mine...*it said. *Mine.*

He'd beat that message into Killion by his fists alone. The image of that rose as he found every bruise and every scrape. He leaned in and brushed his lips against my tender flesh. I closed my eyes as he whispered. "Just let me take care of you." And brushed the inside of my thigh.

"Caleb," I whispered, my throat blazing to life.

"Just give me this, princess." He gripped the backs of my knees and pulled me against him. I buckled, but he caught my fall, lowering me to the floor.

He cupped the back of my head and kissed me. I closed my eyes, engulfed by the warmth of his mouth. He was hungry. So goddamn hungry, and I was an empty well he could fill by his mouth alone. My ass hit the cold, hard floor before he pushed me back.

That's how it was with Caleb. Dark. Desperate. Consuming, until there was nothing else but him.

He broke the kiss, sliding his hands over the warm fleece of the gray sweatshirt until he pushed underneath the fabric. "I'll take care of you," he whispered. "Just let me...give you what you need."

He lowered his head, pressing his face against my breasts. I melted at the brush of his fingers over my nipples, my body taking over from my mind. *Yes*...I closed my eyes as his hands travelled down, skimming over my thighs until he stroked my core.

"Watch me, princess. Watch us. The way I sink into you. The way I work your body."

He pulled me back from the emptiness, making me look down. In the gloom, my focus sharpened, finding his fingers as he slid them over my clit.

"I'll take you away from here..." he promised. "The only way I know how."

I trembled with the intensity of his words, watching as he slowly sank his fingers inside me.

"Jesus," he panted, biting his lower lip. "Christ, you're a good girl. Look at how good you are."

Everything melted away with the touch of his hand. There was no room, no blinking red light. There was just this. Just us. I lifted my hips as he slowly thrust, stoking that spark to life. His fingers thrust, glistening in the faint light before he pulled them free, lifted his fingers to his mouth, and sucked.

"That's the way, little sister," he panted, sliding his fingers back inside me. "Give me this."

I clutched hold of his shoulders and rode his touch as Caleb slid his finger along my slit and lowered his head, kissing me.

"I want to eat you out," he murmured. "Will you let me, princess?"

"*Yes,*" I panted. "*Yes...*"

He held my stare and lowered his mouth to my core, licking, probing. Making me feel things I shouldn't feel, not with the weight in my chest. Tobias's face rose as my desire grew. It was that same hard stare I saw in Caleb's. That savage, ravenous need. The same one that made him hate me...until we were consumed by his rage.

I moaned and dropped my hand to the back of Caleb's head, opening my thighs wider.

"That's it." Caleb sucked my pussy, making me writhe. "That's my good fucking girl."

I bloomed with the praise and the hunger swept me away. All I cared about in that moment was his mouth, his fingers, his cock...I wanted to be empty, to be used. I wanted to be used by him. "Caleb..."

"Let yourself go, Ryth." He gripped my ass and sucked before adding his fingers. "You're doing so well...so fucking well."

His praise was wrong...

But fuck, it felt right.

I rocked my body with his thrusts, watching as his fingers disappeared inside me, chased by the warmth of his tongue. "So fucking well."

My body clenched with his words. "Fuck me," I moaned. "Please, I need you to."

I drove his head hard against my core as lightning ripped through my pussy...and I came, *hard*. He licked and sucked, then lifted his head. In the gloom, the muscles of his throat worked as he swallowed. But there was that hard glint in his eyes. "You're fucking mine, you understand that? *You're...mine.* You go into the darkness, I'm right there with you. There's no leaving me, Ryth. Not now, *not ever*...in this life, or the next."

I sucked in hard breaths and felt those words.

He was scared.

More scared now than he'd ever been.

He swiped the back of his hand across his mouth and reached behind him. "Lift your foot, little sister," he urged, turning back with a pair of gray sweatpants. He worked carefully, slowly, more contented now. More...*here*. I was too. I was more here than I had been.

He slid my feet through the openings and pulled the pants higher. "Lift."

I pushed trembling hands against the floor, holding myself higher as he slid the waistband over my ass and around my hips, settling at my waist.

"Your shirt," I whispered, staring at his chest.

He shook his head. "Don't worry about me." Then he pushed up from the floor and walked over to a hospital table in the corner of the room. The crack of a bottle seal sounded as he came back and knelt beside me. "I need you to drink."

The burn...the ache...it was all I felt.

"For me." He pushed the bottle toward me.

I had no choice but to take it.

"Because I cannot lose you too."

I swallowed the cold water, letting it run down the back of my throat until I coughed.

"Easy." He rubbed my back and I was lost to the movement. "More," he urged.

I swallowed again and pushed the bottle away. "Now you."

If this was how I got through to him, then I would. He fixed that self-destructive stare on me. I knew the look well...but this was the only way we were going to survive...*together*. "You don't drink, I don't drink."

He scowled, then reached up, took the bottle, and lifted it to his lips.

That's it...drink.

He finished the bottle before rising and making his way across the room. My gaze was dragged back to that blinking red light in the corner of the ceiling before the sharp crinkle of plastic drew my focus.

Caleb strode back with a sandwich in his hand, then he held half out to me. "Now eat."

My stomach clenched as panic and acid rose in the back of my throat. "No." I shook my head and met his gaze. "No. Not the food." Memories assaulted me from the first time they'd dragged me here. "You can't trust the food."

He just lifted the sandwich to his mouth and took a bite. His jaw worked as he chewed and swallowed, waiting...

You can't trust the food...

FIVE

Caleb

She slept, eventually. Curled in the corner, refusing the bed, just like I knew she would. Her breaths were steady and deep. But her body betrayed her, twitching and jerking, fighting demons in her sleep. I stared at her clenched fists until my eyes burned. But I didn't dare close them...not in this place. Demons didn't just wait for us in our slumber...they waited here, as well.

Somewhere in the hallway the faint snap of a lock sounded.

"No," a woman pleaded, her words faint. *"No, I won't go...I won't—"*

Then there was nothing. I waited, waited so fucking long...

But there was just silence.

Christ, this fucking place.

Red...

Red coated my world. Red lace at my feet. Red that stained these hands. I flexed my fingers, still feeling the pulsing of her pussy. I'd tried to draw her back from the darkness, tried so fucking hard to keep her safe. Look where that had gotten us. I wanted to never see red on her again. I looked her way, desperate to lose myself in those gray-blue eyes until I stopped existing. Maybe then, I might touch perfection.

Because she was...*pure perfection.*

"Tobias," she called my brother's name. "No..."

I winced at the sound and looked away, at the half-eaten sandwich discarded on the floor at her feet. No matter how hard I'd tried, she refused to eat.

"Don't go..." she whispered.

I swallowed that sting and turned away. Still, it stayed with me, as well as the last thing Nick ever said...*fix it. Fix it or you'll lose her forever.*

I'd tried to fix it, and gotten my brother killed. I closed my eyes and inched toward that black abyss waiting for me. I was a dead man anyway, one living on borrowed fucking time. I was under no illusion about that. As soon as they found a workaround for whatever Jack Castlemaine had on them, I'd meet the same fate. Only this time, there'd be no quick end. No, the fucking Priest would see to that. They'd take their time, drag it out...make an example of me, if only to break Ryth. They'd break her and there wouldn't be a goddamn thing I could do to stop it.

I hung my head.

"Don't worry, T," I whispered. "I'll be joining you soon, brother."

My hands shook as fear wormed its way in deep.

"Caleb."

I jerked my gaze her way. "Yeah?"

"I can't feel my foot." She shifted her gaze from my trembling hands and clutched her leg.

I moved in front of her and grabbed her calf. "You've had cramps all night."

She was tight, her muscles quivering as I kneaded until she closed her eyes. "Oh, that's it." She flinched, that crease in her forehead growing deeper. "Right there."

It didn't matter how deep that abyss went for me. This was what I focused on. Caring for her, protecting her, as best I could. I worked her muscles until they slowly eased. She was so small under the fleece, too fucking small. But still she didn't eat.

The sound of heavy steps drew my gaze to the door. My gut clenched and panic rose as the lock snapped and the door opened. Two women dressed in black stepped in. I scanned the lace they wore and their clasped hands as I pushed to stand.

Two guards followed. That was bad enough...until the bastard they called The Teacher followed. He scanned the room, that stony gaze settling on Ryth. "Ms. Castlemaine. It's nice to have you back with us."

Ryth pushed to stand beside me. "Fuck you."

She glanced at the women as the last guard through locked the door behind him.

"Seeing as our normal clients are unable to visit us, you will assist us in their training," The Teacher said carefully. "After all, it was due to the disruption you caused."

"What?' The color drained from Ryth's face.

"No." My pulse raced as I moved in front of her, glaring at the guards. "You heard what her father said. She's not to be trained."

"No." The Teacher shifted that empty stare my way. "*She* won't be trained at all. But you *will* assist us in *their* training."

Sonofabitch...

"After all, you've already given us a taste of what we want, haven't you?" He looked at the CCTV camera in the corner of the room.

I clenched my fists. Rage burned deep. The piece of shit had been watching. Even with my back to them to shield her, they'd watched it all. I bet they fucking enjoyed it too.

"Amber," The Teacher directed. "Get on your knees for Mr. Banks."

Blood rushed from my face, leaving me cold and empty.

"No." Ryth's hand found mine, her tone dangerous. "Take a fucking step and I'll kill you."

The Teacher smirked. But he said nothing, just reached into his pocket and pulled out an image before turning and sticking it to the wall behind them. It took me a second to realize what the image was...then I did.

"You bastard." Ryth lunged. I moved fast, catching her before she did any damage. *"You were watching us?"*

The Teacher just held her stare. "Always."

Always...

I stared at the image on the wall, remembering that night like it was yesterday. It was right after our parents were married, when all four of us were left alone in the gardens outside the reception...and Nick was on his knees.

"You watched us." I repeated her words. "How *fucking* long?"

"From the very first night."

The very first night...the breath was snatched from my chest. This wasn't just a spur of the moment reaction to what we'd done with Ryth, was it? *No...this was planned from the very beginning.* From the beginning.

From the beginning!

Still, I couldn't stop staring at the image taped to the wall. It meant something and more than the realization this shit ran deeper than a woman and her daughter turning up on our doorstep in the middle of the night with nothing more than a garbage bag for their clothes.

No, this image said *more...*

My gut clenched as T's face rose in my head. T was dead...and Nick...Nick was...

"You have him, don't you?" I met his stare, finding that fucking glint shimmering a little brighter.

"No..." Ryth whimpered.

I wanted to reach for her hand, but I couldn't move. I was frozen by the curl of those hard lips. My gut dropped, falling hard.

"Where is he?" I forced out the words.

Still, he said nothing. I took a step closer and the guard moved with me, stepping in front and shaking his head. But I didn't care about him. *"I said, where the fuck is he?"*

"Amber." The Teacher held my stare. *"On. Your. Knees."*

Movement came in the corner of my eye as one of the women stepped closer and stopped in front of me, then slowly sank to the floor. But this wasn't about their training, was it? They already knew what to do with their mouths, and their hands, and their pussies.

No, this was about training *me.*

I didn't flinch, didn't move, as Amber reached for the buckle of my pants. I saw myself in this woman. I was made to perform, jerked and manipulated by men like this.

Crawl.

Killion's voice resounded in my head as she unbuttoned my trousers. I glanced at the photo of Nick on the wall. The threat couldn't be clearer...*do this...or else.* I closed my eyes...

My zipper lowered. My gut clenched. I was going to be sick...I was going to be...

"Perfect." That sick voice filled the room as a warm hand closed around my cock. "This is the art of seduction, correct?" The Teacher spoke and all I wanted to do was throw up. "Where we empty the vessel of our own being and fill it with the pleasures of another. You do not exist in this moment. You are not here. It is only about them...their wants, their needs. You are nothing more than a mouth to suck and a cunt to fuck."

"*No!*"

I snapped open my eyes as Ryth whipped her hand backward and slapped Amber across the cheek. The woman fell sideways and her hand lifted to her face.

"You *fucking touch him!*" Ryth jerked that savage glare to The Teacher, stabbing the air with a finger. "You fucking touch him, and I *swear to God, I'll murder you all.*" She glared at Amber and the woman had the good sense to cower.

My little sister moved in front of me protectively, just like I'd done for her. This time the roles were reversed...

Or were they?

That sick fucking smile on The Teacher only grew wider. "You don't like the training I provide, Ms. Castlemaine?" He motioned to the floor at my feet. "Then by all means, fulfill the obligation yourself. This *is* our training exercise for the day and it *will* happen, whether you like it or not." He stepped closer, towering over her.

I clenched my fists, taking in the sight. The coldness. The way he looked at her, like he knew exactly how she was going to react...*because the bastard had planned this all along.*

A wounded sound tore from the back of my throat. I shook my head as I understood this wasn't about me. Nor was it about Nick or Tobias. It never had been. It was only about her. "Ryth." My heart pounded. "It's okay."

She shook her head, still holding that bastard's stare. "No, it's not. They're not touching you, Caleb. They're not touching you, because *you* belong to *me*."

"Then by all means," The Teacher murmured, his hand tilting, motioning for her to kneel.

Slowly, Ryth turned.

"No." I shook my head.

What we had wasn't meant for this...or them. Still, she fixed those stormy eyes on me and stepped closer, past Amber, who shoved back from us, clutching her cheek.

"Mine," Ryth's voice cracked as she stopped in front of me. "Only mine."

My pulse was booming as she knelt and, lowering her gaze, reached for my pants. Her damn fingers shook, but Christ, if I didn't want to take this over another fucking woman's hands on me. I'd done some dark, fucked up things...*but not that*. I never wanted to do that.

She stopped, her hands shaking so fucking bad as she reached for me. It was all I could do not to come apart. "Do you remember the last time we were together, little sister?"

She closed her eyes for a heartbeat, and nodded.

"Look at me."

She did, obeying my every word, just like I knew she would. That connection between us was instant, just like it'd been since the very first moment we'd been together. The memory of her body raged inside me, my hand over her mouth, my thumb finding the panicked flutter of her pulse as I'd dragged her backwards into the pantry.

"You're doing so good." The words came out of nowhere. I savored that moment, then and now, as she pulled out my cock. I reached down, dragged my fingers through her hair, and stared at her throat. "So damn good."

They said nothing as she bent and opened her mouth for me, sliding the head over her warm tongue. A lick, and I shuddered. My voice turned husky as I cupped her head as she took me in. Warm, so fucking warm. "In the bedroom." Deeper...sliding her tongue along the length, her small hand gripping the shaft. "My hands around your throat while I fucked you." She took more, driving that fist along the shaft all the way to the base.

Christ.

I grew hard. "You hated me." I tried to focus, tried to help her through this. "Still, you were fucking wet when I fingered you, weren't you? Your sweet, perfect fucking cunt was dripping. Fuck, I loved fingering you, loved how shy you got. How that mark on your cheek still burns when I push into your pussy. I love the way you squirm, clenching around my fingers like a good, fucking girl."

Deeper.

Slicker

My fingers sank through her hair as her head bobbed. "That's it, princess." I closed my eyes. "Worship me."

Her mouth grew wet and I looked down, clenching my fist in the strands of her hair and pulled out just a little. Strings of saliva came away with me. She met my gaze with that look of innocence, so goddamn sweet. So fucking *pure*.

Pure enough to ruin.

Christ, I wanted to ruin her.

I wanted to ride that sweet body.

I wanted to fuck her until she screamed.

And in those perfect moments when she fully gave herself to me, I wanted to take her into my darkness and make her mine.

Make her mine...

The eye of my cock twitched. The head blushed and glistened from her mouth, making my breaths deepen. I pushed her back down. *My hand around her throat. My cock in her ass. I wanted her to watch us in the mirror while I filled her with my come.* I closed my eyes as she took all of me. "Fuck. That's it, little sister. That's it, swallow."

One hand gripped my thigh, the other pumped my shaft as she pushed her head down, forcing me to the back of her throat. My balls tightened with the rush. My hold was relentless, taking every inch she was prepared to give. Still, she didn't buck...as I... "*Ugh...ughhh.*" I opened my eyes and looked down, coming hard in her mouth.

Her throat worked. That throat which had felt my grip. I leaned down, pulling my hand from her hair to clamp around her windpipe. But it wasn't to hurt. I just wanted to feel. "Swallow, little sister."

She did. Those muscles working under my hold, tightening, moving, taking every drop down. "My good little whore, aren't you? My sweet, perfect whore of a sister..." Hard breaths consumed me as I stared into her eyes. "Fuck, I love you."

Her lips parted, and slick coated her tongue as she stared at me. It was just us...just this—*always this*.

And behind us...the slow fucking clap of praise. *Clap...clap...clap...* "Well done," The Teacher murmured, his eyes bright and shining as he smiled. "Well fucking done, indeed. What a shame you're not to be trained, Ryth. You are a goddamn natural if I've ever seen one."

She flinched and pressed against me. My body still twitched, heavy and spent. But I didn't have time for that. I released my hold around her neck and tucked myself back in to my pants. "Let us go." I straightened as Ryth rose to stand beside me.

The Teacher just stared at Ryth like he wanted her on her knees for himself. I lowered my gaze to the bulge in his pants. That wasn't going to happen...

Ever.

"I'm afraid I can't do that," he answered, slowly turning toward me. "But I appreciate your effort, that was...delicious."

"You fuck." I sucked in hard breaths as he just nodded to the guard, who unlocked the door and opened it. Amber pushed upwards and hurried out, leaving the other woman and the last guard to follow. Until there was just him...

Who looked at Ryth once more, before he turned and strode out, leaving us alone...

SIX

Nick

THE DRIED BLOOD ON THE KITCHEN FLOOR BLURRED IN front of me.

I stood there, with the bucket at my feet and the damp rag in my hand, and I just couldn't fucking move. I stared at it like an idiot with the same fucking words resounding in my head. *Dad's dead...dad's dead...dad's—*

Thump.

The sound of a car door outside made me flinch. I shifted my focus to the door behind me. But I'd know the heavy sound of Tobias's steps anywhere, even when he was limping.

I didn't turn around when the rattle of keys came, just stood there pinned to the floor by that fucking stain. Tobias stepped in and closed the door behind him. I doubted he even noticed me, I stood that fucking still.

He just walked in with his head down, then noticed I was there. His head snapped up and he stopped moving. One slow turn of his head and he followed my focus to the floor, then muttered. "I'm gonna take a shower."

I winced at his cold tone, hating how all I wanted to do was meet that dark, savage stare and ask him what the fuck had happened? Was it an accident? Did the gun just fucking *go off*? The memory of that moment pushed in. The glint of steel still in his hand, one that'd been aimed at our father. No matter how hard I tried, I couldn't push the memory away.

I wanted to ask him what he'd done...

No, I wanted to demand to know why the fuck he'd done that.

Why, T?

Why kill him...

But I didn't. Instead, I said nothing as he tossed a set of keys on the counter and limped down the hall. He shoved a hand out as he went, bracing against the wall. I lowered my gaze to the black jeans stuck hard against his thigh. He was hurt...I knew that. Bad, too.

Still, the stubborn bastard refused to ask for help. He just dragged his t-shirt over his head, drawing my focus to the scratches that marred his back. But it wasn't the cuts that made me wince, it was the already darkening bruise across the entire half of his back.

Jesus.

Jesus...

Bang!

I jumped at the slam of the bathroom door. Seconds later, the howl of the water pipes came. What happened...*what the fuck went down?* I was desperate to know. Still, knowing wouldn't change the outcome.

I turned back to that stain on the kitchen floor. One that'd long since dried. I took a step, sank to my knees, and set to work scrubbing, but all the time the question resounded...

What are we going to do?

What the fuck are we going to do...

I tried to come up with a plan, one that wouldn't get us killed, then rinsed the cloth in the bucket before turning back. The constant motion of the rag on the floor lulled me into thoughts of her.

The last thoughts I had of our sister as she raced toward The Order in an attempt to save one of our own. "Goddamn you, Caleb. We should've stayed together, you fucking idiot. *We should've stayed the fuck together.*"

I searched the floor for any trace of blood before I wiped the cupboard our father had leaned on and slowly realized the bathroom was silent...and had been for some time.

Water dripped from my hand when I rose. I dumped the contents of the bucket down the sink before scrubbing that with bleach and stowed the chemicals away. But my focus was pulled toward that hallway. Where it was quiet. *Too damn quiet.*

Something was wrong.

That thought forced me forward, leaving the kitchen behind until I stood outside the bathroom, right across from the bedroom where Ryth had been. I dragged in the air, catching the faint scent of vanilla. Fuck. The place still smelled like her.

That wasn't good—my pulse sped—*no*, that wasn't good at all. Focus. *Fucking focus, Nick.*

"T," I said, my voice husky.

But there was no answer. I stepped closer to the bathroom door. "T," I called louder.

Silence.

The memory of that gun in his hand was stuck in my head as I turned the handle and shoved open the door, finding T sitting on the side of the tub, naked. Water dripped from his body onto the floor.

His leg was bleeding, the bullet wound black and ugly. "Jesus, T!" I closed the distance. "Why the fuck didn't you tell me it was this bad?"

My brother just sat there, staring at the floor, his knees jerking and trembling like he was coming apart. I'd never seen him like this...not this bad—*not ever*.

"We have to get her out, Nick." He slowly lifted his gaze to mine, and all I saw was a ghost. "We have to get her out."

He looked so fragile at that moment, not like a monster at all. He looked like a man pushed to his breaking point, one who was fucking vulnerable. That's what having Ryth in our lives had made us—vulnerable, too vulnerable. That desperation was crushing. "I know, brother," I answered. "I know."

But we were running out of people to ask, except for the one person who knew more than anyone. Elle Castlemaine. I stared at that bullet wound in my brother's thigh. "We have to find Elle. She's the one who can get her out of there. We find her, and we get our sister back."

Tobias lifted his gaze to mine. "And C?"

And C...my heart kicked in my chest. I didn't know...I just didn't fucking *know*. Was he dead already? If he wasn't, then he soon would be. They didn't need our brother. His life meant nothing to them. It was all Ryth, wasn't it? All *fucking Ryth*.

"We do whatever we can to get him back." I held that dangerous stare. "Whatever we can."

T shook his head slowly. "So, we try to find Elle, if they haven't killed her by now."

I scowled, the way he said it worried me. "What are you talking about?"

"She's gone, Nick. After what she did, she's gone."

After what she did? Sent her own daughter to that place? "No," I answered. "They'll need her. They'll use her."

My brother's laugh was chilling as he shook his head. "You don't get it, do you? She's a loose fucking end. One who's shown them she can't be trusted, not even by her husband."

A chill raced through me. "What are you talking about?"

"What do you think I'm talking about?" he snarled. "She killed our fucking father."

My gut clenched as that cold moved deeper. "*She* killed our father?"

But the gun was in his hand, aimed at dad. I'd seen it for a second as I ran through the trees before he'd lunged toward him. I was sure...I was sure—

Tobias flinched, his voice stony. "You think *I* killed him?"

I searched that stare for the truth, but I was sure, I was so fucking sure. "Yes."

He gave a chuff and looked away. "Figures."

"You killed him, T." I didn't know if I was trying to convince him or myself. Was he lying? Was he trying to pin it on someone else? I knew the hate that brewed between them. I sure as hell understood if he—

"Get the fuck out, Nick." Tobias shoved up from the tub, but swayed. He grabbed hold of the sink and dropped his gaze, breathing hard.

My mind raced. "Elle...killed dad?"

He jerked that menacing glare my way. *"Get the fuck out!"*

I stumbled backwards as it finally hit me. "T...I—"

He lunged and shoved me in the middle of my chest, the force knocking me backwards as the bathroom door slammed closed with a *BANG*.

I stood there, unable to move. All I saw was that fucking glint in my head, a memory I now tried to pick apart. Was he telling the truth? Was Elle the one who'd actually killed our dad and all this time I'd thought...I'd thought...*I*—

The door was yanked open and Tobias limped out, still looking fucking pissed. Gone was that vulnerable stare. Gone was that fragile fucking moment. He was the bastard again, the ruthless sonofabitch who could easily have pulled the trigger.

Could...sure, but *would* he? I lowered my gaze to the white bandage around his thigh, that was already specked with blood. "T, you need to see a doctor."

"Save it." He shoved past me to the bedroom at the end of the hall, the one we were supposed to share, and closed the door behind him.

The clang of steel on steel rang out. My brother was searching for weapons and getting ready for war. I wanted to say something, to make this right. But I couldn't. Not now when he was seething.

I turned around, ready to make my way back to the kitchen, and found myself gravitating to that room instead. The one which smelled like her...

The place was a mess. A fucking desk lamp was smashed on the floor. I took a step closer, finding the indent in the wall where it had hit. *No, where she'd thrown it.* I shifted my focus to the ruined bed. The bedding was everywhere, and there was a damp stain on the sheet. I didn't need a fucking blow by blow to know that was our sister's.

So that was how Caleb had fixed it. *With angry sex...*

Of course he did.

I massaged the knotted muscles at the back of my neck and moved closer, running my hand along the crumpled fabric before I sat. Christ, this was a mess...one I didn't know how to get out of.

The bedroom door at the far end of the hall opened and the thudding sound of boots rang out. I rose and made my way to the doorway, finding T already locked and fucking loaded, with the duffle bag full of guns in his grasp.

"Where are you going?" I asked.

He didn't answer, just kept walking.

"T."

He stopped in the hallway and didn't move. Was he just going to leave? "I'm going to find Elle."

"Where?"

He turned, meeting my stare. "The only place there is."

Then it hit me. Home. That's where he was going...he was going home.

I swallowed and nodded, not daring to argue. "I'm coming with you."

He gave a slow nod of his head. I guess that was as good as I was going to get. I headed for the kitchen, grabbed the gun I had left on the counter, and tucked it into the waistband of my jeans before snatching the keys off the counter. I didn't even dare ask where he'd gotten the car from...I sure as hell didn't want to know.

One sharp whistle, and Rebel limped our way. She looked at me with so much fucking love, pressing her little body against my leg before I reached down and ruffled her black ears. "Let's go, girl."

T limped hard as he strode through the door, and I followed, wincing at the sun. A gray Toyota sat parked in the driveway with the windows down. There was a smear of blood on the outside of the driver's door, fresh too, by the looks of it.

"Don't ask."

I held up my hand. "Wasn't saying a word."

He kept walking, heading to the trunk. I yanked open the driver's door and pulled the lever until the latch released. A *thud,* then he was climbing into the passenger seat. I took that as a sign, at least he wasn't going to kill me...*yet.*

Rebel jumped up into the seat and awkwardly leaped into the back. She was a damn smart dog and a damn fighter. She'd had to be. I climbed in, started the engine, and reversed.

"Maybe we don't take Center and Grange," Tobias muttered, closing his eyes and resting his head back. "I'm sure they'll be looking for me."

"I'm sure they will," I agreed, knowing instantly who '*they*' were.

The assholes he'd stolen the car from. Who were probably out for blood.

I stayed away from those streets, instead headed west and made our way to the more affluent suburbs with lush green gardens and their fake fucking smiles. Forty minutes was all it took to replace one shitshow with another. I pulled into the driveway and parked where I always parked, like our entire fucking world hadn't been ripped apart.

I climbed out, leaving T behind me, and made my way to the keypad beside the front door. The place echoed when I stepped in. It was cold now, and hollow. There was no breath of fresh air that our little sister had brought with her when she invaded our home. No excitement at the prospect of teasing and tasting her, either.

My pulse sped as T followed me inside and closed the door.

"I'll take the study," he muttered, striding off and leaving me behind.

I could've told him that searching there was useless. We'd already tossed the place from top to bottom searching for information about dad. But my brother didn't listen, just limped away, his hand fisted at his side.

"Fine," I mumbled, and turned toward the kitchen. "You want to be pissed off, then be pissed off."

My belly howled as though it sensed exactly where I was headed. I yanked open the refrigerator door, pulling out whatever I could find as a heavy *thud* came from the study.

He wanted to be pissed, then let him be pissed. He still needed to damn well heal.

I slathered bread with butter, then added ham, cheese, and mayo before biting down on one, then I turned back and made two more before shoving them both in a snap-lock bag and tossing them on the counter.

Each step was agony as I climbed the stairs, pressing against the wound in my side. I was pretty sure I'd ripped something last night, charging after Ryth. The sharp pain was constant, a fucking stabbing ache. Still, I'd manage, because I wasn't as bad as T.

My focus gravitated upwards to the top floor we shared with our sister, but I didn't want to go there…not now. Instead, I turned and made my way to the bedroom Elle had shared with my father. If she was going to keep any kind of hidden documents, it'd be there.

I turned the handle and pushed open the door before stepping inside. It felt weird walking in. I still expected to see mom's things lined up along the dresser and smell the faint floral scent of her perfume. Not this…

Sure as hell not this…

The room wasn't neat and perfect, it was a damn collision. Clothes were strewn over the floor, the dresser with all her jewelry was sideways across the room as though it'd been dragged over and upended. I kicked an open suitcase still packed with half of her things…designer clothes, shoes, gold necklaces that must've cost dad a fortune. It was easy to see where her things went…

But she didn't take them, did she?

She was in a damn hurry to leave, that was obvious. If she'd left all this behind, then maybe she'd left other things as well. I bent and upended the suitcase, scattering her diamond earrings and rings to the floor before I searched through them.

But there was nothing but clothes and jewelry and my focus shifted to the walk-in closet. Even from here, I could see bags waiting in the corners of the wardrobe. I rose and moved toward them, brushing my hand along the clothes still hanging before searching the pockets.

I wanted information.

That's all.

Clothes. Shoes. I pulled them all down, moving through each of them one by one until I found a small black satin clutch hidden way in the back. One that was heavier than it should be.

I twisted the clasp, to find a small leather-bound notebook inside. "What is this?"

The clutch hit the floor at my feet as I opened the handwritten pages and started reading…

Watching her with her friends, I could almost forget how she came to be, what she represents, and her purpose in all this. But her innocence will be the very thing that makes her perfect for them. As much as I hate thinking about it, I need that more now than ever. I need her innocent and perfect. I need her because I'm backed into a corner, and I'm holding her out in front of me, hoping they'll take her instead.

Because I cannot go back there.

Not to what they are.

Or what they do.

Jack tells me he loves me. He says he'll protect me and he'll keep us both safe. But I don't know what safe is anymore, maybe I never did. He looks at me like Ryth does, they want more than I can give. My soul…my heart. I can't love them…and right now I'm too fucking weak to run.

I stopped reading as a steady thud of steps came behind me. My heart hammered. My mouth went dry.

"Find anything?" T asked from the doorway.

At first, I couldn't speak. I couldn't do anything but stare at that desperate scrawl, the one where a mother tried to convince herself she wasn't the biggest monster of all. I swallowed, then just lifted the diary.

My brother took it without speaking and started to read.

"What the fuck?" he said finally.

I nodded, meeting his stare. "What the fuck indeed."

"She fucking *used her*? She was goddamn collateral. *No, not collateral.* She was fucking *bait, Nick. She was goddamn bait.*" T's words carved through my middle. Still, he kept talking as I tried to hold on. "What does she mean by monster's blood in her veins?"

I slowly shook my head. "I wish I knew."

What I did know was that Jack Castlemaine wasn't Ryth's father, and if he wasn't, then who the fuck *was*?

"This changes everything." Tobias handed the diary back to me. "Trafficking is one thing, but what she's talking about here is some kind of breeding program."

"I know."

"This is bad, Nick." Fuck, he looked scared. "This is real fucking bad, and we've run out of options."

"I know." I stared at the journal in my hand as that crushing weight grew heavier. "We'll figure out something, okay? I don't know what, but we'll figure it out."

The moment I said that, my phone vibrated in my pocket. This was a number that was new, one that no one should have...*so who the hell was calling?*

I pulled it out and stared at the caller ID. *Private.* Goosebumps raced up my arm as I hit the icon, answering the call. "Yeah?"

"Nicholas Banks?" The unfamiliar voice on the other end was careful.

I glanced at my brother. "Who's asking?"

"This is Jack Castlemaine. I hear you're trying to save my daughter...I want to help."

SEVEN

Ryth

I stared at the phone in the middle of the table, unable to look way ever since they'd dragged us into the room and forced me to sit.

My dad was due to call. The Principal scoffed when he called him that. He scoffed and laughed, those sick, fucking, gleaming eyes fixed on my every move. He wanted to see my pain. He *craved it.*

But I *refused* to give in. He didn't deserve to see the real me. None of them did. Caleb was a dark blur at the edge of my vision. He saw me. He comforted me. He took me away from this Hell...even if it was only in fleeting moments of pleasure.

Still, my cheeks burned, remembering the lies The Principal had told me. Lies that my father wasn't my blood and that Tobias...Tobias was dead...

"Remember, say nothing about where you are in the building." That icy tone came at my back. "If I even suspect you're scheming, the call will be terminated immediately."

I didn't meet that sick fucking glint in his stare. I didn't dare... but I felt his gaze burn on the back of my neck. The Principal. The Teacher...The Priest. The three pieces of shit who ran this place. I hated them...almost as much as I hated the man they worked for, Haelstrom Hale.

Caleb glanced my way and reached for my hand. But this time, his touch wasn't comforting. No...nothing could prepare me for this. I inhaled deep, fighting the tension...until the phone gave a sharp, loud chime and vibrated against the surface.

I jumped and reached.

"Wait." The command came.

My knuckles ached. My breath caught until it burned

Still the phone rang...and rang...*and rang...*

"*Now.*"

I snatched the phone from the table, stabbed the icon with a shaking finger, and answered. "Hello?"

There was silence. Silence while my chest ached, then came my father's warm voice. "Ryth, honey?"

My shoulders sagged. "Dad." I couldn't stop the hitch in my breath. "Dad, is that you?"

"It's me, my little lioness." His voice grew louder. "Are you okay?"

Am I okay? I didn't dare look over my shoulder. "For now," I answered carefully.

"I'm getting you out of there, okay, sweetheart? Just hold on."

I pressed the phone hard against my ear. "Okay."

"Riven," he started, then corrected himself. "I mean, *The Principal,* is he watching you?"

That chill prickled at the back of my neck. "Yes."

"Okay, so this is what's going to happen. In a minute, I want you to pass him the phone. I'm going to talk to him, then we're going to get you and Caleb out of that fucking place."

My fingers twitched as I fought the need to rock with relief. "How?"

"Don't you worry about that," he answered, but still the heaviness in my stomach said otherwise. "Whatever happens, you need to leave. Nothing good will come if you stay in that fucking place a second longer."

I glanced at Caleb.

"Promise me." My father drew my focus back. "*Promise* me you'll leave with Caleb."

My stepbrother just held my stare, those dark hazel eyes consuming as I answered. "I promise."

There was a hard exhale before his voice turned cold, colder than I'd ever heard it before. "Good, now put me on to the sonofabitch, and sweetheart..."

"Yes?"

"I love you."

I closed my eyes, letting his strength wash over me. "I love you, too, Dad."

Even though tears welled in my eyes and my damn hands shook, I still turned in my seat and held out the phone.

There was a second where the bastard refused to move, the corner of his mouth twisting with displeasure. I only wished it was his fucking heart—but then I doubted he had one. "He's waiting," I snapped.

That stony stare glinted before he stepped forward and took the phone from my hand and lifted it to his ear. "Yes."

Words were exchanged, ones I wasn't privy to. But I could see it play out on the bastard's face. This time there was no savage bark from The Principal, just a venomous, "I agree to the terms. It's not like I have a choice, now do I?" No. He didn't. And he knew it. "Then I'll look forward to meeting you face-to-face, Jack."

He looked at me when he said those words and I just wanted to scream. This place wasn't safe for dad. I knew that. These men were dangerous, maybe more dangerous than he knew...but then again, the way he spoke, and the things he did—like going into hiding—made me think that maybe he knew exactly what he was getting into.

The Principal ended the call, then turned to the men standing beside him and said the words I'd been desperate to hear. "Get them ready for removal."

Neither of them liked this.

The Teacher jerked his gaze my way. For a second, I thought he was going to disobey the command, that he was going to give one of his own...one where he took me back to that classroom and forced me to my knees.

What a shame you're not to be trained, Ryth. His words resounded in my head. *You are a goddamn natural if I've ever seen one.*

He wanted to train me.

He wanted to do a whole lot more.

But he didn't disobey, he just nodded, his voice so fucking calm. "Peter, see to Ms. Castlemaine and Mr. Banks."

The guard stepped forward, as well as another, who stood at his back. The guard grabbed me by the arm, his fingers cruel as he hauled me out of the chair. "Move."

Caleb pushed out of his seat. "Get your fucking hands off her.

But The Priest blocked his way. "You want to change how this goes, Banks? Because we can just as easily take you out in a goddamn body bag."

"Caleb." I stumbled as the guard yanked me toward the door. "No, it's okay. Look, I'm okay."

But rage glinted in his eyes.

"Say another fucking word, Banks," The Priest warned. "And I'll make good on my promise."

They walked us out of the interrogation room and into the hall, past the room they'd kept us in, and through the automatic doors.

Ghosts stared at us as we passed. Ghosts of the women confined in this place.

"Please." One of them pressed her hand to the glass.

But we were gone before I could even answer. The guard's long steps forced me to take twice as many to match.

"Keep walking." He shoved me forward.

Behind us, Caleb unleashed a snarl. I looked over my shoulder, seeing him and the three men who'd kept us in this place following.

We were close now, so close.

Please. I prayed Caleb saw my plea as I was jerked toward the scanner for another set of automatic doors. A *beep* came before we pushed through. My bare feet were a blur as I hurried. They moved on their own now, quickening as I lifted my gaze to the massive front door and those two terrifying words carved into the black steel, *The Order*.

We slowed, leaving The Principal to step close to the door and press his card against the scanner to open it. With a jerk of his head, he glared at me and commanded. "Out."

I would've walked barefoot across broken glass if it meant freedom for the both of us. It was my turn to all but drag the guard out as I hurried through that oppressive door.

Cold night air rushed around me as I stepped out, my bare feet stinging with the cold stone of the pavement. But I didn't care *at all*.

Silence waited. Caleb stepped out, but they didn't let him touch me, holding me too far away for the connection. I stared down that long, empty driveway to the towering, guarded gates.

My teeth chattered and my knees shook, the sound grating in the night. At least I had a sweatshirt and long fleece pants. Caleb stood there in the same white cotton shirt and black pants they'd taken us in. He had to be freezing, but he never said a word, just fixed that careful stare on me. *Easy, princess,* it whispered.

I gave a nod and turned my attention to that darkened road as we waited, and waited, and waited. Slowly, a seed of doubt sprouted.

Maybe he just wasn't coming.

Maybe…maybe—

He isn't now…or ever was, your father, Ryth. I glanced at The Principal as his words resounded in my mind. *We're not abducting you. We're reclaiming what was already ours.*

But I didn't believe them. All they did was manipulate and tell lies. He was my father...*dad was my father.* He had to be.

In the distance, far back along the road, the tiny glint of headlights shone in the dark.

"Easy..." Caleb whispered, his gaze riveted on the same glimmer of lights.

As the spark grew bolder, I held my breath, watching the headlights come toward the compound. There was a second set of headlights, ones that stayed back from the first, maybe it was backup? Some kind of bodyguard from the Rossis...

The Rossis. My panicked thoughts caught on them as a squeal of metal on metal reached my ears and the gates to The Order slowly opened. The first car nosed in, leaving the second to slow, until it followed behind. But I didn't watch that car. It was the first one...with the driver shrouded in darkness I cared about.

"Well, well, well," The Principal muttered beside me. "So he does have balls after all."

I clenched my jaw at the words. *Fuck you!* I wanted to scream in his face. *Fuck you all.*

He'd get us out, then we'd leave. The faint burn on my cheek lingered. It would bruise too, in the shape of Mother's hand. Pain flared in my chest, but I shoved it down. It didn't matter now that dad was here.

He'd fix it for me.

The first car drove closer to the building, but the second car stopped further back, the engine still running, the headlights on. How could a bodyguard protect him there? I tried not to look ahead. I tried to trust that dad and the Rossis knew what they were doing, and as the engine died and the driver's door of the first car opened, I knew without a doubt, those bastards had lied.

Because the man who stepped out *was* my father.

He couldn't be anybody but.

The *thud* of his door closing was followed by the crunch of footsteps. My pulse was hammering, the sound deafening inside my ears. The cold night air blurred my sight. I blinked, fixed on that dark shape that headed toward us, then in a blink, his face cleared.

"Dad...*Dad!*" I lunged, tearing from the guard's hold.

He let out a snarl behind me, but it was too late.

"Let her go," The Principal ordered.

I tore across the driveway and leaped.

Strong arms caught me with a grunt. Dad was there, staggering under my weight. "Ryth," he croaked, squeezing me until I could hardly breathe.

But I didn't care. I didn't care at all, just buried my head into his neck and wept. "I thought they killed you. I thought you were—"

"I'm right here." He gripped me tighter, his big hands driving my face against his chest. "I'm right here, honey."

The last time I'd seen him, he'd been beaten and bruised...and terrified.

Now I knew why.

"Are you okay, my little lioness?"

I just nodded, my voice breaking. "I am now."

Behind us, the crunch of boots sounded. I stiffened, pulling away and looked into my father's eyes. He grew colder, harder as he fixed his focus on those men. I hated them now even more than I'd hated them before.

They stole and ruined and degraded all for some sick desire of their own.

"Mr. Castlemaine," The Principal's blunt tone shattered the fleeting fear, joy, and worry.

I straightened and slowly pulled back. In front of me, my father became someone else, a man I'd never seen before. His lips twitched, baring his teeth as he set his sights on the monsters.

But he didn't stop at The Principal, and scanned the others beside him. There was a look of disappointment, then that curl of his lips tightened. "Hale's not here, I take it?"

"No," The Principal answered.

"We had an agreement."

Agreement?

"There seems to be a problem with his fiancee," The Principal's voice was filled with contempt. "Apparently she's been kidnapped from an island off Africa."

"Fiancee?" My father sounded surprised. "Then I pray it's a quick and painless death for her. It'll be better than living with a monster."

In my head, I saw Hale as he'd sat in that restaurant, surrounded by disgusting old white men who loved nothing more than to use women like me. He was a monster...a monster with money—a monster they all feared.

"Still." The Principal's voice was caustic. "We had a deal."

I turned then, meeting the bastard's stare as he looked at me. *They had a deal...*what deal?

My father reached back and gently broke my hold, pulling my hands around. "You remember what we said, honey. No matter what, that's what you promised."

"No matter what, Dad?"

But he didn't answer, just gave a nod. The guard at Caleb's back shoved him forward and he stumbled toward us.

Dad's gaze narrowed in on my stepbrother. There was a flare of anger, one he smothered. "Get her out of here, Caleb, and as far away from these goddamn people as possible. And this time, son, *stay the fuck away.*"

Dad stepped away, leaving C to wrap his arms around me. "Let's go, Ryth." He dragged me away as dad headed for them.

"What's happening?" I turned in his arms. "Dad? *Dad, what's happening!?*"

But Caleb's hold never slipped as he pulled me away, past the first car and along the drive.

"Dad, no! *DAD, NO!*"

They closed in like a pack of wolves, swarming him. I tried to tear away from Caleb, to lunge toward dad, who just let them take him without a fight. *What the fuck was happening...WHAT THE FUCK—*

"We have to leave, princess," Nick's voice filled my ears.

Tears came, blurring his face, but I blinked hard and he was there—the sight was a punch to my chest. "Nick?" I stared as he neared. Then, in the wash of headlights, a dark silhouette came. One that limped when he walked...

One that came closer...and closer.

I couldn't look away...

I didn't understand.

Because I was looking at a ghost.

One who looked exactly like my stepbrother.

Tobias stopped in front of me, lifted his hand to graze my cheek with a curled finger, and murmured, "There's my little mouse."

EIGHT

Tobias

"*Tobias?*" she whispered, her eyes widening.

My knees trembled, but I held on. "Yeah, little mouse, it's me."

She took a step closer, flinched at the sound of handcuffs being snapped around her father's wrists, and turned her head. The Principal hadn't wasted a goddamn second. I eyed the piece of shit as he and his goddamn brothers took Jack away.

But the guards turned toward us. We didn't have time for the perfect reunion. Instead, Nick glared at me. "We have to go, *now*."

"Come on, little mouse." I grabbed her hand and dragged her toward the open door. "Into the car."

"*No!*" She fought, just like I knew she would, twisting in my arms, trying to sidestep me. "*We can't leave him!*"

But I left her no room to escape, blocking her in by my size alone as Caleb flung himself into the passenger seat.

"*In the car, Ryth!*" Nick barked, and he climbed behind the wheel, leaving me to deal with our sister on my own.

I tried to be gentle, I really fucking did, even pushing her head down before climbing in behind her. "You gotta trust him now, little mouse," I urged, pushing her back against the seat. "Your father knows what he's doing."

I yanked the door closed and the locks engaged with a *thunk*. We were done taking chances where she was concerned, and that included her goddamn family. I eyed those fucking guards as they came toward the car, wanting nothing more than to aim my fucking gun at each one of them and pull the goddamn trigger.

But I didn't, just shoved across the seat after her, my knee twisting in agony as I went. I bit down on a scream, as the car reversed rapidly back down the drive.

"Rebel." Ryth reached for the mutt as she tried to climb into her lap. She let the beast nuzzle her hand, taking comfort in rubbing her head. She could take comfort in the beast. It didn't matter...*nothing mattered,* as long as we were gone.

Tears shone on her cheeks when she stared out of the window. "Dad."

I swallowed that fucking lump back down, forcing it into the pit of my gut where the rage seethed. "It's going to be okay, little mouse. Just you wait and see. It's all going to be okay."

Lies...

My knee twitched and shook. I grabbed the damn thing in the dark and whispered. *"Yeah, you'll see."*

I didn't know if the words were for her or for me.

But by sheer fucking will, I'd make it true. I looked at those shimmering tears falling from the edge of her jaw and that pain in my leg turned into pure fucking rage.

The blur of the gates came before we tore through them, then the tires squealed and Nick spun the wheel, throwing me against the door. A moan ripped free before I could bite down and swallow the sound. I didn't have time to grab my knee as Ryth was flung toward me. I grabbed my sister instead as she slammed into me.

"Easy." I pulled her close. "I've got you."

Still, the pain was consuming. My world grayed at the edges. But I didn't roar at Nick. I urged him to go faster. "Move!"

"Trying." Nick spun the wheel again and punched the accelerator.

The sedan was a junky piece of shit, used to rolling past corners while money was traded for drugs. Not this...

"We can't just leave him there." Ryth shook her head, looking behind us as we left that fucking place behind. "We can't."

I tried my best to still the tremble in my hands and turned to her. "Look at me."

She did, staring up at me, and everything hit me all at once. Mom's death. Her abduction. My own fucking father...*damn... my own fucking father*. She didn't even know. I glanced at Caleb as I realized he didn't either. Didn't know dad was dead...*and he'd tried to fucking kill me*.

"I thought you were dead," she whispered, shaking her head. "I thought you were..."

"Not even death wanted me, princess," I answered, holding on tight. "Only you...*always you*."

Energy arced between us before she slammed against me, clawing my shirt, grasping my neck, pulling me into her. Fuck, I didn't need to be asked twice. I fisted her hair and kissed her hard, gripping her jaw as I crushed her fucking mouth.

I needed her. Christ, I needed her. I released my hold, palming her breast instead. Her perfect, small fucking breast. Her tight peak grazed my palm, tightening with the contact. I needed to be inside her. I *hungered* to be inside her. To feel her, to lick her. To know she was alive and here and...*mine*.

To know she was mine.

I lowered my head to the crook of her neck and inhaled deeply. The sharp, clinical scent of that fucking place clung to her. But underneath it...was that faint, sweet fucking scent of vanilla.

"You scared the hell out of me." I fisted her hair and yanked, pulling her head backwards, hard enough for her to know I was pissed. "Don't ever do that again. From now on...we stick together. *Do you hear me? We stick together.* Every goddamn second of the fucking day, until we can get the hell out of here."

Fresh tears slipped free as she nodded. The sight of that was a cocked fist to my balls. My callused thumb was too rough for her skin. Still, I brushed the trail away. "They're not going to kill him. He won't let them."

"Yeah, they will." Her voice was so goddamn sure and so...*fucking empty.* "He walked in there to save me."

Nick lifted his gaze and those dark eyes bored into mine.

I shook my head. "If you think he just went in there blindly, then you don't know your father. He's fucking smart, Ryth. He's so fucking smart, and that makes him dangerous to them. The things he's told us, the people who are involved... No wonder they wanted—"

"T." Nick warned, stopping me cold.

My heart hammered. Christ, if she knew the things her father had told us. Things we only guessed after reading her mom's journal. Chilling things. Things that should never see the light of day. The people who were behind this corrupt, twisted shit, it was fucking sickening.

But she didn't need to know about that now. Because that kind of shit would only bring her undone. She watched Nick in the rear-view mirror, then turned to me.

I brushed some strands of hair from her eyes. "Trust us, princess. He's gone in there with a plan."

I didn't know if she believed me. I didn't know if I would, either, in her position.

"Hand me that." Nick nodded to Caleb.

Caleb grabbed the GPS from the dashboard in front of him and handed it over. "Nick...." he started.

"Not now," he snarled, and his tone left no fucking illusion that he was pissed.

We both were.

Ryth blamed herself, but the real person at fault here was our goddamn brother. If he hadn't gone off half-cocked, hellbent on revenge, then both of them wouldn't have been taken.

And maybe our father might still be alive.

I didn't know that for sure.

I met Ryth's stare. What I did know was that we'd be in a very different position. *And none the fucking wiser.* Would knowing what we did now have changed anything? I brushed the hair away from her eyes with trembling fingers—not when it came to how we felt about her.

Nick watched the red marker on the screen and pushed the clapped-out sedan harder to get away.

"They told us you were dead." Caleb was trying to make conversation in the hopes he'd make amends. Fat fucking chance of that. I met his stare, and my own turned dangerous. "Did they?"

Because I almost was...asshole.

There were things we as brothers could come back from. Arguments, rivalry, even where our stepsister was concerned. But this...putting *her* in harm's way like that? That shit I just couldn't fucking forgive. Not even when it came to blood.

He knew...

He saw it in my stare.

We're going to have a problem, you and me, brother. We are going to have a real big fucking problem indeed.

He gave a careful nod, then glanced at Ryth, giving her a weak smile before turning back to the road.

"What's going on?"

I shook my head. "Nothing, princess. Nothing at all."

We followed that marker on the GPS along the winding back roads until it felt like we were the only ones out here. Darkness waited for us, and pain for me. My leg pulsed, shoving a burning fire poker through my fucking thigh, brutal enough for me to catch my breath.

Something was wrong.

I didn't need my brother to tell me that. Nick met my stare in the rear-view mirror until I looked away. *Just get us out of here...*I gripped the armrest, wincing. *Just get us out.*

We couldn't stay around here, not in this car, at least. A rough plan was all we had, but it was better than no fucking plan, which was what we'd had before Jack Castlemaine called us.

So, we'd take it...whatever he could give us, we'd take it and run.

Nick lifted the monitor Jack had handed us in the brief moments we'd had before we left for The Order and glanced at the blinking red marker as the darkness at the edges of my vision started to close in.

"I think this is it."

Those words were all I needed to drive the blackout away.

Nick gripped the GPS and switched off the sedan's headlights. We slowed, heading down the dirt road in the middle of nowhere. I forced myself to fix on the darkened blur of houses through the windshield and caught the glint of lights in the distance.

"There." I pointed. "Lights."

Nick followed the motion, glancing at the screen in front of him. "That has to be it."

He slowed the car and nosed into the stranger's driveway, then turned and headed for a massive barn near the fenceline. It was exactly how Jack had said, all the way down to the oldtimer waiting for us.

I winced with the jolt as Nick pulled up outside the massive double doors.

That hot poker drove all the way into my balls as I yanked the handle and shoved the door wide. "This way, princess." I prayed she didn't hear the whimper, or see my knee buckle when I stepped out.

The world swayed, forcing me to brace against the side of the car.

"Tobias, are you okay?"

I knew the words were coming. My smile was more like a fucking wince, but I gave her all I had. "Yeah, just tired."

I'd slept in snatches of time, fifteen minutes here, thirty minutes there. But it wasn't the lack of sleep that had me worried. It was the bullet still lodged in my thigh. The grating scrape of the opening barn doors drew her gaze, right as the driving agony took another fucking bite. "Go." I forced the word. "Go to Nick."

The look in her eyes told me she wanted to argue, that she knew I was lying. It was all I could do not to beg her.

Go...go to Nick.

She did, leaving me behind. I sagged against the car as she slipped into the darkness inside the barn.

"She's stronger than you think."

I winced. *That* motherfucking voice was not what I wanted to hear right now. "Fuck *you*, C." I narrowed in on my brother on the other side of the car. "Fuck you right to Hell."

He gave a careful nod, then turned and followed her into the barn.

She's stronger than you think...

I sucked in a hard breath and shook my head. She *was* strong, I *knew* that. But this wasn't about giving her more burdens, it was about me. There was no way I wanted to see the same pain in her eyes that I'd seen in mine when I watched my mom become sick...and finally crumble.

I just couldn't do it. Not now...

So I ground my teeth and pushed off the car, forcing the scream back down until the pain was just that grinding throb in the back of my mind.

The interior lights came on from a car parked inside the barn. Nick opened the trunk and rifled through the bags, pulling out one to drop onto the rear seat. "There's clothes for you, princess."

In the wash of the lights, Ryth looked inside the carry-on. "You put this here?"

"No." Nick gave a shake of his head. "Your dad did."

"Dad did this?" She was surprised, but she shouldn't have been.

"Yeah." He grabbed out guns, then handed one to Caleb and another to me before slamming the trunk closed. "We have to hurry."

I took the Sig, tucking it into the waistband of my jeans along with two fresh clips.

Ryth looked around and settled on the open barn door. "There's just us here," I answered.

My hand closed around the weapon's grip. No fucker would dare even look at her. She gave a nod, then tugged the gray sweatshirt over her head...but she was bare underneath.

Her skin was so fucking soft, creamy and hypnotizing. Those pink nipples hardened with the night air. She bent and shoved the sweatpants free, kicking them away in disgust before tugging on panties from the bag, then jeans, a t-shirt, and a jacket.

"Ready?" Nick asked, glancing my way.

I just stared at her as she grabbed her discarded clothes, rolled them into a ball, and fixed her hair. I looked away, Christ, I had it bad.

Caleb climbed into the driver's seat, leaving me to follow Ryth as she slid across the back seat.

I forced myself to move, dropped low, and yanked the door closed behind me before C started the engine and pulled the sedan out of the barn.

"The light's off," Ryth said quietly as Caleb climbed out of the driver's seat and walked around the front.

"What?" I looked her way as she pointed to the farmhouse in the distance.

"The porch light was on when we drove in. Now it isn't."

"He's done what he had to do," I answered as the barn doors closed once more.

"My father did all this?"

"Yeah," I nodded. "He did."

"I don't know who he is anymore."

Maybe she never had. Maybe none of us had, not really.

Nick climbed in, shoved the car into gear, and pulled away from the barn and the house...and everything. Pain pulsed and gnawed, pulling my focus to that heat that burned my thigh. I gripped the armrest, bit down on a moan, and closed my eyes, hoping like hell sleep took me down, and all the while I prayed.

Just hold on...

Just hold the fuck on.

NINE

Ryth

THE CAR WAS QUIET...TOO DAMN QUIET.

Nick scanned the rear-view mirror as we hauled ass from the farmhouse, searching the roads behind us for a glint of headlights. I didn't know where we were driving, but he seemed to have some idea.

In the front passenger seat, Caleb silently stared out his window and beside me, Tobias was asleep. He was acting strange. Not screaming, not threatening. Not at all what I expected after what we'd just been through. I brushed my fingers down his arm and he opened his eyes.

"Princess." He licked his lips, dropping his gaze to my breasts.

One carnal look and my breath caught. Desire followed as it always did with them, making my nipples tighten and my thighs clench. But he never made a move as we drove past farmhouses, skirting the outside of the city, just watched me for a while before he slept again.

I'd expected anger. I'd expected ranting.

But this silence was worrying, fraying my damn nerves. I forced my focus instead to the darkness outside. A low whine at my feet made me reach down and ruffle Rebel's ears. She leaned into the touch, nuzzling my palm as dad pushed into my mind.

Whatever happens, I want you to leave with Caleb, sweetheart. Nothing good will ever come of you if you stay in that fucking place a second longer...

Tobias wanted me to trust dad, said that he'd gone in there with a plan. But I couldn't stop the panic from gripping me tight. He'd just walked in there without a fight. I couldn't shake the image of him being pushed by the guards toward the doors.

Were they hurting him?

I closed my eyes, were they killing him?

My hand clenched against the armrest on the door.

Trust...

It was hard to come by, especially where family had been concerned. But dad had come for me. I touched my cheek and winced, the tenderness still there from my own mother's palm.

Dad had come for us. That meant more than anything. I dropped my hand to the leather seat of the car he'd hidden for this exact moment. The clothes, the guns, the medical kit, all stowed away in the trunk. He knew we were going to run at some stage, with or without him.

But run where? There wasn't a place we could go where The Order didn't reach? That question haunted me as we wound around the hills, inching closer to the city until, in the distance, the faint lights of an all-night diner shone in the dark.

"We'll pull over." Nick lifted his gaze to the mirror. "Get something to eat, find our bearings before we leave again, okay?"

"Sounds good," Caleb answered carefully.

Still, Tobias was quiet, now staring out the window. I lowered my gaze to his hand, clenched around the armrest like a vise. Moonlight caressed his face, bouncing off the sheen of sweat across his forehead. It figured. Here I was, shivering with the cold, and he was hot as ever. I scowled, maybe too hot.

Nick slowed as the diner's lights became brighter. Dust kicked up in a cloud behind us as we hit the shoulder of the road, pulled past a truck parked outside, and nosed the car into the side of the building.

"Everyone okay?" Nick glanced over his shoulder, but it wasn't me he was looking at.

Still, I gave a nod. "Yeah."

Caleb looked, too, his stare finding mine. "Just stay close to us, okay, princess?"

Tobias cracked open the door before I had a chance to speak, then the others moved, climbing out after him.

"Rebel," Nick called, patting his thigh.

She followed his command, lunging between the seats to scurry out his open door. When she leaped out and landed on the ground, she whimpered.

Nick bent and ruffled her ear before checking her back leg. "Easy now, that's a good girl."

He was so kind with her, so careful, making my chest flutter. Empty booths were all I saw as I glanced in the windows of the diner. "At least it's quiet."

The car doors closed with a thud. I shoved my hands into my pockets as Tobias turned his face from me. That hurt. A lot. But Nick was already moving, heading to the front door of the diner, and Caleb followed. I hated leaving Tobias behind, but that pang of guilt in my chest told me he needed space. I didn't like it...no, I didn't like it at all. But I headed to the steps and climbed, following the others.

The bell above the door let out a chime, making me flinch. I glared at the thing before following my stepbrothers inside.

"No dogs." The woman behind the counter snapped as she buffed the counter to a shine.

But Nick didn't listen, just strode close and placed a hundred-dollar bill on the freshly cleaned surface, sliding it toward her. "We'll sit in the back," he said with the kind of tone that was dangerous. "You won't even know she was here."

The woman said nothing, just stared at the money before she slowly reached out, took the bill, and slipped it into her pocket. If she had been the owner, she might've kicked up a fuss, right before she tossed us out. But it didn't look like that was going to happen.

A slow nod from her, and Nick turned. The lone truck driver watched us from the far end of the counter. He scanned us, wiping the corners of his mouth with his napkin before tossing it next to his plate.

We didn't slow, just headed for the last empty booth in the row alongside the widows, like Nick had promised. He stepped aside and motioned for Caleb to slide in first, which he did. I listened to the limping thud of boots coming behind me, then lifted my gaze to the door of the women's bathroom. My breaths were heavy, panic coiled in my stomach, desperate to come out. I needed a second...a second where I could think...

"I'll be back." I left them behind, forcing myself not to lunge for the salvation of a damn restroom.

My steps were silent, when all I wanted to do was scream. I pushed through the door, stepping into the gloom, and for a second I thought I was back there—in the pit of Hell, where the rooms were more like cells and the guards were sick men bent on your destruction.

But then the overhead lights of the restroom blinked on, causing me to stumble for the sink before I stopped, lifted my gaze to the haunted stare in the mirror, and whispered. "What the hell have I done?"

I didn't have time to listen, only spin as the door squealed and that same limping thud of steps followed me in.

"This is the women's—" I started, and froze, the words dying in my mouth.

Tobias's threatening glare was fixed on me. My mouth went dry, my pulse raced. There was a tiny scowl...before he lunged.

He closed the distance between us in a second, his fist in my hair, yanking me backwards to show me who was in control here...*and it wasn't me.*

My jacket gaped open and my t-shirt pulled taut across my breasts, drawing that savage stare.

"Princess..." He purred, reaching up to palm my breast. But the touch wasn't soft or tender. No, nothing about Tobias was tender. I winced as he pinched my nipple hard enough for me to cry out, then raised that fierce glare. "I thought I'd fucking lost you," he growled.

I opened my mouth to speak, but he didn't let me, just slid his hand over my ass, gripped my thigh from underneath, and lifted, hoisting me onto the edge of the sink.

All the fear and the heartache I'd been holding inside tore free. "I thought I'd lost you too."

His mouth was unforgiving and I welcomed it. Every gnash, every bruise, every clench of his hand around my breast. I let out a moan, needing his hard love like I needed air to breathe.

He yanked my jacket from my body and stared into my eyes. "Princess..." he whispered. "I'd crawl through fucking Hell to get back to you, don't you know that by now?"

I melted with his words, lifting my arms as he dragged my shirt over my head. My nipples tightened under his stare. He lowered his head and licked a puckered peak before grazing it with his teeth.

"Oh, God," I whimpered, my hands moving to his clipped hair. "Yes. Yes, Tobias...*yes.*"

Yes, to knowing that.

Yes, to this.

I craved his control, his cruel, manhandling ways. I craved everything about him, from the battle that raged in his eyes, to the torment he took out on my body. Run or fuck, that's all there was. Right now, he was done with running.

His fingers worked the button of my jeans, then spread the zipper wide before he shoved them down. One hard yank and I slipped from the sink until my feet hit the floor.

"T," I whimpered.

He spun me around until I stared into my reflection in the bathroom mirror. But it was his face I saw. His dark eyes that met mine. He slipped his fingers along my crease, yanking the elastic of my panties down.

One hand moved to the middle of my back and gently made me bend. "Spread your legs, princess, and tell me how much you fucking missed me."

My chest pressed against the cold counter as his fingers pushed in. "I missed you," I whispered.

"What was that?" He drove his fingers inside me, then slid them along my crease, reaching between my legs to find my clit. "I couldn't quite hear you."

The force of his body pinned me to the counter. I couldn't move, even if I'd wanted to, and Christ, I didn't want to. I clawed for a hold, opening my legs as far as the jeans and my panties around my knees allowed.

"I m-missed you," I stuttered.

He thrust his fingers inside, stretching me, *fucking me,* stroking that part of me that made me tremble. "How much, princess?"

I gripped the counter as our gazes met in the reflection. "So fucking much."

There was a twitch in the corner of his mouth. This was the punishment he wanted to inflict. Berating me with every thrust of his touch as he reached for his zipper with his other hand. "This cunt is mine, do you understand that?"

"Yes."

"This heart is *mine.*" Those haunting dark eyes were fixed on mine as he grasped my thigh and yanked upwards, splaying my pussy wide. "You know what else is mine?"

My knee slipped, angled against the edge of the counter. He unbuttoned his jeans, shoved them down and, with one hard thrust, drove his cock inside. "Your fucking life. Your..." Thrust. "Fucking... life."

I bucked with the invasion and shoved my hands out, desperate to grab anything as he rammed home.

"No one touches it," he growled and slammed home again. "No one fucking gets to have it...only me...only...*us*."

Us...

My stepbrothers. I grasped the faucets, driving my body backwards, meeting his thrusts.

I barely had a second to adjust to my stepbrother's raw fucking before he pulled out. His eyes were wide. His breaths, savage. I'd never seen anyone so quietly unhinged. "You're mine, Ryth. You've always been mine. No one, and nothing, will take you from me, do you understand that?"

I saw the fear in him then, fear that I'd be taken. Fear that I'd be killed. All he'd known was loss. He was stained with it, from his anger to his consuming need. He drove himself to the edge for me and beyond. Maybe there was no coming back for him... maybe there was no coming back for any of us. But I was here. I was here and there was no going back for me. Not now...not ever.

"Then make me yours."

His breath stilled, and the whole world stilled with it. My skin prickled with the intensity of his gaze as he slowly looked down to my pussy on display, still clenching and pulsing from the brutality of his hunger. He reached out, splayed his fingers wide, and cupped my ass.

His touch was slower, softer and searching. As though I hadn't been real until this moment. The muscles of his throat worked as he swallowed.

"They won't take you from me," he said with chilling certainty. "*No one* is going to take you from me."

He slipped his fingers along my crease, spread my lips, then entered me again. I bit my lower lip and bent my spine, reveling in the feel of him.

"Do you hear me, little sister?" he urged, thrusting more slowly this time. "No one is taking you from me."

I moaned with that slow, demanding stroke and drove back against him.

"Open your eyes, princess. Watch me as I fuck you."

I did, finding that unfathomable stare in the reflection. He was the brother who'd hated me, the brother who'd gone out of his way to be cruel. Now he was the brother who'd kill for me.

The faint clutter of pans pushed in from outside. For a second, I'd forgotten the world outside this bathroom existed—in this moment there was just him—*and this*. I shoved reality aside, focusing on the feel of his big cock inside me.

He leaned forward and grasped my throat. "You like to be fucked hard, little sister?" he grunted, driving into me. "You like the way Caleb drives you?"

I nodded, jolting hard.

"Then consider yourself owned."

"Yes..." I drove back hard against him, meeting his thrusts, driving him deeper and harder.

He owned me.

They *all* owned me.

He reached up and gripped my jaw, turning me to stare into my eyes. "Say my name, little sister."

"Tobias," I moaned.

"Again," he demanded.

"*Tobias.*"

He bucked his hips, driving me against the sink. I had nowhere to go, no room to breathe. It didn't matter anyway. His breath was my breath. His touch, my *everything*.

The intensity in his stare tipped me over the edge and as my orgasm quaked inside me, the door to the bathroom opened.

Tobias was an animal, reaching around his back to whip the sight of a gun at the person who entered the room.

But it was Nick.

"One second, brother," Tobias growled, turning his attention back to me. "That's it, princess. Take it. Take what you need."

I lowered my chest to the cold surface as my pussy clenched. "Oh, God...*oh, God.*"

"That's it, baby," Tobias grunted.

I met Nick's stare in the reflection as my world exploded.

The gun clattered as Tobias shoved it onto the counter, giving one long moan as he thrust once and stilled. His cock kicked. Warmth bloomed Inside me, making me whimper and clench tight.

"Fuck, little mouse," Tobias gasped, the sheen of sweat on his forehead shining. *"Fuck."*

His heavy breaths consumed the space as he stared at me. I'd brought him undone, I knew that now. I glanced at Nick.

No.

I brought *all* of them undone.

Just as they did for me.

"That was just a taste, princess." Tobias drew my focus back as he slid his cock from me and looked down. His fingers went between my legs, sliding in the slick as he pushed his cum back inside. "Make sure you make yourself available to me, day and fucking night. Consider it your punishment for leaving me and don't even think about cleaning this up. I will fucking stain every inch of you by the time I'm done."

My pussy throbbed, the heartbeat clenching around his fingers. But that predatory stare said it all. I would have this. Maybe more than I was prepared for. This was my stepbrother's punishing way.

Make myself available...

My knees trembled. My will was weak.

"Have something to say to me, little sister?" Tobias demanded.

I tried to control my panicked breaths. "No." I licked my lips. "Not at all."

A nod, and he reached down, shoved his cock into his jeans, and zipped up. "Nick?"

Cum coated the inside of my thighs. God, I almost whimpered when Nick stared at the mess his brother had made. "Not yet." He licked his lips as he answered. "Although, seeing you bent over the sink like that is making me reconsider."

Tobias leaned forward and braced his hand against the wall, earning a scowl from Nick.

"I came to tell you the food is ready."

Tobias nodded, then met my stare. "You go eat, princess. I'll be right behind you."

"T," Nick warned.

"I said I'll be right there." Tobias bared his teeth.

Something passed between them. Something I didn't understand. I reached down, tugged my panties and jeans upwards. "What's going on?"

Nick stared at T.

T just looked at me, shaking his head. "Nothing."

But it didn't look like nothing. It looked like a whole lot of something. But no one pushed Tobias. No one told him what to do. He was too damn stubborn for his own good.

"Fine," Nick answered.

"*Fine*," Tobias answered back.

"Men," I muttered, buttoning up my jeans and shaking my head. "No, *brothers*."

They both started after me as I pumped the soap dispenser and washed my hands, tearing off a piece of hand towel and eyeing them as I went. Nick followed me out, and the moment I did, the smell of food hit me.

I hadn't eaten in that place and barely had anything to drink. But I wasn't the only one. Caleb sat waiting, the massive plate of food in front of him untouched. Rebel chewed and gnawed a thick, raw steak on the floor as I slipped into the booth opposite him.

"Better?"

I met Caleb's stare as he searched my face. I knew he saw the marks his brother had left behind. "Not even remotely," I answered, lowering my gaze to the massive cheeseburger and fries waiting. "I'll be better when we're safe and I hear from my dad."

He picked up his knife and fork and carved into his steak. He attacked his food with complete precision, carving, chewing, never once making a mess. I knew he must be starving. He hadn't eaten himself after that one bite of the sandwich.

That place corrupted everything. Nick strode toward us, but instead of sitting down, he kept walking. I took a massive bite of the burger and moaned with the taste, licking the grease and sauce that dripped down my hand, and glanced over my shoulder, watching as Nick spoke to the woman behind the counter.

She lifted her hand and pointed to something in the shadows next to the door. I barely saw my plate as I reached, just grabbed two fries and dragged them through the ketchup before sliding them into my mouth and turned back.

It was a phone. One of those old landlines that stranded motorists with no cell phone reception used. But Nick's phone sat on the table in front of us, with full bars of service.

I chewed, swallowed, and grabbed more, this time without even looking. Instead, I watched my brother as he punched in numbers and spoke into the handset, to who, I didn't know.

"Who is he talking to?"

"Hell if I know," Caleb answered.

I didn't believe him. I met his stare, searching those hazel eyes for the truth. "What's going on?"

One brow rose as he chewed and swallowed, then grabbed the napkin and dabbed the side of his mouth. "Do you want the long version or the short version, little sister?"

He was playing with me. I looked to the closed door of the ladies' room. Tobias still hadn't come out, and all of a sudden, I wasn't hungry, I was worried and pissed.

"Here he comes," Caleb muttered. "You can ask him yourself."

Nick sat down next to Caleb. I didn't wait, motioning with my head to the phone. "Who was that?"

Nick just smiled and glanced at my plate. "You're not hungry, princess?"

"No." I placed my burger down on the plate. "Are you going to answer me?"

There was a twitch in the corner of his mouth as he shook his head. "If you're not hungry, then we'll grab the rest to go."

He waved the waitress over and this time she was only too accommodating, even smiling as she neared. He never once looked away, just held my gaze. "Can you wrap the rest of this up? Add in three more steaks for the dog and six bottles of water, and we'll leave."

She just gave a nod, then reached forward and grabbed my plate, as well as Tobias's untouched food. "Sure thing."

She'd barely left before the clatter of plates echoed through the doorway of the kitchen. Seemed like she was only too happy to get rid of us.

"You want to tell me what's going on, Nick?" I demanded. "I deserve to know."

"You do." His smile was sad this time. "And I want to tell you, but first we need to get you somewhere safe. Somewhere where they can't track you. Somewhere where they can't find you. Only then will we tell you what's going on, and why."

The bathroom door opened and Tobias stumbled out, only this time he limped a little harder. That sheen of sweat was more obvious now as he made his way to the table. "Are we leaving?"

"Yes," Nick answered.

"Good." Tobias seemed pleased with that and kept on walking past the waitress as she returned, grabbed the two remaining plates, and left.

Barely a minute later, and she returned, carrying a plastic bag filled with containers of food. Nick reached into his pocket, slipped out another hundred-dollar bill, and left it on the table before sliding out. "Thank you."

He grabbed the bag and motioned toward the door. "Ryth."

He didn't call my name like that. Not normally.

I grabbed a napkin off the table in front of me, wiped my hands, and left it behind as I slipped out of the booth and followed them outside.

Tobias had barely made it three steps ahead of us before we caught up. I stepped down onto the first step as he wobbled and reached for the railing.

Only he missed it.

"Tobias," I cried out.

He took a step, and another, before finally, his knees gave way, sending him crashing to the ground. Panic surged through me as I lunged. "Tobias!" I called his name...

But this time, he didn't get up.

TEN

Vivienne

They were out there, on the other side of this damn door...someone was, at least.

I was sure of it.

I *felt* them more than heard a sound. The air was charged, rippling with that unmistakable tension of male. I was starting to *hate* that fucking stain. I took a step toward the door, then glanced at the sheer black curtains covering the window. I'd throw myself through the damn thing, even from up this high...if I had anywhere to escape to.

No. My hope of that had disappeared in the rear window of the car that *bastard* had abducted me in. Ryth and her stepbrothers were left far behind. I didn't even know if they were still alive. She would be, of that I was sure. The Order wouldn't risk their property.

And that's all we were to them.

Property.

I fixed my gaze on the sheer curtains, pulled aside enough for me to glimpse the darkness outside...again.

Again.

The word resounded. Three days they'd held me here. Three days to pace the floor and come up with every vile thing I wanted to do to that man...*and* his fucking sons, the moment I could escape. I was London St. James's prisoner. There were no two ways around that. I'd tried the locks on the windows, but the plastic cutlery he left me with proved useless.

Still, I'd managed to get one of the locks bent enough to look like I could escape. That would piss him off and ruin his perfect bedroom...*one he'd set up for me.*

Did he think the darkened, moody tone was sexy? I lifted my gaze to the black felt headboard on the king size bed and the soft pink Egyptian cotton sheets. Did he think I'd like *anything* he bought me? The perfect sheets drew my gaze. Sheets that felt like satin as I slid between them.

Right now, only the fitted bottom sheet was there. I looked down to the same dusty pink wrapped around my body. Because the other one was occupied. I tucked the corner back in place around my hips and checked the knot at my back. It seemed like his expensive sheets weren't only good for sleeping on, they also came in handy to wear.

Black, paired with blood red, and soft pinks filled the expansive room. No, I hated this room and everything in it.

Ward.

That's what he called me. But that was just a pretty name for a captive. His...own personal slave. Only he hadn't forced me. Not yet, at least. I pressed my palm against the door, then tried the handle. The lock caught, the steel, unforgiving. *"Let me the fuck out!"*

I slammed my fist against the wood.

Outside, there was a whisper of sound.

A scrape of something on the other side.

Terror pricked at the nape of my neck, standing my hair on end. "I know you're there." I pressed my palm against the painted wood. "I can hear you breathing."

"Can you?"

I flinched at the voice and pulled away. But the voice wasn't London's. It was the son, only which one was it? Their identical faces filled me, only everything else was a blur. "Your name." I stared at the door. "What is it again?"

Silence. Before a tiny chuff.

That sound pissed me off. "I say something funny to you?"

Still there was nothing.

The corner of my lip twitched. "You can't keep me here forever. I'll get free. I might even kill *daddy* while I'm at it, what do you think about that, asshole?"

I knew he heard me, but still, he said nothing. That only incited my rage.

"*Answer me!*" I screamed, beating the door until it shuddered. "*Answer MEEE!*"

But he didn't. Because he wasn't there, not anymore. There was an emptiness he'd left behind. It was a vacuum of silence. Just like this fucking place. A crushing weight...a heaviness in my gut. Because I'd disappeared, again...hadn't I?

Just like the first time, when my family got rid of me the first opportunity they had. I'd fought and kicked when they'd tried to drag me to some fucking convent. I'd lashed out, begging to stay when they realized their threats to me were nothing more than words.

To be fair, they'd never loved me.

Hell, they'd barely even tolerated me.

Because they weren't my blood. No one was.

I should consider myself lucky that I hadn't been in the foster care system. No, instead I'd been raised by parents who had the emotional connections of fucking robots.

All I had was me. My wits. My strength. *My cunning.*

That had to be enough to get me out of this.

I didn't have a choice, did I?

The slow thud of footsteps echoed from the stairs. I dropped my hand from the door and stepped backwards. I'd had this moment in my head for hours...but now I wasn't so sure.

I glanced down at the sheet wrapped around me and stepped backwards until the backs of my legs hit the edge of the bed as the lock clicked and the door opened.

Then the devil himself walked in, carrying a tray of food.

Of course, he locked the door behind him. Nothing could be that easy. He didn't glance my way, didn't even speak as he placed the tray on the desk next to the half-eaten sandwich and the empty water jug. "Good." His words were careful. "You're starting to learn."

"Fuck...*you.*"

That impenetrable, icy stare cut my way as he straightened, then his gaze slowly lowered. I didn't fight the surge of satisfaction at the look of distaste that followed. "Where are the clothes I provided?"

"I threw them out the window."

He flinched, his gaze shifting to the curtains behind me. "You did what?"

I smiled wider. "I threw them...*out* the window."

His nostrils flared. His eyes narrowed, drawing attention to the faint lines near his temple that showed every bit of his age. I jutted my chin higher. "If you want someone to dress like a whore, then you should wear the fucking clothes yourself...*Daddy*."

He went still. So still he looked like a damn statue, then he moved across the room faster than I could track. His hand lashed out, gripping me by the throat, forcing me backwards until I fell onto the bed.

He was on top of me in an instant, leaving no room for me to escape.

"Those cost me a fucking fortune." His cultured, stony tone made fear flutter in my chest, as he looked down to the sheet hugging the curve of my breasts. "The next time you decide to throw away something I buy you will be the last time you get the freedom to perform such an act. Do I make myself clear?"

A shiver passed through me.

He cut that deadly stare to mine, his grip tightening, until I fought the urge to cough. "I said...*do...I...make... myself...clear?*"

"Yes," I whispered.

Slowly his hold eased before he pulled away and stood. That chilling stare fixed on my body, the way my hard breaths pushed against the fabric. I felt a trickle of cold air, a slither that caressed my hip where the sheet gaped open. The graze of his fingers made me shiver as he pushed the sheet aside for it to fall between my parted thighs. One more inch to the left and he'd see everything...revealing the nothing I wore underneath.

Because that's what he wanted…wasn't it?

My body bare.

Open.

Exposed.

Waiting for the brutality of his touch.

He licked his lips, his chest rising.

I saw it now. London St. James had a breaking point, and I'd finally reached it.

That flutter in my chest sank lower, until it settled between my thighs, tucked a little deeper than the sheet. My pussy clenched with the throb. I hated that, hated how, instead of beating him with my fists and screaming in his face, I wanted him to push that sheet wider.

I wanted him to see me.

To fucking use me.

To take me back down to that basement and make good on his threats.

Oh God…

My cheeks burned. The heat only made that heartbeat between my legs throb harder. I didn't need a mirror to see my own humiliation, I saw it all on his face. There was a twitch at the corner of his mouth as he fed on my shame like a vampire.

"Now, I want you to eat the food I bring you…and Vivienne."

"Yes?"

He glanced at the fabric hugging my pussy, his voice edged with need. "I've had it with your attitude. One more display from you and I'll take you downstairs. Do you understand what I'm saying?"

Throb...

I swallowed and slowly nodded, my pulse frantic in my chest.

"Good," he murmured, meeting my gaze. "Now eat. I'll return later for the tray."

He spun on his heel and went to the desk, then picked up the plastic sandwich plate and water jug before heading for the door.

I didn't dare breathe until the door locked behind him. I just waited for it to *snap* before the air left my lungs in a *whoosh*.

"Jesus." I dropped my hands to the comforter and fisted the softness.

That was close...

That was real fucking close.

Throb...

Throb...

I shifted my thighs, the faint brush of fabric, tickling the sides of my pussy. I was wet...and *aching*. I reached down, dragged the edge of that expensive fucking sheet aside, and sank my fingers in.

"*Ohhh*," I moaned, closing my eyes.

I wasn't soft, wasn't warm. I didn't move first for my clit in an attempt to get myself ready. I just sank two fingers in, as far as they'd go—it wasn't far enough. *Not anywhere near enough.* I parted my thighs wider and thrust again.

I've had it with your attitude.

A moan tore free, low and guttural, sounding like an animal.

Take you down to the basement.

*Take you...take you...*I quickened my thrusts, sliding out of the slick to find my clit. Fuck, I was wet...wetter than I'd ever been in my life. "No." I clamped my eyes tighter. I didn't want to be, but I couldn't stop this, not even if I tried.

I wanted this. I wanted...*him.*

My clit pulsed, my pussy clenched.

As my mind screamed for release.

I drove three fingers into my cunt and stilled, bucking my hips up from the bed. I'd let him fuck me in that moment...him *and* his two sons. I'd let him do whatever he wanted...

Fuck.

I came harder, pulsing, clamping, warming against my hand. I closed my thighs together and rolled, clamping my fingers in place still inside me...and as my mind slowly came back to reality, I heard that sound outside the door again.

The weight of him.

Whoever he was...

And knew he'd heard everything I'd just done.

"Fuck you," I gasped. "Fuck you all."

I slowly slid my fingers free, lifting them to my mouth. Salty, sweet. I liked my own taste. My eyes focused, finding the tiny hint of black peeking out from under the edge of the pillow.

I didn't want to move, but I did, stretching up to snag the edge of the garment and dragged it free...lifting it into the air in front of me.

This wasn't lingerie. This was pure fucking entertainment...*his entertainment.*

The high-waisted harness panties were mostly straps at the back. Thick around the waist to dive down to thin straps, they were supposed to hug my hips. I was guessing the two plunging ones were supposed to crest the curve of my ass and dive underneath, perfect to pull me open.

He wanted me to wear this.

No, he *demanded* I wear this.

For my humiliation and nothing more. Because he couldn't break the contract. If he did, then I'd be gone for good. That's all that stood between me, that monster, and the stark white walls of The Order. One pathetic slip of paper and his goddamn signature.

I bet I'd even hate his fucking scrawl.

Was London St. James a man of honor? No. But he was a man of consequence. I swallowed hard, still feeling the strength of his grip around my throat. That I already knew. Break his oath to the monsters who ran The Order and there'd be hell to pay.

I stared at the flimsy mess in my hand.

If he wasn't prepared to break the contract...

Then why the hell did he want me to wear this?

I'll take you down to the basement.

His threat still lingered.

He might not be able to invade my body, but that wouldn't stop him from degrading me in other ways. London was a man hellbent on my destruction. The only question was, would he claim my desire as well?

ELEVEN

Caleb

"TOBIAS?" RYTH CALLED AND STUMBLED FORWARD. *"Tobias!"*

I just stared at my brother on the ground, trying to figure it out. "What happened?" Fear kicked in, making me reach behind and grab the gun from the waistband of my pants before I spun, searching the empty parking lot for movement. "Was he hit?"

Nick let out a snarl and lunged, falling to his knees beside T.

"Nick!" I roared. "Was he fucking hit?"

Ryth looked up at him as she gripped Tobias's shoulder and rolled him onto his back. I risked a glance, searching my brother's chest for blood until Nick blocked my view. "He hasn't been hit. He hasn't...*been hit.*"

I sucked in hard breaths as his words hit home. *Jesus...* Still, I didn't trust anyone, not any more. Not where my family was concerned. I aimed the muzzle towards the rig parked outside and swung to the darkened tree line that surrounded the diner.

"Tobias," Ryth pleaded. "Can you hear me? *Please, say something.*"

"We need to get him to the car." Nick glanced my way. "You need to help me."

Tobias's breaths were so shallow his chest barely moved. Christ, he didn't look good. No, he didn't look good at all. I gave a small nod, tucked the gun back into my waistband, and headed for them.

Nick was still hurt. The stab wound in his side was barely even stitched. There was no way I was letting him hurt himself more. "I'll grab his shoulders, you take his feet."

"Give me the keys, Nick." Ryth pushed up from the ground and held out her hand. "I'll open the doors."

He searched his pockets, handing them over before she hurried away to where the car was parked alongside the diner.

"Rebel." Nick gave a jerk of his head. "After her."

I wanted to tell him the command was pointless. The dog was barely a pup, and even if it did under— I'd barely opened my mouth, and the damn thing limped away. I shook my head in disbelief, then strode toward my brother's head, bent, and slid my hands under his armpits. "Ready?"

"When you are."

My muscles seized and my back strained as I drove my boots into the ground and lifted upwards. "Christ, T," I grunted. "You're a heavy motherfucker—

Memories pushed in. When T and I sat in the seats outside the surgery while we waited for someone to fucking tell us if our brother had survived. T when he'd stood beside mom's casket, and when he'd taken on two goddamn bouncers inside that club when they'd come for me.

He was always fighting.

Fighting dad.

Fighting life.

"You better stay alive, you stubborn bastard," I muttered, staggering toward the car. "You better...stay a-fucking-live."

Ryth waited beside the open back door with a terrified look on her face. I wanted to say something to comfort her. But any hope I had to offer was weak at best.

"I'll climb in, just hold him, okay?" I almost dropped his shoulders as I backed into the seat and dragged him in after me.

She was gone in a heartbeat, scurrying around the rear of the car to open the other door for me to pull him all the way inside. "The light," Nick urged. "Get the goddamn light."

I stabbed the switch above and the interior of the car was filled with a weak glow. Still, it was enough...enough to see the shine of blood that had soaked through his black jeans.

"What the fuck happened?" I stared at Nick as he unbuttoned Tobias's jeans and yanked them down.

"We just..." Ryth started, stopping as we glimpsed the top of the white bandage. "Had sex." She finished, slowly shaking her head.

"Sex didn't do this, princess." Nick tugged my brother's pants lower. "A bullet did."

The lower they went, the worse the sight became, until there was barely any white left on the gauze. It was stained with blood instead.

"Jesus," I hissed. "Why the fuck didn't he say anything?"

Nick jerked his gaze to mine. "You've met our brother, right?"

That said it all. "Stubborn motherfucker," I snarled as Nick tugged down the top of the bandage and stared at the dark, oozing wound.

"Fuck." Nick closed his eyes for a second, and when he opened them, all I saw was fear.

"Oh God. *Oh God...*" our sister whispered. "We need to get him to a hospital."

"*No hospital,*" Nick and I answered in unison.

"What do you mean, *no hospital?*" She pushed in around me, stabbing her finger toward the wound. "Look at it, that's bad... *that's real fucking bad.*" Her voice broke, until there was nothing...

Nothing but silence.

My stomach clenched tight, driving the taste of that steak into my throat, because I *was* looking at it. The gauze glistened. The wound was black around the edges. It looked bad...real fucking bad.

I did this.

There was no way around it.

I caused all of this. If I hadn't gone after Killion—if I hadn't left them behind.

The car seemed to sway under the weight of consequence. I closed my eyes as that heaviness pressed down on my chest. We had nowhere to go now, and no one to trust. We couldn't go to the hospital. We sure as hell couldn't stay here.

"There's a doctor."

I opened my eyes.

Nick licked his lips and met my gaze. "This guy."

I scowled. "What guy?"

My brother straightened, dug into his pocket, and pulled out some kind of business card, muttering, "A friend of a friend, apparently."

I narrowed in on the damn thing in his hand. "A friend? What fucking friend?"

But Nick didn't answer. He just shook his head and stared at me weirdly. I didn't like that look at all. *"What fucking friend, Nick?"*

A rasp of a breath was followed by a moan. Tobias slowly opened his eyes. "What the fuck happened?"

"You collapsed." Ryth pushed around me, climbing into the footwell, and I moved out of her way as she barked. *"Why the hell didn't you tell me you'd been shot?"*

But the smartass just gave a weak fucking smile, saying nothing as he closed his eyes. The moment he did, that smirk turned into a wince.

"We need to call the doc," Nick answered.

Tobias cracked open his eyes, staring at our sister. "Can't...trust anyone."

"Yeah, well, we're running out of fucking options," Nick snapped. "I sure as hell *am not* losing a brother *and* a fucking dad all on the same day."

And a fucking dad?

I flinched. *And* a fucking dad? What the hell did that mean? Did Dad...*did he...*

Nick's eyes widened as though he realized instantly he'd just dropped a goddamn bomb.

I swallowed, forcing myself to focus on T. "This guy is a doctor?"

Nick just gave a slow nod. A doctor and the loss of a father. Looked like my brothers had been busy.

That cold edge came back in my voice. "You sure we can trust this guy?"

"No." Nick stared at Tobias's shallow breaths. "But right now, we don't have a choice."

"Then call him," I answered carefully. "Call him and we'll deal with whatever comes."

As long as T is alive.

I didn't care what happened to me. Not one fucking bit, as long as they were safe.

My brother stepped away, leaving Ryth to reach over and brush Tobias's cheek. "You fucking idiot." She rested her head against his. "Why the hell didn't you tell me you were hurt?"

"Do you think you could've stopped him?" I answered for him as Nick's voice drifted through the open car door, sounding careful…and relieved.

"Help me," I said to Ryth as I gripped my brother again, tugging him further in. "We need to be ready to move."

She wrestled with his jeans, pulling them high enough so she could slide in around his legs.

The crunch of boots came closer as Nick returned. "We have an address. A cabin about an hour's drive from here."

I held T's shoulders and carefully closed the door. "An hour?"

"Thirty for me. But an hour for the Doc." Nick rounded the car and climbed in behind the wheel, reaching through the gap between the seats. "Keys, princess."

I hurried after him, yanking open the passenger door to climb in. I called Rebel to me and held her on my lap to keep her out of the back seat. The sedan's engine roared to life before the headlights splashed against the side of the diner.

We peeled out of the parking lot, scattering rocks in our wake. The fucking drive was agony. My focus was divided between the road and my brother. But still, my mind raced.

This guy better be fucking trustworthy.

He better keep our brother alive.

The GPS glowed in the darkness as Nick steered with his forearms and pulled up the map. "Fuck, I can hardly tell which road is which out here."

A twitch flared in my jaw. That wasn't what I wanted to hear. "Just don't get us fucking lost."

A quick glance between the seats to where Ryth was cradling Tobias and he turned to the road. "I won't."

Silence pushed in, leaving me to scan every road we passed, and all the while, that panic seethed inside me...*We weren't going to make it... We weren't going to make it... We weren't—*

"I think this is it."

I searched the road ahead, catching sight of a turn off, before glancing at the GPS. "You sure?"

"That's what the map says."

I had to trust Nick knew what he was doing as he signaled, then turned. We traveled along that road for a good twenty minutes.

All I saw were trees and darkness and not another damn house in sight.

Nick was riveted to that screen, slowing the car until we were at a crawl as we passed by a faded yellow mailbox.

"That's it," he muttered, glancing at the screen and back up. "DeLuca."

We turned in, taking it even slower along the rutted driveway that was designed for a four-wheel drive and not a damn sedan. The tires skidded and we slipped sideways. Still, there was no one better behind the wheel.

Nick handled the car with precision, turning into the slide, then gently correcting as we inched toward a large cabin set against the trees.

"Must be some kind of family retreat." Nick leaned forward, scanning the grounds. "Doesn't look like anyone's here."

Tobias whimpered behind us, then mumbled something I didn't catch.

"I think he's dreaming," Ryth murmured.

I could only stare at my little brother, trying to figure out exactly when our world had started to fall apart.

It was him…

Dad.

He was the catalyst.

His betrayal of Mom.

And now Ryth.

The fact he was apparently now dead tore me apart. Part of me was satisfied, the other was still his damn son. I wrestled with that as Nick pulled up alongside the cabin and killed the engine.

I climbed out, leaving Ryth and Nick along with Tobias in the car. The moment I looked at those dark windows, listening to the wind howl through the trees, I felt a chill crawl along my spine.

Maybe coming here was a mistake after all? "This doesn't feel right." I looked around and slowly made for the cabin.

"We don't really have a choice, do we?"

No, we didn't.

Mounds of fallen leaves stacked against the outside of the cabin, blown in from the trees. The place even *felt* empty. I was starting to think we'd wasted time driving all the way out here... time we didn't have.

I turned and opened my mouth to tell Nick we should go back, that we'd find something, a pharmacy...or a damn doctor we could abduct in an effort to save our brother's life, when the wash of headlights cut through the trees and flowed over me.

The heavy throb of an engine followed as a dark four-wheel drive skidded and rolled down the driveway toward us.

I reached around, grabbed the gun at my back, and neared the car. The hulking vehicle came closer until, with a skid, it pulled up hard, parking beside the sedan. The headlights stayed on, blinding me as I neared.

"Nick," I warned, lifting the gun as I stepped closer.

The *thud* of a car door followed....

And I didn't know if they were friends, or foes.

TWELVE

Ryth

The glare of headlights flooded the car from behind us. Nick winced and shied away from the beam in the rear-view mirror before climbing out and leaving me alone with the pale, shivering form beside me.

"T," I croaked, brushing his arm. "Can you hear me?"

Nothing. Not a wince, or a lie of a smile, not even for me. "It's going to be okay," I whispered. "It's going to be okay."

If a lie was all we had to hold onto, then I'd dig my claws into it and cling tight with all I had. I'd *make* him okay...because for me, there was no future without him. I climbed out, biting down on the tremors.

"Behind me, Ryth," Caleb commanded as the four-wheel drive skidded coming toward us.

I rubbed my arms, easing the goosebumps, and moved on instinct. I was so used to them protecting me, always putting themselves at risk. I took a step and realized I didn't want that.

Not anymore.

I wanted to stop this tormenting ride of guns, betrayal, and loss. I wanted to get off...and never come back. I wanted us to disappear, to step out of this mayhem and never come back. Not for Dad, or for Mom. Not for anyone but us.

Protect them...

The need howled inside me.

Protect...them.

Headlights bounced against the sedan my father had left for us. I turned as the gleaming black Range Rover came to a stop and the engine was switched off. The driver's door opened and a man climbed out. But he didn't come toward us, just stood in the open door, scanning each one of us before he looked at someone in the passenger's seat and spoke in a hushed tone. "It's okay, it's safe."

It's safe?

Was he talking about us?

The passenger's door opened. I didn't know who I'd expected to climb out, but it wasn't the pretty young woman who took one look at me and smiled.

"Nick." The strange guy nodded to my stepbrother. "Is he?"

"In the car," Nick answered, striding to the door I'd left open. "Kit, grab my—"

But she was already moving, heading to the rear of the four-wheel drive. "On it."

The stranger pulled out his phone and pressed the flashlight, shining the beam on T as he leaned into the car. I held my breath and stepped closer, my arms wrapped tightly around my body, desperate to hear every word this man had to say.

"He's going to be okay." She spoke as she headed our way, her smile widening just for me. "Just you wait, my brother is the best emergency doctor in the state."

"*Kit.*" The soft bark came from inside the car. "What have I told you about saying things like that?"

She just gave me a wink and instantly the breath I was holding released as she muttered. "Always tell the truth?"

I liked her...

No, I more than liked her.

I needed her.

Her faith. Her smile. Her warm, brown eyes as the stranger straightened from the back seat. "We need to get him inside."

"Caleb." Nick raced around to the other side of the car.

"Come on." She jerked her head toward the cabin. "You can help me open up."

She heaved the massive black tactical bag filled with medical equipment from their vehicle. I stepped closer. "Can I help with that?"

One look at the desperation in my eyes, and she nodded. I grabbed the handles and pulled it closer, almost crumbling with the weight. But she never gave me an option, just hurried up the steps to the wide veranda and disappeared into the gloom. I followed, listening to the grunts of my stepbrothers behind me as they carried Tobias to the cabin.

The *clunk* of a lock sounded before light spilled out of the open front door, illuminating the way.

"Second door on the left down the hall, that way." She pointed deeper into the cabin.

I raced forward, hurrying through the space as Tobias unleashed a roar that made my stomach clench and my heart hammer. I flung open the door and reached around, flicked on the light, and stepped inside.

It was some kind of surgical room, fitted with monitors, equipment, and cupboards of instruments.

"Get him on the table," the doctor barked over Tobias' scream.

I heaved the bag onto the long counter that stretched along the wall, and turned, rushing to his side. "I'm here." I grabbed my stepbrother's hand. "I'm right here."

He gripped the side of the stainless steel table with his other hand and fixed a wide, terrified stare on me. His panting breaths blew my hair as the doctor directed, "We need to get these jeans off."

"Ryth," Tobias gasped.

"I'm not going anywhere." I fixed my gaze on his. "Look at me."

He did, clinging to my hand as Nick unbuttoned his jeans and pulled down his zipper. The stranger moved the bag I'd hauled in, opened it and rifled through, pulling out a plastic case full of vials. He grabbed one, then a syringe, and filled it with the contents. "Kit."

"It's ready," she answered, drawing my focus.

I hadn't even seen her in the room, but she was pushing an IV stand closer to the table.

"We're going to need that hoodie off, as well." The doctor nodded to Tobias.

"Help me?" she asked.

I dropped Tobias's hold only long enough to yank the sleeve and pull his hoodie over one shoulder and his head. Then his clammy grasp was mine again.

"I need to hook this up," the doctor said as he worked, tearing open an alcohol swab and cleaning the crook of Tobias's arm. "Small sting," he muttered, sliding the needle in deep.

Kit moved fast, crossing the room to yank open a drawer and come back.

"Here." She tore a strip of tape and placed it over the IV line as the doctor injected the drugs into the port.

"It'll ease the pain," he said, staring at Tobias. "Hold on now."

Tobias bucked with the agony, gripping the table tight as they pulled his jeans down. But not once did his hold on my hand tighten. No, he made sure of that. Even in agony, his first instinct was to protect me.

"I always w-wondered about living in a cabin like this," I blurted, my words punctuated with harsh breaths. But they were the only words that came to me. Right now, I didn't care.

Tobias stared at me. "What?"

"A cabin." I kept talking. It didn't matter, as long as he was focused on anything other than his brother's efforts. "I wondered what it'd be like. You know, hunting, hiking, fishing. The only problem is, I hate fish."

T's brows creased. "You...hate...*fish.*" He groaned as Nick lifted his leg while Caleb tugged his jeans down. "Who hates fish?"

"Me," Caleb added. "I detest it, actually."

"*Fuck.*" Tobias bucked as the doctor took a pair of scissors to the bloodied bandage wrapped around his thigh.

"Lucas?" Nick glanced at the guy.

The doctor winced. That wasn't a good sign. "I'm going to need to get this out."

He moved, heading to the open bag once more. More drugs were pushed into Tobias's veins, but these worked fast. His eyes started to close, drooping until they were barley slits, then nothing.

Just the slow, steady rise of his chest.

"You might want to step out for this." Lucas looked at me when he spoke.

I just shook my head, clasping Tobias's weak grasp in mine. "I'm staying."

"Suit yourself."

He didn't waste a second, squirting gel on his hands and set to work opening sterile packs. He picked up forceps. I looked away at the last minute, focusing on Tobias instead. "You're going to be okay," I whispered. "You're going to be okay."

THIRTEEN

Nick

She didn't leave his side, even long after the Doc had removed the bullet and finished stitching his wound. Instead, she stayed there, gripping his hand, her eyes wide with fear as she stared at him.

"He needs to rest now." Lucas fixed the end of a bandage in place and adjusted the electrodes fixed to my brother's chest. "I'll stop in and check on him. Right now, there's nothing more you can do." He stepped closer, placing his hand on my shoulder, his voice somber. "Apart from taking care of yourself."

I stared at the bloody instruments laid out on the hospital table next to my brother, my head a damn mess of all the *what ifs*. *What if we lost him...what if I lost them all.*

My dad was one thing...

His own fucking betrayal pulled the trigger on his damn life.

But my brothers?

That would be too much to bear.

The door opened behind me and his sister's gentle voice followed. "Food's ready."

"Good." Lucas smiled at her. "Because I'm starving."

My stomach growled at the mention of food. The diner food was still sitting in the car, long forgotten. It looked like Rebel was about to have a huge meal. I didn't want to think about food at a time like this. Still, there were more than me in this. I moved close to her side, brushing her shoulder. "Princess?"

She shook her head. "You go, I'm staying here."

I wanted to argue, but one look at the woman sitting beside my brother and I knew it was pointless. Wild horses couldn't drag her away. "I'll bring you something to eat."

She would've nodded to anything in that moment. I doubted she'd heard me at all. I waited while the others left, then I followed, giving her the space she needed. Kit was already in the kitchen, the clatter of pans drawing me along the hallway.

She had to be the stepsister the doc told us about back at the safehouse, the one that was in trouble, enough trouble to make him gunshy around Benjamin Rossi.

Caleb stood next to the fireplace, watching the first faint flickers of flame erupt from the starter. I hadn't seen him leave, that's how out of it I was. I'd barely seen the place when I'd carried T in. But I did now. It was bigger than expected, filled with stone and timber and the scent of pine.

I crossed the living room and headed for the kitchen, now drawn by the heady scent of bacon and eggs. Lucas grabbed a plate piled with fresh buttered toast, eggs, and a mess of crispy bacon and handed it to me.

"Thanks." I watched his stepsister carry another plate to Caleb, who took one look at the food and shook his head. Stubborn motherfucker.

But she was feisty, shoving the damn thing at him until he took it.

Good.

I almost smiled, watching as she shook her head and carried another plate back along the hall to the room we'd just left. I saw Ryth in her, maybe a little too much. Sweet and bratty at the same time. I took a bite of toast, chewed and swallowed, then felt nauseaous.

Were we really safe here? Or had we dragged these people into our own goddamn mess. The thought of that made me feel fucking sick...

"She's lovely." Kit drew my gaze as she ruffled Rebel's ears, then glanced my way. "Where did you get her?"

Her howls in that fighting ring pushed into my head. "Nowhere good," I answered.

"Aww." She turned back to the pup, stroked her head, and pulled her in for a cuddle. "But she's good now, isn't she?"

"Yeah," I answered, desperate to protect them all. "She's good now."

"There's a main bedroom at the end of the hall." Lucas drew my attention back. "It's big and separate from the rest of the cabin. You and your...family are welcome to whatever you need."

I gave a nod, chewing my lip, then swallowed. "I can't thank you enough."

"No thanks necessary. We all need help every now and then. But those men, Nick. They're still coming, aren't they?"

I winced. "Yes."

"For revenge?"

I shook my head, that sinking feeling weighing me down again.

"Because you have something they want," he said carefully. It wasn't a question, more like a confirmation. I waited for the question.

"Do you at least have a plan to get out of this?"

I placed the plate on the counter. "Oh, I have a plan. Just one you won't like."

One brow rose. "Tell me."

I met his stare and said the one name he didn't want to hear. "Benjamin Rossi."

There was a twitch in the corner of his eye before he looked away. He didn't like the idea of bringing in the Stidda Mafia boss, but right now, I was all out of options.

The Rossis were tied up in this somehow and as much as I wanted to push and find out the real story between them, I needed to mind my own damn business.

"Then you gotta do what you gotta do," Lucas said carefully.

He went quiet, chewing silently until he moved to the sink. The silence was empty and awkward. I needed to say something... but what was there to say?

He placed his plate in the sink, leaving it unwashed, and stepped away before stopping and glancing my way. "I take it you have...protection?"

"Yeah." I answered, remembering the bag of guns in the trunk of the sedan.

Lucas walked over to his stepsister, who was still loving on Rebel, and brushed his hand along her thick curls, murmuring words I couldn't hear. She rose and gave Rebel one last pat on the head before she glanced toward the hall. "She hasn't come out."

She met my stare, concern blooming. "I took her food and she said she'd come out, but she hasn't. I'm a little worried."

I nodded. "I'll check on her."

"I'll get our things from the car," Caleb offered before heading for the door.

I left him and turned for that room as Lucas and his sister headed for a hallway on the other side of the cabin, urging myself to mind my own business. I cracked open the door to the surgical room, listening to the same *beep...beep...beep* that haunted me. But the moment I stepped inside, I stopped.

Ryth had her head on Tobias's arm, the plate of food untouched beside her. She was asleep, her breaths slow and deep. Fuck, she looked peaceful. I didn't want to wake her.

The heavy thud of Caleb's steps carried down the hall, heading to the master suite. He returned, stopping behind me and looking over my shoulder. "Damn," he said, staring at our sister.

"Yeah," I agreed. "Damn."

I moved to her side.

"Nick, let me."

I gave a nod. The last thing I needed was to tear myself up further carrying my stepsister. But as Caleb picked her up and cradled her against his chest, I fought a pang of jealousy.

He carried her to the room at the end of the hall and I followed. The massive king-sized bed sat in the middle of the room. There was a bathroom off to the side.

We worked in silence, taking off her shoes and jeans before tucking her head on the pillow in the middle of the bed. I kicked off my boots and pushed down my own jeans before slipping in beside her. Caleb moved to the door and flipped off the light.

A second was all it took for the bed to sink on the other side. Warm fingers brushed my hand, finding my grasp. Ryth was the only person who could bring us together, even in our hate.

I closed my eyes as darkness pulled me down, but before I slipped completely under, I heard the faint thud of Doc's steps as he checked on my brother. Then I was falling, and with her hand clasping mine, I slept.

FOURTEEN

Ryth

A grunt woke me. The sound was a low growl in my ear, pulling me from the darkness.

"Princess..." Nick groaned in his sleep, his tone desperate.

*I'm right here...*I answered. But the words never reached my lips. Instead, it took me a heartbeat to remember.

Nick.

Nick was beside me.

I reached out, my cold fingers touching his warmth. I exhaled as the bed shifted behind me, drawing me to the heat. Caleb was here as well, huddled on the other side of the massive bed. I searched for him, brushing his chest, my touch lingering for just a moment, my thoughts dreamy and slow. We were together. We were safe...until the memory of Tobias hit me.

His screams followed, tearing me from the comfort. I shoved upwards, scanning the gloom. My heart hammered as everything hit me. *Tobias...Tobias in the bathroom of the diner. Tobias as he crumbled and fell...*How could I have forgotten? How could I sleep without him?

I shoved against the pillow, moving to the foot of the bed before leaving the two sleeping forms behind. The moment my feet hit the icy wooden floor, I caught my breath. A shudder tore free as I wrapped my arms around my middle and searched the room.

I didn't think. I just *moved*, stumbling forward until I hit a wall and searched for a handle. My fingers hit steel. One twist and I was out. The hinges squealed, making me wince. I held my breath and gently closed the door behind me.

All I cared about was finding him...

*Come on...*I searched along the wall in the dark until I found another handle, then turned. The faint beep of a monitor made me still for a second. I breathed in the sharp tang of antiseptic, then slowly stepped in.

But there was only silence.

He was still alive.

I knew that.

But still, I didn't like the quiet. It made me feel...*alone*.

"Tobias?" I whispered, moving further into the room and closing the door behind me.

There was no answer. I took a step, then another, reaching out so as not to hit the machines, until the hoarse whisper came through the dark. "Scurry... scurry, little mouse."

I jumped, my pulse pounding. "You scared the shit out of me."

In the faint glow of the monitor, I caught the curl of his lips. "Can't sleep?"

I moved closer. "I did a little. But I can't now."

He gave a nod, stilled for a second, then gripped the edge of the bed and shifted to the side, enough for me to lie beside him.

Because it was always for me.

I was careful as I climbed up and swung my feet, but I bumped his leg and he stiffened. I winced, searching his face. "Sorry."

He gave a nod, then he lifted his arm, letting me curl against him.

"Sleep, Ryth," he murmured, closing his eyes. His voice was etched with exhaustion.

I did, drifting...

But I didn't for long, opening my eyes to the darkness. Peace slipped away, leaving me to listen to Tobias's heavy breaths. I loved that sound...*I craved that sound*. It was the sound of life, of comfort, driving away all the things that had happened to us. Everything hit me all at once. Mom. Dad...I lifted my gaze to T's peaceful face. Him. I'd almost lost him...I almost *lost*...

I shoved the image of him lying on the ground outside the diner aside and slowly rose, making sure I didn't wake him. Instead, I slipped from the bed and padded out of the room.

It took a second for my eyes to adjust as I headed out of the hallway and stopped. Moonlight spilled through the kitchen window. The soft glow was enough for me to find a light switch. Overhead lights blinked on. I looked around, taking in the wood and stone of the sleek, expensive rustic kitchen. The entire cabin was like this, well maintained, neat, and earthy. I traced my fingers along the gleaming countertop, stopped at the sink, and stared out into the night.

It was still early, too early for me to be awake. The moon was low and ripe in the sky, spilling through the edges of the forest. I looked down at the dirty dishes in the sink and almost sighed with pleasure to have a purpose. I set to work, filled the sink with water, and started washing.

I opened cupboards, searching until I found a pot and ground coffee. Before long, the heavenly, heady scent of fresh coffee filled the air. I poured myself a cup, warming my hands on the mug before sipping, oblivious to the thud of steps behind me until someone carefully cleared their throat. I spun, eyes wide, and found the doctor from last night...*Lucas*...right behind me.

"That smells good." He gave a weak smile and nodded to the machine. "It's unusual to find somebody up earlier than me."

I smiled, swallowed my damn heart, and slowly nodded. "I couldn't sleep," I answered, turning to pour him a mug before handing it over.

"That's understandable." He took a sip, then closed his eyes. "Oh, that's damn good."

"I figured we'd need it strong."

He opened his eyes and nodded. "It's a staple of any doctor's diet."

I watching him, his hands, his demeanor, remembering how careful and focused he'd been last night working on Tobias. "I never said thank you."

He smiled and shook his head. "No need. It's my calling. He's okay now?"

"Asleep," I answered.

He gave a nod, sipped his coffee, and slowly lowered his cup. "It seems you've made quite the impression with my sister."

Kit. She was a damn blinding light, making me smile as I drank. "As she has with me. She's lovely."

He nodded carefully. "She is."

"And she's lucky to have someone like you looking out for her."

He said nothing, just drank, thinking about that. "As are we. We would've—we would've lost him without you," I continued.

His brown eyes darkened. There was an ache there, one that hit me hard. "It's a very dangerous game you're in. I've seen far too many deaths."

My dad.

My mom...

Creed. Jesus...*Creed.* "You saw him, didn't you?" I searched the hallway, just in case, then went on. "That's how you met. You were there when Creed died."

"Yes."

I nodded slowly, sipping the coffee that now tasted bitter. "I don't want this, this helplessness."

I leaned against the counter, listening.

"I feel like I..." My chest ached. "Like I'm being crushed inside."

"A lack of control will do that to you, make you feel helpless."

I nodded.

"But you can get a measure of control back," he continued. "These men, whoever they are, took your power, but all it takes is one thought. One action. One...desire."

In the corner of my eye, Kit stumbled toward us, her cropped white shirt pulled taut across her full breasts as she scratched her messy bed hair.

"And one reason to keep fighting," he muttered.

The carnal way he looked at her made heat rush to my cheeks. I looked away, a bystander to such a private moment. Whatever Lucas was going through, I knew *she* was his reason, even if she didn't have a clue herself.

"Morning," she mumbled, oblivious.

"Morning," he answered, crossing the kitchen to pour her a cup of coffee and hand it over.

She smiled at him and there was a knowing glint...a *budding* attraction, or maybe one that'd lain dormant forever and was now breaking through the surface.

"I'm about to make pancakes and bacon." I focused on the rim of my mug. "If anyone wants some."

"Oh." Her brows rose. "I do...but I get first dibs on the bacon because Lucas eats it all."

"Do not." He scowled.

"Dooo...*tooo*," she countered, pinning me with her stare. "He's like a bottomless pit where bacon is concerned."

"Why, you little...." he started forward.

She let out a tiny squeal, holding up the sloshing mug of brew as she stepped backwards around the end of the counter. "Don't make me *spill* it."

He stopped, grinning, letting her get away with it...*this time*.

I placed my coffee down and set to work. Under the directions of Kit, I found all the ingredients I needed as Lucas walked away, then returned a few minutes later. I cooked while he was gone, and as I poured batter into a skillet, I had time to think about what he'd said.

A purpose, that's exactly what I needed.

"You are so far away right now." Kit poured herself another cup, then refilled the water and grounds before it started brewing again.

"I'm thinking about something your brother said."

"Oh, yeah?"

I nodded as I slipped a perfectly browned pancake onto the stack. "He said to take back my control I needed a purpose."

"That sounds like him."

I placed the spatula down and met her gaze. "I think I've figured out what that is."

She was intrigued. "Go on."

"I want Lucas to teach me how to save a life."

She stilled, thinking. "How to save their lives, you mean?"

I swallowed, nodding.

"Then you've found the best teacher imaginable. He's good, Rye. He's really good."

Rye...mom had called me that, and if it was anyone else, I might've cringed. But not her. Not Kit.

"He's just got a way about him." She kept talking, but I doubted she even noticed I was here at all anymore. "He's so good…"

I smiled, grabbed the bacon that was crispy on the edges, and piled it onto a plate.

"Perfect timing." Lucas smiled as he crossed the room.

"See what I said?" Now she looked my way, nodding to her brother. "Bacon. That's all he answers to."

I wanted to take in their banter, but this need hummed inside me and, as Lucas helped himself to the food, biting down on a piece of bacon in front of her, I turned to him. "I know my purpose."

"Yeah?" He looked my way.

Kit smiled behind him as I spoke. "I want you to teach me. Can you teach me how to keep them all alive in case something like this happens again?"

His chewing slowed, as he looked surprised. "You want me to teach you trauma medicine?"

"Yeah," I nodded. "If you'll teach me."

His eyes widened and there was a hint of a smile. "I hope you're a quick study."

That's all I needed. I nodded. "I'll need to be."

"Then I'll teach you all I can."

FIFTEEN

Tobias

SHE WAS GONE WHEN I WOKE UP AND, FOR A SECOND, IN that cruel silence where one beat of my heart replaced the next, my mind played tricks on me. Maybe it was all just a dream? Her, us...the Hell we'd descended into and somehow crawled out of. Caleb. Nick...*Dad*. Panic filled me. The kind that was...*crushing*. I winced and shifted in the bed, and as I did, it all came rushing back.

The pain...

And the terror.

And her.

I closed my eyes and released a moan. A sickening wave of pain bored through my thigh, making me quake. My hands dropped to the sides of the bed and gripped the cold steel rails. But I wanted the agony...*no, I fucking hungered for it*. Hungered until I was sick with need.

I opened my mouth to scream *her name*.

Her name...

Always her goddamn name, resounding.

LITTLE MOUSE!

The terror cracked—and the door opened…and she stepped through, carrying a plate of food. One I didn't even see. My throat thickened and tears threatened to blur her face. I pushed them away because I couldn't waste a second, not one fucking beat.

All I saw was her. Her messy hair. The dark circles under her eyes. The haunted gleam in those gray-blue eyes, and the mark on her cheek that was paler than it should be.

She hadn't slept, I knew that with one fleeting look. Not wedged between my brothers, or curled under my arm. Had she eaten? *Had she*—she met my stare and froze. "Tobias?" The crease deepened between her brows. "You okay?"

I licked my lips, my breaths furious. "Yeah," I nodded. "I'm okay."

"Hey." She forced a smile.

My voice was husky as I gave her a weak smile. "Hey."

Don't let her see you panicking, she'll only worry more. Just touch her, smell her. Hold her and tell her it's all going to be okay—

"I figured you'd be hungry."

I swallowed the burn in the back of my throat. "Starving."

Heavier footsteps thudded, not Nick's…or C's. I scowled as the familiar male came into the room. *The damn doctor? How the fuck did we get here?* First Dad…and now this. Jealousy slammed into me as I looked at Ryth, then him. I tried not to think about the guy around my stepsister as he strode closer, not missing a fucking beat.

"How's my patient today?"

Patient?

I looked around, taking in the machines and the medical equipment. "Where are we?"

The doctor pulled the sheet from my legs. "Safe."

Safe...

I slowly exhaled, met Ryth's concerned stare, and nodded. *Safe...she was safe.* I didn't look away when cold air caressed my legs, or when he lifted the back of my knee to remove the dressing around my thigh. I just fixed my sight on her.

"How's the pain?" he asked.

"Manageable."

I caught the rise of his brow. "Tough guy, huh?"

But I didn't care what he said. The last thing I needed was to be slow when they came. Because they *were* coming, and when they did, I needed to be ready. Instead, I shifted my focus to the light blush of blood on the bandage. At least that was under control.

"Then I take it you don't want anything to dull the pain you don't have?"

"That's right." I stared at the doctor, then shifted my gaze to the doorway as my brothers stepped inside and took one look at me, then at my damn thigh.

"T." Nick met my gaze.

I just gave a nod and clenched my fist around the edge of the bed when the asshole started prodding.

"Ryth, grab some of those gauze squares over there, Kit will show you which ones. And you'll need the Betadine, as well."

I flinched, watching as a young black woman crossed the room behind him and started pulling out drawers. *Who the fuck are you?* I wanted to ask, but I was more concerned with the way Ryth was taking control, grabbing the dressings the young woman handed her, as well as the bottle of antiseptic, before turning to the other side of the bed.

One look at my brothers, and I could see they were equally as stunned. As the doc gave her instructions, our sister set to work. I didn't flinch when she gently cleaned the angry red wound on my thigh, didn't looked away, just watched her, amazed at how careful she was.

"Damn." The doc leaned close, looking at her work. "You're a natural."

She flinched at the words, and the mark on her cheek turned even paler than it was before. "And I didn't even have to be on my knees," she mumbled.

Caleb looked away, drawing my gaze. Something had happened between them, something I wasn't privy to. *What the hell did that mean, C?* I clenched my jaw, willing the bastard to look at me. *What...the...fuck...did...that... mean?*

"Perfect. You can use this Tegaderm dressing, then you just follow the same process tomorrow. You good with that?"

"Yes," Ryth answered.

She was so proud of herself, straightening her spine, jutting her chin in the air. She looked my way and all I wanted to do was crawl inside her head and find every little thing I didn't know about. *Especially what had happened in that place.*

"You must be hungry." The doc interrupted my thoughts.

"I have food." Ryth grabbed the plate and handed it my way.

But I couldn't stomach the shit, not when I was starved for her goddamn demons. I wanted to kill those men who hurt her, consume all her terror and her pain. More than anything, I wanted to protect her from anyone else who tried to tear her away.

"T?" she murmured carefully, that smile falling fast.

I took the plate, giving her a wink. "This looks perfect, little mouse." And I forced myself to eat, chewing and swallowing, but all the while, I was fixed on that seething darkness. I wanted to know what had happened in that place—I glanced at Caleb—and I wanted to punch my brother in the goddamn mouth for almost getting us killed...or worse, *used*.

They could've used her.

Could've made her wear...*red*.

"T?"

I jerked my gaze to Nick, who looked at me strangely. "Yeah?"

"The doc was asking if you felt strong enough for a shower and a more comfortable bed."

I just nodded, my focus slipping to Caleb across the room. The fucker felt it, too, glancing my way before scowling. "I'll, ah, give you some space," he muttered. "Glad you're feeling better, T."

I clenched my jaw, forcing the words between my teeth. "You sure about that, *brother?*"

Because he sure as fuck wouldn't be for long.

He left, and the tension in the room became awkward.

"I can give you some painkillers that won't make you drowsy, how about that?" the doc asked.

I just stared at the door Caleb had left through and nodded.

"Ryth," he called, gesturing her to the drawers filled with drugs.

I turned to her, took the pills she offered, and put them in my mouth before swallowing them with the glass of water she gave me.

"Okay, then let's get you into the bathroom."

My body howled the moment I moved, but I gripped the sides and pulled myself up.

"You can lean on me." Ryth held me steady as I sat for a moment. I wrapped my arm around her shoulders and leaned on her while I slowly tried to rise.

Sparks ignited behind my eyes the moment my foot touched the floor. My thigh clenched, driving the agony deeper. I sucked in hard breaths, gripping her tight. She didn't flinch, didn't move. She was a goddamn tower of strength, supporting my weight as I limped toward the door.

Step by step, we left them behind and made our way toward the open door at the end of the hall. Once we were inside, it was just her and me.

"I'll help you into the shower."

I nodded. "Thanks."

By the time I'd reached the bathroom, I wanted to vomit from the pain. How fucking long did those painkillers take to kick in? I almost regretted not asking for something stronger, until I remembered... then I made peace with the agony stabbing through my thigh.

Ryth flicked the light on, holding me as I limped to the sink. I gripped the vanity and slowly lifted my gaze to the haunted fucking face in the mirror. "Jesus," I groaned. "I look like fucking hell."

"You look like you've been shot and walked around with a bullet still in your thigh, that's how you look," she muttered as she stepped into the shower stall and turned on the water.

Then she turned to me and our gazes connected in the reflection.

A bullet I'd carried around to save her.

We didn't need the words to hear the truth. There was that flicker of pain in her eyes once more. "I wish you'd told me."

"I don't."

The muscles of her jaw flexed and that fire in her eyes burned brighter. Fuck, she was pretty when she was angry. A nod of her head, and she exhaled hard and slow. "You're starting to learn, little mouse."

There was a hint of a smile, just a little one. At least she'd kept her sense of humor. Steam drifted from the shower, making me take a step forward.

"Let me help." She moved closer and dropped to her knees, and I couldn't help but feel fucking tuned on. The way she reached up, grabbed my boxers, and tugged them down, was hot as hell.

I reached up, yanked my shirt over my head, and dropped it to the floor as she rose. Her breath caught and a moan tore free. "Tobias..." she whispered.

I didn't stop, just limped forward. "It's not as bad as it looks."

But I caught the movement before the faint brush of her fingers on my back. "This doesn't hurt?"

A throb came at her touch, low, aching, hitting all the trigger points. I swallowed and shook my head, not trusting myself to speak.

But she knew. "I'm helping you."

That throb seemed to travel upwards and lodge in the back of my throat. I let her step into the stall with me, let her run her fingers along my shoulders as I turned and faced her. Her wide eyes took in every scratch and every mark. I was a mess...I knew that, but it was the kind of hurt I'd feel a thousand times over for her. Didn't she know that by now?

She stepped out, grabbed a clean washcloth from the vanity, and stepped back in, soaking it before she grabbed the soap. Silence filled the space. The heat thrummed against my shoulders and her hands lulled me into a sense of comfort I hadn't felt in a while...not since they took her.

Not since they—

Sodden strands of hair stuck to the side of her face. I brushed them away as she ran the cloth over my chest and under my arms, nearing the deep bruising over my ribs. "This has to hurt," she whispered.

"Not when I'm looking at you."

Her cheeks blushed before she looked away.

"You can look, Ryth." My voice turned husky. "You can touch, you can do anything you want with me."

Fuck if that wasn't too close to the goddamn truth.

Anything she wanted.

Fuck me.

Hit me.

Hate me...

Just never *leave* me. Not again. Not ever again...

"Head back," she demanded, squeezing a clump of shampoo into her palm, a little surer of herself now.

I smiled and did as she commanded, letting the heat sluice through my clipped hair. She had to stretch, her body grazing mine as she rose on her toes and wobbled. It was instinct to grab her, but fucking hunger to pull her against me.

I grew hard with the friction. Christ, I wanted to be inside her, to feel the stretch her pretty little pussy gave as she adjusted. The memory of the diner rose, her hands braced against the sink, me fucking nailing her from behind.

Still, it wasn't enough.

It'd *never* be enough.

My little taste of the forbidden.

I stared into her eyes as she gently worked the shampoo in and rinsed my head.

She was my stepsister.

No, our *stepsister.*

At least my father did this one thing right before he died. "Fuck, I missed this."

She met my gaze, sinking back down off her toes. "Me, too."

"We're never going back there," I said as desperation rose. "Not to our home or our life. Everything will be new from now on, you, me...us."

"I'm sorry about Creed."

I winced and looked away. "I'm not. He did it to himself."

"Will you tell me what happened?"

I stiffened and thought about lying to her, or telling her I didn't know. But there were too many lies and half-truths. I didn't want that between us. "Elle killed him right in front of me."

"My m-mom?"

Fuck, I hated the tremble in her voice. That sting. That...*betrayal all over again.* "Yeah, your mom."

"When?" Her breathing deepened.

I met her stare, scowling. "When they took you."

She was silent, thinking. "She ran, didn't she? She was running."

"Yeah, she ran."

Ryth lifted her hand and cupped her cheek. "She was breathless when I saw her, panicked, her eyes wide. Then she hit me."

"She *hit* you?" I grew cold.

There was a nod and she met my stare. "Then she let them take me. They told me..." she looked away. "Never mind."

But I wasn't about to let this go. I captured her chin and turned her face toward me. "Tell me."

With a glint of fear in her stare, she answered. "They told me that my father wasn't my father."

Her innocence will be the very thing that makes her perfect for them. I need her perfect, because I'm backed into a corner, and I'm holding her out in front of me, hoping they'll take her instead.

Those fucking words roared back to me. Words that made me sick to my stomach. Words I wanted to beat with bloody fists from my mind. But I couldn't, because I knew the woman who'd written them.

Give her up. Elle's voice filled me, chilling me to the bone. *She's as good as dead anyway.*

She's as good as dead...

As good as dead...

As good as—

"He's your father, Ryth."

Hope filled her stare. "He is?"

I eased my grip on her chin and grazed my callused fingers along her jaw, catching drops of water on the way. "Blood means fucking nothing. You should know that by now."

She did. I knew she did. This woman standing in front of me wasn't the kid our parents dumped in our house anymore. No, she was stronger, harder. She was *ours*.

Ryth swallowed the pain and nodded. "You're right. Fuck what they say."

I smiled. "That's it, baby, fuck what they say."

I dropped my hand, reached around, and hit the tap, ending the spray. Water ran in rivulets down my chest, drawing her gaze. I saw her desire, saw the moment her breaths deepened, and that perfect fucking mark on her cheek blushed.

"You want to touch me, little mouse?"

Her eyes darted to mine and she nodded. I stood there with the cold closing in, making my damn leg shake. Still, I didn't let her see that. My nipples tightened. She liked that, brushing her soft fingers across my chest. A tremor rippled through me. Fuck, she was dangerous. She was so fucking dangerous and she didn't have a goddamn clue.

No one got this close to me.

Not even blood.

She stepped closer and lowered her head. Her warm tongue brushed my nipple, making me close my eyes. My pulse thundered, booming in my goddamn ears. But she lifted her head with barely more than a lick and stepped backwards, reaching for the towel instead.

"I'm taking care of you, Tobias." There was a sternness in her tone.

Tobias?

Okay...

The corners of my lips tugged up as she dragged the towel across my body. But I knew what she was doing, masking the exploration of my body with this need to comfort and care for me.

"Arms up," she muttered.

That birthmark grew a little redder as I did, letting her run the towel down over my hard muscles and grazed skin. She winced at every cut, and her nostrils flared as she gently dried over the bruise. "I'll get you to the bed."

I gave a nod, leaned on her, and limped out of the bathroom. Agony drove deep, causing me to stumble and fall onto the bed. I hit hard and lay there, catching my breath. Then I inched backwards, drawing my legs onto the bed.

"I'm sorry," she moaned.

I forced a smile through the pain. "It's not your fault, princess." I patted the bed. "Climb up."

"I'm dripping."

The words only made me grin. I opened my eyes, finding her standing beside the bed, and patted the mattress, this time more softly. "Show me." She shook her head, but she didn't leave. No. She didn't leave. She was thinking about it. "I want to see what you showed Nick that day in the car."

That blush deepened.

Fuck.

"When you were in his Mustang, leaning your head back, your fingers in that—" I licked my lips and lowered my gaze. "That perfect cunt."

"T..." she whispered.

She liked it when I talked like that, liked it more than she wanted to. "A good girl who likes her cunt looked at."

She bit her lip, dragging those teeth across the soft, plump flesh. Then she moved, climbing onto the bed with my brother's t-shirt stuck against her breasts.

"Take the shirt off." I dragged my gaze over her. Her tiny puckered nipples tightened as I spoke.

She glanced toward the door.

"No one's gonna come in, Ryth. No one who doesn't want a taste of you, at least."

She trembled at those words. Her fingers were shaking as she dragged the sodden shirt off and let it drop beside the bed. I lowered my gaze to the equally wet boxers she wore. "Pants, princess."

Her gaze was fixed on mine as she reached down. Fuck, her skin was so perfect, her cute plump ass, the softness between her thighs. Any other man would only see flaws—for a second, until I gouged his fucking eyes out at least.

But not me...or my brothers.

She let the pants drop onto the shirt and hugged her body.

I fought every urge inside me to crawl across the bed toward her. I wanted to cage her in with my body and part those sweet thighs. I wanted to ram my cock home and make her buck in ecstasy. I wanted to hear my name on a shuddered breath.

"Show me, princess. Show me how my brother took care of you in that fucking place."

She flinched, her eyes widening. "You know?"

"I know him," I answered, even if the ache of betrayal was there. "I know the guilt would eat him alive. I also know he'd channel that guilt into the only thing he could, and that's taking care of you."

Pain raged in her stare. I hated the turmoil inside her, hated seeing her battling her own demons because of what my brother did when he delivered her to them.

"I would've wanted him to," I added. "If he hadn't taken care of you, then that'd make this a thousand times harder. So I'm glad he was there. I'm glad he took care of you."

"You are?"

I nodded, lowering my gaze to her thighs. "Yeah, princess. I am. Now, show me. Show me how he took care of you."

That excitement returned, making her slowly lower her hand until her fingers pushed against her mound. I eased back against the pillows, pulling them up higher as she slowly parted her thighs, showing me a glimpse of pink. "Jesus, that's it." I was riveted by the way she danced her fingers over her lips, sinking in to the top of her slit. "Part yourself, baby. I want to see your clit."

That tiny nub peeked out as she slid two fingers down and splayed them. I divided my focus, unable to know where to look, from the shine in her eyes, to the hard rise of her chest, or those thin fingers dancing around the center of her pleasure.

Slow. So fucking slow. I watched her embarrassment give way to tiny jolts of desire. Around and around she skirted, before she slowly slid down and slipped a finger in.

Jesus...

My cock jolted watching her knuckle come away wet. "You wet for me, baby?"

She nodded.

"Then show me." I lowered my gaze to her pussy and reached for my cock. "Show me how you come."

She sank two fingers in this time and I had to bite back a moan, gripping my shaft instead. Her nipples tightened with the arch of her back. She braced her other hand behind her, gripping the edge of the mattress while she rode her fingers.

"Fuck yourself," I growled, driving my own fist down. I didn't want my own touch, all I wanted was to see her drip all over the fucking comforter. But I ached for the release.

Her eyes fluttered closed as momentum took her, stealing her away for a moment at least. Until, with a buck of her hips, she cried out, her fingers still inside.

"Open," I grunted. "Open your fucking thighs, Ryth."

She did, letting herself gape open. Creamy come coated the tips of her fingers. I released my hold and shoved forward, ignoring the roaring agony as I grabbed her hand, pulled her toward me, then slowly slipped her fingers into my mouth.

Salty.

Sweet.

I chased the taste with my tongue and sucked before easing my hold. "Mine," I reminded her. "Your come, your pussy, your fucking heart."

She eased forward, staring into my eyes. "As are you, *brother*." She pulled away and slowly eased down.

Her hand wrapped around my cock. I lowered my gaze, watching as she wrapped those lips around the head of my cock and licked before sucking. "Fuck, little mouse." My groan was husky.

I already wanted to come. I wanted to fill every fucking hole until she was sated.

Until I was sated.

She sucked, driving her fist down to hit the base. I drove my fingers through her hair, cupped her head, and pushed her down. "Take it, little sister. Open your mouth and take your brother's cock."

Fuck, she did.

Stretching her mouth wide, saliva dripped from the corners as her head bounced. The veins kicked as warmth spurted. I held her there, sucking in hard breaths, using her mouth in the most delicious way. She didn't fight, didn't gag, didn't jostle my thigh, like a good fucking girl.

I groaned and released my hold, letting her rise and lick her lips before falling against the mattress beside me.

"Jesus, baby," I groaned, dropping back against the pillows. "Jesus."

She curled her body against me, tucking in when I lifted my arm. "Did I hurt you?" she asked.

I shook my head. "No, baby. You could never hurt me."

But she could, with barely a word. But I shoved that fear away, willing myself back to reality, and closed my eyes. I'd just sleep, just a little…then I'd fucking destroy that pussy of hers…

And she'd destroy me. One. Fucking. *Swallow at a time.*

SIXTEEN

Nick

Kit glanced toward the hallway...for the fourth time in as many minutes. Her brother's voice droned in the background as he talked to Caleb about the hospital where he worked. My brother listened intently, but while he was focused on the doctor, I was watching Lucas's stepsister become a little too intrigued *with Tobias*.

A scowl creased her brow, and there was a blush before she muttered under her breath. "Maybe someone should check on them." And she moved...a little too damn fast.

Shit.

The moment she made for the hallway, so did I, striding around her to block her way. A shake of my head and I murmured, "You don't want to do that."

Lucas snapped his gaze my way. There was a flicker of annoyance as he looked from me to her. Jealousy burned in the doc's stare for an instant before he leashed it. Yeah, the guy could be dangerous if he wanted. "Kit?" He muttered. "Everything okay?"

She glanced at the entrance to the hall. "Just thought someone should check on them is all."

Lucas cleared his throat as he followed her stare, lingering on the spot behind me. A highly strung asshole like T and someone like our little stepsister alone in a room together? Wounded or not, the doc knew what they were doing. He also knew his sister was too damn inquisitive for her own good.

"Maybe you could check our supplies?" There was a huskiness in his tone as he shifted his attention back to his own stepsister. "Nick and I are going into town. We want to be well stocked."

There was a crinkling of her nose and a pout that reminded me of Ryth when she'd landed on our doorstep and it was hard to believe that was mere months ago.

She'd been so damn young.

So damn naive.

But she wasn't anymore.

No.

They'd made sure of that.

"Fine." Kit glared up at me, knowing I wasn't about to move out of her way. "I'll make the damn list."

"And when they're gone, I might see if you can show me around the place." Caleb drew her attention. "I bet you know this place like the back of your hand."

She smiled at that, her eyes lighting up. "Yeah, I know it really well. There's a creek and a swimming hole not far from here and the biggest boulder I've ever seen, I call it the lookout."

"Sounds good," C muttered, glancing my way.

He would keep her busy, making sure she didn't wander. Although the doc didn't seem to like that idea at all. I slowly stepped away, keeping the firecracker in my line of view, and crossed the kitchen. "She'll be safe with him," I murmured, meeting Lucas's stare. "Don't worry about that."

He was...

And there wasn't a thing I could do about that.

Caleb had an air of darkness about him now, a savagery that was the ice to T's fire. I glanced left and saw him now as he crossed the room. "I can give you a hand with that list too, if you want?"

She looked at her brother, and he gave a slow nod. *Go,* the motion said. *You're okay.* She did, glancing back one last time before heading for the kitchen.

"He's dangerous."

The words were so quiet I almost missed them. But I didn't miss the look the doc gave me, a look that said far too much. It was my turn to look away, my turn to try to ignore the howling in my head. One that said even though Caleb was the quietest of all of us, he was also the most dangerous.

Dangerous to us...

And to Ryth.

"I'll meet you outside," I muttered, and headed after them.

The place was nice, but damn quiet. The chirping of birds in the trees was all I could hear as I stepped out and headed back along the veranda, kicking leaves as I went. I stepped down and strode to the sedan Jack Castlemaine had left for us in a stranger's barn in the middle of nowhere.

No. Not for us...for himself.

I opened the driver's door and yanked the latch for the trunk. Guns were fixed under the lid. I wedged my fingers under the carpet and yanked up the flooring, staring at the weapons stowed in the spare tire well. This wasn't fitted out to last, just to get them to the next one hidden away on a map Ryth's father had in his head.

A map for them to use to run.

And leave us behind.

I braced my hand against the side of the trunk and felt the world sway. They'd leave us...*he'd make her leave us*. Even the idea of that was too much for me to think about. An ache filled my chest. The kind of ache that was crushing. Spears ripped along my arm...I couldn't breathe...*I couldn't breathe*. I—

"You ready to go?"

Lucas stepped up out of nowhere and took a look at the guns visible in the sedan, then at me. He scowled, his gaze moving to my fist pressed against my sternum. "You okay?"

"Think I'm having a damn heart attack," I groaned.

He moved close and pressed his fingertips against my neck, his gaze unfocused for a moment before he dropped his hand. "You're fine."

Still that ache pounded, shredding my damn chest. He looked at the open trunk once more, his brows rising. "Impressive haul. Looks like you're equipped to run."

"Not us," I forced the words, and the moment I did, that ache grew real, tearing words from my mouth. "Ryth's dad."

"And Ryth, I take it?"

I nodded, unable to say the words out loud.

"How about we drive?"

I lifted my gaze, then nodded and slammed the trunk closed. "Sounds good."

Before I climbed into the passenger's seat, I glanced at the cabin once more. T and Ryth were busy, probably asleep by now. C and Kit were off getting the layout of this place. They were safe for now. *We* were safe for now. That's all I cared about as I climbed into the Range Rover and closed the door.

The engine throbbed as he gunned it, switched the dial to reverse, and backed out, swinging sharply. The road tires weren't meant for the loose terrain, but they caught alright as he nosed the four-wheel drive forward along the dirt road.

"This your place?"

"Grandfather's," he answered as the vehicle slipped into a rut. "Not by blood, and we keep it in his name so it's safe and fairly untraceable."

"Fairly," I forced the word through clenched teeth, holding on.

He cut me a look. "Nothing is one hundred percent safe."

He was right. I fixed my focus on the road as we straightened out and picked up speed, tearing past the mailbox that had a name printed on the side. I guessed if anyone was going to track him this far, then a damn name amounted to nothing.

If they wanted us bad enough, they'd come.

Because nowhere was really safe. Not on our own, at least.

As we drove, my thoughts turned to Jack Castlemaine, where he'd been hiding and how the hell he'd gotten out of prison. I had too many questions...the most nagging one dragged me to that damn notebook I'd found in Elle's closet. *Watching her with her friends, I could almost forget how she came to be, what she represents, and her purpose in all this.*

What purpose?

That's the thing that kept me panicking, it was like living with a ticking time bomb. The only problem was, Ryth didn't even know she was dangerous herself.

"—you haven't heard a word I've said, have you?"

I jerked my gaze to the doc behind the wheel. "Sorry."

He gave a nod. "I was telling you that we'll be leaving first thing in the morning."

"You're leaving?"

He gave a nod and focused on the road. "You're calling Benjamin Rossi, right?"

I scowled. "Yeah, we don't really have much of an option here."

"I understand that, but I have to look out for my own."

There was that remark again, and the fear where the Rossis where concerned. I knew Ben, knew he could be a hardass and a ruthless motherfucker, and I also knew Lazarus was the kind of guy you didn't want to mess with. So what the fuck did the doc actually do?

My thoughts returned to money. "If you're in some kind of money trouble," I started.

He glanced my way and scowled for a second before shaking his head. "I wish. No...it's..." he sighed. "It's Kit."

"Your sister?"

"She gets defensive, especially when it comes to people she thinks of as friends."

Now I was intrigued. "Go on."

He didn't want to, growing red in the face as he scowled. The guy had pulled a bullet out of my brother's thigh and hauled the dead body of my father into the back of his car, and yet his stepsister being defensive made him flinch?

There had to be more. But I said nothing while he wrestled with the words.

"Let's just say my stepsister is the one standing in the way of Benjamin Rossi and love."

"And love?"

He looked my way. "Literally. Love Hartman is a trauma nurse Mr. Rossi met through an acquaintance." He winced at the word.

A friend of a friend. "I take it that acquaintance is you?"

He nodded. "Yeah."

I dragged my fingers through my hair. Now that made sense.

Not the part about Benjamin Rossi falling in love. That I struggled with. I'd never seen him so much as look at a woman, let alone a damn trauma nurse. But I did understand how the fiery young woman we'd left behind at the cabin could make the doc's life difficult indeed. Especially when there were other women even remotely near the guy.

Because he was a good-looking guy...and the way she looked at him...

Damn...

"Here we are," he muttered, drawing my focus to the quiet country town. "There's a payphone in Meg's Diner, you can use that while I load the car with everything you might need."

He signaled and pulled the four-wheel drive over, nosing into a parking spot in front of a large sporting goods store. I still had no idea why he was helping us, but right now I was damn thankful. I'd make it up to the guy, that was for sure.

Right now, I'd take everything he offered. I climbed out of the car and headed for the corner, stepping into the small diner. The place was empty, except for an elderly couple enjoying milkshakes, who eyed me as I searched the room and saw the payphone at the back of the store. I headed over to the thing, put my money in, and the number I'd memorized.

"Yes?" Benjamin Rossi answered cautiously.

"It's me."

Silence, then carefully. "I take it you're safe?"

"For now. But we need to meet."

The sound of a jet's engine roared in the background and the heavy thud of boots rang out on a steel platform. "Unfortunately, that is going to have to wait. I'm dealing with a situation here."

Concern filled me. "What kind of situation?"

"Nothing I can get into over the phone. Give me three days and I'll be back in the country. Until then, hang tight."

Hang tight? I didn't like it. But the man wasn't giving me an option. "Will do," I answered. "I'll see you then."

"See you then, and Nick..."

"Yeah?"

"Head down, son. Stay safe."

With those words in my ear, I hung up. The old couple were still watching me when I turned around and headed back toward the door.

"Get everything you need?" the waitress behind the counter asked.

"Yeah...well, actually." I stopped, my eyes drawn to three fresh pies under the counter, and nodded toward them. "I'll take those."

"A piece?" she asked, wiping her hands on a white towel and reaching for a knife.

"No, all three of them."

One was decadent, chocolate and whipped cream, the second was caramel, and the last was the best-looking homemade apple pie I'd ever seen.

"Okay, sure." She smiled and grabbed boxes from behind the counter.

By the time I walked out, I felt at least worthy. Now all we had to do was stay alive and careful for three more days...and plan our run for good.

SEVENTEEN

Vivienne

I STARED AT THE ARMANI OUTFIT LAID OUT NEATLY ON THE end of the massive king-sized bed and suppressed a shudder. Fear mingled with my rage. It was a dangerous cocktail. One I swallowed down. Still, I was unable to look away from the *things* he expected me to wear. The wide-leg caramel slacks were split thigh high, partially hidden under the see-through cream-colored top. I leaned forward and flicked the tie, meant to be around my throat.

Just like his hands, right?

That was the effect.

Wrapped around my throat.

Controlling me.

My gaze darted to the lingerie laid out separately. The soft pink lace bra sat on top of the satin thong, the front so fucking narrow it'd slip between my lips with the first step. Revulsion burned, making me feel sick. Everything about this was calculated, right down to the fucking material. My breaths were hard and heavy. At least it wasn't red. That color, I couldn't stomach.

This was the third day...and the third outfit, each one expertly chosen and displayed for me like I was some kind of dog in training. *Wear the pretty clothes, Vivienne, and do exactly what you're told.* I gripped the bedsheet still wrapped around my body. Three days I'd worn the same thing...and I was starting to smell.

I glanced over my shoulder at the locked door.

I didn't want to be here.

Not in this room...or in this place.

But refusing him would only have me locked away forever. He'd never let me free, not until I played by his rules. I turned back to the clothes waiting for me. Because that's just the kind of man London St. James was...

A vile fucking bastard.

Hate moved through me, trembling and snarling. I strode for the bathroom, working the knotted sheet from around my body and let it fall to the floor. Cold tiles stung my toes as I moved into the bathroom and stepped into the shower. The hiss was instant, the hot water steaming up the stall. I inched closer to the spray, dropping my head backwards, letting the heat pound against my shoulders and carry me away from this hell, for a few seconds at least.

Until the bitterness moved in.

It invaded with a thought, and then the past followed.

The past where I was a nobody, not seen, not heard. Certainly not wanted. I opened my eyes, squeezed shampoo into my hand, and lathered my hair.

I'd tried so hard to keep away from the past. The months I'd spent at The Order were focused on surviving the present. Still, in the quiet of the night between the rounds of the guards, the past had crept in. First it was the house I was meant to call home and the couple who were not my parents. They were barely in my life at all, apart from the rules...so many fucking rules.

No answering the door...

No giving out your address.

No speaking to anyone not approved by your mother or myself.

Rules and laws.

Still, it had been better than the flickers of memory from before them. The *'place'* they'd kept us in was no more than a jail for kids. My fake parents told me it was foster care, that my real mother had *'issues'* relating to drugs and had abandoned me at birth. Not wanted. Not worthy...

Only to be used.

And that's exactly what London St. James wanted to do. I was under no illusions about that.

Ward, he called me.

Ward with limitations, though.

He couldn't fuck me, the contract wouldn't allow it.

I raked conditioner through my hair and set to work scrubbing and shaving. At least this time I was alone. I lifted my gaze to the small, neat camera fixed in the corner of the bathroom and fought the need to flip the bastard off. That wouldn't get me out of here though, would it? Wouldn't get me free...

Wouldn't let me...*run.*

The word hummed in my head as I dragged the razor along, then between, my legs. I glanced up at the camera. Was he watching? I'd bet he was. I straightened and dropped my head backwards into the spray. I'd bet he was fucking riveted to the screen.

I hit the faucets, switched off the water, and stepped out, my gaze moving to the expensive bottles of perfume and makeup lined along the vanity as I grabbed a towel from the warming rack and dried, buffing my tawny skin.

La Prairie and Guerlain. The names meant nothing to me, but I knew designer when I saw it. I draped the towel around my body and stepped closer, dragging my fingers across the purple Raptain jar and shimmering platinum vial next to it. I hadn't allowed myself to touch them before. I hadn't even allowed myself to even look at them. I didn't want to acknowledge what they represented...or the bastard who'd bought them.

My fingers trembled for a second before I lashed out, smacking the glassware. Bottles scattered, clashing before they tipped and rolled. The moment they did, that panicked feeling ignited inside me. I stumbled forward, grabbed the vials, and righted them, shifting the goddamn things until they were perfect once more.

Perfect...

I picked up the colloidal serum and opened the lid. A silver drop trickled into my palm before I touched it with my fingers and leaned close to the mirror, spreading it across my cheekbones and watching the glimmer sink in. "Oh, shit, that's fucking nice."

I pulled backwards, eyeing the gorgeous shine as I turned my head this way and that. "No." I lowered my hand, shaking my head. "Just no. I'm not using this, not playing his fucking game."

Be smart about this...I stared at my reflection, then shifted my gaze to the locked bedroom door behind me. I wasn't getting out of here. It was that simple. No matter how much I hated it.

Wear the makeup.

Wear the clothes.

But make sure I remain in control. I glanced at the camera above me...

That incensed look in his eyes when he'd had me on the bed returned to my mind. I was the one in control here. I was the one he wanted...

He could force me.

But would he?

My pulse thundered...no, I didn't think he would. He wanted this game, wanted me...*yielding*.

I licked my lips. Yeah, that's what he wanted. Me on my fucking knees.

I turned back, my focus drifting to the foundation that had the gold undertone for my skin and set to work...making myself beautiful. My past trickled in, the same hurt...the same sense of abandonment. This was just another one of those times, the same rejection. The same fucking power play.

But that game I was well versed in...

I could play, just as well as he could.

Dark, smoldering eyes, the highlight of bronze against golden skin high noon my cheekbones. I yanked open the cupboard, found a hairdryer, and set to work, rubbing product in and blowing the strands out until they were sleek and shining. "It'll do," I murmured. "It'll do."

Control slipped in as I made my way back to the bed. It wasn't a trickle, or a rush. It was jagged and savage, sawing a gaping hole inside me to push its way in. I didn't think, just snatched the panties from the bed and yanked them on, then I followed with the rest of the clothes and stepped into the nude Prada heels.

I fought the urge to turn and look at myself in the full-length mirror opposite the bed. I didn't want to see myself in his clothes, didn't want to see him in the soft material as it brushed my skin. I didn't want to see him...

But I did, unable to help myself. My gaze shifted, catching the peek of tan. One step and the split widened, revealing my thigh. My knees trembled, my pulse turned sluggish and slow. Humiliation moved through me and dragged with it desire.

The woman in the mirror wasn't me.

Not the fighter...or the loner.

No, she was the whore.

The *'vessel'* they'd created at The Order.

One I'd use any way I had to. "I hate you," I whispered, scanning her jutting breasts, small waist, and olive skin. "I fucking hate you so much."

That hate stayed with me as I moved toward the door. But I didn't scream or wail this time. No, I was done with that. Instead, I lifted my hand and rapped my knuckles softly against the wood. The sound barely reached my ears, yet the lock snapped open almost instantly and the door slowly opened.

He was there...

Dark eyes glinted with that criminal fucking stare. He slowly lowered his gaze, taking in my face, breasts, and my waist, then slowly lowered to my thighs and heels. I looked away, then my focus fixed on that cold stare. Heat rolled through me as his stare lingered between my legs, then shifted to my breasts...

Was he thinking about the thin strap between the cheeks of my ass? I hoped so...*I really fucking hoped so.* I swallowed hard, hating how good he fucking looked right now. He was always so infuriatingly immaculate. The charcoal gray suit was buttoned, the pressed white shirt spotless underneath. I wanted to ruin that shirt, wanted to smear the makeup I wore all over it.

The thought of that assaulted me. My cheek pressed against the white shirt, the dark smear left behind. My pussy pulsed, clamping tight. No. Just fucking *no*. I forced the tremble from my voice. "I want out of here."

He didn't answer, just pushed the door wider and stepped to the side.

My pulse stuttered and my gaze darted to the top of the stairs. Freedom waited...freedom and es—

"The front door is alarmed and is wired to trigger an alert to my phone, as are all the windows. Try to escape, Vivienne, and see what happens."

I flinched and jerked my gaze to his. He couldn't hear the stuttering of my pulse, couldn't hear the thoughts in my head. He couldn't *know me*.

But he'd just given me a fuck-around-and-find-out ultimatum, hadn't he? I couldn't quite catch my breath with all the implications. Still, hope waited, and it started with an open bedroom door. One nod of my head, and he lifted his hand, motioning for me to advance.

I did, heels clicking on the tiled floor until I grabbed the handrail and stepped onto the first step. Silence swallowed any sound of my steps. The stilettos sank into the plushly carpeted stairs. I made my way down the three flights, eyeing the glass wall of the elevator in the center of the house.

A shiver raced through me. I'd been in this house before...but my time here had been fleeting, barely making it past the foyer and the downstairs hall. I'd never made it up here...*never anywhere personal*. I gripped the cold steel railing and made my way down. I wondered where his bedroom was...

Was it close? My gaze darted along the first floor hall...*there? Was it there?*

There was a second when those thoughts entered my mind before a wave of dizziness hit me. *His bedroom? You're wanting to know about his goddamn bedroom?* I clenched my jaw and hit the last stair, stopping at the edge of the foyer. Shimmering Italian tiles, cold and sleek. All I saw was my face pressed against them...and the two sets of boots in front of my eyes.

I warned you, Vivienne...I told you there'd be consequences...

A pang tore across my chest, fiery and brutal. I gripped the railing, unable to move. Fear rooted me to the spot. I couldn't look away. The panic. The humiliation.

"Thinking about running?"

My knees trembled, but I forced myself to move and turned before stepping backwards. He descended like evil itself, those cold, unflinching eyes seized me in his stare. Flecks of silver sparkled at his temples as he stepped down to the foyer and cut through the sunlight. I met that sickening stare, then looked away. "No."

"Good."

I flinched, powerless, *trapped*. What exactly did you think was going to happen? The thought rose...

He stopped in front of me. "I need to work."

I jerked my gaze to his as fear turned to anger. "Then go to work."

There was a twitch at the corner of his lips. My stomach clenched, my breaths almost panting. He was volatile...so fucking volatile. I waited for him to lunge, to grab my throat and drive me across the foyer. I waited for his wrath, the one I saw shimmering under the surface.

But none of that came. Just a twitch at the corner of his mouth. Don't tell me the demon was fucking impressed? One nod of his head and he turned, his steps slow enough to be a command of their own. He expected me to follow, like a good little whore.

Hate was a fist in my belly, driving up through my ribs, but I followed, glancing at the closed basement door as we passed. The electronic lock flashed red against the door on the outside, just waiting for him to enter his goddamn code and drag me down there.

Only, he kept walking, cocking his head to the side. Listening. That's what he was doing, waiting to see if I'd crumple. I tried to quell the thunder in my chest and kept moving, striding past the elegant chef's kitchen that gleamed, and moving deeper into the house. I was surprised anyone lived here. It didn't look like it.

Not a speck of dust.

Not a fingerprint left behind.

He turned at a hallway and stepped forward, and I was scared to follow. Being in a confined space with London...

Didn't think this through, did you?

I tried to catch my breath as he opened a door at the end of the hall and disappeared, leaving it gaping behind him. I hadn't thought about this...hadn't thought he'd actually...*open the door*.

But I couldn't run, couldn't even think about turning around and fleeing. If I did, then he'd know he'd won.

No fucking way was that happening.

I clenched my jaw and strode forward.

My gaze took in the sleek black bookshelves that ran across the back wall as I stepped inside. Books filled the space, a lot of them. Perfect as usual, not one out of place.

"The door, Vivienne."

I jerked my gaze to him sitting behind the desk, head down, focused on the pages in front of him. Indignation seethed. *Fuck you, do it your goddamn self*...the words didn't reach my lips as I took in the black leather gloves he wore. His jacket was gone, the white shirt rolled up against strong forearms.

I looked away, stepped in, and closed the door. The study was big...and breathtaking. A blood red plush velvet sofa sat toward the back of the room, facing the most stunning black gas fireplace I'd ever seen. Black filled the rest of the room, black furnishings, black steel everywhere else, except for a small section of books far in the back corner...no, they were pink. Everything was the same colors as my bedroom.

I turned around, catching his attention shift to me without lifting his gaze. I unnerved him with my presence alone. He lifted his head, dark eyes darting my way before he fixed on the massive iMac screen in front of him. One click of the mouse, and a printer started at the edge of the desk. He rose without a sound and turned. I was drawn to the paper upturned on his desk, the one he seemed so intent on.

I took a step, my pulse racing as I was drawn to that document. But the closer I came, the more I realized it wasn't what I'd thought it was...it was some kind of—

"Help you?"

I jerked my gaze high. Those dark eyes bored into mine. I looked away, shaking my head. The moment I did, I caught the edge of a stack of pages peeking out from the middle of a leather embossed folder. *Ooks,* the word drew me. Unconsciously, I knew what it was. But still, I had to see for myself. I reached out...

"Vivienne..." the warning came.

But he didn't move. Testing me. I glanced at the word...*ooks*...

My hand trembled as I reached out, grasped the edge, and jerked it free.

He moved fast, crossing the study in a blur to grasp my wrist from the other side. But it was too late...my own name was printed right there in front of me.

Vivienne Brooks...

I scanned the words.

The party must hand over the subject immediately or risk litigation and/or further unlawful consequences. Failure to do so will result in action against the party, including, but not limited to, harm.

Including, but not limited to, harm? Had London St. James just threatened The Order?

"You're playing a very dangerous game, Vivienne."

I stared at his hand clasped around my wrist, then met his stare. Yes, yes he had. "Aren't we all?"

EIGHTEEN

Ryth

Tobias was finally asleep. His breaths were deep and steady, and it seemed that pain no longer had control. I waited for a heartbeat, then gently eased his arm from across my body and rose. The mattress dipped as I slipped off. But he didn't stir as I quietly made my way to the stack of clothes piled in the corner of the room. Clothes that Caleb had pulled from the getaway sedan that morning. Clothes my father had brought for me.

Pinks and purples littered the floor at my feet, but at least he'd had the good sense to make sure the jeans were black.

I tugged off my shirt and boxers, still damp from Tobias's shower, and dropped them on the floor before pulling on a soft cup bra, panties, shorts, and a t-shirt that looked like it was about two sizes too small. I thought about wearing Nick's oversized black shirt but then realized they had even less clothes than I did.

So I tugged on the shirt, hating how it rode high, and gathered our dirty clothes. I wanted to make good use of the time we had in this place. Washing our clothes, learning how to keep us alive, those tasks would give me purpose...that's what I needed now. Purpose. Momentum. *Peace.*

Peace would come, when we were safe.

When we were *all* safe.

My thoughts turned to dad as I moved quietly to the door. I tried to keep the image of his beaten face and gentle eyes from my mind. But no matter how hard I tried, I couldn't. He was right there, smiling with that sad smile right before he strode toward the men who wanted him dead.

I twisted the handle and eased the door open before slipping out.

"Is he asleep?"

My heart leaped, driving into the back of my throat. I bit down on a cry and spun around, finding Kit standing in the hallway behind me. "*Jesus,* you scared the crap out of me!"

But her gaze shifted to the door and stayed there. "You sleep with your stepbrother, don't you?"

Heat rushed to my cheeks. I swallowed the flare of heat and answered. "Yes."

"Just him?" She met my stare, those wide brown eyes demanding the truth.

I swallowed. "No."

Her brows pinched, like she wrestled with her own demons about that. Then she leashed the inquisitiveness and turned away. "Lucas wanted me to show you where the antibiotics and painkillers were, just in case you need to know for next time."

Next time? I hoped there'd never be a next time. I hoped for a lot of things, but hoping and planning were two very different things. I knew that. So I followed her as she opened the door to the treatment room and went to the drug cabinet.

I dumped the damp and dirty clothes on the floor beside the door and shifted my attention to her. But she was quiet, not yet reaching for the drawer.

"Do your parents know?"

I jerked my eyes to her. She hadn't moved, just stared at the counter.

"Yes."

Kit lifted her gaze my way, her eyes widening. "Really? And they just...let it happen?"

Let it happen? I thought of Tobias and the way he'd narrowed in on me, his hate, his anger...and his love. "They didn't really have a choice," I answered carefully. "It wasn't something we planned."

She gave a slow nod. "It never really is, though, is it?"

"No." I moved closer, narrowing in on all the things she *wasn't* saying. "Is everything okay, Kit?"

She forced a smile and nodded. "Sure. I just wanted to know. I wasn't sure how you..."

"Love all three of them?" I tried to fill in the gaps. "Or love them because they're my stepbrothers?"

"Yes."

Yes...

She didn't distinguish and I was too lost in the past to stop the flood of emotions. "They didn't like me, not at first."

"They didn't?"

I shook my head, meeting her stare. "No. Especially Tobias. He was...angry and hurt."

"And then they did."

I forced a smile. "I guess so."

"Lucas said you might need these." She reached out, grasped a stack of long white pill boxes, and pushed them my way.

I didn't need to look at the labels to know what they were. I picked up the top one and opened it, sliding out the sheave inside. "Kit, are you on the pill?"

She blushed and slowly shook her head.

"Do you want to be?"

The answer burned in her eyes. My pulse stuttered and raced at the sight. There was so much emotion, so much turmoil...so much need. I didn't want to overstep my place, but she looked like someone who could use a friend right now. Someone to talk to about what she was feeling. Someone who wasn't her stepbrother...

"I've seen the way he looks at you," I murmured. "And the way you look at him."

She swallowed hard. "You have?"

I gave a nod. "Yes."

"And does he...look at me the same way your brothers look at you?"

A smile tugged at the corners of my mouth. "Yeah, Kit, he does."

She blushed again, then turned away for a second before pointing to the overhead cupboard. "The antibiotics are on the top shelf. I can't quite reach."

I opened the cupboard, then reached high. My mind was captured by the past, on the way Tobias had hated me, before that hate had become an inferno, as a touch came across my stomach. The sting burned across the tattoo they'd carved into my skin.

"That's pretty." Kit stepped closer, her eyes fixed on my stomach. "H inside the O. What does it mean?"

Terror descended, dragging me back there, to that place and *that room*.

Hold her down!

HOLD THE BITCH DOWN!

I cried out and stumbled backwards, slapping a hand against my stomach, the other shoved out in front of me.

In the blur of my panic, Kit stepped toward me. "Ryth?" She reached toward me. "Are you okay?"

Hold her down...hold her...THE FUCK DOWN!

I couldn't speak, couldn't scream. My heartbeat exploded, punching against my ribs.

I saw everything, the way she reached for me...the way she *moved*. She became them. Their hate, their cruelty. Their *need*. I had to get out of there. Had to...

Run...

I spun around...and lunged. The doorway was a blur, so were the living room and the front door of the cabin, and even when I hit the sunlight, I still didn't stop. Because I couldn't.

"*Ryth! RYTH! I'm sorry!*"

Hard rocks stung the bottoms of my feet as I lunged from the veranda and hit the ground. By the time I hit the treeline, I was in full sprint. Branches lashed my face, stinging my cheek, blurring the forest through my tears.

"*Ryth!*" Caleb's roar came far behind me.

I caught the faint sound of Kit's panic. But I was too far gone to care, ripped away from the sunshine and slammed back into the dark.

And the cold.

And the empty room...

And their empty stares.

She's ruined...you like to be beaten? You like to be fucked...

A hand across my mouth, a hand around my throat, pressed against the wall. *I bet I could make you fucking scream...*I had to run. I had to escape. I had to—

"*Ryth!*"

Hands grabbed me and pulled me backwards as I scurried over a fallen tree.

"*Ryth, it's me!*"

A hard chest was at my back. A deep growl was in my ear and the rage, so much fucking rage. It bubbled up inside me, too, ripping free until the burning screams were all I could feel. I lashed out and kicked, bucking against the arms wrapped around me.

"*It's me!*" The roar boomed. "*Ryth! Ryth, it's me. It's Caleb!*"

I clawed, fighting against the hold. "*No! NO!*"

But he didn't let go...he...didn't let go.

"It's me. Baby, it's me." Strong fingers bruised my arms as he turned me around. Through the tears I saw...*him*. His dark hazel eyes gripped me. "It's me, princess. It's me."

"Caleb?"

He gripped me hard, pulling me against his chest. "It's me, baby. *It's me.*"

Still the tears flowed, sliding salty down my cheeks and into my mouth. "I *c-can't stop it. I c-can't.*"

"Then don't."

I squeezed my eyes closed and wrapped my arms around his neck.

"Don't fight it." The bass of his voice sounded beside my ear. "Just let it roll through you. It's just me...in that place with you."

I buried my face against his neck, drawing in his scent.

"Me touching you." Those words of comfort turned into something darker, something...*else*.

Heavy breaths claimed me.

His hand slid between my legs.

"Say my name, princess."

"*Caleb,*" I whispered, my voice husky. "*Caleb.*"

"That's it. Again," he demanded. I closed my eyes. "Caleb."

"That's the way, princess." He slid his finger along the crease of my jeans. "I'm there, right? You can see me in that room you can't escape. You can see me."

I could only nod, my arms wrapped tight around his neck. His hand moved upwards, his fingers working the button of my jeans. "Gonna take you away from here, princess." He pushed in, sliding under the elastic of my panties. "Gonna take you far away."

He dipped low, burrowing inside my panties to drive his fingers inside me.

"Fuck, baby." His voice was a growl. "I've been waiting for you to come to me all day."

My body responded to him. To his darkness...to his *savage need*.

"Breathe against my neck while I finger you, Ryth."

Oh God, my body trembled...and my pussy quaked, pulsing against the invasion.

"Jesus, that's it," he murmured, sliding two fingers inside me.

His other arm held me steady, drawing me down to the ground with him, until he pulled away, just enough to stare into my eyes. "Gonna need to be quiet out here, princess. You think you can do that?"

My ass hit the ground. He loomed over me as I was pushed back on the sticks and the leaves. But his fingers never stopped those slow strokes inside me as he placed a hand over my mouth. "Gonna need you to be really quiet now," he repeated, but there was an edge to his voice.

A coldness...

Sinking into depravity.

And it seethed in his stare.

I flinched at the pressure over my mouth. My body bucked as that fight rose inside me...until he looked down. My jeans were shoved open, his fingers using me the only way he knew how. I stared at him, captured by that infernal gleam in his eyes as he whispered. "That's it, baby. That's so fucking it, look how fucking wet you are. Christ, you love this...*you need this*."

I moaned with his praise, starved for his *wickedness*. My panting breaths warmed his palm, which only made him clench tighter and shift that savage glare my way.

He needed me.

Needed to use me.

Needed to keep the beast at bay.

And I needed him, too.

"I'm going to use this cunt." His fingers came away wet when he withdrew them. Stars glittered in the hazel abyss of his stare. "Over and over and over again, I'm going to use you. My perfect fucktoy." He leaned down to growl against my ear. "My needy little stepsister."

He reached for the button of his pants, yanked the belt, and shoved the zipper down. His hard cock sprang free as he pulled backwards, grabbed my waist with both hands, and lifted me. I was spun, my knees dragging against the ground as I was dropped back down.

His hand moved to my throat. His fingers were a cage as he surged against me, driving me against the trunk I'd so desperately tried to climb. I shoved out my hands, bracing myself against the hard surface as he wound his other hand around my hips and thrust.

"*My* cunt."

Thrust.

My spine bowed with the invasion as he filled me.

"*My fucking sister.*"

My legs trembled. My nails clawed, peeling bark. But his grip around my throat steadied me, holding me in place as he rammed his thick cock home.

"I'm gonna use you, princess," he growled again, driving me against the tree. "I'm gonna use your body...gonna take your soul. Gonna steal that heart right out of your chest...*the way you've stolen mine.*"

I slammed my eyes closed as my body clenched. The end swallowed me, taking me down into that room. To the darkness...*to his need.*

"You see me, princess?"

His voice was a growl. I nodded, driving myself backwards to meet his body. My knees lifted, my pussy quaked. I couldn't stop this feeling, couldn't fight this hunger...

Not anymore.

A savage sound ripped along my throat. My elbows buckled, suspending me by his hold around my throat as I gave into him. His brutality. *His cock.*

He used me.

Fucking me like I needed to be fucked.

I climaxed...*hard.*

He grunted, his fingers pressed against the vein in my throat. Darkness swam, sending me soaring...

Until he released and I crashed back down.

"I got you." His chest punched against mine with heavy breaths. He pulled me on top as we fell to the ground. "I'm right here, princess. Right here."

I closed my eyes, my body spent, empty...and yet full, all at the same time. His touch was real, drawing me back from that place. I shivered, turned to curl into him, and wrapped my arm around his waist.

"I'll always be there in that place with you, princess. Whenever you need me...I'll always be right there."

That was the truth. He would be.

Just him...

Only him.

My Caleb.

NINETEEN

Tobias

"Ryth! Ryth, wait, I'm sorry!"

I cracked open my eyes and shoved upwards, crying out as a sickening wave of agony ripped through my thigh. *Ryth...Ryth...*I scanned the room, finding the empty space beside me on the bed before I jerked my gaze to the door. *"Fuck!"*

"Come back!" The female voice sounded, along with panicked steps that faded.

For a second, I forgot where I was, where *we* were. Until Caleb's faint roar reached me. *"Where is she?"*

But that motherfucker, I knew.

I shoved out of bed, nearly screaming with agony as my foot hit the floor. His betrayal...and his selfish fucking ways. It all came rushing back as I stumbled around the foot of the bed. The Order. Her dad. The diner...and the doc. I gripped my thigh and bent over, moaning as I snatched a pair of cut-off sweats from the floor and yanked them on.

If Caleb hurt her.

"I'll kill him..." I grunted, yanked the waistband high, and stumbled for the door, slowing long enough to grab a gun from the dresser, then tore out the door. "I'll fucking kill him."

I half-stumbled and half-ran, tearing through the living room before I plunged outside. The sun hit me like a blow, boring into my eyes, blinding me for a second. "Fuck."

I lifted my hand to shielding myself from the glare. Trees blurred all around me. I tripped and staggered, calling out as I ran. "*Ryth! Ryth, where are you!*"

I focused on the blur of the forest and the silver sedan that glinted in the sun. I didn't know where I was running, didn't even know where we were. But I couldn't just stand there. I sucked in hard breaths, letting instinct take over, and scanned the towering trees.

"*Ryth, stop!*" Caleb called from deeper in the forest.

I gripped the gun, catching movement in the corner of my eye. The doc's sister stood there, staring into the forest as I raced past.

"I didn't mean to scare her." Kit said, fighting back tears. "I didn't mean..."

I don't think she even saw me. I gripped the gun and left her behind, charging through the trees. Sticks snapped under my feet. Pain followed, biting.

She needs me...

She needs...me.

Gone was the forest. Gone was the pain. Ryth was all I thought about. Movement came from somewhere deeper, hidden behind a bush. The flicker was nothing more than a blur. Still it was there, leading me forward. I tore around a tree, pivoting, and caught sight of a rotting fallen trunk stretching too far for me to go around. I drove my feet into the ground and lunged, only for my knee to buckle the moment I hit the other side.

A moan burst free as I slammed to the ground.

"*Ryth, stop!*" Caleb roared.

But the sound was closer…

Just through the group of trees in the distance.

I ground my jaw against the agony, using it to propel me upwards. But I had no strength anymore. I had nothing. I slammed the gun against the tree, using it to brace myself, and shoved forward. My feet blurred as the ground seemed to tilt.

"No…don't you fucking *dare,*" I growled.

I drew on my last ounce of strength to keep myself upright and lifted my gun.

"*No! NONONO!*" she screamed. "*Get off me! GET THE FUCK OFF ME!*"

All I heard was her terror. All I felt was her fear. I clenched my jaw and wrapped my finger around the trigger.

Caleb unleashed a curse, his muffled words growing deeper and softer the closer I came, until I rounded the thick clump of brush and saw them.

"It's me, baby." He held her, kicking and thrashing, against him. "It's me, princess. It's me."

"*Caleb?*" she moaned.

"It's me, baby," he repeated, turning her around.

"I *c-can't stop it. I c-can't,*" she cried, sounding so fucking broken it killed me inside.

"Then don't." I flinched with the coldness of his tone. "Don't fight it."

My lips curled as I narrowed in on him, watching them together from behind the trees.

"Just let it roll through you. It's just me in that place with you."

She pressed her face into his neck and I swallowed a pang of jealousy.

"Me touching you." He slid his hand between her legs. But she didn't need that, because we'd just— "Say my name, princess."

"*Caleb.*" Her moan was a punch to my chest.

"That's the way, princess. I'm right there, right? You can see me in that room you can't escape. You can see me."

He unbuttoned her jeans and pushed inside. My damn heart thundered, both excited and fucking savage watching them. Something was happening between them, something more than just sex.

"Gonna take you away from here, princess. Gonna take you far away."

What the fuck?

I took a step forward.

"Fuck, baby, I've been waiting for you to come to me all day."

I stopped. *Sonofabitch...*

"Breathe against my neck while I finger you." Her arms wound tight over his shoulders, clinging to him while he dug inside her pants. "Jesus, that's it." I couldn't move as he lowered her to the ground, pushing her backwards against the fallen tree. "Gonna need you to be quiet out here, princess. You think you can do that?

He shoved her jeans open, and tugged her pants low. "That's it, baby. That's so fucking it, look how wet you are. Christ, you love this. You *need* this."

He fucked her with his fingers, then pulled away, shoving his trousers open. I didn't want this to happen...didn't want to share her with him. Because he...didn't deserve her. Not after what he'd done.

He leaned over to growl in her ear. "I'm going to use this cunt... over and over. My perfect fucktoy. My needy little stepsister."

Something savage moved inside me. I clenched my grip on the gun as he lifted her, turning her around to face the tree. In a blinding second, I was back at that place, lying on the forest floor, staring up at my father as he aimed his gun at me as I now lifted mine, taking aim at the back of my brother's head.

"*My cunt.*"

He drove inside her. That savagery inside me pushed to the surface.

"*My fucking sister.*"

He gripped her around the throat, driving her hard against the trunk. But she didn't fight him...she didn't even cry out. She gave in, letting him fuck her like an animal. *Because she needed this. She needed him...*

The thought stopped me cold.

She needed the way he was. His darkness. His control.

Because that place had changed her.

It had corrupted her, stained her, left a part of her craving the kind of darkness Caleb could give. I winced, unable to fight the sting that carved through the center of my chest. *I could be that for her. I could...*

No.

I couldn't.

Because it wasn't just about the sex, was it? She cried out, her fingers clawed the bark of the tree on front of her as she climaxed. It was about that place. That place that Caleb had dragged her into. I hated him for that, hated him more than I had before.

But I didn't want him dead. Because that would hurt her even more. I lowered my gun and took a step backwards as my brother came inside the woman I'd given my heart to. No, I didn't want him dead...

I wanted him gone.

TWENTY

Ryth

My body pulsed as I came back from oblivion, that darkness sated for a little while as Caleb pulled me against him. "I'll always be right here."

Right here...right here—

Snap.

The sound invaded, wrenching me from that numbed state. Panic slammed into me as I jerked my head upwards, scanned the trees, and froze. Tobias stood in the distance, watching us with a gun in his hand and a savage glare in his eyes. "Tobias?"

There was a twitch in the corner of his mouth before he surged forward. I was drawn to the glint of steel in his hand as it rose. All I could see in my head was that bloodcurdling look of betrayal in his eyes. I was frozen as Tobias charged toward us, swapped the gun to his other hand, and cocked his fist.

"You fucking took her from me!" he roared, and lashed out, catching Caleb on the jaw. *"YOU PUT HER IN THAT PLACE!"*

Caleb stumbled backwards with the blow and his hand rose to his jaw as he settled a chilling stare on his brother. "T—"

"You fucking broke her," Tobias gasped. "You *fucking broke HER!*"

I shook my head, reaching for Tobias as he went for Caleb once more. "No! *Stop this!*" I screamed. *"Stop this!"*

But there was no holding back Tobias's rage now that the walls were cracked, and it all spilled out. At that moment, it was brother against brother. And I was trapped in the middle.

"Fuck you, Tobias!" Caleb screamed. "You self-righteous piece of shit!"

"Self-righteous?" Tobias's voice was stony as he stepped in front of his brother. "Self-fucking-righteous?"

Tobias's lips curled into a sneer. Even though he had to look up at Caleb, I knew who was the deadliest here...and so did Caleb. "You're fucking *weak,* C. You let your emotions get the better of you, and you put Ryth in danger."

Caleb held that deadly stare, never once flinching. "That's fucking rich coming from you. Your entire fucking life has been one temper tantrum after another, *little brother.*"

A chill raced down my spine.

My stomach clenched.

There was no stopping this.

Not now.

Not after this...

Tobias's grip tightened on the gun and something inside me broke. I surged up and forward, yanking Tobias away, to push in between them. "No...no, this isn't happening."

"Oh, it's happening," Tobias answered, but it was Caleb he stared at. His glare was a promise of all the things he wanted to do to him. Things I'd never let happen. "It's been a lifetime in the fucking making."

"Caleb, leave." My words were hoarse.

"No, Ryth, we—" he started.

But I jerked my gaze to him, imploring him without words. He met my stare and flinched. There was a second where my heart felt like it shattered in two, where it was ripped from my chest, the two halves beating and pulsing, bloody in my hands.

"You fucking leave now and this is done," Tobias warned carefully.

Caleb held my stare for a heartbeat, as confusion mingled with desperate pain. Then he took a step backwards before he strode toward the trees.

"That's it!" Tobias roared. "Fucking walk away, like you do all the time. That way you never have to face the consequences, right? Just like *fucking Dad!*"

Caleb froze with his back to us. I thought he was going to turn around and bite at Tobias's cutting words, but he didn't, he just took another slow step forward and left.

"That was cruel," I whispered, turning back to the brother I loved with all my heart but hated in this moment. "And uncalled for."

"Yeah?" He swung that savage glare my way. "You hurt for him, *little mouse?*"

The way he spoke hurt me, like he wanted to watch me bleed just to prove a goddamn point. "I love you," I whispered. "But I don't like you at this moment."

"Looks like we've come full circle then, doesn't it? *Minus the love.*"

He turned and walked away, striding after Caleb. But I had to stop him. I had to *save him*.

He didn't get it. He didn't see. When one of us bled, *we all fucking bled, until there was no stopping the flow.*

Sticks snapped as Tobias followed Caleb. He didn't limp as bad now, fueled by cold, hard rage. "Come back here, C!"

I hurried after them, cutting through the trees to head back toward the cabin. But the closer we came, the colder Tobias became. "Come back here!"

He moved faster, lunging over a fallen tree to land on his good leg and hop until he was steady once more. "You fucking walk away! *You don't get to DO THAT!*"

I raced to catch up to them as the sound of a four-wheel drive headed our way. Sunlight glinted off chrome, and there was a blur of black skidding across the loose gravel to pull up beside the silver sedan. Tobias was limping hard now, pressing the gun in his grip against his thigh.

He was in pain, and it bled out in his words. *"Leave, Caleb! Keep on fucking walking. We don't want you here, you hear me? I WANT YOU FUCKING GONE!"*

"Tobias!" I skidded down the driveway after him as the four-wheel drive narrowly missed them, skidding sideways. *"No!"*

But Caleb stopped walking, spinning around to face his brother. That cold, brutal look settled in his stare as he lunged forward, grabbed Tobias by the arm and pulled him closer. "You want me to leave? *Is that it? Leave so you and Nick can have Ryth for yourselves?*"

"Yeah," Tobias answered coldly. "I do."

"Well, guess what, T?" Caleb stepped even closer until he towered over him. "Even if I left, she'd still follow. She needs me, brother. I give her something you can't. I fuck her *just how she needs it*. So, maybe *you* better get used to that."

Oh shit.

Oh shit...

Car doors opened. "What the fuck is going on?" Lucas barked as he stepped out.

But Nick was there, striding around the rear of the vehicle to move in front of him. "You don't want to stop this, Doc."

I glanced at Kit, who stood there with her mouth agape, watching this all unfold. I hated that this was happening in front of them, but their emotions were too high. Wounded or not, Tobias unleashed a roar and lunged, swinging his fist to catch Caleb on the jaw. The *crack* was sickening, freezing me to the spot. I couldn't move, ripped open and torn down the middle watching the two men I loved go head to head.

"You fuck her right, huh?" Tobias drove his fist into his brother again.

Panic filled me as Caleb stumbled backwards and hit the ground. But Tobias wasn't stopping. That savagery inside him only seemed to grow until he was almost unrecognizable, falling on top of Caleb.

"You wanted her there!" He grabbed Caleb's shirt, cocked his fist, and lashed out once more. *"You wanted her there for yourself!"*

Crack!

"STOP!" I screamed until I tasted blood. *"Stop this, NOW!"*

I sucked in hard breaths, my mind splintering as that darkness waited, beckoning me toward insanity. "He did *not* break me." I slowly lifted my gaze to where Tobias had Caleb's blood-splattered shirt in his fist. A slow trickle of blood spilled from Caleb's nose, catching the sun, and I was mesmerized by the sight, unable to look away as I slowly delved into that place. "He saved me."

The world seemed to stop.

"He saved me the only way he knew how." I shifted my focus upwards until I met T's murderous stare. "*You* broke me, don't you see that?"

Tobias flinched and his chest rose hard, then fell with a heavy breath. I stepped toward them, empty and hollowed and hurting. "They told us you were dead." Closer still. "And I wanted to die too."

His throat muscles worked as Tobias swallowed hard. "They told you I was dead?"

Pain lashed deep. I reached out, closing my hand around his clenching Caleb's shirt. "Yes. They wanted me broken, pliable. They wanted to..."

"Ryth," Caleb whispered.

But I couldn't meet his stare, because if I did, then I'd fall apart.

"Maybe no more now," Nick urged, stepping closer. He looked at me, then Tobias. "Let's just all calm the fuck down so we don't say shit we'll regret later. Then tomorrow, when we've cooled off, we can talk about this?"

But Tobias didn't look away, his gaze unflinching. He didn't know. I saw that now. He had no idea what they'd told us, or what we'd had to do to survive. Or what they did to me. No one did.

I'm going to fuck you until you see stars...

My stomach clenched with the memory of those words.

"Okay, T?" Nick pushed.

"Okay," Tobias answered.

I sucked in deep breaths, staring at him. It was too late to claw back the things that had been said. I only hoped that, somehow, we'd find a way past them, for all our sakes.

"C?" Nick turned to Caleb.

"Fine," he said, swiping at a bead of blood that spread out from the corner of his mouth.

Tobias took one look at Caleb before he unfurled his fist from his brother's shirt, then slowly slipped his hand away from mine. "I would *never* have let you let near that place," he said carefully before turning and limping away.

I looked away.

"I'm sorry," Kit said, coming closer. "This is all my fault."

And something inside me snapped. I shook my head and turned to her. "You've got nothing to be sorry about. This was going to happen eventually."

"Well," Lucas muttered behind us. "Maybe pie might help? Nick grabbed some from Meg's Diner and she makes the best I've ever had. Kit will vouch for that."

He motioned to the car. "Help us with the groceries...*Nick?*"

"Sure," Nick answered, glancing at Caleb before he turned away and headed toward the four-wheel drive once more.

Caleb followed, leaving me to turn and pull Kit into my arms. "It's okay. It's all going to be okay."

I didn't know if I was trying to console her or myself. But she hugged me back, then followed me as I trailed the others as they went inside.

Kit cut the pies, which looked decadent and delicious, but I wasn't hungry. Food was the last thing I wanted. Instead, I carried a piece on a plate to the bedroom we shared and stopped outside the closed door. He needed space, I knew that. But still, knowing he was right there, yet out of reach, hurt. I placed the pie on the floor outside the door and straightened. "There's pie here for you."

Thump, the sound of an axe came as I turned and left, meeting Lucas in the middle of the hall, carrying two plates. He handed me one and motioned to the treatment room. "Want to go over some more drugs in case you need them?"

Thump.

"Sure." I glanced toward the window.

"Nick's working off some frustration, I believe." He shook his head. "You've found yourself some hot-tempered stepbrothers, haven't you?"

Thump!

"You can say that again." I placed the untouched pie on the counter.

Thump!

He started talking, pulling down vials and sliding sleeves of pills from locked drawers before he stopped. "You haven't heard a word I've said, have you?"

Thump!

"Sorry." I gave myself a shake. "I'm listening, I am."

He gave a small smile. "It doesn't matter." He glanced toward the window. "Go to him. That's the key to survival, anyway. Find your people and hold onto them." He reached toward his piece of pie.

I started toward the door. "I will, thanks, Doc."

He gave a chuff and shook his head. "No problem."

When I stepped out of the room, instinct made me glance toward the door down the hall. The pie was gone. I didn't know why that small thing made me feel a little more secure, but it did. If he had the pie, then maybe we were okay, somehow? I held onto that hope and hurried out, leaving everything behind.

Thump!

I headed for that sound and found Nick beside a chopping block back against the trees. Sunlight shone on his hard chest, drawing my focus to the white bandage on his side before I met his gaze.

Pain and desperation mingled as he gripped the axe and sucked in hard breaths. I took in his golden brown eyes and the dark hair that had grown in the months we'd been together and was now long enough to stick to the sweat on his temples. He stood tall, his long, muscular body so fucking perfect. I'd never realized how beautiful he was until now.

"He had pie." That's all I said, standing there like an idiot. Pain and desperation swirled inside me as I stared at my stepbrother in an exhausted and confused haze. "At least he had some pie."

Nick seemed to understand, glancing behind me at the open door, then at Caleb as he approached from the parked cars. There was a twitch in the corner of his eye, a blink before he looked away.

We kept busy, trying our best to avoid saying anything that would only inflame the situation. When the sun began to set, I went inside and helped prepare dinner. Steaks were cooked on the grill, with steamed vegetables and fluffy mashed potatoes.

I carried a plate to the bedroom door and knocked gently. This time, he opened it, took the plate from my hand with a sad smile, and handed me the one from before.

"Little mouse," he started when I turned.

I stopped. "Yeah?"

"Will you sleep in here tonight?"

I turned around. "Do you want me to?"

He gave a small nod. "Yeah, yeah, I do."

It was a start, so I gave him a smile. "Then I will."

"Good" He gave me a smile in return and lifted the plate. "Thanks for the food."

I nodded again. "Anytime."

We were almost like strangers. Civil. Careful. That hurt more than anything. This man had grabbed me with both hands and dragged me into his world filled with angst, love...and desperation, yet still I craved more. But there was a sadness about Tobias. One I didn't know how to heal.

I left to sit with the others, taking a few small bites when Nick and Caleb glared my way, then helped clean while Lucas grabbed extra bedding and Caleb started a fire. It hurt my heart to see him set up a bed on the sofa.

"Don't worry, princess." Caleb brushed the hair from my face. "The fire will keep me warm. You look like you could do with some sleep. So go, we'll fix this tomorrow, okay?"

I hated leaving him, but I did, nodding before I followed Nick into the room we shared with Tobias. He was lying in the dark, waiting for us, watching as I stepped into the bathroom, wound my hair on top of my head, and stepped into the shower. I wanted the banter, the ridicule even, not this…the quiet was too cruel.

After Nick stepped in, I dried and dressed in one of his t-shirts before climbing into bed. Tobias lifted the comforter for me, then rolled over and gave me his back. I snuggled against him for a moment, then leaned forward to kiss his shoulder.

"Sleep, Ryth," he urged. "We both need it."

We did. I lay there, waiting for sleep to come, and listened as Tobias's breaths turned deep and steady. The bathroom light flicked off and Nick climbed in on my other side.

"Can't sleep?"

"No," I whispered, my voice husky with emotion.

He lifted his arm, letting me curl against him as he pulled the comforter over us.

"I don't understand," I whispered. "Tell me what I did wrong?"

"Nothing, baby. You did nothing wrong."

"Then why does it feel like I did?"

He had no answer, other than to tighten his hold around me. I pressed closer, needing his strength as well as his warmth. The slow caress on my arm moved higher, his touch warmer, charged with more. I lifted my head, meeting his stare.

"I missed you," he whispered, and I realized that somehow, he'd been shoved aside.

It was Caleb, and Tobias, that had consumed my attention, and all the while Nick had waited for me to notice him. *My Nick.* "I missed you, too."

He leaned forward, lowered his head, and kissed me. Warmth spread out from my mouth. I closed my eyes, relishing the quiet carefulness. He deepened the kiss as he pushed me back against the pillows, and I was reminded of how it was with them.

Each of them demanding, in their own perfect ways.

My body and my heart.

I slid my arms around his waist as he rose above me on the bed. "Are you still sore?" I asked as I brushed my hand across the bandage.

"No, Ryth," he murmured.

A drop of water dripped from his hair to plop on my cheek before he dipped low, slid his hand over my thigh to burrow under his t-shirt, and push it higher. I was bare underneath, shivering as he palmed my breast and dragged his thumb across my nipple.

"Fuck, I missed you," he murmured, lowering his head.

His tongue danced around my nipple, over and over again, until I shivered. Even in my pain, Nick found me, the only way he knew how. He sucked gently, drawing me deeper into his mouth as that ravenous stare pinned me to the bed.

But it didn't need to—I let out a moan, my back arching, driving my nipple deeper into his mouth—because I wasn't going anywhere.

"Missed you so fucking much." His husky words sank into me as he moved lower. "How about I show you just how much?"

I watched him as he sank lower, kissing my stomach and my hips. Freezing when he reached the tattoo, then grazing his lips across the raised red flesh. "Ours," he whispered, meeting my gaze. "Always ours, princess."

He sank further, sliding his hand under the back of my thigh to lift my leg.

There was no stopping Nick, no taking control.

He was the rush of the tide, coming, claiming, no matter what.

I could only let him happen.

He widened my legs, then moved in to lick, finding the part of me that pulsed, and drew it into his mouth.

"Oh, God," I moaned. "Oh, Nick."

"Mhmm?" He didn't stop, just kept dipping, caressing, parting my body to claim me with his mouth.

The rush was instant, like lightning tearing through me. My body wasn't mine when Nick was in control. No, every cell, every quiver...every climax belonged to him.

"You're all I want," he growled, sliding his tongue in deeper. "All I fucking need, princess." He slid his finger along my slit and pushed in, fucking me and ramming those words home. "There will never be a moment without me, you understand that? Never again. I don't care if I have to chain you to my bed, Ryth. You belong to us." *Deeper.* "And you are never leaving us again."

I shivered as I rocked my hips against him and closed my eyes. "Never," I croaked, my hips thrusting against his touch. "*Never.*"

He slowly slid out, kissing that tattoo once more before he rose. Our gazes connected as he surged his hips forward and drove his cock inside. My breath caught. I stiffened with the shock as my body adjusted. He was so big...*and hard.*

"Ours." He punched his hips forward, driving me hard against the mattress, making me bounce. *"Ours...ours...ours."*

I grabbed his shoulders, pulling him against me as my body gave over. Every thrust, every grunt from him stroked the flare higher. I wound my arms around his powerful shoulders and hung on. "Oh, Nick," I groaned as the end rushed over me.

And with his next savage thrust, I came apart underneath him.

My body pulsed and quivered.

"Such a good fucking girl," Nick growled. *"A good little sister."*

With a growl, he came hard, driving deep inside me.

Warmth spilled, filling me.

In the rush of hard breaths, I floated. Nick rolled, falling to the other side. His heavy arm wrapped around me, pulling me hard against him. "Sleep, princess," he murmured, already closing his eyes. "You're gonna need it."

My body quivered, pulsing, but still, I felt myself crashing hard. He sat up swiftly, grabbed the end of the comforter, and pulled it over us.

In the warmth of his body, I finally gave myself over and fell... even harder than I had before.

In the darkness...and in love.

TWENTY-ONE

Nick

NICK!

NICK!

NO!

I wrenched open my eyes. My panic thundered, booming in my ears as I took in the murky darkness of the room and the woman beside me. But inside my head, I was still trapped in that warehouse, controlled by the events that had rippled from that moment. I looked down, found Ryth sleeping soundly beside me, and a wave of relief slammed into me, hitting me so damn hard my body shuddered.

Princess.

Her screams faded in my mind, but my body still responded, hardening, aching. Needing to fuck her once more, to remind myself that she was here and real, and not just a figment of my imagination. We'd almost lost her. I lifted my gaze to my brother on the other side, curled around her. We'd almost lost everyone. Tobias was deep asleep, his lips parted, an arm wrapped around her waist. He needed rest and her, now more than ever.

But sleep was now gone for me, fading with her screams in my head. I rolled over and climbed out of bed, then grabbed a pair of sweats and a t-shirt before heading for the door.

It was still dark when I stepped out. The only sounds were the crackling of the fire and the faint growl of an engine fading away. I headed along the hall, glancing around the murky gloom and finding the faintest trace of sunlight through the kitchen window as I yawned.

"They're gone."

Caleb moved, standing near the fire, wearing the same clothes from yesterday. A scan of the sofa and I found the comforter still neatly folded, lying across the arm. Looked like he hadn't slept at all.

"You don't seem surprised about that."

I met his stare and raked my hair back from my face. "I'm not."

"So you knew they were leaving?"

"Yeah."

"Which is why you said to leash it until today." I didn't answer, because I didn't need to. "There's fresh coffee in the pot."

"Thanks." I headed for the kitchen, hating how it felt like we were strangers.

Blood or not, it meant nothing when it came to betrayal.

"Nick." He stopped me.

"Yeah?"

"Are we ever going to move past this?"

I stopped in the middle of the kitchen, unable to look at him. "I hope so, for Ryth's sake."

He left me to pour a cup and stare out the window, wondering how this all had gone so wrong. It wasn't just betrayal here. It was the secrets I couldn't get past. So many fucking secrets, too many. It made it hard to trust and this *couldn't* work without trust, no matter whose heart was on the line.

I turned around, staring at Caleb as he watched the fire and drank his own coffee. The meeting with Benjamin Rossi was in two days. Two days until we got answers, real answers. Only answers wouldn't keep us safe, if anything, they'd be more like a target on our backs.

I thought of running, really running, leaving all of this behind. I had enough money to make it happen. Maybe it wouldn't last forever, but it'd carry us through until we made a new plan.

A plan that would keep us together.

I stared at my brother...

If we made it through this.

Movement from the hallway caught my focus. Tobias glanced toward Caleb, then headed for the kitchen.

"T," I muttered, motioning to the half-filled pot.

He wasn't limping as much today, which surprised me after the workout he'd had yesterday beating the shit out of our brother. But he held back. I knew that. I'd seen T consumed with rage and for a second, when we'd rounded the driveway yesterday, I'd thought for sure the Doc was going to add one more dead body to our cold pile.

But as I'd climbed out of the Range Rover and headed their way, I knew that wasn't going to happen. Not then, at least. I knew that because of who'd stood in his way.

Our sister.

She'd *never* let that happen, not to them…or because of her.

All three of us turned now as Ryth came out of the hallway, yawning, then stopped halfway between the kitchen and the living room, looking at each of us intently. A blush crept into her cheeks as she looked around and headed for the kitchen.

"Morning," she mumbled.

"Morning." T turned and handed her the freshly poured cup he'd just taken a sip from.

I stared at the offering, then him. He looked the same and even moved the same. But the man standing in front of me wasn't the brother I knew. He was different, older and rawer than I'd ever thought possible. I glanced at Caleb as he watched them together with an aching fucking look in his eyes.

Christ, our little sister had changed us all.

She took a sip, wrapped her hands around the mug, and turned around. "Any sign of the others?"

"They're gone," I answered.

"Gone?" T glanced my way.

I gave a nod. "Gone."

"Where?" Ryth looked nervous.

I pushed off the counter. "Back home. He said he had some things to take care of and preferred not to be around when Benjamin Rossi came."

"Oh, is there bad blood?" she asked.

"More like a misunderstanding," I answered, focusing on her. "Which leaves us two days before the meet."

"Two days?" she whispered.

"Two days," T repeated as he leaned down to whisper in her ear. "Let's hope we all survive, huh?"

She paled, the birthmark blushing before she covered it while taking another sip. But then she lowered the cup and found his stare. "If we don't, *brother*, then you'll be the first one I take out."

"Sibling rivalry, huh?" he bit back.

"No." She shook her head. "You're just the asshole of the family."

"Ouch." He feigned a blow, jerking his head to the side and rubbing his jaw. "That one hurt."

It was strained, but fuck, it was nice to feel even a little of the light-hearted banter we'd had before our lives went to hell.

"In that case," she muttered, "I'd better feed you."

"I'll help." Caleb headed toward us, and instantly T went cold, that laughter now a cruel glint in his stare.

"And suddenly, I'm not hungry." Tobias placed his cup down on the counter and turned, striding away without a glance in our brother's direction.

"Tobias," Ryth called.

But it was too late, he was gone, his heavy limping thud echoing down the hall.

"I'll go after him." Ryth took a step.

"No." I stopped her. "Let him go, he'll come to you in his own time."

"As long as he comes to me."

"Oh, he will." I sighed, knowing when he did, she'd better be prepared.

We cooked and ate, then I walked out, checked the sedan, and made plans on how far and how long we could run. I spent the day thinking about that, taking the car into town to refuel and gather supplies before I returned.

When I did, the tension was palpable.

I strode into the cabin to find Tobias standing in front of Caleb with a cold, hard look in his eyes. "You want to do this, brother? So let's do it. Let's have it all out in the open...let's hear exactly how you fucking saved her. But I swear to you, if you hold back or lie, then I'll cut you out of my life...and you'll never see me again."

Oh shit...

This was going to be fucking messy.

TWENTY-TWO

Ryth

"Tobias." I placed my hand on his chest as he stood in front of Caleb. "Please, you promised."

He glanced my way, his stare stony. "This is me holding up that promise, little mouse. Believe me...I'm very much in control." My pulse thundered as Tobias glared at his brother. "So how about we start at the beginning...with the clubs you went to."

Nick walked in from outside, returning from somewhere in town. He took one look at Caleb, then Tobias, and muttered. "Okay, we're really doing this."

Tobias glanced his way. "Oh, yeah, we're fucking doing this."

"You really want to start there?" Caleb questioned, glancing at me.

There was a flicker of fear there, like he was scared for me to know the truth. The *real* truth and not the part I knew, or thought I knew. That same sting of betrayal came roaring back and I was dragged to the fight we'd had before he left to go after Killion.

I'd been out of control then, throwing lamps and anything I could get my hands on at Caleb because all I saw was his betrayal. I couldn't do that again, no matter how much it hurt to hear what had happened, even if the sex...*Oh God,* I stared up at Tobias—had been incredible. But this wasn't about sex, not really. It was about betrayal and trust, and trust started with the truth. I inhaled deeply and nodded, letting Caleb know that I was ready.

But Tobias wasn't backing down. If anything, he seemed to be gaining savage momentum. "Yes, *brother. I* really want to start there."

"Fine," Caleb responded.

"Fine," Tobias didn't flinch.

I shifted, panic swirling inside me, rolling under my skin. Tobias saw, grabbed me, and pulled me close. His hand moved to the middle of my back, his thumb moving in slow circles, like he needed the touch to keep himself grounded.

It was annoying at first, aggravating that coiled tension inside me...until slowly...slowly...that irritating touch seemed to ease the thrumming of my heart. My breaths slowed, moving deeper. My stepbrother glanced my way, those dark eyes searching mine. I hated how he knew what I needed better than I knew myself. "Go on," he urged his brother.

"I contacted Evans after Ryth was taken. He'd been the one to introduce me to Killion, several years ago. Even though at the time, I'd wanted nothing to do with the kind of men they were, I knew after the capture, they'd be my way into The Order."

The way he said it was so clinical, like he was giving us the bare minimum. Still, the mention of Killion's name sent chills down my spine. Whatever desire I'd felt a second ago was replaced by the sickening promises Killion had snarled in my ear as he'd pushed me naked against the wall in The Order. *I'm going to fuck you so hard you'll see stars, you ruined little bitch.*

My fingers trembled as I touched my throat, still feeling his fingers. Tobias saw, shifting that cold stare from his brother to me. His brow furrowed, narrowing in on the movement.

"So I asked for a re-introduction." Caleb continued carefully. "And he did, taking me to meet Killion at the same club I'd gone to that night..."

"The night your almost got us all killed." Tobias turned back to him.

"Yes."

But there was no edge to Tobias' voice anymore. Instead, he swallowed and murmured. "Go on."

"That first time, he made me sit and watch while a woman of The Order was raped and degraded."

The temperature in the room plunged. Tobias scowled, and that glint of rage danced in his eyes again.

"It was a test," Caleb continued as Nick stepped closer, drawn to the darkness. "My first test...but not the last, or the worst. I made it through that night, knowing if I so much as flinched at the things they did, that I'd lose my only way in. So I played along."

"Something you do very well," Tobias muttered.

"And thank God for that," Caleb bit back. "We got her out, didn't we?"

Tobias was the one to flinch that time, but he didn't give Caleb an inch, pushing him again. "The rest, C."

At least we were back to calling each other by our names, and Caleb noticed. "The second test was another woman, one

Killion expected me to fuck, and not just fuck, either. He wanted to see how I *'played'*."

I turned away, unable to look at him.

Still, he continued, even though I heard the pain in his voice.

"He wanted proof I was one of them. That I liked to humiliate and degrade."

"And did you?" Nick asked. "Did you fuck and degrade?"

I wrenched open my eyes, turning to Nick.

Caleb glanced my way and swallowed hard. "Fuck her, no..."

But he did degrade her, right?

I tried to stop the onslaught of images that followed, where Caleb had his hand around the throat of the woman at The Order, growling in her ear how he was going to choke her and ride her until she passed out. My stomach hardened and my clit throbbed, my senses at war with each other.

"Evans fucked her instead," Caleb whispered carefully, regret staining his words. "He didn't want to. He was sick doing it. But he did, because he knew what was at stake *for us.*"

Me...

That's what was at stake. He'd done it for me.

"And that's what got me in." Caleb glanced at me, his vice softening. "And Ryth out."

"Until you fucked it up," Tobias finished.

We'd almost had him, almost pulled him back to us, until that last moment.

"That was...*is* my only regret." Caleb met his brother's stare. "If I could go back and do things differently..."

"We've all done things we regret," I added carefully as my own screams of rage came roaring back. The way I'd hit Caleb, the way I'd hated and trusted...

"You killed, T," Nick's voice was so quiet I barely heard it. "I stood there and watched you kill a man."

But Tobias did hear, and slowly turned to face Nick. He was so cold in that moment, so utterly fucking terrifying. "A number of them, actually," he added. "And I'd do it again. I'd kill and I'd keep on killing, I'd leave a river of fucking blood, brother. But there is one thing I'd *never* fucking do, and that's put *her* in danger."

He shifted that deadly stare my way and his control trembled. "Because if I did, the next man I'd kill would be myself."

His love was murderous, and consuming.

My heart throbbed hard in response, even as he held my stare and asked. "But that's me, isn't it, C? It's not you. Not the dominant lover she needs, right?" He looked from Caleb to me, and I saw fear in his stare, real fear. The kind I never thought I'd see in someone so threatening. "I want to know what happened between the two of you."

I flinched and snapped my gaze toward him. "What?"

He dropped his hand from the middle of my back, distancing himself. "I need to know how he saved you." He rubbed his jaw. "How he..." *gives you what you need*. He didn't have to say the words, because the air was charged with them.

For a second, I couldn't speak, unable to stay the words he so desperately needed to say.

How could I put it into words?

I closed my eyes, praying Caleb or Nick would say something...*anything* to fill the void.

But they didn't.

I winced. Because this wasn't their truth to tell...*it was mine.*

My throat thickened. I swallowed the fear.

"You've got my heart in your hands, little mouse," Tobias whispered huskily. "Careful there."

I opened my eyes as a charge ignited inside me. Love. That's what this was. Ground-shaking, heart-tearing, *all-consuming love*. Tobias would *never* stop choosing me. I saw that now, saw it all in that dangerous, moody stare. He would *never* stop loving me, fighting for me, ...*bleeding for me.*

My voice trembled when I spoke. "He protected me. He..." I licked my lips. "Lured Killion away from me by touching another woman, by telling her exactly what he wanted to do to her..."

"To you, Ryth. They were all the things I wanted to do to you," Caleb cut in.

But Tobias never looked away from me. "Let her finish, C. Go on, little mouse. I want to hear everything."

It all came pouring out of me and I couldn't stop it. "I thought he'd betrayed me. Thought he...wanted her. I didn't know what felt worse that night, the image of his hands on another woman...or the one of his back when he left."

Caleb shook his head and turned away.

But I couldn't protect him, not at that moment. I had a heart to save. "But he came back, and after that...day with the both of us, I knew how much he'd risked to save me."

"And when you were back there?"

A pang tore across my chest. "When we were back there, they told us you were dead...and that Nick was captured."

"What the fuck?" Nick whispered.

"They tried to break us, forcing us to believe your life hung in the balance. They wanted to use me...to make me...perform for them. But they couldn't, because of my father."

"He threatened them," Tobias clarified.

I gave a slow nod. "So they hurt me instead, making a woman kneel for Caleb. She almost...she tried to..."

"Fucking bastards," Nick growled. "They made Caleb fuck a woman in front of you?"

I held Tobias's stare. "No." That same panic rose. "I would never let that happen."

"So you did it instead, didn't you, little mouse?" Tobias whispered. "You fucked him in front of them."

"I kneeled for him, yes." I couldn't stop this crash, no matter how hard I tried. "And in those moments when I was broken, when I thought my mind had shattered with the loss of you, he brought me back. Touching me, drawing me back to my body. Because I can tell you, Tobias. My heart was the last thing I wanted to be anywhere near."

His powerful chest rose on a massive breath.

"I wanted to die," I whispered. "I prayed for it, screamed for it...*I*..."

His chest stopped moving.

Stopped rising.

Stopped *everything*.

"He brought me back, dragged me by his touch and desperation."

"And you clung to him," Tobias whispered. "You clung to each other."

Tears welled, blurring his face. Tobias took a step closer, so close his chest pressed against mine. He leaned down, making sure I understood this was what all this was really about. "Now I want to see how he fucks you, how he is the one you run to when your world is falling apart. How he—" He stilled, sucked in a breath, and continued. "How he gives you something I don't."

"Then in that case, *I* want to see how *you* fuck her," Caleb declared. "How *you're* the one she goes to for comfort and not just sex. I want to see how *you* give her that. Because, *brother*, while she clings to me, fighting the darkness of that place, she is forever occupied by you. Just in case you don't see that."

Tobias jerked his head up, those dark eyes flaring wide as it slowly dawned on him.

"She needs us...*all of us*," Nick added, turning to me. "Don't you, princess? Each of us in our own way."

I nodded, the roar of my pulse deafening in my ears. "Yes. I need all of you." I looked at each one. "In your own way."

Nick shook his head slowly, and chuckled. "You are both the death and the making of us."

"As you are to me," I whispered.

"So, the question is, little mouse..." Tobias leaned down to whisper against my ear. "Are *you* gonna be *good for us?*"

Good for us?

My breath quickened, mingling with the fluttering of my heart as he pulled backwards.

"What?" I glanced at the others. "Now?"

"Now," Tobias answered. "Unless you have something else on your schedule?"

I swallowed hard. I didn't and he knew that.

"You want us to move past this," Nick added. "Then this is how. We *all* watch, we *all* participate, we *all* take care of your needs."

That wasn't a request...it was an ultimatum.

They wanted to fuck...

I inhaled hard.

So, we'd fuck.

"Okay."

Nick smiled as I grabbed the bottom of his t-shirt and dragged it over my head, standing there in nothing more than panties. Cold swept across me instantly as all three of my brothers lowered their gazes to my body.

"Fuck me," Nick whispered.

"You wanted it." Caleb stared at my breasts and licked his lips. "Then we make it good."

"Exactly what I was thinking," Tobias growled, then he stepped forward, grabbed me around the waist, and lifted me.

"Tobias," I protested, pushing against his shoulders. "Stop, your leg."

"The only leg I care about right now, little mouse, is the aching one between my fucking thighs. Wrap yours around me and shut the fuck up. This is happening."

I did as he demanded, clinging tightly as he limped toward the bedroom at the end of the hall...and his brothers followed. Déjà vu slammed into me as Nick closed the door. This was just like the first time, when I was so damn terrified and excited all at the same time.

They'd taken me into their room...and made me theirs.

Now it was my turn.

My turn to bring us together, any way I could. Tobias gently tossed me onto the bed, watching me bounce with the impact. I braced my hands against the mattress as all three stared between my legs.

Tobias yanked his shirt free as Caleb did the same, his hair still damp from the shower he'd had before all of this started, tousled and darker now when he worked the buttons of his clean white shirt. Sometime during the early hours of the morning, he'd taken care of the laundry, leaving it neatly folded.

He'd always been good like that, pristine, neat...

But certainly not vanilla.

He stepped closer, dropped his shirt to the floor, and unbuttoned his pants. "Our brother wants to watch us, little mouse. So how about we make it worth his while?"

My body trembled as he pushed his pants and boxers low, as Nick stepped closer.

"It's only fair, princess. You take our clothes, and we take your ability to walk...for a while, at least." Nick grinned, dropping his t-shirt to the floor. "Two days until the meet...how the fuck are we gonna pass the time?"

"I have a few ideas," Caleb offered as he climbed onto the bed and slid his hand around the back of my neck, staring into my eyes. "You ready?"

My erratic pulse was out of control, but I nodded.

The corners of his lips quirked as he leaned down. I'd expected darkness, and maybe danger. I'd expected his hand around my throat. But there wasn't any of that. Goosebumps raced along my flesh as he lowered his head. I closed my eyes and waited for the kiss...only it wasn't on my lips.

His breath warmed my neck as he eased my head to the side and kissed me. I couldn't track him, couldn't anticipate what he'd do. I'd expected dominance, but this wasn't dom—

His teeth pressed over my vein and drove down, hard enough to make me flinch. I released a yelp, feeling his hand move up from the nape of my neck and grasp a handful of my hair.

"Gonna mark you, little sister" he murmured against my throat as he yanked my head backwards. "Gonna show our brother what a *good fucking girl you are.*"

"Ohh," I moaned.

Panting breaths consumed me as I stared up at the ceiling. Heat lashed my scalp, but it wasn't a cruel heat, just enough for my pulse to race and my body to respond.

"She fucking likes that," Tobias murmured.

A touch came between my legs, as Tobias's finger dragged along my panties before he slipped under the elastic and pushed into me. "So fucking wet."

"Hear that, princess?" Caleb's voice was colder. He angled my head so I stared into his dark brown eyes. "Our brother likes to see how perfect you are. How about we show him a little more?"

I could only pant and try to nod against his hold.

He smiled...

And that wicked glint just made my pussy clench.

"Fuck me," Tobias sighed, slowly thrusting his finger inside me.

Caleb pressed his hand over my mouth, muffling me. "Are you going to be good for us?"

I nodded, strands of my hair pulling taut.

"How good?"

So fucking good...I opened my mouth to say the words, but caught myself. My senses fired, and somehow, I knew that had been a test, one I'd caught just in time.

Caleb's smile only grew wider...

And I grew wetter, my body taking over to drive against Tobias's fingers. "Christ, you have the most perfect cunt," he muttered.

I knew he watched me, riveted by Caleb's hand as he pulled it away. "Open your mouth, princess."

I obeyed on instinct as Caleb rose up, gripped his cock, and aimed it for my mouth. Our gazes connected, searing with intensity, as I took him inside.

"So good." He drove deeper, forcing me to open wider.

The careful stroke of his thumb against my cheek came, so soft, so caring, before his hand went around my neck once more...and he pushed me backwards against the bed. "Tobias," he murmured. "I think our little sister needs more than one hole filled."

"You want that, Ryth?" Tobias checked.

All I could do was nod and stare into Caleb's eyes. He smiled... and that flicker of happiness only made me want to please him more. Whatever he wanted, I'd do. He could use me and keep on using me. He could do anything he wanted...*and he knew that*.

He cupped my head, pushed it back against the pillow, and swung his leg over to straddle my face. I opened wider as he thrust even deeper, pushing his cock all the way to the back of my throat. Panic kicked in, but that rush only made me hyper-sensitive. I couldn't hold back the moan as rough hands gripped the edges of my panties and dragged them down.

"I fucking dream about this pussy," Tobias growled. "About how I want to fucking fill it."

Movement came from the corner of my eye as he tossed them to Nick. My nostrils flared as I sucked in hard breaths as Caleb thrust, pulling out only to slowly slide back in.

I turned my head, seeing Nick as he leaned against the wall, my panties in his hand. He gave me a smile and slowly nodded. "You know how I like to watch, princess." He licked his lips, his gaze shifting to Tobias and Caleb as they rode my body. "I could get used to this show."

I didn't want to leave him out, desperate for our connection, until Caleb leaned forward and I was drawn back to the feel of him.

"That's my girl." He tightened his grip and leaned forward, using his other hand to brace against the mattress.

I gripped his waist as Tobias parted my thighs and pushed them apart.

"Eyes on me, princess," Caleb urged.

I couldn't look anywhere else. My throat clenched as he thrust, saliva pooled and ran down the back of my throat, and all I thought about was him coming. Tobias thrust inside me, driving me upwards, but Caleb's hold against my neck kept his cock seated.

"That's it, little brother," Caleb encouraged. "Use her."

"Fuck," Tobias growled, and drove in harder.

"Use that sweet cunt," Caleb whispered, staring down at me.

Tobias stretched me, sliding in with the slick. "Fuck, little mouse," he grunted, gripping my hips and driving in harder.

I bounced against the bed, pinned by Caleb's cock as he thrust in my mouth. I opened my legs wider as desperation rose.

"No coming, princess," Caleb grunted, his brow creasing with concentration. "Not yet."

Then he pulled out, leaving me to gasp and moan as Tobias slammed in all the way to the hilt, filling me. I was going to come...I knew that. My core clenched as Caleb slid his hand from under my neck and gently pinched my nose shut.

"Not until you've had your fill." His voice turned dangerous. I gasped, drawing in a breath through my mouth before he plunged his cock back in.

I couldn't breathe, couldn't breathe...*couldn't breathe.* I bucked, my body clamping down on Tobias as he thrust in. This was just the same as his hand around my throat and panic drove me closer to the edge as Caleb released his hold, leaving me to gasp and groan. My body quivered as the end rushed toward me.

"Princess?" Caleb watched me intently as he pulled free.

I nodded, closed my eyes, and whimpered. "I'm going to come. I—"

He smiled and pinched my nose again as he grabbed his cock with his other hand. "Open."

I parted my lips wider, feeling the stretch. He was so hard, so ready, that desperate gleam twinkling in his eyes as he ran the smooth skin on the head of his cock around my mouth. I licked, and lifted my head, desperate to feel him in my mouth.

"Fuck, C, I'm going to—" Tobias groaned.

Caleb thrust back in, keeping my nostrils clamped shut. He trembled, released a moan, and set his cock it at the edge of my mouth. The head quivered, pulsing, before that thick vein jerked and warmth filled my mouth.

My brothers moaned, both guttural...*and perfect.*

And I couldn't hold back any longer.

Cum slipped down the back of my throat. I swallowed, desperate for air, and came *hard*, quivering and whimpering as Caleb released my nose and whispered, "That's my girl."

TWENTY-THREE

Vivienne

I CHASED THE LAST DROP OF JUICE AROUND THE RIM OF THE plastic cup, then set it back on the tray alongside the flimsy plate and cutlery. It'd been three days since they'd let me out. Supervised, of course. My every move was watched by *him* and the damn cameras, but we still hadn't worked our way up to real metal utensils. Because the sonofabitch knew I'd take them to his goddamn face.

Him and his goddamn sons...

I stared at the tray, then turned toward the door to follow him. He let me accompany him downstairs to the study, even answered some of my questions about the house with clipped answers. Yes, his sons lived here. Yes, he knew about Ryth and her brothers. No, he wasn't about to divulge her location or if they were even back at The Order.

He wouldn't really tell me a goddamn thing.

Frustration seethed inside me.

But he knew...

Oh, fuck yes, he knew.

My mind shifted to the medical reports he poured over. If there was anything I was starting to understand about London St. James, it was that he was fucking conniving...and powerful. The DNA printouts had *highly confidential* stamped all over them.

He obsessed over them, scanning each one before moving on, then printed more. That only intensified my interest.

I wanted to know what he was looking for...

I wanted to know what he wanted.

And I wanted to know about Ryth...

Where she was, if she was safe...*if she was even alive.*

They wouldn't kill her, that I was pretty sure of. No, The Order wouldn't dare risk one of its captives. Still, I knew there were worse things than death. *Like being locked away by a monster.*

Darkness waited outside my window as I turned away from the new tray. It was night...late, too. Stars sparkled in the sky, glinting around a full moon. I made my way to the window, tracing my finger along the electronic locks, ones he'd made sure he mentioned, just in case I thought again about trying to escape.

Just like the door, right?

I glanced over my shoulder at the bedroom door.

He needn't have bothered. Even if I escaped this hell, I had nowhere to run. No family was looking for me, no brothers desperate to get me back. Not even a goddamn friend I could call. Ryth had been the closest thing I'd ever had to a friend, and I'd lost her.

I turned away from the window and crossed the room, habit driving me forward. I didn't know why I even tried. Every night the bedroom door was locked, and every night I went to sleep frustrated. But as I reached out, I realized one tiny detail. *I hadn't heard it click.*

The door lock clicked at the same time every night. Set by a timer, I'd assumed. The tiny *thunk* always came just after he brought me the tray. I tried to think, tried to pick apart the minutes since he'd placed the tray on the dresser then turned to watch me with that hungry stare, and remember...

I hadn't heard it.

I was sure.

My breath caught as I reached out, closed my hand around the handle, and pushed.

But instead of catching...it unlocked, bearing down until the hinges softly creaked.

My heart leaped, slamming against my chest. I eased the door closed, then froze. *What if it was broken? What if the damn thing had somehow malfunctioned and if it was now fixed...if it clicked, then I'd have missed my chance.*

I looked at the red blinking light of the electronic lock. It didn't look right. Normally, the light was on, a solid red. Red for locked, green for open. It was broken...

I twisted the handle once more, praying with all I had that this wasn't a joke, and it inched open slightly before I released my hold and dropped my hand. Darkness waited out there, on the other side of the door. Darkness and silence.

Was this a test?

It'd be just like him. He'd be waiting, watching to see what I'd do. I took a step away from the cracked open door, my mind racing. What would he expect me to do?

Run...

That's what.

He'd expect me to slip down the stairs and try the front door, maybe even search the house for the back door. My mind skipped over the basement. Fuck, no, I wasn't going down there. I wasn't even thinking about that room...

Still, that *machine* rose inside my head, sending shivers along my spine. I reached out and hit the light switch, plunging the bedroom into darkness, then I stepped backwards, made my way to the bed, and sat down.

It was a test.

I was sure of it now.

See if I'd run.

See if I could be trusted.

I pulled my feet upwards and lay my head down, curled on my side, staring at that slither of inky blackness on the other side of the door and tried to think of all the possible reasons...and the outcomes.

Run...

Leave this house and these people.

And I'd have to keep on running, because it wouldn't be just The Order after me, would it? No. There was no way London St. James would allow me to even get through the door before he dragged me back, kicking and screaming...

Try it...his cruel fucking tone filled me. *Try and escape and see where that gets you.*

I knew where it'd get me. My body quivered and my core clenched. I closed my eyes, willing the image of that *thing* away.

He threatened me with it, promised it to me. "No," I whispered, and opened my eyes. I wouldn't let that happen.

So, I wouldn't run...

But I sure as hell wasn't about to stay a prisoner, either. Fuck that. I slowly sat up, slid my feet to the floor, and rose. My steps were light and soundless as I made my way to the open door. One careful push and I waited, standing in the doorway, my pulse thundering until the sound was all I could hear.

Only no one pounced.

I took a step out of the room and scanned the darkness, my senses hyperalert. Hard breaths consumed me as I waited. But there was nothing, not a hand reaching for me, not a stalker outside my door listening. I took a step forward, heading to the stairs.

They blurred as I watched in my peripheral, taking another step, then another, until I reached the railing. They weren't here, weren't waiting. Embolden with confidence, I moved faster, stepping down, keeping my footsteps light. I scanned the floors as I passed, finding a flicker of light coming from under a door on the second floor. I stopped...*listening.*

There was only silence.

Silence and the booming of my heart.

I kept going, stopping only when my bare feet hit the cold tiles of the foyer. I didn't even look at the front door but kept walking along the hall until I made my way further through the house toward the kitchen. The tiny red light blinked on the electronic lock outside the basement, the same way the broken sensor blinked on my door. It had to be a malfunction.

I kept going, driven by those reports he seemed so obsessed over...and the contract hidden under his journal. The contract he hadn't allowed me to see. I knew he couldn't hurt me, knew I was nothing more than a *'ward'* in his home. I belonged to The Order, still wearing black and not to be touched.

But if I knew anything about the vile bastard who held me prisoner in his home, he was tenacious. If there was a way around the contract, he'd find it. I swallowed hard as I turned along the hallway that took me to his study.

He'd find a way around it, that was a given...

So I had to protect myself.

I had to make sure I knew what I was in for...and plan for a way out. I stopped at the door, looked over my shoulder to the gloom, then turned back, to that same red flashing light on the door. My hands were shaking as I grabbed the handle and pushed. It moved. It fucking moved.

I hurried, stepped inside, and closed the door quietly behind me before I reached for the light switch. One tiny *click,* and the room illuminated. I almost smiled...almost thought I'd finally *won*...until I turned around, and in the middle of the room stood *his sons*.

"Well, well, well." The one with platinum blond hair muttered, his blue eyes fixed on me. "Told you she'd come."

I jerked my gaze to the other, who leaned against London's desk with his arms crossed. That topaz stare shifted as he looked away.

But it was his twin who stepped forward and did all the talking. "Looking for something?"

I stiffened, panic racing as I looked at the quiet one once more.

"Don't look at him." Blondie flanked my side, moving to lean close and whisper against my ear. "He won't help you." Panic punched through me as he moved fast, lashing out to grasp the front of my throat and pull me back against him. "No one will help you with us."

I bucked, clenching my fist. Instinct roared, screaming at me to fight. But I didn't...I stayed still, leaving his hand around my throat while terror howled inside.

"Look at you," Blondie whispered, his breath against my ear. "Looks like we have the perfect daughter. Obedient. *Submissive.*"

"Fuck you," I snarled quietly.

He yanked me hard against his strong chest. "Defiant, too. He's gonna like that."

He...

I sucked in hard breaths, fighting the terrifying need to scream and kick and claw. Instead, I scrambled for whatever I could use. *The contract...I could use the contract.* "You c-can't t-touch me," I declared, my gaze moving to the silent one still leaning against the desk.

"Can't?" his brother repeated at my back. "It's just you here." He reached around and palmed my breast, growling. "Pretty sure we *can* do whatever we want. There's no one to stop us...no one to stop us from having a taste of a *daughter.*"

Daughter?

It was the second time he'd called me that. "I'm *not* your fucking *daughter.*"

He just chuckled, and no matter how hard I tried to hold onto the training The Teacher had forced into us, something inside me *snapped.* I clenched my fist, cocked my arm, and drove my elbow backwards into his stomach.

He gave an *oof,* his hold releasing enough for me to punch his arm and stumble away, lifting my clenched fist in front of me. "You just s-stay the fuck way from me."

Blondie grinned, his focus fixed on me as he rubbed his stomach. "Looks like we got ourselves a wildcat here."

"Fuck you," I spat.

His gaze snapped toward mine and in an instant, that stare turned deadly. "How about I fuck *you*, instead?"

Cold plunged into my center.

He strode forward, no longer playing or teasing. No. He was an avalanche rushing toward me. I stumbled backwards, lifting my hand to shield myself. There was no amount of training that could protect me now, no amount of *yielding* that could stop a monster.

He grabbed me under the jaw, his fingers digging in each side until pain flared. There was nothing but darkness in that pitiless stare. "I can *fuck you* anytime I want. I'd take you kicking and screaming if it came down to it. In fact, I'd probably enjoy that a whole lot better. So the next time you decide to slink out of your room, *wildcat,* just remember...*we're always watching.*"

The study door opened quietly behind him and London St. James entered carefully, his gaze moving from the monster in front of me to his mute goddamn brother, then to me. If the asshole with his hands wrapped around my throat was aware of the intrusion, he didn't let it show. Instead, he moved forward, driving me backwards until I hit the black fireplace in the middle of the study.

My hand went back, bracing against the cold steel.

"Carven," London said carefully. "Everything okay here?"

"Fine," the monster answered, not once shifting his gaze from me. "We went mouse hunting and found a hellcat instead."

"You were meant to be hunting something else," his father said quietly.

Shallow breaths. A racing heart. The dim room bled to gray at the edges, but I refused to lose control. I wouldn't crumble...I wouldn't fall apart. I just stared into the eyes of a madman as he answered. "We were...we're close, we'll have the address by morning."

He seemed to gain control of himself and released his cruel hold that still throbbed long after he dropped his hand and stepped away. I touched my jaw, massaging the deep throb. Still the asshole stared at me, drinking down every wince and flicker of fear that crossed my face.

"Then I suggest you keep at it," London urged.

He might be their father, but it was clear in that moment that he had no control over his sons...how could he when they were nothing more than rabid animals?

"Until next time, hellcat," Carven murmured, and looked me up and down, stopping at my breasts. "Maybe then we'll get to play."

"Colt," London muttered, and the quiet one pushed up from the desk where he'd just stood by and watched this all play out. "Control your brother."

Carven gave a chuff and turned away, glancing at his father before they went to the door and left.

Shudders wracked my body as the door closed behind them.

My shoulders sank and my body almost collapsed as I sucked in hard breaths. "Thanks," I whispered, before I realized who I was thanking.

"Oh, don't thank me, Vivienne." London strode forward. That steely control was now sparking too cold, hard rage flared as he grabbed my arm and yanked me forward. "I want you to explain yourself instead. What the fuck are you doing in my goddamn study?"

My panicked gaze went to his desk...then to the black leather binder sitting neatly on the edge.

"Well?" His grip tightened as he stared down at me, rage sparking in his eyes. "Answer me."

I lifted my gaze to his. "Get. Your. Fucking. Hands. *Off me...*" I snarled.

His brows rose for a second as surprise flickered. I was betting London St. James wasn't used to many women biting back. He sure as *hell* wasn't used to me. But he released his hold.

My mind was frantic, clawing at anything I could to keep him leashed. "You signed the contract. You can't...can't..."

"Can't," he mocked as he stepped forward to push me back and off balance. I hit the edge of the sofa behind me. *"Fuck you, Vivienne. Is that what you're trying to say? I can't—"* He lowered his gaze and sucked in a heavy breath, then took a step forward, driving me against the rolled armrest of the black leather sofa. "Make you wear red."

A whimper slipped from me. But I swallowed the sound and answered. "Yes."

There was a twitch at the corner of his mouth. "Believe me... there are ways around any contract. Don't push your goddamn luck. *Now.* I suggest you return to your room...unless you wish to have another encounter with my sons."

That thought terrified me more than anything. I shook my head.

A jerk of his head, and he eased backwards.

I pushed up from the sofa, stumbled sideways, and hurried for the door.

"Goodnight, Vivienne," he murmured at my back. "Sleep well."

TWENTY-FOUR

Ryth

The stack of sterile dressings blurred on the counter in front of me. My hands trembled when I hit the faucets and squeezed antiseptic wash into my palm before scrubbing them. Tobias's dressings were changed, his wound flushed pink and healing...and for some strange reason, I was proud of that.

"*Little mouse!*" Tobias bellowed.

My head snapped upwards at the sound.

"*You better be drinking!*"

My lips curled as I shifted my focus to the almost full bottle of electrolytes on the counter beside me as I rinsed, turned off the water, and called out. "Doing it now!"

"Better be," he snarled from the bedroom. "Don't make me spit it in your mouth."

Oh...God.

My body pulsed after this morning, pushed to its limits by all three of them, and I was now feeling the aftereffects, especially from Tobias. The man was...*insatiable*.

I grabbed the bottle and tipped it to my lips. The slightly salty taste of berries slipped down the back of my throat. It hadn't been just the sex. Tobias needed me...

Touching me.

Murmuring to me.

His love blindingly real.

And consuming.

I swallowed again and again, until my belly was heavy, then swiped my mouth with the back of my hand. "All gone!"

"About time," he muttered from the doorway, those dark eyes fixed on the empty bottle in my hand.

I jumped with shock, staring at his bare chest and black boxers. "Jesus, T. You scared the shit out of me!"

He barely limped now, striding forward until he pushed me back against the counter. That flicker of fear always came when he looked at me like this. My stepbrother was an undeniable force. He reached up and brushed a strand of hair from my face. "The next time you hide your exhaustion from me will result in a spanking, got it? One that you won't enjoy."

Heat flushed, and my lips curled as a chuckle tore free. "Yes."

"Good." He wasn't joking when he said it. Then he captured my chin, tilted my face to his, and kissed me soft and slow before pulling away. "You taste like fucking berries...and I love it."

The sound of skidding tires invaded, making him scowl and jerk his stare to the doorway. "What the fuck?"

Rocks peppered the side of the cabin, sounding like a spray of gunshots. But the car's engine didn't switch off as the thunder of heavy boots descended. *"They're coming! They're COMING!"* Nick roared. *"WE LEAVE NOW!"*

Tobias moved toward the doorway.

"Ryth! RYTH!" Nick screamed my name. *"Where the FUCK is she?"*

"I'm right here," I cried as Tobias strode out of the treatment room and slammed into Nick tearing along the hallway.

"Whoa!" Tobias grabbed hold of Nick as they stood in the middle of the hall. "She's right there! *Look!*" Tobias pointed my way. "She's right there, brother. *She's safe.*"

But Nick jerked his gaze to mine. I saw fear, *consuming* him. His nostrils flared, those golden-brown eyes wide. "We gotta leave," he gasped. *"Now."*

Heavy steps came from the veranda outside. *"Nick!"* Caleb called. "What's going on?"

"They found us." Nick tore his gaze from me to Tobias. "They fucking found us...get whatever you can...and *get in the car.*"

We all stood there stunned for a second...*until we moved.*

Our panic was a tornado. I snatched what I could, calling out. "Rebel! *Rebel!*"

We were out in a blur of terror, piling into the car and slamming the doors closed.

Dust and rocks kicked up behind us, swallowing the sight of the cabin as we skidded around the corner of the driveway and hit the road. I turned around, tearing my gaze from the place that'd been a haven for us for the last few days, and looked at the road ahead.

"And he didn't say who it was after us?" Tobias snapped, sucking in hard breaths as he lifted his gun and checked the chamber.

"No," Nick snarled, his focus fixed on getting us away as fast as possible.

Tobias tugged his shirt down, that'd been thrown on in a hurry. His jeans were still unbuttoned, his boots barely hanging on.

The remainder of our clothes had been shoved in a bag and tossed into the back, along with the mess of pills I'd grabbed as we raced out of the cabin. I sucked in hard breaths, willing away the bright sparks of panic behind my eyes. Rebel whined and pushed against me as Nick expertly handled the car, turning hard and gunning the engine.

"Did he say if it was The Order?" Caleb asked.

"It has to be," Tobias snapped beside me. "Who else could it be?"

My hands still shook, clutching the bottle of antibiotics I'd grabbed as I ran. I tried to process everything. Nick had gone to call Benjamin Rossi...expecting the Mafia boss to be on his way to meet us...

But it looked like that had all changed. *Because now we were running.*

"Those fuckers," Tobias snarled softly, then turned his gaze to mine. "I'll kill them all before I let them anywhere near you."

I tried to stop the panic, but I was tipped off my axis...one step out of balance and I couldn't get myself together. All I saw was...*him.* Tobias.

"And he said this warehouse is protected?" Caleb asked in front of me.

Rebel climbed down to the floor to curl around my feet.

Nick watched the rear-view mirror as the white lines on the road blurred beside us. "He said it's as protected as we're gonna get."

"Somehow that doesn't sound very convincing," Caleb muttered, turning around to look at me. "You okay, princess?"

"No, she's not okay," T snapped, rage sparking in his eyes.

"I didn't get everything I wanted." The words were out before I knew it.

"What?" Tobias asked.

I turned to him. "The dressings for your thigh, I left them all on the counter."

He scowled, then shook his head. "We're told The fucking Order is after us and you're worried about my damn leg?"

I just nodded. "Yes."

Caleb turned to face the road ahead. "We'll get you more, baby," he assured me. "Whatever you need."

Whatever I need...

I looked at Nick, then Tobias, whose stare was deadly. I wanted us to be safe, was that too much to ask for? It seemed it was. It seemed like the universe conspired against us. It wanted us fighting. It wanted us running. It wanted us desperate to survive.

Nick pushed the sedan harder, his focus divided between the road ahead of us and the rear-view mirror. I glanced over my shoulder to the long stretch of road behind us, and tried to breathe...as we headed back to the one place we didn't want to be...*back home*.

"IS THIS IT?" Caleb glanced around.

"This is it," Nick answered.

The loud rush of air brakes made me jump. I looked behind us at the massive grill of the refrigeration truck behind us, all gleaming chrome and polished paintwork. I turned around, staring at another towering beast in front...and three more that passed us on the way to the city.

We were sandwiched between the metal giants as we crept toward some kind of dispatch yard outside the city and, by the looks of it, the only car in sight.

"This is his, isn't it?" Caleb asked. "Rossi's?"

Nick just nodded, then leaned forward and turned off, nosing the car up to the security gatehouse at the entrance of the massive yard. "Yep."

"Smart," Caleb sounded impressed. "Very fucking smart."

The whir of the driver's side window filled the space and the roar of truck engines invaded. Nick waited for the guard to approach, giving his name and Benjamin Rossi's.

"Wait here," the guard ordered, turning and heading back inside the small hut. He returned a minute later as the boom gate in front of us lifted. "Through the gates, all the way to warehouse five. Mr. Rossi is waiting for you."

A nod, and Nick drove through. Trucks were everywhere, in and out. Anyone else trying to get in here would stick out like a sore thumb. It seemed we were safe here...for a little while, at least.

We pulled into an empty parking space outside a massive warehouse. A ten-foot chainlink fence topped with razor wire surrounded the yard. Men dressed in neon yellow vests and hard hats walked to and from the buildings. For some reason, it made me feel a little more settled, like maybe we had a chance of survival here and Benjamin Rossi had some kind of plan.

"Princess," Nick called as he killed the engine. "You okay?"

I glanced his way as Tobias climbed out and tucked his gun into his waistband at the small of his back. "Yeah," I answered. "Just nervous."

"We're right here." Caleb opened my door and closed his own. "We're not letting you out of our sight."

Nick shoved open his door and stepped out. "Rebel, come," he called.

She jumped up instantly and scrambled between the seats to follow him out the driver's door. We headed for the warehouse entrance, scanning the workmen as they stared, until the powerful figure strode out of the gloom and headed our way. It felt like forever since I'd seen the man my father worked for, but Mr. Rossi didn't look like he'd aged a day. If anything, he looked even more dangerous.

"Nick, thank fucking God you made it." He nodded, reaching out to shake my stepbrother's hand. "Any problems?"

"No," Nick answered.

Benjamin turned to Tobias. "Tobias, how are you, son?"

"Pissed off, if you want the fucking truth," Tobias snarled.

But Benjamin Rossi didn't seem at all surprised at the outburst. In fact, he gave a slow, sad smile and nodded, then stepped forward, grabbed Tobias, and pulled him close. "I was so goddamn worried."

I hadn't known what to expect, but the fatherly hug made me smile. Then Mr. Rossi turned that careful stare to Caleb, then to me. "Ryth, honey."

"Mr. Rossi," I murmured.

"Ben," he corrected. "You're to call me Ben. Come on, let's not talk out here." He scanned the yard and turned, leaving us to follow him back inside.

He led us through a mechanical workshop to a massive office in the back. The moment the door closed behind us, the deafening sound of truck motors and clanging tools dulled.

"Sit." Ben motioned to the sofa at the end of the room, but none of us took him up on the offer. Instead, Tobias crossed his arms, scanned the desk and photographs pinned to the cork-board, and turned around.

Ben noticed, scanning us in the corner of his eye as he opened a refrigerator and pulled out cans of soda, tossing one each to the guys and an extra one to Tobias for me.

"Laz?" T asked.

Ben Rossi gave a hard sigh, aging in a second. "He's safe. They're all safe."

"Good," Nick said, setting his unopened can on the small table in front of the sofa. "Because we're running out of options here."

"I know," Ben nodded.

"Do you?" Nick stepped closer. "Do you really? Because we need answers. Who the fuck is behind this and how the hell do we get them to stop?"

If there had been anything kind in Ben's eyes, it died away... leaving something menacing behind.

"Was today The Order?" Nick's stare was fixed on the older man.

"I'm not sure." Ben shook his head, earning a snarl from Tobias. He winced at the sound, glancing at T before he continued. "I have men watching the compound, and more on the ground listening for anything that sounds even remotely like they're hunting. For all we know, it could be Killion. The bastard is ruthless and sneaky."

I flinched at that name, my blood running cold.

"What I do know is that this is no longer business." His voice turned colder. "It's now personal for those men. If they can't get Ryth back, then they'll set an example of her. Make sure no one else tries to take what they feel belongs to them."

"I'll fucking kill them before they come anywhere near her." Tobias' words were devoid of emotion. But I knew the rage that burned under the surface, and so did everyone else in the room.

"You said Ryth's father was working for you." Nick tried to find some sense in the mess of threads we had. "All the information we've found said he stole a shipment of drugs."

"Lies."

I flinched, my heart thundering as Ben met my gaze. "Yes, your father worked for me and had done for years. He was loyal, to a goddamn fault, and I consider him one of my closest friends. I need you to understand that...*all of you.*" He sounded almost desperate. "Because he did *not* steal from me. Not a fucking dollar, not a gram of cocaine. That weekend he left to go south, he wasn't working for me."

I stiffened as a phantom sting lashed my cheek, still burning from the imprint of a hand. "So, everything my mom told me..."

"More lies." Ben's gaze was fixed on me.

"And every time I saw your man drive past our house?" I whispered as pieces started to fall into place.

Ben's voice softened. "And at school. We were trying keeping an eye on you, making sure you were safe...until your mom..."

"Burned down our house," I responded, the truth finally hitting home.

He didn't answer, because he didn't need to.

"What was her father involved with?" Caleb enquired.

"I don't know. He was handling private matters." Ben looked away. "Ones he didn't confide to me."

"Are you saying he was working for someone else?" Caleb tried to read between the lines.

"Working for, or with."

"Who?" Nick asked.

Ben just shook his head. "I don't know."

"Mr. King," Caleb whispered, staring at nothing.

But the name alone made Benjamin Rossi flinch and scowl. "What did you say?"

There was a second, one where Caleb tried to think. "That night...when he saved my goddamn life, he called those bastards at The Order and he said a name...*Mr. King*. He said, *I'll have the FBI and the CIA on your doorstep by morning, well before Mr. King can get to you*."

Caleb narrowed in on Ben, we all did.

"Who the fuck is King?" Nick asked.

Ben shook his head slowly. "I don't—"

"Bullshit," Tobias snarled. "You fucking know."

"No." Ben shook his head again. "No one does. I know the name...and I have the good sense to stay away. If you're smart, so will you."

Tobias strode forward, glaring at Rossi. "Kind of hard for us to do that, don't you think?"

"Whoever he is, he's the one who they're afraid of," I spoke slowly. "He got my father in there to save me, so he can get him out, right?"

"It's a dangerous game your father's playing now," Ben answered carefully. "But I'd say yes, if King got him in there, then he could also get him out."

"Then he can get to Hale," Nick added.

"If my son doesn't kill him first."

"What?" Tobias narrowed in on him.

Rossi held his stare. "That's what I've been trying to tell you, the reason why I was away and couldn't help sooner was because Lazarus seems to have fallen head over heels in love...with Katerina VanHalen."

Nick paled. "Hale's fiancee?"

"Yes."

Nick winced. "Fuck."

Silence filled the space while we tried to piece it all together. "So Hale and this Mr. King are at war, somehow my father was pulled into this mess...and I'm—" I whispered. "The cause of it all."

"You're one piece of a puzzle" Ben answered. "A very important piece."

"Of what?" I needed to understand.

"Only your father knows." Ben murmured.

"And your mom," Tobias added, meeting my stare. "She fucking knows."

Ben nodded. "We're looking for her. Believe me, the moment we find her, you'll be the first to know."

"Right now, we need somewhere safe to stay, and protection." Nick raked his hand through his hair.

Ben turned and headed for his desk, grabbed a set of keys from a stack of paperwork, and tossed them through the air. "This will get you somewhere safe, and inside you'll find all the protection you'll need." The Mafia boss met my gaze. "I'm going to get your father out, Ryth, trust me on that, and I'll find your mom. We'll get to the bottom of this. We'll keep you safe."

"No." Tobias shook his head. "We'll do that. You get us a way out of this…and we'll take care of our stepsister."

"Deal," Ben nodded, grabbing another set of keys. "Something a little sturdier and faster, new phones, clothes, and money are in a bag inside. Keep your phones on you. I'll call as soon as I know anything…and guys." Ben was deadly serious. "Stay the fuck alive."

"Gonna do our best." Nick glanced our way. "Believe me on that."

TWENTY-FIVE

Nick

I lifted the remote and pressed the button. Lights flashed on a towering black beast parked three spots away from the sedan we'd driven in. I barely saw it, my mind still captured by the things Ben Rossi had divulged to us. The secrets. The lies...more importantly, the fucking betrayal.

How the hell could we get out of this?

We were all quiet as we made for the sedan, each one torn between the reasons why Jack Castlemaine would be connected to someone like King...and what the fuck that had to do with Ryth.

Only, none of that really mattered. My only priority right now was keeping us alive until we could get the fuck out of here. The moment I popped open the trunk and stared at the mess inside, I realized this affected one of us more than the rest. I turned my head as Ryth opened the back door and climbed inside. She grabbed the packets of dressings and the fucking antibiotics, then straightened.

Her damn knees wobbled, making her brace against the door, then turn a panicked gaze my way. I looked away, fighting the urge to pull her into my goddamn arms. She stared my way, then straightened, thinking I hadn't seen her fumble.

But I had...

And I didn't like it one bit.

"Wait...you're not saying anything," T muttered, and cut me a stare. One jerk of his head toward the massive four-wheel drive and he added, "Don't tell me you're not impressed."

Ryth followed the comment, glancing my way again as I bundled up the mess of clothes tossed into the trunk. "As long as it keeps us safe, I don't give a shit what I drive."

I strode toward the thing. "Rebel, come girl."

The pup scrambled after me as I yanked open the back door and tossed the clothes on the floor, eyeing the bulging duffel bag I assumed was full of money, guns, and new phones. I bent instead, grabbed our girl, and lifted her to the floor. "Need you to look after Ryth, okay?" I murmured in the mutt's ear and gave her a scratch on the head. "She needs you."

Then I turned around and froze, witnessing something I never thought I'd see in my life. Tobias reached out to take a woman's hand like it was the most natural thing in the world. Ryth let him, glancing toward Caleb, then me.

Desire flooded me, desire, and fear, and desperation. I had to find us a way out of this, no matter what it took. I stepped backwards, grabbed the dressings and bottles of pills from her hand, and helped her into the four-wheel drive. Tobias rounded the vehicle and climbed in the passenger seat, leaving Caleb to sit beside Ryth in the back.

"Address is here," Tobias called from the front, "as well as new phones and some cash."

Caleb opened the duffel bag between the two of them. "Clothes, enough to change into anyway."

"Good." I walked back to the sedan, then scanned the area around us before I grabbed the guns from under the false floor, and closed the trunk, then I tossed the keys onto the driver's seat and left the sedan behind.

Once we left the yard, we were on our own. Benjamin Rossi's reach only went so far. I climbed behind the wheel, stowed two guns under my seat, and handed the others to my brothers. "Got the address?"

My pulse hammered as I reversed the car and watched Ben and one of his men head toward us. He gave a nod as we left, motioning for his man to take the sedan. We needed no trace left behind, of us or where we were headed.

That thought haunted me as I drove out of the compound and back into the flow of refrigeration trucks. I looked in the rearview mirror when I turned off and headed for the city. Tobias scanned the cars in the side mirror, a gun in his grip, pressed against his thigh.

Rebel whined, sensing the tension in the car, as I took the quiet backstreets to the address Ben had given us. There were manicured lush gardens and massive houses set back off the street. There was green as far as you could see until I turned the corner and slowed the car, staring at the looming black and gray four-story mansion that sat at the end of the cul-de-sac.

"Jesus," Caleb muttered from the back seat.

Jesus was right. I pulled into the driveway and rolled down the window as the towering black metal gate opened and two men carrying semi-automatic weapons strode out. I searched their faces, not finding a familiar stare, and muttered. "You know these guys?"

"Yeah," Tobias answered as one neared my window.

"Briar," T called.

The guy leaned down and met my brother's stare without saying a word, then shifted that steely glare my way, then to the backseat. "Tobias," he said slowly. Ex-special forces, that was easy to see, even before I caught a glimpse of his eagle- globe-and-anchor tattoo. "Mr. Rossi told us to expect you. We're to provide protection while you're under his roof, for as long as you need it."

He met my stare when he said it.

Friendly, I didn't give a shit about.

But being trained…now that's something we could use.

"Parking's around the back. You have the code to access the house in the details Mr. Rossi left for you. There're panic buttons in each room that send an alert straight to us if anything happens. Rest assured, we're not letting anyone in that doesn't belong here."

A hard exhale and I felt some of the tension ease

"Ms. Castlemaine." The bodyguard turned to Ryth. Tobias stiffened beside me, and I caught Caleb jerk his gaze from the house to the Marine as he softened his tone. "I just want you to know I'm personally invested in this. Your father…your father was a good friend to me. He was the one who introduced me to Mr. Rossi and who helped me when I needed it. I'll keep you safe."

T narrowed his gaze on the Marine. "Thanks, Briar," he snarled. "We already got that covered."

The Marine gave him a nod and stepped away. I smothered a flare of jealousy, hit the button for the window, and pulled the four-wheel drive inside.

"He'll keep you safe," T muttered under his breath. "What the fuck does he think we've *been* doing?"

I'd would've smiled at the venom in his tone if I didn't feel the fucking poison in my own chest. I glanced at the rear-view mirror, catching Caleb as he scowled and stared out the window.

"He seemed nice," Ryth said quietly as I pulled the SUV around to the rear of the house and parked. "I don't even know my father's friends."

"And that's the way it's gonna stay," Tobias snapped as he climbed out, muttering, "if I have anything to do with it."

I caught her smirk as Ryth shoved open her door and called, "Rebel, come on."

T was jealous. Fuck, we were all jealous. The bodyguard better keep his focus on the grounds. I didn't want to have to put the bastard down. But I would—I rounded the four-wheel drive, catching Caleb looking behind us—we all would.

Tobias neared the electronic keypad, punched in the number in his hand, and opened the door. He limped a little as he headed inside. I grabbed all I could while Caleb gathered up the rest and we followed.

If the house had looked impressive from outside, the inside was stunning. Black and chrome, with polished concrete floors. All I heard was Rebel's nails tap, tap, tapping as she ran inside.

"Rebel!" Ryth called out, following her into the gloom.

But as beautiful as the place was, I just didn't care. My focus was fixed firmly on the future, on *our* future. I headed inside through the short hallway, dumped the stuff from the car onto the stone kitchen counter, and turned to scan the area.

"There's a weapons room filled with some impressive shit back there," Tobias muttered, gesturing over his shoulder as he made his way further into the house.

"Rebel!" Ryth called as she came from deeper in the house, only to throw her hands into the air when she neared. "I can't control her."

I forced a smile. "Then don't." Her belly released a loud growl, causing her to wince. "Hungry?"

"Fucking starving," Caleb answered as he cut across the expansive living room from the floor-to-ceiling tinted glass windows. "How about I make us some food?"

"I'll help," Ryth offered.

I left them and made my way deeper into the house, catching sight of a glass-walled elevator beside the wide set of stairs. I took them, climbed up to the second floor, and slowly made my way through the house. Five bedrooms, one with an open bathroom that looked like a Bali oasis, complete with rainfall shower and a pebbled floor with real-life oversized plants, and off that what looked like a...sex room.

I gave a chuff, closed the door to the Mafia boss's private sanctuary, and kept moving onward. The top floor looked like it was for guests to close themselves off in private luxury. But that wasn't us.

This wasn't a damn holiday. This was survival. Instead of the bedrooms upstairs, I went back down to the second floor as smells of butter melting in a frying pan, then onions and garlic, drifted up the stairwell. The lower floor bedrooms would be where we stayed. The last thing we needed was to be woken up and having to scramble down three flights of stairs to get the hell out of here.

The bedroom doors were already open as Tobias strode out, his limp a little more noticeable. "There's two bedrooms here, as well as Ben's study."

"Perfect," I answered. It seemed like I wasn't the only one thinking about an escape plan.

T glanced toward the stairs, then moved closer and kept his voice low. "Who is after us?"

"Now, you mean?"

He nodded.

"I'm not sure yet, I need to talk to Caleb."

Tobias scowled. "Why?"

I licked my lips. T was a fucking grenade right now and the last thing I needed was to pull the damn pin. "Let's just say I need more information."

My brother moved in front of me, his scowl turning darker. "Information about what?"

I hated to say the name, each time I even thought of it, chills ran down my spine. "Killion."

T flinched, the corners of his lips curling as a savage glint sparked in his eyes.

"You think he's behind this? You think he's the one The Order sent?"

"I think Ben's right. He paid good money for something that he doesn't possess."

"That something *is our fucking sister."*

"I know..." I met his deadly stare.

Ryth's laughter cracked out as scurrying sounds of the damn dog shot from one side of the house to the other. Fuck, she almost sounded happy. Almost sounded...*normal.*

"Then we talk to Caleb." Tobias turned toward the sounds. "Then we plan."

"Then we plan," I agreed.

Tobias jerked his head toward the kitchen as Ryth let out a low moan that was followed by, "that's so damn good".

He limped harder, as he made his way back down the stairs. The image of him holding Ryth's hand was stuck inside my head. My brother had looked happy, at least, as happy as he could be in this whole fucked-up situation. I'd never seen him so much as take a woman on a second date, let alone hold her damn hand. But here he was...

My brothers' voices mingled with Ryth's, echoing in the space. I left them to enjoy that small sliver of normality and instead, turned my focus to Ben's study. I grabbed the new encrypted phone from my pocket as I walked and punched out a message to the Mafia boss.

I'm in need of a PC, any way I can use yours?

Then I hit send and moved to slip the phone into my pocket as I opened the study door and stepped into the dim room.

Rossi: Figured as much. There's a new MacBook in the study, internet password and other details listed on top. Let me know if you require anything else.

The damn Stidda Mafia boss thought of everything. I made my way to the bookshelf and found the new laptop waiting in the open, along with all the passwords I'd need. Laughter reached me through the open door as I got to work setting up the laptop and started logging in to my accounts.

I was lost to the familiar glare as I opened secure portals and worked my way into all the crypto accounts I had, as well as my electronic wallet. While the happy sounds of my family thrummed in my chest, I got down to work liquidating and cashing out every asset I ever owned...

To buy us a way out of this.

It felt like just seconds when the soft thud of bare feet drew my focus to the doorway. Ryth stepped in with a smile, carrying a plate. "I helped with the tasting, but that's about it, I'm afraid. Caleb is a much better cook than I am."

I turned as she neared, took the plate, and even though I'd passed starving four hours ago, I pulled her into a hug. "Don't be upset, Caleb is a much better cook than all of us. Did you eat?"

"A little."

"Good." I smiled as she leaned down and kissed me.

I wanted more, a lot more. But she needed food and I needed to work, so as much as I hated it, I broke the connection with a soft slap on her ass. "Now, go eat, and let me work."

She gave a smile and left, but stopped at the door to murmur. "I love you."

Jesus...

My pulse thudded as I stared at the woman who'd stolen our hearts. "I love you too, princess."

She gave me the most perfect fucking smile before she turned and walked away. I held onto that smile and used it to fuel me as my fingers flew across the keyboard. It'd taken me years to accrue this much wealth, years of watching the crypto market, buying when it was right, then trading out when it wasn't. Years of watching, of hunting, of being ruthless, and I was about to undo all of that in a single night.

I opened up secure messages and typed out an email to my stockbroker, as well as a young real estate hunter who'd been after the apartment complex for the last twelve months. I was ready to sell...*tonight.*

By the time I sat back and took a deep breath, I realized I'd forgotten the food Ryth had brought me. Food that was now long cold. Still, I ate, then went back to work until my fingers ached and a heavy throb started in the base of my skull.

When I looked up from the screen, it was dark outside. Shadows no longer hovered in the corners, they now consumed the room, and silence came from the doorway. I swallowed a flare of annoyance, hating I'd lost the time with her, but this was important. I helped myself to a glass of Scotch from Ben's cupboard and returned to the screen, watching the market rise slightly before I pressed *sell.*

Sell...

Sell it all...

Every last thing.

Everything I fucking owned.

I logged back into the messages and found one from the real estate hunter who sounded like he'd almost tripped over himself to get his hands on the keyboard. *Name your price.* That's where we were at now, he'd chased me that long. We were well past niceties and desperation, so I punched in a figure, one that was outrageous and three times what it was worth...

But there was potential.

So much potential, which is what had made me purchase the property in the first place.

A property I'd thought I'd eventually own with my wife.

Thoughts of Natalie tried to push in, but none of them were good. None even compared to what I'd found with...my damn sister.

Beep.

I glanced down at the response. *Sold. I'll have the contracts drawn up in the morning. I'd say it was a pleasure, Nick, but I just paid out the ass for this. I doubt I'll sit properly for a goddamn month.*

There was a twitch at the corners of my lips as I logged out. "Yes, you did," I muttered. "And I appreciate the money, believe me."

Movement came from the doorway. She moved like the damn shadows, this woman, as she stepped in slowly, dressed in my old hoodie with her bare legs peeking out underneath. *Christ, she moved me.* I glanced at the clock and it was almost midnight, no doubt the others were long in bed.

"Can't sleep?"

She shook her head.

I pushed the chair back. I'd done all I could tonight. Sold it all... now it was just a matter of waiting for the money to come in. Money that would buy us a future...*with her.*

I opened my arms as she rounded the desk and stepped between my thighs. She took a look at the scrolling numbers on the screen. "Sorry if I interrupted you."

The thunder in my chest only grew louder. "Princess." I lowered my gaze to my damn clothes that covered her perfect body. "You can interrupt me any damn time, especially when you look like this." She gave a small smile as I wound my arms around her waist and lifted, sitting her on the edge of the desk, then pushed the laptop backwards. "Our brothers?"

"Passed out." She shook her head. "Caleb's asleep in one of the bedrooms and T is out like a light on the sofa. I put a blanket over him and a cushion under his head. But once they ate, they were basically gone."

"Figures." I smiled and shook my head, running my hand along her bare thigh and under the hemline of the hoodie. "I like you wearing my clothes."

"You do?"

That throbbing sensation in my chest swelled. "Yeah, baby. I do." I focused on the feel of her and that hunger inside me pushed to the surface. If she only knew how much I fucking loved her...

If she only knew...

Her touch came along the edge of my jaw, her nails grazing my stubble as she tilted my gaze to hers. In the wash of the flickering light from the laptop, I met her stare. The sight was compelling, slamming into my chest, and my body responded instantly. I'd never felt this way before, never so...*fucking raw*.

I slid my hand between her knees, parting her thighs. "My brothers have been a little rough," I murmured, searching her eyes for the truth as I asked. "Is your pussy sore?"

She started to shake her head, then stopped. "A little."

I gave a nod, and kissed her warmth. "Then let me lick it better."

Her fingers spread out against the back of my head. I kissed her skin and slid the hemline of my hoodie up as she parted her thighs. That same urgency that had filled me all those months ago resurfaced. We were back in the Mustang the day after our parents announced their engagement, sitting in the park...and that same demand still lingered between us. "Show me, princess." The same words escaped as I lifted my gaze to hers. "Show me."

She sucked in a hard deep breath, then widened her legs for me, still holding my stare.

My throat tightened, choked up with emotion. This...slip of a woman made me feel. Fuck, she made me feel so much.

More than I wanted.

Yet, here she was...

I was the one to break the stare, my voice husky. "I'm going to find a way out of this, princess. I'm going to find a way."

She answered instantly. "I know you will."

There was so much faith in her voice, pure conviction. It only made that brushing pang in my chest move deeper. She loved me...she loved all of us. I lowered my gaze to the elastic of her panties and slid my finger underneath.

Love...

It consumed me as I tugged her panties aside and kissed the top of her slit. I wanted to do more than fuck her. I wanted to taste and relish and drink her down. But as her hand cupped the back of my head, I realized this wasn't going to work. I wanted more. I grasped the waistband of her panties and dragged them down. "Lift, princess."

She braced her hands against the edge of the desk and her heel found a hold against Ben's drawer before her ass rose enough for me to slide them off. I dropped the lace to the desk, wanting my line of sight as I placed my hands on her knees and parted them.

Pink waited between her thighs in the flickering light. Her body trembled under my touch, making me seek her stare. Was she nervous... *scared?* Was her body thrumming like mine? "Is this okay?"

She nodded as I slid both my thumbs over the lips of her pussy, gently pressing them together, and dragged all the way to the top. I never pushed in, never looked away, just went back down, sliding over her slit, then moved up again once more. Over and over, without parting her lips, and each time when I neared her clit, I eased that pressure just a little, watching the sparks of nerves in her stare turning into something a little hungrier.

She wiggled her ass a bit.

I shifted my focus to the movement of callused thumbs. My hands weren't meant to touch anything so goddamn perfect, so...*pure*. "I've never wanted to fuck you more than I do right now."

Her body rocked as I stopped my touch on either side of her clit and massaged. A moan tore free, low and guttural, and her fingers trembled as she reached for something to hold on to.

"You can hold onto me," I murmured, then lowered my head and licked the top of her slit. She whimpered as I slid my thumbs over her flesh to dance around the sensitive area of her clit. Fuck, she was wet...*glistening* in the goddamn lights.

And as the numbers flashed across the screen, selling my millions in possessions, I bent my head to lick her again. "Mine," I whispered before I parted her pussy lips and drove my tongue into her core. *Mine.*

Her body bucked, and her hand drove my face harder against her. I reached up, grabbed the soft flesh of her ass, and yanked her forward until she balanced precariously on the edge of the desk. "Lie back, princess," I demanded.

The thud of her elbows hitting the desk followed. I splayed her out against the mafia boss's desk and licked the mess I'd created.

"Oh, God." She lifted her leg, bent her knee, and opened wide for me.

I gripped her ass and licked that sweet pussy from ass to clit, then pulled that tiny nub into my mouth and felt her body pulse. "That's the way, princess," I murmured, releasing one hand to gently slide two fingers inside.

She bucked and quivered. I couldn't look away as she came apart under my touch.

This was more than sex.

More than desire.

More than love....

Because there weren't the right words to capture this.

Her pussy clenched around my fingers as creamy slick flowed.

"Fuck, you're beautiful," I whispered, watching my sister come. "So fucking perfect."

She moaned, and her hand moved to cup mine, with my fingers still buried inside, and as I watched her, I was slammed with a wave of terror, one so brutal it snatched the air from my lungs. I slid my fingers free and clenched my fist, holding onto her desire as hard as I could.

She seemed to sense something was wrong. Her head lifted from the desk and those gray-blue eyes found me in the dimness. "What is it?"

I couldn't say the words, couldn't find a way out of the agony that gripped my chest. She pushed up, fear moving in her eyes, alive and real and *hungry*. "Nick?"

I looked away at the lights shimmering off her thigh. "One day, you'll want more," I started. "You'll want a husband and a family. You'll want more than we can give you." Fuck, the words felt like acid, searing the back of my throat. "When that time comes, we'll step away. You have my word on that."

We'll step away...

We'll step away.

We'll step—

"What the fuck did you say?" She shoved upright, her voice faint and fierce and trembling all at the same time.

I forced myself to meet those innocent eyes. "Ryth, we're your—"

"Family," she declared forcefully. "Lovers. Brothers. *Mine.*" The bottom of my hoodie fell as she cupped my chin. "There is *no* stepping away for me, don't you get that by now?"

The soft chuff was reflex, as was the small shake of my head. "You're young—"

"And you're stupid if you can't see I've fallen in love with you. Nick. I've fallen in love with all three of you. I don't care about marriage, or kids. But if I did want to have kids…and if you did, as well…then…then we'd explore that together."

Kids?

A family?

Dried, bloody smears on the floor pushed in. Not like the one we'd had with our own father. A real family, one not built on lies and betrayal…but on love.

On what we had…

Even if it was forbidden.

"Got that?" she whispered.

I gave a nod. "I got it."

"Good. I don't want to hear that ever again and I'm going to pretend I didn't hear it now. I'd get down and ride you right now if I was sure my legs would take my weight."

A smile tugged at the corners of my mouth. "It's only fair," I responded. "You steal my hoodie and I take your ability to walk...for a second, at least."

She smiled, then chuckled as she lifted her arms. "Then it looks like you'd better carry me to bed."

I rose from the chair, closed the laptop, and reached for her. "Whatever you want, princess...whatever you want."

TWENTY-SIX

Vivienne

D*AUGHTER*...

The word dragged me to the surface. Higher and higher I rose, until the panic set in and I remembered exactly where I was. I cracked open my eyes, blinked until the blur went away, and fixed my sight on the tiny blinking red light of the electronic lock.

Daughter...

I pushed upwards and scanned the room as that haunting word lingered.

Daughter.

Not his daughter. I tried to grasp the loose threads of my memory, still caught between the waking world and my dreams. No, they hadn't said *his* daughter, but they'd called me that and I didn't understand why. I shoved the plush bedding aside and rose, wrapping my arms around my body as I shivered. It was cold this morning. One glance at the soft morning sunlight and I realized it was early...

Too early for *him*.

Thoughts of last night pushed in, panicked at first. Why the fuck had I gone down there? What the hell did I hope to find? Nothing that could save me...that was for sure. Not from this hell, or The Order.

I walked into the bathroom and glanced up at the cameras, hating that panicked feeling of him watching me, and tugged the pale pink nightdress over my head. *Traitor.*

I winced, tossed the garment to the floor, and wrapped my arms across my breasts before I stepped into the shower. I wore his clothes now. I used his makeup. I did what he told me, even as that screaming *thing* inside me kicked and bucked and howled in response.

It didn't matter.

None of it mattered.

Steam rose instantly as I hit the faucets, filling the shower stall, leaving me to drop my hands and turn around. As I lifted my gaze, that blinking light on the camera dulled, smothered by the fog on the glass. I tilted my head backwards and stared at the shimmering blur until I finally closed my eyes.

I washed, shampooed, and conditioned, each strand smelling like he wanted. What he demanded. What he *controlled*.

I *had* to get out of here.

The need thrummed.

I had to find a way to get my control back, because if I didn't... I'd lose myself forever. The thought of that was terrifying. I turned around and hit the faucets, ending the spray. The steam lingered, warm and wet, as I sucked in a breath, opened the shower stall, and stepped out.

Only I wasn't alone...

He stood there.

Arms crossed.

Dark eyes fixed.

Malice burned in his stare.

Which made me shiver.

London never spoke as he grasped a thick white towel from the top of the pile and stepped toward me. Fear nailed me to the spot, even as my heart hammered and my knees turned weak.

"What you did last night was reckless," he started, and dragged the towel over my shoulders. "But I can understand why you did it. It was a momentary lapse of judgment on your behalf. A remnant from your time in The Order as you adjust to your new surroundings. As you adjust to your place."

Your place.

That venomous tone hit me.

"Lift your arms," he ordered.

My hands trembled as they rose in the air, leaving him to wipe the beads of water that coursed down the sides of my breasts. He moved my long hair to the side, scrunching the strands as they dripped. I hated how my mind took over, how he made me feel young and weak and afraid and vulnerable.

"So, I'm going to overlook your error." He dragged the towel down the line of my back and over the curve of my ass, lingering. My senses were on fire, tracking that crippling stare as he took in my body.

He can't touch me...

He can't fuck me...

He can't hurt me...

Thump.

The towel dropped to the floor at my feet. I stared at the wall as he moved, grabbed a bottle of expensive lotion on the counter, and opened the lid. "Otherwise, I might assume you required some adjustment, Vivienne." He squirted the creamy white lotion into his palm and moved back to me. "That this spirited need inside you requires a …heavier hand."

I closed my eyes as his touch moved along the underside of my arm.

"Lower."

My throat clenched, and revulsion burned as he smoothed the mess across my stomach. I knew instantly where this was going. His hand cupped my breast, spreading the lotion underneath with his fingers as his thumb grazed my nipple.

He never looked away.

Because he liked this.

The degradation.

The pain.

He lowered his gaze as he brushed my nipple once more. It tightened, puckered. Excitement glinted in that sickening stare. "I need to do your legs," he instructed, his voice devoid of the emotion that raged in his eyes. One he hid from me. *"Now."*

He hid it from me.

Now.

Just like he had last night.

Like he'd done before.

Every time he's near me, like he's fighting something, pushing me away and yet drawing me back, unable to stand the thought of me and yet...yet...*yet he craves me*. That thought punctured my mind like a thorn as he stepped to the side and jerked his head toward the bed. I *saw* it now, saw past the control and cruelty. I saw that man, the hotblooded man who invaded my room. I stepped into the bedroom to find my clothes laid out neatly on the bed.

The man who sets my clothes out every morning, and who rules what I wear to bed.

Who'd come to my rescue when I was lured out of my room by the two men he called *sons*.

Who'd abducted me from The Order...

And forced them to give me to him.

"Sit."

I turned around and did as he instructed, lowering myself to the bed. He didn't look my way, intent on the task at hand now that I was pliable and meek.

I was pliable...and meek.

He sat on the side of the bed and patted his thigh. "Your foot."

I froze and my heartbeat thrashed in my ears as I whispered. "No."

He jerked his gaze to mine, the shine savage and feral. "No?"

"N-no."

There was a second of chilling silence before a twitch came at the corner of his eye. Then he lunged in an instant, twisted to grab my throat, and drove me back against the pillows. "NO?" he roared, and fury filled his stare as he loomed over me. "There is no *NO* in your vocabulary when you speak to me, do you understand that?"

I couldn't move.

His hand clenched tighter as he shook me. *"DO YOU UNDERSTAND!"*

No...

No, I didn't understand any of this.

His gaze narrowed as he pinned me to the bed. Sawing breaths came in the wake of his anger, the heat burning as he fixed on my parted lips, then lowered to the hold around my throat. It eased, no longer crushing. "You think I'm playing fucking games here?" He shifted that violent stare to mine. "You have no idea of the things I've done to have you. No idea of—"

He stopped himself, scowled, and looked at my mouth before he clenched his jaw and eased backwards. "So when I tell you to lift your fucking foot, Vivienne, *lift your foot.*"

He eased backwards further as he released his hold. I didn't move, my gaze fixed on him as he straightened, composed himself, and said, "Let's try this again. Your foot."

He bent, grasped the bottle of lotion from the floor, and straightened.

But if he thought his outburst had scared me...

Then he was wrong.

He was wrong because he couldn't break me.

Because he didn't *know me.*

Because I had no brothers to come save me and no mother who'd ever cared.

Because I had me...and only me.

I lifted my foot as he straightened and placed my heel on his thigh. But I didn't rise from the bed, didn't cover myself, or hide myself at all. When he turned his head, I lifted my other leg and parted my thighs, letting him see what he wanted to see...

"You want me so bad," I whispered, reaching down to cup my breast. "Then have me."

He stared, clenching his jaw, his gaze riveted on the juncture of my thighs.

"You know I fucked myself when you left the last time," I whispered. "Because you watched."

I moved my hand down past my stomach, to my navel, brushing the top of my mound.

"You want your cock inside me. You want to feel me, taste me."

He licked his lips.

"You want to take me down to your basement," I pushed.

With every flare of his jaw.

Every second of silence.

I grew stronger.

Until with a snarl, he tossed the lotion on the bed beside me, rose, and walked out.

Boom!

I flinched at the slam of the door.

My heart echoed the sound.

Panicked and heavy in my chest, until, with a roll of my stomach, I pushed upwards and ran for the bathroom...to be sick.

TWENTY-SEVEN

Ryth

The sudden draw of a breath woke me. A feather-light touch brushed along my arm, pulling me higher and higher to the surface. Warmth pressed against my back, driving harder with every breath. I opened my eyes, to find Nick's big hand gliding down to swallow mine. I was caught by the sight of those hands, long fingers curling. Fingers that made me feel so fucking good. Just the sight of them made me tremble. Heat flared with the memory and, for a second, there was bliss, where the world was perfect and still, until through the cracks of my mind, a whisper slipped in.

One day you'll want more.

You'll want a husband and a family.

When that time comes.

We'll step away.

Step away.

Step away...

I shifted, hating how those words hurt, and in the cage of his arms, I rolled over. Golden brown eyes met mine. "Morning," he murmured.

"Morning," I forced a smile, hiding the sting.

"Sleep well?"

"A little. You?"

There was a flicker of something careful. "Yeah, I did."

"We're back home." I said, more to remind myself.

"For a bit."

"Did you get your work done last night?"

"Yeah, baby." He captured my chin. "I got it done."

I closed my eyes as he kissed me, then pulled me close, but this wasn't about sex. It was about connection. About love. About finally taking a breath amongst the chaos. I didn't just take a breath...*I took his.* Rising up, I kissed him once more, slid my arms around him as I sank back down and rested my head against his chest.

The heavy thud echoed in my ears, steady and slow. I realized I'd never felt a more perfect sound. Thoughts of last night pushed in, his hands, his mouth, then the study. I wanted to ask him what had been so important that he'd closed himself off from the rest of us, feeling like everything at this moment was somehow important. I didn't want to be left out.

Like the way you leave them out, you mean?

The words snatched away that feeling of perfect desire. Heat moved through my cheeks. Nick's hands moved across my shoulders. But I was frozen from the sensation, plunged deep into the cold.

When are you going to tell them the truth? The real truth...

I closed my eyes and squeezed them shut.

The memory of a hand around my throat.

Pushing me back against the wall.

Those fingers.

Those cruel fucking fingers.

I'm going to fuck you so hard you'll see stars.

My body clenched in revulsion as Nick's voice filtered in.

"Hey."

I swallowed, opened my eyes, and tilted my gaze to his.

There was a flare of concern, one that creased his brow. He opened his mouth to speak, and I was filled with terror. *Please don't ask me...please don't make me say...* until the thunder of footsteps invaded and Tobias's roar filled the air. "He's fucking *gone!*"

Nick jerked his gaze to the bedroom doorway as Tobias burst through, wearing running shorts and dripping sweat. But it was the rage in his stare that gripped me as he barked. "I swear to God, if he does anything...*if he so much as—*"

"Who?" Nick shoved the bedding aside.

"Fucking Caleb, who the fuck do you think?" Tobias dragged his fingers through his hair, narrowed in on me, then glanced at the bed.

I looked from Tobias to Nick and slowly shook my head. "He's gone?"

"The car."

"Ours is there, but one of the Rossi's is gone. He fucking took it."

Nick bent down, grabbed his crumpled jeans beside the bed, and yanked them on. "How long ago?"

"I don't know," T snarled, thinking. "I didn't hear him when I got up. I thought I'd use the gym..."

"It's okay." Nick left the room, not even bothering with a shirt.

I followed, sliding out of the bed to hurry after him.

"If he went back there," Tobias snarled. "If he went back to The Order, we're fucking leaving him."

I snapped my gaze to his as fear punched through me. "Don't say that." I clenched my jaw. "Don't you dare say that." *If you knew...if you only fucking knew...*

We tore through the house, turning at the kitchen to take us to the massive six-bay garage. Silver and black gleamed when Nick flicked on the lights. I instantly narrowed in on the empty space, and so did Nick.

"Shit," he muttered.

Shit...shit...shit...

"What if they took him?" I whispered, staring at that empty space. "What if they..."

Nick grabbed his phone, pressed a button, and held it to his ear. "Yeah, this is Nick. The car that left this morning, where was it going?" The guards...that's who he was calling. It had to be. "Yeah, Ben sent him...and he didn't say where? He didn't tell you anything?"

Nick's voice grew colder and darker the longer he spoke. T paced the garage between the black Maserati and the sleek silver Audi.

"Yeah. Thanks," Nick replied, and ended the call. "The guard said Ben sent him somewhere."

"Ben?" I whispered looking from Nick to T. "Why would he send Caleb? I didn't think he knew him that well?"

Tobias stopped pacing, staring at the floor. "Neither did I."

"So, we call Ben," Nick decided. "And we ask him what the hell is going on."

Something slithered along my spine at the words.

Something that didn't feel right.

A gnawing...an aching.

A remnant of thoughts from moments ago.

What did Ben want with Caleb?

Nick had grabbed his phone, his finger hovering over the button, when the garage door jerked, then slowly rose. I flinched at the movement, watching the silver Mercedes ease toward us.

"I'll fucking kill him," Tobias muttered under his breath as Caleb pulled in and switched off the engine.

Nick was the first to move, striding across the space as Caleb got out. He grabbed his brother by the shirt and shoved him back against the car. *"Where the fuck were you?"*

But Caleb didn't answer.

He was back to that cold, stony stare, the one I knew so well. One glance my way and my stomach dropped like a stone.

"Answer us, C," Tobias warned, his hands in fists at his sides. "Answer us right fucking now."

"I came back, didn't I?" Caleb answered.

At first, I didn't understand what he meant...until it hit me. He came back, and if he came back, then he went...

"You went there? To that *fucking place?*" Nick snarled, shoving Caleb back.

Only, he was pressed against the car, leaving Nick to be the one to create the distance. He took a step backwards. "Did you make a deal, is that it? Did you make a fucking deal?"

Pain cut through Caleb's stare. "No, and I never went to The Order."

"Then if you didn't go to the compound," Nick countered. "Where did you go?"

Caleb glanced my way once more, and that sinking feeling carried me down as he answered. "I went to find Killion."

Tobias stiffened. Nick went still. "Why?" He took a small step toward his brother. "Why go there...and why fucking go there on your own?"

"He didn't say."

Nick leaned closer. "What do you mean *he didn't say?*"

But Caleb stared at me.

"You wouldn't just go there on his say so," Nick pushed. "Not without a reason, a *good* fucking reason."

There was a small shake of Caleb's head as though he was saying *I'm sorry*...until a buzz came from his pocket. His eyes grew sadder as he reached in and pulled out his phone.

"On speaker, Caleb," Nick warned. "Or I'm going to assume the worst here, and I don't think you want that, *brother."*

There was no choice.

He had no choice.

I saw that as he pressed the button and answered the call. "Ben."

"Caleb." The deep growl came through the phone. "You have the information I'm after?"

"I do," C answered. "But there's a complication."

"Complication? What kind of complication?"

"This kind," Nick answered, staring at his brother.

There was silence on the other end.

"Want to tell me what was so urgent you had our brother out on his own and to hunt down a piece of shit like Killion, of all people?"

"Nick," Ben started. "He, ah..."

The way Caleb looked at me...the way he was desperately trying to hide the reason why. But I knew...maybe deep down I'd always known it'd come to this. To that day...that moment. That fucking room as Killion ripped that white nightgown from my body after he signed the contract The Principal gave him.

"It's the recording, isn't it?" I whispered.

Silence descended. Nick turned his head toward me, followed by Tobias.

And through the speaker Ben answered. "Yes."

I gave a slow nod, then turned away.

"Recording?" Tobias snapped. "What fucking recording?"

I took a step.

"What fucking recording, Ryth?"

There was pain in Tobias' voice, pain and fear.

"Ryth." Ben's voice through the speaker stopped me. "What do you want me to do here? Say the word, and I'll take the bastard out. This can all go away here, right now. At this moment. This damn thing all goes away."

I closed my eyes.

Why?

Why now did he release the recording...what did he hope to gain?

The answer was simple; his property.

That's what he saw me as. That's how he controlled. He degraded, he used. He...he...*he*...

"Ryth?" Ben repeated.

It was too late now, too late to hide the truth, because the only people I needed protecting from seeing it were standing right here in this garage.

"We want to see it," Caleb murmured. "Ryth, look at us...we want to see it. *We have* to see it."

I squeezed my eyes closed so damn tight my head trembled, until something inside me *snapped*. I spun around, staring at each of them. *I've never asked you for anything,* I pleaded inside my head. *Never so much as asked you for a goddamn thing and this is me...this is me—asking.*

"We will always wonder," Tobias whispered. "Always envision the worst. Is that the kind of future you'd want for us? Believe me...my own mind is a fucking beast."

The way he said it, so quiet, so controlled. It tore something inside me. He was right. I knew he was right. The monster Tobias could create would tear him apart. It'd tear *us* apart.

Could I allow that to happen? Could I allow what we had to just...tear itself apart?

"Send it," I whispered. "Send them the recording."

"Ryth..." Ben murmured.

"They need to know, so let them know."

I couldn't stand the silence, or the *beep* when the notification came.

I was trapped between staying and going, nailed to the spot by the moment as Nick and Tobias moved closer and Caleb played the recording on his phone. *"Stop! STOP! Get your fucking hands OFF me! GET YOUR FUCKING HANDS—NICK! NICK!! TOBIIIAAASSS! TOBIAS PLEASE...TOBIAS PLEASE! Tobias...Tobias please—You like that? Yeah, you fucking like that. Your cunt is so tight even after taking all three of them. Did they fuck you good? Ugh—did they finger your cunt like this? I'm going to fuck you...I'm going to fuck you until you see stars...Ryth! RYTH! The fuck...NO! He's not to be harmed, by order of The Principal."*

I closed my eyes as it all played out. My fingers trembled as they touched my neck, still feeling his hands. When the recording went silent, I thought I'd never hear sound again. Apart from my heartbeat. That I heard. *Thud...thud...thud...*

"I take it back," Tobias whispered. "I take it all back. There's nothing that compares to that—"

"Ryth," Nick called.

Tears came, slow and silent, stinging as they ran down my cheeks.

"Ryth, look at us."

I lifted my gaze, finding my three stepbrothers staring at me. Sadness. Pain. That's what waited.

Nick gave a small shake of his head. "I wish you'd told us."

A hard chuff tore free. "Why? So you could look at me the way you're looking at me now?"

"If I'd only been faster," Caleb moaned. "If I'd only fought back."

"But you didn't, and I didn't, and a million other things that could've changed what happened didn't happen at all. Nothing happened. Nothing but *him*."

With those words, sadness left.

With those words came something else.

Something that started inside *me*.

Cracking.

Shattering.

Reforming once more.

I was a different person when I'd stepped out of that room. I knew it, had felt it. Like death and rebirth all at once. I undressed as a person, then slipped from my innocence, only I wasn't reborn. I was...*nothing*. Empty. Hollow. *Lost*. When they told me Tobias was dead, I became even more lost, even emptier. Even more afraid.

I shifted my gaze to the man who held the phone.

The man who'd brought me back.

Who'd molded me with his own fingers into someone new.

"This doesn't change anything," Caleb started.

"Then what happened to me was for nothing." I held his gaze as I answered. "And feels worse than the rape."

He flinched.

Just like before, I felt that shift inside me, that *slipping*. Moving, creating. My hands clenched on their own. That thrumming inside me wasn't a desperate need to flee. It was a need to *run to*, to grab this newness that trembled with the first flicker of life and slam it into me.

To smother me.

To *become*.

"I'm going to kill him," I whimpered.

"No." Tobias stepped forward and closed the distance between us. When I looked into his eyes, I saw that *newness* staring back. "*We're* going to fucking kill him."

"That's why I went looking," Caleb explained. "That's why I tracked the bastard down. I wanted it to be *us*."

"Ours, princess," Nick growled, his hands curled into fists. "You are ours...and we take care of our own."

"Then we take this piece of shit out." Tobias never looked away from me. "Then we bring you home and show you just how much you mean to us."

I lifted my chin, and whispered. "*Yes*."

TWENTY-EIGHT

Tobias

TOBIAS! TOBIAS PLEASE!

Her screams rang inside my head. They were all I could hear. She'd screamed for me...*she'd screamed for me.* The sound of it shattered something inside me. Still, I gripped her chin and stared deep into her eyes. *Be the man...be the man she needs you to be. Be that fucking man or I swear to God...I'll eat that goddamn bullet myself.* "We take care of our own, little mouse. You understand me?"

There was a tremble in her eyes, a glistening of fresh tears even over the savage gleam. "Yes."

We take care of our own...

Hate moved inside me. I'd tasted that hate. In the darkest hours, when they'd taken her from me, I'd swallowed it down. The bitter tang bloomed now in the back of my throat. But as I stood there and stared into her eyes, I welcomed the taste. "Then we take him out."

"All of us," she agreed.

She was holding onto that hate, tasting it for the first time. Fuck, it felt like a freight train hit me. Seeing her like this, her hands clenched at her sides, and that look of pure, cold rage.

Pure...

She was pure to me.

First her virginity.

Now her hate.

But the thought of her—I lowered my gaze to her perfect fucking hands fisted against her thighs—the thought of her carrying blood on those hands was almost too much to bear. "I can do it on my own if you want me to."

Those words were quiet, too fucking quiet for the malice they intended. I'd never felt like this with anyone before, never felt so raw and open. I'd never felt so...*selfless*.

"No," she answered and shook her head. The muscles of her jaw flexed. "I need this."

"Then we do this our way, got that, little mouse? Because if you think I'm taking one more fucking risk with you, then you're in for a goddamn surprise."

Her eyes widened.

"It's our way or not at all."

She scowled and fuck me, if this conversation wasn't so dangerous, it'd be cute. "Fine," she gave in.

"Fine," I answered back, then turned to find my brothers. "Agreed?"

Nick glanced at Ryth, and so did Caleb. They didn't like it. No, my brothers didn't like it one little bit. They wanted her as far as possible from this bloody fucking mess as I did. But like me, they understood.

Our little sister was finally one of us.

"And this time, we're using the fucking Rossis," I added.

I'd use their damn snipers and their former Marines. I'd use whoever I could to make sure she got through this safe...because after hearing that recording, hearing what that vile, scum-sucking motherfucker had done to her—there was no way we were leaving that piece of shit alive.

"Agreed," Nick answered.

I shifted my focus to Caleb. Our loyalty was rocky...too damn rocky. Still, he gave a slow nod of his head. "Agreed."

"Then that's that." I turned and brushed my lips across her cheek. "I'll make a plan and come find you."

She just nodded and I'd never felt fucking prouder in my life. It was pride that stayed with me as I left my family behind and strode back to the gym in the east wing of the house. But I had no intention of climbing back on the cross-trainer. My damn leg had been pushed to the limit as it was. Instead, I used the quiet, pulled the phone from my pocket, and hit Ben's number.

He answered with a sigh. "I've been waiting for your call."

"That predictable, huh?"

"Not at all. I'd call it...invested, how's that?"

I clenched my grip around the phone and that old familiar weight of betrayal settled on my chest. "You should've come to me."

"Really, why's that?"

The bastard almost sounded indifferent. "Because...because..."

"Because you're invested, Tobias."

"We're *all* fucking *invested*," I snarled into the phone.

"Yes, but Caleb knew when he was in trouble. He knew that one wrong move and you'd do what you do best. You'd destroy him. Besides, Caleb knows these men better than you ever could."

Heat burned in my face. "You saying my brother can protect her better than I can?"

"Not at all."

He was so careful, so fucking controlled. I wanted to reach through the damn phone and strangle him. Pain flared through my chest. Cruel enough to make me catch my breath and curl my shoulders. I closed my eyes as the thunder in my head took hold. "Because I can protect her. I can keep her safe."

"I know you can, son, better than anyone else alive at this point."

I opened my eyes with the words.

"Because you love her," Ben added. "I knew that the second I saw you. I knew it with one look, one word…one threatening phone call."

I shook my head. "I haven't threatened you."

"No? Is that not what this is about?"

"No," I shook my head, but deep down, I knew he was right. "I called because I need your help."

"You know you have it, you've always had it. Tobias, you are a son to me, anything you need. Anything I can do, all you have to do is say the words."

"Your men. The ones guarding the house. We need two good ones."

"Done," he answered, then added. "But I want you to be careful on this, Tobias. Those men are dangerous. The connections... the reach. It's not like what you're used to. Hell, it's not even like what I'm used to."

There was fear in his words, real fear. The kind of fear I never thought I'd hear from someone like Benjamin Rossi. I knew he'd gone to help Lazarus and I also knew the asshole was tied up with the man who owned The Order. "Laz?"

"Is safe," he said, and a hard rush of air filled my ear. "As is Katerina VanHalen. But Hale is a man who's savage and dangerous, and right now he's licking his wounds. You don't want to cross a man like that. You don't want him as an enemy."

My mind was racing, searching. "You spoke about that guy, King. He seems to be the kind of man Hale doesn't want as an enemy."

"No, he doesn't."

That thrumming in my head only grew louder. "And you can't reach out to this King? To see if there's a way to get her dad out?"

"I've reached out, but so far, I haven't heard anything back. But everything I've heard about this guy tells me he's a ghost. It's just whispers."

"But he's invested, right? He's invested in her dad." There was silence on the other end, the kind of silence that made me pull the phone from my ear and check the connection. But the timer was still counting. "Ben?"

"Her dad isn't the real reason for this guy's investment. One of the few things Jack told me about him was that the man only helped him because of Ryth."

"Ryth?" My blood ran cold. "Why?"

"He never told me."

I forced the words through gritted teeth. "And you didn't push?"

"How the hell was I to know she'd be important to you? As far as I knew, it was a private matter from one of my closest friends, he asked me to stay out of it, so I respected his wishes."

How was he to know? How were any of us to have known?

"All I remember was that King wanted to meet her."

The words rocked me backwards. He wanted to meet her, had set up private deals and threatened those bastards to get her free. A man like that, tied to others like Haelstrom Hale, only meant one thing...*he wanted Ryth for himself.* "That's never going to happen." My words were hollow and strange. "Do you understand me? That's *never...going...to...happen.*"

"I understand," Ben answered, and for a second, I forgot who this was. I forgot this man loved me like a father, like a real father and not the kind that'd kill his own blood to save his skin. "Dad was..."

"Weak."

I swallowed hard. "Yeah, he was."

"I'll never betray you, Tobias, you don't have to worry about that from me."

Relief slammed into me. "I know."

"Good. I'll have my men ready, all you have to do is say the word and, son."

"Yeah?"

"When this is done, I want you back. I want you to put whatever beef you have with Lazarus behind you and I want you back, okay?"

Fuck. My throat tightened, the lump too big for me to speak. I could only nod. Maybe that was enough. Maybe that was all he expected as he continued. "Blood means nothing. Not when your heart is on the line. Protect yourself, son. Protect yourself and keep your family safe. Call me if you need anything else."

"I will," I croaked, then lowered the phone and ended the call.

TWENTY-NINE

Ryth

"You know what you have to do, right?" Tobias didn't look at me, his focus was fixed on the dark blue Explorer parked further down the street. Its headlights were off, but there had been movement a while ago behind the dark tinted windows. Someone was in there, two someones we assumed.

I swallowed my breath, trying to quell the shallow pants.

We were parked a street behind our target. We'd been sitting here, behind the overgrown brushes of the corner house, for the last hour. But it didn't matter how long we sat here, I still couldn't stop the shakes, not from my fingers or my knees. I gripped them, crushing my fingers as my legs smashed together.

"We'll find another way." Tobias turned and met my stare. "It's okay. We'll find another way."

I shook my head. "No. I want to do this."

He shook his head, and that spark of anger ignited inside me. "Tobias."

"Our way, little mouse," he reminded me. "You promised."

Fuck.

I turned my focus back to the dark Explorer, and seethed.

"If we don't do this, T, then we may as well start running now," Nick's voice was low and careful as he sat behind the wheel, staring at the same car we did. "She'll never be safe, never stop worrying. We'll never know when that fucking recording will surface again. You want that for her?"

He shifted his gaze to the rear-view mirror to see his brother.

Come on...come on...

My knees jerked and bounced no matter how hard I clenched.

"If anything happens," Tobias murmured. "Anything you're not prepared for—"

"Then I'll scream," I answered, drawing his focus to me. "I'll scream and you'll come running, and then the bad guys will be dead."

He knew it. I knew it. There was no way anyone inside or around this house was getting out of this alive. I only prayed we would, that we would get that recording and get out, and fuck everyone else. Because Nick was right, there was no running from this. How could you run from a threat? The answer was simple; you couldn't.

You eliminated the threat.

You countered the threat with violence and death.

Fighting for peace.

Tobias's dark eyes were haunted, fixed on mine, as he whispered, "I can't lose you."

"Then don't lose me."

He searched my stare, desperate to find a reason why we should just turn tail and run. I straightened my spine and clenched my jaw, determined he'd find no weakness in me.

"Fine," he muttered.

"Fine," I answered, then held my breath and looked away.

He wouldn't see it...because I *refused* to let him see it. I eased my grip on my knees, feeling the throb as blood rushed back into my fingers, and I reached for the door handle. But before I pulled, Tobias murmured, "I'll be right there, little mouse. Right fucking there."

I turned my head, meeting his stare once more. "I know you will." Then I yanked the handle and opened the door.

The interior light didn't come on, at best there was a tiny *clunk* before the door pushed open and I all but fell out. My legs were made of jelly, for some reason my knees were nowhere to be found. I jerked and stumbled, finally found my feet, and slowly, achingly slowly, headed for the house.

I forced myself to stare at the sidewalk as I rounded the bush and cut across the corner of the yard. The dark green grass and the tops of my boots were all I saw. I wore jeans, because there was no way in fucking hell I was letting that man get anywhere near me.

Never again...

Never...again.

I felt their stares on me, burning a hole in the back of my head as I strode past the four-wheel drive and then, at the last minute, I veered off, hurrying along the sidewalk.

"What the fuck?"

I caught the mutter as I crossed the sleek wooden entrance, mounted the stone steps, and stopped at the massive black door. My fists were already curled. I didn't even think, I just acted, slamming them against the door. "Killion, *open up. Open up, it's me. IT'S RYTH!*"

Footsteps sounded inside, growing louder.

"Get the fuck away from the door!" Came the bark behind me.

But I didn't move. My focus lifted to the camera above the door and the tiny red blinking light. "It's me," I said to the lens. "You know...the woman you paid for."

Click.

The door cracked open, then he was there, stepping out of the doorway, those sickening blue eyes fixed on me.

Stall him...stall him...stall him...

I didn't want to look at him, not at the pressed white shirt he wore, the sleeves rolled against his forearms. Nor at the tight smirk that grew bolder as he whispered, "Well, well, well. Look what dragged itself to my door."

"Mr. Killion, sir," the bodyguard snarled behind me.

"It's fine," the vile fucking demon answered, never once taking his gaze from me. "She's fine...just not what I was expecting. Why are you here, Ryth?" He searched the street behind me.

"I have n-nowhere else t-to g-go," I stuttered, wrapping my arms around my body as I shivered. "My brothers...they..."

"They left you, right?" he answered for me, narrowing in on his kill. "The attention became too much and they decided they were their father's blood after all."

I clenched my brow, looked down, and prayed to God I looked sad, because inside I trembled with rage. "Yes."

"Figures." The snide remark made me flinch. "They were always lowlife scum."

I clenched my fists so hard I felt the sting of my nails cutting into my palms and fought the urge to lunge forward and claw his fucking eyes out. But it'd come...it'd come...*it would.*

"You'd best come in then, the last thing I want is my three-million-dollar investment catching a goddamn cold."

Three million dollars? I jerked my gaze to his. That's how much he'd paid for me? That's how much my body, my mind, and my soul were worth to him? Three million dollars. I thought of Nick as Killion stepped to the side and motioned me forward.

But I pushed my brother from my mind. I had to be careful now. I had to be smart, and strong. I had to keep my wits about me, especially in a place like this. I scanned the foyer and stepped into the house as the door clicked shut behind me.

"I have to say, Ryth, I'm surprised to see you. In fact, you were probably the last person I was expecting on my doorstep."

"Yeah, well," I muttered, watching another bodyguard come from further inside. "I wasn't exactly planning on being here either."

I stared at the holster strapped to the guard's chest. My focus fixed on the silver weapon, calculating in my head how much time it'd take for him to draw it.

"Still, it's a *very* pleasant surprise." The voice came from right behind me.

Killion lashed out, grabbed my arm, and shoved me forward. I didn't have time to think. Memories collided. Me in that room, with his hand around my neck and his fingers inside me. *Tobias!* TOBIAS!

I battled the howling need to fight back, just throwing my hands up as I hit the foyer wall. His hand was at my back, tearing at my shirt as he tried to yank it up while he reached around and gripped my throat with the other. *No! No!* His hand clenched around my throat, his fingers bruising as he snarled. But he had to work at exposing me. Nick's long t-shirt was tucked in tight, pushed all the way down and cinched by the belt around my waist.

"What the fuck is this?" he growled, then snarled as he reached around instead, mauling my breast and pinching my nipple as a *thwack thwack...thwack* came from outside the front door.

Thud.

"Christ, don't tell me he's here," Killion exclaimed, and pulled away, turning to the front door.

Crack!

I flinched at the shot, but this time the sound hadn't come from outside the door...it was inside the house.

Movement drew my gaze to my right. Three dangerous men were a blur of menacing black, striding from the rear of the house, all three gazes fixed on me.

The bodyguard lunged from the doorway, looked at my brothers, then drew his weapon from his holster and spun. "Fuck! *Get in the panic room!*" he screamed at Killion. "Get in the *goddamn panic room NOW!*"

But it was too late, for him and for Killion, as Tobias took aim. *Crack!*

The bodyguard spun and staggered backwards, slammed again and again by bullets to his Kevlar vest. But he didn't go down, and he kept hold of his gun. Harsh breaths sounded as he lifted the weapon and took aim.

"Kill them!" Killion screamed, his eyes wide with panic. *"KILL THEM NOW!"*

Crack...crack! The guard fired back, making my brothers scatter. Two went one way, and Caleb went the other.

"Fuck!" Caleb roared.

He was on his own now. On his own in a house with only God knew how many bodyguards, cut off from his brothers while the hallway was peppered with bullets. Panic roared inside me. My own panting breaths were a rushing noise in my ears. But still, I dropped down and my trembling fingers yanked the bottom of my jeans leg up and pulled out the knife from inside my boot. We'd had to get a way in, and we'd known Killion would open the door if I was the one knocking.

They knew I'd find a way inside.

"Kill those fucking bastards!" Killion roared beside me, his spine pressed flat against the wall. He didn't even look at me, didn't even see me. He was too busy hiding behind his men, who opened fire at my brothers as they drew their focus. *You'll have one chance, princess.* Nick's words filled my mind. *One chance and we all get to leave that place. One chance, and we're done. Can you do that? Can you be like us?* Yes. Yes, I could.

I rose on trembling legs, took one look at Killion, and froze. He was so close, so close, stabbing his finger in the air and screaming. "Fucking kill that betraying bastard."

Crack.

Crack.

Crack.

The nearest bodyguard opened fire as thunder came from deeper in the house. *Thud...thud...thud...*footsteps echoed as two more came from the rear of the house. It was now or never...now or we were all going to die.

And I wasn't about to let that happen.

I gripped the cold steel in one hand, my knees trembling as I lunged. Only it was *my* turn to grab Killion by the throat, *my* turn to press my body against his back with the point of the knife at his neck. He stiffened instantly, understanding the mistake he'd made.

Crack! The bodyguard fired, only my brothers didn't fire back. They wouldn't because I was here...

"Tell them to stop shooting," I gasped, then drove the point harder against his neck. "Tell them to stop or I'll stab you."

He didn't dare move his head.

He didn't dare breathe.

"Ryth—" he whispered.

But I didn't care, gripping his neck with one hand while I pressed the point against his vein with the other. All I thought of was that recording. All I cared about was getting it back. *"I said, tell them to stop."*

Killion lifted his hand into the air. "Stop..." I eased the knife a bit. "Stop it." He croaked louder, drawing the attention of the guards.

The bodyguard stiffened, staring at the knife in my hand. He sucked in hard breaths and glanced from Killion to me. "What's going on?"

"We want the recording, that's all."

"Recording?" Killion turned his head, pressing against the blade.

"That's all we want," I urged, staring into his hate-filled eyes. "That's all we're here for."

Killion motioned to his bodyguards, urging them to lower their weapons. Silence. That's all my brothers needed, silence and...*a way in*. Tobias stepped around the edge of the doorway to draw the bodyguard's gaze. He lifted the gun in his hand, barely taking aim before he squeezed the trigger.

Crack.

The bodyguard stumbled backwards, then dropped to the floor, blood spilling from a hole in the center of his forehead. Killion stared at the sickening sight...then slowly turned his gaze as Tobias strode toward us, with Nick right behind.

Crack...

Crack.

Two more guards were hit. One went down, while the other stayed upright.

Crack!

Crack!

The wounded guard tried to shoot back.

"Don't bother," Tobias snarled. His head was down, his shoulders rock hard as he took one more step and lunged. He charged forward, slammed into the male before fists and fury raged. My hand trembled at the sheer brutality of my brother as he used his knuckles as weapons, driving into the bodyguard's face over and over and over again.

The male could only take the punishment.

Crunch. Crunch.

His head snapped backwards. Blood sprayed from his nose.

"Next time." *Crunch.* "Pick a better employer!" Tobias roared, and drove his fist so hard into the bodyguard that his head rolled back and he slumped to the floor.

"T," Nick called, sucking in deep breaths as he aimed his gun at the two remaining bodyguards.

Tobias didn't answer, and he didn't stop...until I called his name. "Tobias."

His fist froze in mid-air, the knuckles dripping with blood as he turned that brutal gaze to me and it softened.

My hand with the knife trembled. He looked from me to the man I gripped around his neck and in an instant, he let the dying guard go. The male slumped to the tiled floor and didn't move. Killion stiffened as Tobias stepped over the body and headed our way. "Ryth?"

"I'm okay," I whispered, tearing my gaze from the bloodied mess that was once a man. "I'm okay."

But Tobias didn't take my word for it. He gripped my chin, sliding his bloody thumb along my jawline as he turned my head to the side, then lowered his gaze to the throbbing area left from Killion's hold. There was a flare of rage, a promise of violence. "Did he do that?"

I swallowed hard, my hand trembling as I answered. "Yes."

Killion flinched, paling as Tobias fixed that merciless stare on him.

"Uh-uh." Nick shook his head as a bodyguard tensed, looking for an opportunity to make a move. "Don't be fucking stupid."

He seemed to think better of it, scowling before he glanced at Killion.

"The recording," Caleb demanded, stepping around Nick to face Killion. "Where is it?"

"Recording?" the bastard snarled. "What fucking recording?"

Caleb's jaw tensed and hate burned in his hazel eyes. He took a step closer as Tobias gave me a slow nod. "We'll take it from here, princess."

"We know you leaked it," C growled. "All we want is the master copy, and every one you've made."

Killion flinched as I stepped away and Tobias took my place. He glanced at Tobias, trying to shift away as he answered. "I don't know what the fuck you're taking about, Banks. But I can tell you right now, you're in fucking deep shit." He glanced at the unmoving mess on his perfectly tiled floor. "I'll have your ass for this."

"You don't know about the recording?" Caleb repeated, his voice careful and controlled, and I'd never heard him so deadly.

"No, I don't know about any fucking recording. Now, get the hell out of my goddamn house!"

Caleb gave a slow nod, then he carefully turned his head to Tobias, who lifted his gun, took aim at the bodyguard in front of Nick, and fired.

Boom!

I jumped at the sound. The bodyguard slammed against the doorframe, then fell to the floor.

"Now," Caleb murmured. "Let's try this again."

He was so cold.

So careful.

So utterly terrifying.

"I don't know about any recording." But there was a tremble in his voice, one that could only be the telling of a lie.

"Now that just makes me disappointed." Caleb stared at him. "Because I know, and you know, there is no way you wouldn't keep something like that in your sick treasure trove. Nick..."

"Yeah?"

"I think it's about time we showed Mr. Killion here how serious we are."

"My fucking pleasure."

Nick barely moved, just lifted his gun and took aim at the last bodyguard.

"No...*no...no!*" the guard roared, lifting his hand in the air.

Boom!

"You don't get to touch what's ours," Caleb declared, staring at Killion. "You don't get to look at her. You don't get to watch... you don't get to survive."

Tobias grabbed Killion by his shirt and dragged him backwards. The bastard stumbled, crying out before he fell and landed on his ass on the floor.

"Get up," Tobias growled, moving toward him.

"Wait...*wait...wait a minute,*" Killion stammered, his eyes wide, turning from one of my brothers to the other. "Okay. Okay, I'll... I'll give you what you want."

Tobias stilled, looking down.

Killion didn't even look my way. "You can have the little cunt."

Ice plunged through me, making my belly clench tight.

Tobias's brow furrowed. "What the fuck did you say?"

"The bitch is yours," he continued hurriedly. "You fucked her anyway. She was supposed to be a virgin. I paid for a fucking virgin. Three million dollars. Three fucking million and I didn't even get to make her bleed."

My brother turned ghostly white standing over him.

Revulsion burned, rocking me where I stood.

"Her cunt is dry anyway," Killion started...and that's where it stopped.

Tobias unleashed a sound that was primal. He cocked his fist in the air and lunged, driving it down into Killion's face. The sickening snap of bones made me jerk in surprise.

"The...*fuck*...DID...YOU...SAY?" Tobias roared. His eyes were black pits, his body a weapon honed by violence...and love as he drove his fist into Killion's face once, twice, three times before he snapped out of it.

I didn't even get to make her bleed...

I didn't even get to make her bleed.

My hand trembled, still clutching the knife. Nick raged forward, moving like a blur to grab Killion by his shirt and lift his body from the floor. "Where is the goddamn recording!" he screamed. "Give it to us NOW!"

But Killion just whimpered, which only seemed to enrage him more.

Nick unleashed, driving his fists into Killion's face, then he pressed his fingers into his neck on some pressure point that made Killion pale then buck in agony.

"You think you can bargain with her life?" Nick leaned close to him. "You think you can trade her away like she's some piece of fucking meat?"

I tightened my hold around the knife, my whole body trembling.

"She is our sister, our lover. She is ours to protect and ours to save."

"And we are hers," Caleb joined in, turning his gaze to mine. "For now...and always."

"There is no...fucking recording," Killion hissed, staring up into Nick's eyes.

My brother flinched, then eased his hold and dropped Killion to the floor. "Then we have no use for you."

The ringing in my ears was a deafening drum. I moved on instinct, striding forward. "Only for me."

Tobias's head snapped toward me, followed by Nick's. "Princess," Nick murmured.

But I couldn't answer, because I wasn't here. I was trapped in that room, held prisoner by that man's hands and his violence. I needed to find myself, to pull myself back any way I could. I stepped closer, drawing Killion's stare. He thought so little of me, nothing more than flesh to poke and prod any way he chose.

I'd survived then...I survived that room and I survived him. I lowered myself to the floor, kneeling, and pressed the edge of the knife against the buttons of his shirt. But Killion wouldn't survive me. I'd make sure of it.

Pop. A button tore free with a jerk of the knife. I flicked again and again, slicing them off. "Tobias," I whispered.

"Yes, little mouse?"

I didn't look away from Killion as I demanded, "Take his pants off."

There was a second of silence, until he understood. Then with a chuff, he moved. "Whatever you need."

"Wait!" Killion spluttered, and flecks of blood flew through the air as he batted Tobias's hands away.

"He needs to be restrained," Caleb directed, glancing at Nick.

Revulsion burned in my brother's eyes. But he couldn't do it. "If I touch him, I'm going to kill him."

One shove, and Nick rose.

Caleb was the one who grabbed Killion's arms as Tobias yanked open his belt and unbuttoned his pants, Caleb whose unflinching stare drove Killion's panic even more.

"Stop this!" he bucked and fought.

But it was useless. One hard jerk and Tobias tore his pants down. He wasn't gentle when he ripped his shoes free and cast them aside to hit the barely breathing, beaten bodyguard. I moved over Killion, straddled his thighs, and looked down at his white cotton underpants. "So fucking unoriginal, aren't you?"

The worthless apology for a male blubbered, his hands held back by Caleb.

"You are just a weak, pathetic excuse for a man."

"I'll pay you. Whatever you want, I'll pay you."

I pressed the knife against his tiny cock, it was barely big enough to make a mound against his underpants. "What did you tell me? *'I'll fuck you until you see stars?'*" I looked down and pressed the knife harder. "Not with this, you wouldn't."

He moaned when I dug the blade down even harder. "You disgust me." I pressed more firmly. "Fucking vile piece of shit." My hand trembled.

"We're right here, our lioness," Tobias murmured. "Right fucking here."

I didn't know if I'd ever told him what Dad used to call me. Maybe I'd told Nick once. I couldn't remember. But the familiar pet name triggered something inside me. Something that had already been pushed to the surface. Harsh breaths moved deeper as I fixed my sight on Killion. "You won't hold me prisoner anymore."

I drove that blade down again, pushing it all the way to the inside of his thigh, until the blood ran and my hand shook. Then I jerked the knife back.

"That's all you needed, princess." Tobias lifted the gun in his hand. "I'll take care of the rest."

Boom!

THIRTY

Ryth

The perfect tiles were a mess. Blood was neon red against the white. There were bits of something, shards scattered, and at first, I didn't understand. I couldn't look away, until it hit me...

That was bone.

Bone blown by the bullet that had entered one side of Killion's skull and exited through the other. Bone that shimmered white against the crimson mess. There were other bits, too. Other bits that when I glanced at them, I wanted to puke...

In fact, I *was* going to puke.

"Princess."

My belly tightened and acid burned in the back of my throat.

"Princess?"

Boom...boom...boom...

The deafening sounds were above me and inside my head.

"Ryth, we have to go now."

*Christ, don't tell me he's here...*Killion's words repeated in my mind. "He was expecting someone."

"What?"

I lifted my gaze to Nick. "He was expecting someone."

His eyes darted to the front door, and his grip adjusted around his weapon. "Are you sure?"

The hollow boom of my heartbeat thudded in my head. I pushed through the fog, battling the rock in my stomach and the rancid tang in the back of my throat, and tried to sharpen my memory of the seconds of chaos. "Yes. He said, *"Christ, don't tell me he's here."*"

Nick glanced toward the hallway as Tobias strode out wielding a baseball bat. Where did he get that?

"I went through the scumbag's bedroom," Tobias snarled. "Now I feel like I need to shower for a fucking week." He stopped, stared at Nick, then glanced at me. "What?"

"He was expecting someone," Nick answered. "So we need to wrap this up."

"If he was expecting someone, then the bastard never came." Tobias gave a chuff. But concern moved through his eyes as he glanced at the front door.

"I have his phone and his laptop." Caleb strode from deeper in the house carrying the items with one hand and a black bag in the other. "As well as a mountain of cash."

"He was expecting someone," Nick repeated.

C glanced at the front door. "Then I guess that's our sign to leave." He shifted his gaze to me. "Ready?"

I frowned, and glanced at the body lying at my feet for the last time. Empty eyes stared back at me. "Yes."

"Come on." Nick stepped closer and wrapped his arms around me. "Let's get you home."

Home…

I didn't know where that was anymore. Still, I let him lead me out the front door and along the walkway.

"Watch your step," Nick urged.

I'd almost kicked the body lying in the dark. Black on black shifted And I jerked my gaze up, flinching at the movement.

"It's okay…it's one of ours."

One of ours…one of ours…the bodyguards that protected us stepped out of the gloom. One of them met my stare and gave a slow nod. I remembered him from the house, the house we stayed at. "He knew my dad."

"That's right, princess. He knows your dad."

My feet moved, Nick's hold around my shoulders the only thing driving me forward. We made it to the four-wheel drive and the door opened for me to climb in. Then I realized. "My knife."

"It's right here, my lioness." Tobias neared, grasped my hand gently, and pressed the hilt into my palm. The metal was warm, and now, sickeningly familiar. "Keep it on you, just until you can work through the thoughts in your head."

Work through the thoughts in my head?

How was I ever going to do that?

I climbed in, then locked my seatbelt down as my brothers followed, and before I knew it, we were pulling away. Leaving it all behind, every last…sickening image.

I just killed a man…

The words resounded, along with the memory of the spray of blood. I looked down, and saw the smears still on my arms and felt the wetness on my jeans. The cloying, meaty scent surged into my throat. "I'm going to be sick."

"Fuck," Nick snapped, then jerked the wheel.

Hands gripped me as I was thrown sideways. Tobias dove across me, yanked the door handle, and shoved it open. Acid spilled in the back of my throat as I clawed the clasp of my seatbelt and threw myself out of the car. Heat burned, carving all the way up as liquid shot from my mouth. I stumbled and threw my hand out to brace against the car, but Tobias grabbed my arm, steadying me, and murmured. "That's it, let it all out."

The asphalt blurred in front of me as Tobias held me gently. His other hand went to the middle of my back, caressing, stroking. "You did so well, princess. So goddamn well. I'm so fucking proud of you. Look how strong you are."

"I don't feel strong," I spluttered as my belly clenched and I heaved.

"Oh, but you are. How many women do you think could do what you just did?" His words praised. "How many women go through their entire lives feeling powerless and afraid? You did it for them. You did it for you."

I shook my head as real tears began to fall.

"You are so fucking strong. I don't think I've ever met anyone as strong as you. You make me proud. Even if you hadn't done a goddamn thing tonight, you are breath-taking."

The vise-like grip on my belly eased, so I swiped my mouth with the back of my hand and turned my gaze to his. Even with my vomit glistening on the tops of my boots and strands of my hair stuck in the corners of my mouth, even with smears of blood on my arms and more sticking my jeans to my thighs, he still looked at me with the kind of hunger that made my cheeks burn.

The car's engine throbbed. Nick and Caleb were waiting.

"So, we move on," Tobias murmured. "We move on and we grow stronger, okay?"

I nodded.

Tobias dropped his hand from my arm and held it out instead. "The first step is getting back in the car."

I swallowed, hating the taste. Still, I took his hand and climbed in. Rocks kicked up as Nick pulled away the moment the doors were closed. I gripped Tobias's hand, holding on tight as we sped through the backstreets and made our way back to the Rossi house.

My legs weren't shaking anymore when we pulled up and I climbed out without help. In fact, I felt steadier, surer. Still a little like a toddler finding my feet, but that strength stayed with me, as did Tobias's words. The guards stayed at the gate and I saw more of them now, probably ready in case there'd be a problem and retaliation from Killion's men.

But there was no one coming for us, not at this moment, at least.

Killion's men were all dead, even the one Tobias had beaten with his fists.

He was dead…they were *all* dead.

"Yeah, it's me," Tobias muttered on the phone as the garage doors closed behind us. "We're back safe. No, we didn't get what we wanted. He didn't have it, said he didn't know anything about a recording. No…I don't know." Tobias glanced my way as I followed Caleb and Nick inside the house. "I guess we'll keep looking. *Someone* has that recording and we want it back. Yeah, I will. Okay."

I hung on every word as we headed into the kitchen. Nick grabbed four glasses. Caleb opened the cupboard doors and pulled out a bottle of Scotch. Amber splashed in the bottom of a glass before Nick handed it to me. I shook my head. "I don't—"

"Tonight, you do." Those golden-brown eyes bored into mine.

I took the glass and swallowed, coughing and spluttering as my brothers watched.

"Again," Nick urged, curling his finger under the bottom of the glass and tilting it to my lips.

I could only swallow. This time, the searing swill stayed down. The heat seeped out until the most delicious wave of warmth spread through me.

"There you have it," Nick murmured approvingly.

I swallowed again while all three watched, until they were satisfied. Only then did they take a glass themselves and downed the contents in one gulp. I winced. "How the hell can you do that?"

"Practice, little sister." Caleb gave me a wink, and even if it was sad, it still felt good. I finished that glass and half of another until that delicious warmth grew fangs and took a bite.

"Oh." The room blurred, then sharpened.

"Okay, lightweight." Nick took my glass. "That's enough for you."

I scowled. "But I haven't *finshed*," I slurred.

"Oh, believe me," he muttered. "You've finshed alright."

Caleb downed his second glass, or was it his third, tugged open the black bag he'd brought from Killion's house, and upended the contents all over the counter. Stacks of one-hundred-dollar bills hit the counter with a thud.

"Damn." Tobias leaned forward, eyeing the bundles. "How much is that?"

"Twenty, thirty grand," Nick muttered.

"It was sitting there in his study, like he planned on paying someone."

"The someone he was expecting," Nick answered, drawing my gaze.

My thoughts were slower, grasping the threads.

"Someone who didn't turn up," Tobias added, and drank from his glass.

"Anyway." Caleb reached over and stacked the bundles. "It's ours now. We need it more than he does, whoever it is."

I swayed a bit on my feet, making Nick grasp my arm. "Whoa there. Shower and bed for you, okay?"

"I'll help."

"I'll help her."

Tobias and Caleb answered as one, then glared at one another.

"I'm fine," I muttered, patting Nick's arm. "I'm a big girl. If I can kill a man, I sure as hell can shower by myself."

"Stab," Tobias corrected. "Technically, you just stabbed him."

"Sure," I nodded, then staggered as I left. "Technically."

But I wasn't stupid. I knew what he'd done and why he'd done it. The pang in my chest was brutal as I headed to the stairs and climbed. I didn't even know where I was going, just that I was... going somewhere. I made it to the first floor and somehow found a bathroom.

The overhead lights were blinding, making me wince as a dull throb came at the back of my head. "Technically stabbed him," I muttered as I unbuckled my belt and exhaled with relief. I kicked off my boots and peeled my jeans off, wincing at the smears of blood they left behind on my thighs.

I needed to get it off...*just get it off...*

I lurched to the shower and hit the faucets, not bothering to wait for the hot water before I stepped in, still in my underwear. Cold water slammed me, instantly making my teeth clench.

"Here," Nick murmured.

I jumped, jerking my gaze to his, but the alcohol and the cold did nothing to change the fact of what I'd done. "I killed him, no matter what Tobias said or did, I still killed him."

"He's just trying to protect you." Nick adjusted the faucets, then tested the water with his hand before meeting my gaze. "The last thing he wants is for that to be on your conscience."

"But I knew what I was doing." I searched his stare. "Lucas showed me...he showed me where the veins were. He told me that a bullet or a puncture there would result in death. I knew... and I still did it."

"Then you killed him," Nick answered. "You killed him and you take ownership of that act. We've all done things that've changed us. Now you need to decide what happens with that. Do you let it destroy you or do you rise above it, knowing that a man like Killion will never harm another woman again?"

His words hit me.

He slowly reached for the back of my bra and unhooked it. His touch was so gentle, catching the straps as they fell, then he turned his focus to my panties, sliding his fingers under the elastic and tugging them down. Seeing him kneel in front of me reminded me of the night our parents married. That seemed like a lifetime ago, another me...another them.

I reached down, caressed his strong jaw, and whispered, "Stay with me."

He did, through the undressing and showering. We took our time, giving comfort more than anything. He held me when I cried, standing outside the spray so the warmth hit my back and ran down my shoulders, and when we were done, he switched the water off.

No words were needed. He ran towels over my body and squeezed out my hair, toweling the strands before he searched the drawers for a comb. When he was done, I was clean and dry. He led me out with a towel wrapped around his waist. Tobias strode out of another room, also wearing a towel. Those dark eyes met mine. Somehow, they just knew.

We made our way to the bedroom, climbed under the sheets, and just lay there. Caleb came in, tossed the phones onto the table, and undressed before he climbed in. I reached out, caressing Nick on one side and Tobias on the other, as Caleb sprawled out across the foot of the bed and caressed my leg.

The bedroom was silent as I closed my eyes. I didn't sleep, I *drifted*, but I didn't replay the things that had happened tonight. Instead, I thought of Mom, and Creed, and all the women still trapped in that hell that was The Order.

Someone had to do something about it.

Someone had to get them all out.

But not me and not us. Not tonight, at least.

Tonight, warm bodies lay beside me. A faint brush against my arm and a stroke of my leg drew me back to them. There were no sounds, no questions, not even a conscious thought when I turned to Nick. He was waiting for me, reaching down to cup his cock with one hand, as he slid the other around my waist.

I leaned up, slid my leg over to straddle him, and climbed on top. His thick head pushed into me as I eased down. God, this was what I needed, what I wanted. I rode him, letting Nick steady me with his hands on my hips. Tobias rose up, slid his fingers through my hair, and kissed me. I leaned down and reached for his cock, needing them...needing all of them.

"Fuck," Tobias growled as I gripped his length.

Then Nick shifted, slid me from on top, and knelt behind me. One thrust, and he was inside. I looked up as Tobias slid the slick head inside my mouth.

"Jesus, princess," he moaned, looking down and watching as I sucked and fisted his length.

He'd killed a man for me tonight. I wasn't under any illusion that it was the first man either. There had been many, I was sure of that, and I didn't doubt there would be many more. Because that's how Tobias loved.

I slid my fist down, working T's length as Nick's thrusts grew harder and more savage. He leaned over me, driving my body down as he claimed my pussy.

Hard breaths filled the space.

I sucked harder, desperate to have, desperate to taste.

Tobias's hand cupped the back of my head as he gave a grunt and held my head down. "Christ...*Ryth*..." Warmth filled my mouth with the taste of saltiness.

Nick gave a grunt, then a groan, as he slammed me hard against the bed and stilled. "Fuck...*I'm sorry*," he groaned.

They'd both come so fast, leaving me aching when Nick slipped out.

"It's okay," I murmured.

Nick moved to the side, sucking in deep breaths, and muttered. "C?"

I looked over my shoulder to the silhouette behind me.

"Princess," Caleb murmured as he ran his hand along the outside of my thigh, then slipped it between my legs and found Nick's mess. "Look at how you made my brothers come." I closed my eyes and unleashed a groan. "Such a wet pussy." He slipped his fingers in the slick, spreading it all along my crease.

"You going to be good for me?" He murmured as he pushed Nick's seed into my ass. My body clenched around the invasion. The warmth of the alcohol hummed in my veins. I rocked backwards, driving against his touch, and whispered. "Yes."

"How good?" He pushed in deeper and a flutter came within my core.

"So good," I moaned. "So fucking good."

"Good girl," he growled as he slipped his finger from my ass. "Such a perfect cunt, such a tight little hole. Fuck, I love this hole." He drove his cock against the tight ring of muscle, spreading me before he eased away, running a trail with his fingers from my core up to my ass before he tried again. "Breathe, princess."

I tried to focus, but my mind was soft with Scotch.

"Breathe..." he grunted, then drove inside me.

I bucked with the intrusion, fisted the sheets, and squeezed my eyes shut. His thick head stretched me, making my ass grip tight around him.

"Jesus Christ," Tobias groaned.

Caleb gripped my hips and slid out as his hand caressed my ass. Something cool and slick dribbled down, finding that burn. "How good?" he asked again, dragging his cock through the slick to push back in.

The burn and the wet…and his words collided.

"So fucking good, Caleb," I whimpered. *"Please, I'm going to be so fucking good."*

He gripped my waist, pulling me hard up against him until I rested against his chest. His arms wrapped across my chest as he jutted his hips, driving deeper in my ass. Stars ignited, casting white sparks behind my eyes as he drove all the way inside.

"Yes," he groaned, bucking upwards. "Yes, you are."

My core clenched, twitching, quivering, and pulsating. "Oh God."

My eyes flew open as Nick wiggled around, his feet against the pillows now as he lay on his back. "Open your legs."

"Oh, fuck, that's it," Caleb growled.

Restrained, I did as they wanted, widening my thighs apart as Nick settled between my legs and licked my core. I clenched, invaded and wet, rolling my hips as Caleb drove me against Nick's mouth. His tongue invaded my pussy and his thumb grazed my clit. The sensation tipped me over, making me ride Nick's mouth. I squeezed my eyes closed once more as Caleb unleashed a savage sound, bucking harder and harder and harder…

Until a cry tore free. I spasmed again and again, arching my back, giving over to them. My body, my heart, my soul, as Caleb gave a grunt and filled me. It was just them at that moment. My body trembled, warm and pulsing. Caleb's hold slowly eased.

His hard breaths were a rush in my ears. Nick slipped out from between my thighs, swiped his fingers across his mouth, and looked up at me. "Christ, you taste good."

"And you fuck well, too," Caleb growled, as he gripped my hips and slipped his cock free. "You fuck really well. Such a good fucking ride...."

THIRTY-ONE

Ryth

An irritating buzzing sound intruded. A moan followed, deep and snarling, before the bed shifted and shook. I let myself drift, falling back toward the blissful darkness until Nick mumbled. "Yeah?"

I fell…

Plunging back into a dream, one where I was sucked into a void I couldn't get out of, no matter how hard I fought—until a name snapped me back.

"Elle…she called you?"

I jerked my eyes open, forcing myself back into my body. The bed shifted again, and this time Tobias muttered. "What is it?"

Our room came into focus, sharpening at the edges, drawing me away from sleep. I rolled, then pushed myself upwards, and found Nick sitting on the edge of the bed.

"Of course she wants protection. It's not like she's ever fucking shown she cares about Ryth."

I flinched at the words. My pulse raced, tearing me further and further away from sleep.

"We want to talk to her." Nick pushed up from the bed.

Caleb rolled over, shoved upwards, and slipped out the other side as Tobias followed Nick, leaving me all alone with the sheets sliding from my body.

"What is it?" Tobias growled, his voice husky.

"Where? The Pier. How long until they get there?"

The Pier? Why was mom going there?

"You want us to head there?" Nick turned away, shielding his face from me, not that I could see anything in the dark. Still, it hurt, the tiny pang of rejection raw and real.

I knew it was because of Mom, and fought the need to touch my cheek.

"Okay, well, we'll just wait for them. You'll call the moment you hear…yeah…yeah, she's okay. I get it. Sure."

He lowered his hand and I was riveted by the movement. No one spoke…not for ages, until Tobias broke the tension. "What is it?"

Nick turned, his focus aimed at me. "Ryth's mom reached out to Ben, apparently she's in fear for her life and needs protection."

"Of course she did," T snarled.

I swallowed hard, hating how I was caught on every word. "Did she…did she ask to see me?"

Silence.

Silence that spoke louder than words ever could.

I turned away.

"Princess." Nick started.

"It's okay." I pushed the sheets away. "I don't know why I expected anything different."

"Maybe she's just scared right now," Caleb offered. "Once she's safe, she might want to reach out."

The memory of her palm burned on my cheek. I knew the truth. "I don't think so."

"Even if she doesn't want to see us, we sure as hell want to see her," Tobias snapped. "And I don't give a *fuck* if she doesn't. We want answers." He was riled, pacing the floor at the foot of the bed. "We want to know what the fuck she's hiding and why she'd send her own daughter to that fucking place and leave her there...but mostly...we want an explanation of what's in that goddamn diary."

"Diary?" I whispered, looking from Tobias to Nick as he flinched.

"T," Nick snarled softly. "You fucking idiot."

"What diary?" I asked again.

"Shit." Tobias turned away.

But I was already striding toward them, naked and growing cold. "What fucking diary, Tobias?"

"Princess." Caleb reached out for me.

But I stepped out of his reach as Nick flicked the bedroom light on and turned to me. All I saw was guilt.

"What she writes doesn't make a whole lot of sense," he started. "There's some things in there that are pretty fucked up...things I don't think you should read."

I didn't care what he thought. I needed to know. "Do you have the diary?"

"Little mouse," T protested.

I snapped my glare his way. "You fucking lied to me. At best, you hid the truth. You were the one demanding honesty, and now I find out you've read...this diary. So, I'm going to ask you again, and so help me God, if you tell me a goddamn lie, I'll kick you right in the balls."

He didn't flinch at the threat.

But his stare grew darker. "I don't want—"

"I don't give a fuck, T. Answer the question. Do...you...have... the...diary?"

But it was Nick who answered, Nick whose shoulders sagged as he nodded. "Yes."

"I want to read it."

I waited for him to fight me. He didn't. Instead, he reached down, grasped his boxers, and tugged them on. "Then you're going to want to get dressed," he muttered. "Because I guarantee, once you start there'll be no more sleep."

A tremble raced through me as he reached for his jeans.

Then I followed.

THIRTY-TWO

London

My ring clinked against the tumbler as I lifted the rim to my lips and swallowed the top-shelf Jack. Lights flickered on the monitors in front of me. The screen on the far right was divided with the black-and-white livestream footage around the outside of the house. The one beside it was mostly shadows. But every now and then, movement danced at the edges, just out of view. But those I watched were mostly asleep. Just like everyone should be asleep...

Everyone, except for her.

I shifted my gaze to the other screen in front of me, the one I watched in full color. It was the only one whose occupant was still awake...and right now pacing like a lioness in her room. She thought she was clever, thought she was brave. But she wasn't. She was my pliable target. My defiant, headstrong weapon. I'd use her...use her to get what I wanted. I'd use her to obtain my control.

I'd break that will in her.

Crush it under my own hunger.

And feed it like a drug back to her.

I'd give her just enough.

Just a taste of freedom.

A lick of love. Enough for her to obey me.

I crossed my legs, watching her glance over her shoulder to the fake camera installed in the corner of her bedroom, then turn back to the door before testing the lock. The toughened steel held. The camera narrowed in on her face. Dusty lips, brown eyes. Hellcat, that's what my sons called her...*hellcat*.

She was a little hellcat, wasn't she? I dragged my teeth across my lip. A hellcat that required taking. She looked so much like her father, the same brown eyes and searing gaze. I caught the movement of her lips as she snarled *sonofabitch*.

A tight quirk came at the corner of my mouth. If only she knew...

I reached out with my other hand and caressed a key on the keyboard in front of me, then glanced at the other monitor at my left, the one that watched every angle of the inside of the house, and weighed the consequences of what I was about to do.

Just like I did every time.

I glanced at the phone beside me, the one with a secure, untraceable SIM...the one with the recording of a very private affair. Instead of pressing the button on the keyboard, I grabbed the phone and unlocked the screen. The woman silently cursing me on the screen in front of me had no idea the lengths I'd gone to to get her here.

But I knew.

I pressed the button, reliving those moments, and the hidden room I sat in was filled with screams, *TOBIAS! TOBIAS*

PLEASE! TOBIAS! I pressed the button once more, ending the sounds. Still my heart kicked. Sounds like that, handed to the right kind of people, would be a trigger...the kind of trigger I needed...

I lifted my gaze to the monitor. The kind of trigger I desired. Just like her...

FUCK YOU! Vivienne howled, those consuming dark eyes sparkling with hate. She looked over her shoulder once more, and stared at the camera...then walked up to it, her focus fixed on the blinking red light that acted as a decoy and—gave it the finger.

My pulse thundered. My cock twitched.

At that moment, she looked every bit of her nineteen years.

Young.

Resistant.

I couldn't help myself and reached down to grip my hard cock through my pants. She spun around, her hands clenched into fists. The light from her bedroom hit her face just right and I was drawn to the splattering of freckles across her cheeks and the bridge of her nose. Those fucking freckles.

"Christ."

I looked away, hating that flare of uncertainty. There was no room for weakness here...no room for desire. No room for hunger. Just a cold savagery. A cutting cruel grip. There was no room for anything other than the objective. I'd come this far, risking it all...and I was so fucking close now.

I turned my focus to the monitor and even though my stomach tightened and those panicked thoughts rose, I reached past my phone to the keyboard and hit the command, *unlock.*

Click.

The lights from the electronic lock blinked. The sight and the sound drew her gaze. She spun, standing there under the fake camera, and scowled. *What the fuck?*

"What the fuck indeed, Vivienne," I murmured. "Take the bait, hellcat."

She was tentative, glancing at the camera, then turned back to take a step, and then another, until she was at the door. She reached out and her hand hovered over the handle. Only this time, she opened the door like I thought she would...no. She pulled her hand away, and moved to the tray I'd carried in hours ago with her dinner.

I scowled and leaned closer, riveted, as she shoved the plastic cups and utensils away and reached to grab the tray itself, lifting it, testing its weight, before she swung it over her shoulder and brought it back down, cutting it across her body. "Clever girl," I muttered. "Feisty, clever girl."

Only then did she move with purpose, hurrying to the door to twist the handle and yank it open. She was ready, hoisting the tray upwards. If anyone was waiting for her, they'd catch a tray to the face.

I grabbed my phone from beside me, my real phone. The SIM on it traced back to me. That one I was very careful about. There were no 'special recordings', no texts that sent it to Mr. Benjamin Rossi, either. There was just them. I brought up the tracker and found the flickering lights as my sons hunted.

I wanted them to hunt.

Had trained them to hunt.

It was what they were bred for.

Movement drew my focus back to her. She was a blur in the night vision cameras, racing down the stairs with that damn tray poised over her head. If she tripped like that, she could hurt herself. I clenched my jaw, my muscles flexing. My fingers moved to the keyboard and punched in the keystrokes I wanted, switching cameras, following her path all the way to the study.

I hit the command, unlocking the study door well before she got there, just like last time. Only then, I hadn't planned on my sons coming home so soon. They'd come from the garage and the click of the lock on my study door piqued their interest.

It was damn lucky I'd gotten there when I had. There was no telling what the brothers would've done. But the tracking signal on my phone told me they were far away this time, out at night, stalking my prey. On the screen, Vivienne shoved open my study door and swung the tray in front of her, pre-empting an attack. Only there was no attack tonight. Not from my sons...or from me.

I re-crossed my legs, picked up the tumbler, and drank, relishing the warmth as it spilled through my body and into my veins. I almost felt...*giddy* when Vivienne scanned the room, stepped inside, and closed the door.

"So fucking young, aren't you?" I whispered, my voice husky and strange as my gaze moved down her body. I knew for a fact she was brand fucking new. "Christ, I wonder what your cunt tastes like."

My balls tightened and my cock twitched, bulging against my pants. I'd already had a whore today and I still felt on edge. I grabbed my phone as Vivienne glanced around the study and moved to the desk. She watched the door, hurrying now, as she wrenched at the drawers and found them locked. "Move the mouse, Vivienne," I murmured. "Move the goddamn mouse."

I opened up my contacts and flicked through the numbers for the high-end escorts I used. The names blurred as they scrolled. They were all too familiar. I needed something new, something fresh. My gaze shifted back to the monitor as the hellcat braced her foot against the side of my five-thousand-dollar red cedar masterpiece, gripped the handle on the top drawer, and fucking heaved.

"Jesus Christ," I groaned. She was going to cost me a goddamn fortune, this one…I could feel it.

A nerve twitched in the corner of my eye. I cast the phone back onto the desk in front of me and it hit the surface with a *thud*. I didn't care about pussy or about getting my dick sucked at that moment. I dragged my fingers through my hair, riled up and furious at the goddamn tornado in my office as she unleashed a silent scream and kicked my goddamn leatherbound journal clear across the room.

I winced. I should've locked it away. Furious, I tried to think if there was anything in there that I didn't want her to know. It was a new journal, with only a few jotted entries. Nothing of any real importance. If she spent the time scanning the pages, she would come away furious.

Even more furious than she was now.

Somehow, I didn't like the sound of that.

Then she swatted my Montblanc Royal pen and it spun, hitting the wireless mouse before it slammed against the keyboard. In an instant, the iMac came to life. The monitor had been left unlocked for this exact reason. But she wasn't expecting it, was she? Her gaze narrowed as she looked around the room. I could see her body tense.

"Press play, hellcat," I urged.

Crush it like a drug and feed it back to her. That's what I wanted...and this was the first step in doing that.

She chewed her lip and scanned the study, then leaned close to the monitor and pressed play. She flinched. Once, twice, three times, and she stumbled backwards. I knew instantly what she was listening to. In my head, the sound played out.

BANG! BANG! BANG! *You don't get to touch what's ours!*

Her eyes widened and her mouth gaped.

Then she lunged forward, gripped the monitor, and tilted it harshly. I winced, she was so goddamn rough with the equipment, so fucking inconsiderate. Such a goddamn...*brat.* She slipped down hard into the chair, staring at the monitor as Ryth Banks and her stepbrothers exacted their revenge.

It was the first time she'd seen Ryth since I'd brought her here.

Now she knew two things:

One, that Ryth was alive and with her stepbrothers...

And two, that she was looking at a house that couldn't possibly be monitored, not with the feed sent directly to my computer. The first thing hit her instantly. Her shoulders sagged with relief, her head dropped forward, and I swore I saw a shudder. If I did, it didn't last very long, as the second realization hit home.

Her spine slowly straightened. Her gaze was unmoving, fixed on the screen. I caught the heavy rise and fall of her chest before she slowly scanned the room...narrowing in on the false camera high in the corner of the room.

It didn't matter that she looked at the wrong camera, didn't matter that she slowly rose and stepped around the desk until she stood underneath the blinking light. It didn't matter that she said nothing, did nothing.

Because what did matter was that she realized now.

How far my reach was.

And the things I'd do.

I glanced down at the phone beside me, the one with the recording of Killion and Ryth. I'd unleashed her brothers like a weapon, taking out one of the pathetic few. I loathed Killion. The vile, cheap bastard wielded his cruelty like some fucking carnival sideshow, bringing in men who consumed like a goddamn plague.

Only I was different. I was *selective*.

And my reasons were my own.

Vivienne slowly lowered her gaze and turned around. What, no flipping the bird this time? No obstinate screams? A smile tugged the edges of my mouth as I watched her stop. Something had caught her eye, something deeper in the study...something on the shelves.

I knew instantly what she'd seen.

My stomach clenched.

The beginning of satisfaction died faster than it had come.

"No." I leaned forward as she stepped forward and reached for the small pink notebook tucked away in the back of the shelf.

She shouldn't have noticed it.

She shouldn't have cared.

She shouldn't be fucking reading as I watched her open the pages and flick through.

Goosebumps raced along my spine as I watched her, even if I tore through the house and lunged down the stairs, it'd be too late. Just like it was already too late. Vivienne's head slowly nodded as she gently closed the notebook and slipped it back into place.

I uncrossed my legs and slowly rose. My focus shifted to the door as my phone started to buzz. *"Not now,"* I forced the words through gritted teeth.

On the monitor, Vivienne made her way to the study door, opened it, and slipped through. I tracked her just like I had before as my phone buzzed and buzzed and buzzed. I snatched it up and stabbed the button. "What now?"

"We have a location on Elle, Pier Ten, east side of Mossman."

East side of Mossman...

That was unexpected, even for someone like her.

"The Order has her location as well," Colt added. "What do you want us to do?"

What to do...

What to do?

My mind raced with a thousand possible scenarios, but none that would help me on my path. "Observe only."

"You sure?"

"Are you questioning me?"

"No...I just..."

"Then *observe only,*" I ordered.

"Will do," he muttered. "I'll report back if anything happens."

On the monitor, Vivienne reached the top of the stairs and headed for her room. "I'll be waiting," I said, staring at her, then lowered my hand...and ended the call. "I'll be waiting right here."

I'd barely ended the call before my phone beeped again. "What the fuck is it this time?" I snapped, not wanting to look away from the woman on the monitor...the one who now knew more than I wanted her to know as she slipped into her bedroom. But I did, and glanced at the screen...

To a message that made my blood turn cold.

A low, savage sound erupted. I shot upwards, knocking my glass and spilling the contents. *"Fuck!"* I roared. But it wasn't about the expensive goddamn alcohol...

It was because my entire plan...had just been blown to hell...

I ran from the room, punching numbers into my phone, praying to God I could salvage this...and left Vivienne, and her satisfied smirk, far behind as I raced for my car.

THIRTY-THREE

Ryth

He never did tell me...

I realized that as I stood there clutching my mother's diary in my hand. When we'd left the diner, before Tobias collapsed, Nick had promised to tell me the reasons why Mom had handed me over to those sick fucking pieces of shit. But as I stood there, holding the small leatherbound notebook, I realized he never had...

As the words blurred on the page in my hand, now I wished he never had.

I swallowed hard, trying to find my voice, only to whisper. "Breeding program." I lifted my gaze to Nick's sad stare. "That's what I am?"

"No." Caleb shook his head. "That's not *what* you are. All that is, is how you came to be."

"They were *bred*, Caleb," I whimpered, and lifted the journal. "My mother, other women, they were *bred*."

"And if they had the chance, they'd do the same to you," Caleb added.

You're a natural.

A natural.

A nat—

The kitchen spun, blurring under the savage rush of my panicked breaths. *Oh, God...oh, God...*

"Easy." Tobias gripped my arm, shooting a savage glare C's way. "A little bit of fucking tact, huh?"

"Tact won't give her answers," Caleb bit back. "And it sure as hell won't keep her safe."

Tobias shook his head as anger burned in his stare. "And you think scaring her half to death will?"

Caleb turned away, raking his fingers through his hair, his unbuttoned crumpled white shirt flapping as he turned, and paced the length of the kitchen counter. "Fuck, this is a mess."

I thought it was a lie.

That it was *all* some sick, twisted lie. But it wasn't, was it? Not only *wasn't* it a lie...it was far worse than I'd thought. "I don't know whether to throw up, scream, or get drunk."

"We can try all three at once if you want," T muttered beside me. "'Cause that sounds like an average Saturday night out partying to me."

I let out a bark of laughter, shooting him a glare. "Way to crack a joke at a time like this."

There was a quirk at the corner of his lips as he gave a shrug. "Hey, it worked, didn't it?"

I was about to give him a jab in the ribs, but Nick's phone vibrated on the counter. Then what little laughter I had inside me died away in an instant. Nick glanced at me, then pressed the icon on his phone, putting it on speaker. "We're here."

"My guys are almost there to pick her up." Ben Rossi's deep growl echoed huskily through the phone. I doubted he'd had a second of sleep. "Thought I'd give you a heads-up."

Nick stared at me, then reached out, his finger hovering over the phone. "Thanks. Keep us informed."

"Will do."

I surged forward. *"Wait!"*

Nick stilled from ending the call. My heart hammered, my chest was tight. "Can you stay on the line?" I asked. "I just want to make sure she's safe, that's all."

"Ryth," Nick cautioned.

There was a sadness in his stare. One I didn't need to see right now. "I'm not getting my hopes up," I muttered. "I know what she did was wrong. But if this..." I lifted the diary. "If this doesn't speak volumes as to her state of mind, then I don't know what does."

"She seemed fine when she had them abduct you from that warehouse," Nick growled.

"She also seemed fine when she shot our fucking dad," Tobias snarled.

I flinched at the words. After Tobias told us what had happened that night, I couldn't believe it. That...murderer wasn't the woman who'd given birth to me, who'd raised me...who'd cared for me. She was a stranger. A—I gripped the diary in my hand—by-product of vile men.

Hate seethed in the kitchen, making goosebumps race along my arms. I hugged my body as Ben's voice came again. "Let me call my men on the other phone. I'll put them on speaker and as soon as we have her, then you can rest easier."

He knew. I didn't understand how, but he did. "Thank you," I whispered.

I waited as sounds filtered through the phone, until the voices of other men echoed. *"Yeah, we're coming up on the Pier now."*

"Do you see her?" Ben asked.

"We're looking...there's..." his man started.

"What the fuck?" Ben snarled.

Nick snapped his head up at the sound. "What is it?"

"I just got a goddamn text from a private number...there's been an explosion."

"Wait!" his man's voice cracked through in the background. *"Wait, WHAT THE FUCK!"*

Crack!

Crack...crack...crack crack crack.

I flinched at every sound. Panting breaths consumed me. "What is it? *What's happening!"*

"Nick!" Rossi roared. *"Get the fuck out of there NOW!"*

Crack!

I stared at the phone on the counter, but the screen was dead now...the call disconnected.

Crack!

"What the fuck?" Nick snapped as a blur of movement came in the corner of my eye from behind me.

I spun as Tobias whirled around, and found three men dressed in black and wearing balaclavas striding toward us with their guns raised in the air.

Crack! The shot rang out as Caleb lunged sideways. Tobias was savage, pushing in front of me, protecting me with his life as the men spread out, each one of them going for my brothers. But it was the middle one who shifted the gun in his hand, taking aim at Tobias's head.

Until Nick unleashed a savage roar, vaulted clear across the kitchen counter, and kicked the gun from the attacker's hand. *Crack!* The shot went wide, hitting the counter next to me. There was a second where Tobias jerked his gaze to mine, then found the bullet hole, then turned back to the asshole.

"You fucking *bastard!*" he screamed and lunged, driving his fist into the black mask. *"You almost hit her!"*

Thump!

Thump!

Crunch!

Rebel's savage snarls came from around the corner of the dining room. Her black lips were curled back, and rage shone in her midnight eyes. She lunged at the attacker as he lashed out at Nick, sinking her fangs into his leg. He bucked with the pain, kicking out. But there was no way she was letting go. If anything, she held on even tighter, thrashing her head from side to side.

"The fuck!" Nick's gunman screamed.

They were an unmerciful blur of fists and balaclavas and a savage pup who was my brother's protector. I shoved away from the counter and stumbled backwards as all three of my brothers fought for our lives. But I wasn't running. *No fucking way...*I was done with that...I was *so* fucking done. I rounded the edge, moved into the kitchen, and grabbed one of the butcher knives from the block instead, then turned back to them.

They were here to abduct me...

No. They were here to kill them...

I gripped the knife tightly and plunged back around as grunts and snarls and the sickening sounds of fists on flesh followed.

"Shoot this *motherfucker!*" one of the attackers roared.

Nick was throwing fists, then swept out his leg to take the gunman down. But he was so focused on Tobias that he took a fist to the jaw. He stumbled backwards, then went down himself, while the other man went for Tobias's wounded leg.

"I'm gonna kill you!" Tobias roared. *"I'm gonna fucking kill you!"*

Crack!

A gunshot rang out, deafening in the space. I gripped the hilt of the knife and searched the walls to see where the bullet had hit. But it hadn't made a hole, not in the walls or the counter. Instead, Caleb tumbled backwards, blood blooming neon red at edge of his shoulder.

They'd shot him.

They'd shot Caleb!.

Something savage unleashed inside me. A feral, uncontrollable rage just...*snapped*. I lunged across the dining room and drove the knife through the air as Caleb stumbled, trying to stay upright. The gunman snapped his head toward me. But it was already too late as I plunged that wicked point right into him.

The blade carved deep, sinking steel into flesh until there was no more steel left.

Numb, I stared down at his middle, where the glint was swallowed by black, then lifted my gaze to his. There was a stunned widening of his stare as the grunts and howls of my brothers came behind me.

"Ryth!" Caleb grabbed my arm, tore me away, and pulled me behind him. "You fucking touch her…" he warned. "You fucking touch her and I'll kill you."

But the gunman just looked down and stared at the big knife embedded in his middle, then he gripped the hilt and pulled it out. *Wait!* The cry ripped through my head. But that's where it stayed. The idiot jerked the knife free, carving upwards and all I could hear in my head was Tobias as he'd showed me just where to stab. *Jerk it up, little mouse…do more damage that way.*

And it did do more damage.

Crunch.

Crunch.

Thud!

Tobias lunged, driving himself between us and the man whose blood began to flow out from under his black shirt to enlarge the pool of his blood already on Ben's beautiful floor. "Game over," Tobias snarled, wrenched his fist backwards, and unleashed it right into the man's face.

Nick joined us a second later as the gunman dropped to the floor. "We have to go."

"Where?" I whispered, staring at all the blood. "We have nowhere to go."

Nick's phone vibrated on the kitchen counter where we'd left it. He crossed the space, grabbed it, and answered the call. "Yeah?"

There was a second of sickening silence, where the only sounds were the choked off crackle of escaping air and the slick sound of dripping blood. I don't think I really heard that, or maybe it was my mind playing games. Still, I was riveted—like we were *all* riveted to Nick as he turned pale and muttered, "What the fuck?"

"Speaker!" Caleb demanded as he lurched toward him.

Nick lowered his hand instantly and hit the speaker icon. "Say that again, Ben."

"Something's gone down at The Order. There's been an explosion. Jack...Jack's" *dead, right? Dad's dead.* "Escaped and headed this way."

I jerked my gaze upward. All three of my brothers stared at me as the mafia boss kept talking.

"Ryth, honey...there's no easy way to say this, but your mom's dead."

Mom's...dead?

"When my men turned up, so did three men from The Order. They killed her, right there in front of my men. They opened fire, but by the time they got there, it was too late."

It was too late...*too late*. My knees trembled, but Tobias was there, wrapping his arm around my waist, holding onto me like I was about to become adrift.

"But her dad is alive," Nick insisted, drawing me back to the only flicker of hope I had left.

"Yeah, and he's on his way here."

"How the fuck did they get him out?" Caleb stepped closer and braced his good hand against the counter.

"How the fuck do you think?" Tobias snarled next to me. "It's King…King, who seems only too happy to help him, as long as he can get to Ryth."

I flinched and jerked my gaze to his. Those dark brown eyes sparkled with malice. "He's not getting anywhere near you, little mouse," he promised. "No one is."

"Then we're heading your way." Nick gripped his phone and turned toward us.

"Take the back roads," Ben warned. "Call me when you're close."

"Will do," he acknowledged, then ended the call.

I looked down at the blood that had almost reached my bare feet and flinched, before pushing into Tobias. He followed my stare, then pulled me away.

"I'll get the car started," Nick growled. "You get the guns."

"Hurry, princess," Caleb urged. "Grab your clothes and we're out of here."

But I turned on him, searching body. "Your shoulder."

He looked down, the smear of blood on his shirt hadn't grown. "I'm okay, just a flesh wound. Grab your things, princess. We have to move."

Fuck the things. "Rebel?" I searched the space, finding her sitting near the end of the counter, panting hard. I lurched forward and dropped to my knees beside her. "You okay, girl?" I ran my hands over her head and gently searched her body. "Did you hurt yourself? Did you tear a stitch?"

"In the car, princess," Nick snapped, gathering our attackers' weapons and searching their bodies. "I'll get the dog."

I pushed upwards as my pulse boomed in my ears and snapped me out of it. "You're right. I'll be quick." I didn't bother to look behind me as I rushed for the stairs.

"Five seconds, Ryth!" Nick roared behind me.

Five seconds. Five damn seconds. I took the stairs two at a time and the deafening sounds of heavy steps behind me closed in. Strong hands around my waist lifted my feet from the stairs and thrust me faster up to the first floor.

"Hurry, little sister." Tobias gently shoved me forward.

But he didn't follow me. I didn't slow long enough to see where he went, just raced to the room I'd been sharing with my brothers and grabbed every piece of clothing I could find before yanking on jeans, boots, my bra this time, and a shirt, then grabbed my jacket.

I wasn't five seconds...but I was damn fast.

I stumbled out of the room, finding Tobias waiting at the stairs with a heavier duffel bag filled with guns. Corded tendons strained in his neck with the weight. Still, he motioned me first, leaving me to slip around him and race down the stairs.

The heavy throb of a car's engine beckoned. We were heaving our bags into the rear in a blur of movement, climbing into the car...and tearing away from the Rossi house.

THIRTY-FOUR

Nick

I punched the accelerator, clipping the garage door as it rose.

"Where are we heading?" T snarled from the backseat.

But I didn't have time to answer as I braked hard at the closed electric gate and stared at the body of one of Rossi's men at the edge of the driveway, his automatic weapon in his hand. Another one of his buddies lay not far away. Christ, this was bad...

"I'll get it." Caleb shoved open his door and climbed out.

I scanned for assholes in balaclavas, ready to step out and start firing at the first sign of movement. C hurried to the fence, gripped the iron, and heaved himself over.

"I don't know," I answered T's question.

"Not the shipping yard, that's too far out of the city."

"I don't know..." I snarled, panic filling my head.

The gates rolled open before C hurried back out. I shoved the four-wheel drive into gear and rolled through, stopping only long enough to pick him up before I tore away from the house.

Beep.

I jerked my gaze to my phone as Caleb snapped his seatbelt shut and reached for it sitting between us. I divided my focus, pushing the four-wheel drive hard as I tore along the back streets.

"Silks District," he muttered, jerking his gaze to mine. "That's where he wants us to head."

"Silks?"

"The abandoned warehouses that were sold by the city."

"And bought by Ben, no doubt," T muttered in the backseat. "At least it's not the shipping yard."

And not that far away. I pressed the button on the GPS in the middle of the console system, narrowed in on the back streets where we were, and dragged the map right until it came to what was still marked as factories in the upper west section of the city. It'd take us...about twenty minutes. "Tell him we'll be there in ten."

Caleb's fingers flew across the keyboard as I yanked the wheel and punched the gas, heading to the highway. I focused on the street in front of us and the rear-view mirror, waiting and watching for the next onslaught.

"How the fuck did they find us?" Tobias snarled, turning in his seat, watching the blur of overhead lights.

"Hell if I know," I muttered, turning the car onto the on-ramp and gunning the engine. "But they did, so we need to be prepared."

T lifted his gun and checked the round with a *clack*. "Oh, believe me, I'm fucking ready."

I concentrated on getting us there in one piece, my mind racing. But no matter how panicked I was...I was still drawn back to her. "Princess?" I cut my gaze to her in the back seat. She was quiet, too damn quiet.

She glanced my way, the splash of streetlights making her washed-out blue eyes even paler. "Yeah?"

"You okay back there?"

She swallowed hard and nodded. T reached over the dog, gripped the back of Ryth's neck and forced her gaze to his. "No falling apart on us, little mouse."

She shook her head, even though those wide eyes were filled with fear. I pushed the car harder and slipped onto the off-ramp, taking the next exit.

Beep.

I winced. Fuck, I was starting to hate that sound. "What now?" I growled, my focus dragged back to the moment tonight had gone wrong.

Those men in black were The Order, they had to be. The bomb. The fucking assassination. This was them cleaning house and taking back what was theirs. My gaze went to the rear-view mirror as C answered. "Yeah?"

But Ryth wasn't theirs...

She was ours.

"He's there?" Caleb glanced my way as I took the next left and headed to the Silks District. They were a bunch of abandoned warehouses that were once a thriving factory that specialized in top-end materials...hence the name. Now it was a carcass...a lonely, desolate, abandoned carcass.

I looked up at the empty apartment building that towered over this block, searching for movement, and turned in.

"Over there." Caleb pointed to three cars parked outside the gates of the closest section.

I nosed the four-wheel drive toward them, mounted the curb, and killed the engine. "I don't like being this exposed," I muttered as I scanned around.

"Neither do I." Tobias shoved open his door and climbed out first, taking his time to check out the surroundings. "Okay, Ryth. You can get out."

The screech of metal pierced the night, coming from the old roller door just ahead of us. I jerked my focus toward the sound, seeing two silhouettes against the weak inside lights. Ben stood there, right beside—

"Dad?" Ryth whispered.

She took a step, then another, before she lunged.

"*Ryth!*" Tobias snarled, leaping for her.

But he wasn't fast enough, and our princess was scurrying as fast as her legs allowed. Rebel gave a bark and charged after her as both of them tore through the open gate and raced toward the men.

"Shit," Tobias snarled.

Panic kicked in my chest. *"Ryth, wait for us!"* I called out, shoving the door closed as I surged after her.

We needed to stay together...

Tobias was already hurrying after her, leaving everything else behind, including me. I hurried after him, my attention moving to the shrouded figure of Jack Castlemaine. He strode forward and opened his arms, and Christ, if I didn't hate the thought of another man touching her—even if it was her father.

Not really her father, though, was he? I strode through the gate, Caleb right beside me. We were almost at a damn run along the concrete drive to the open warehouse door.

"Dad," Ryth moaned, wrapped in Jack's arms. "I thought we'd lost you."

Her head was pressed against his chest, leaving him to lift his gaze to mine. No words were spoken, but that sad glint screamed a helluva lot.

"We need to get inside," Ben muttered, catching my stare. "No one followed you?"

I shook my head. "I made sure of it."

"Good." He stepped away, motioning inside.

I glanced over my shoulder at the cars parked just outside the fence, then followed. The shrill sound of the hinges followed as we moved inside, Ryth still clutched in her father's embrace. But once the doors closed, she turned to him. "How did you get out?"

He gave a chuff and shook his head. "You wouldn't believe me if I told you."

"Try us," I answered for her.

All heads snapped my way. But I didn't care if my words sounded harsh, not when it was her life in the balance.

"King…" Jack started.

Beep.

Ben jerked his phone up and scowled at the screen.

"What is it?" Jack stepped away from Ryth, his attention fixed on Ben.

But the Stidda Mafia boss didn't answer right away, instead he punched the icon and lifted the phone to his ear. "How bad is it?" He stiffened with whatever was said.

Ryth glanced my way, knowing instantly. Fuck if it didn't make my heart swell when she stepped our way. "Nick," she whispered.

I reached out to her at the same time Tobias lifted his gun and stepped forward. "Behind us, little mouse," he muttered.

"There was no way they tracked us," Ben snarled into the phone. "No way they knew this place was even on the radar. Fuck. The others, how far away are they?"

I didn't know what was said, but I knew it wasn't good when he slumped his shoulders. "T," I hissed.

"The guns are in the car." He strode forward, leaving us behind. "I'll be back in a second."

And it hit me.

The resounding punch of déjà vu all over again.

I was back there in the fucking dark, watching my brother race to his goddamn death. *"Tobias!"* I roared.

He stopped and turned, his gaze automatically shifting to Ryth, as though his entire fucking purpose was to look to her first.

"If we go," I ordered. "We all go together."

Ryth stepped forward as Ben ended the call. "I agree."

"They're coming." Ben shook his head. "And we're on our own."

We're on our own.

Those words should have chilled me, and if I hadn't been standing there with both my brothers and Ryth, they would have.

"We'll be back." Ryth hurried after T, leaving Caleb and me to follow.

"Ryth," her father called. "Honey, stay here, let them go."

She stopped at her father's insistence, then turned her head and answered. "Never, Dad. Where one of us goes, we all go."

"Ain't that fucking right, princess," I growled as I gripped her arm and drove her forward.

Where one of us went, we *all* went. There was no falling behind, no going off on our own. No bed we slept in alone. Not anymore. Tobias yanked on the chain hanging from the roller door and it lifted just enough for us to slip through.

"How long do we have?" she asked, half running, half walking to match my long strides.

My senses were tuned, finding the throb of a car's engine driving way too fast. "Not long," I answered as Tobias yanked open the driver's side rear door of the car as we hurried toward him.

"Heads up," he barked, tossing an automatic rifle toward me, then another to Caleb, who searched the streets.

"And me," Ryth urged, glancing from Tobias to me. "I want to fight." T scowled and started to glance my way, before Ryth stopped him. "You can either give me something to fight with or I'll ask my dad."

I flinched. *Shit.*

T didn't like that, not at all. He reached into the bag and pulled out a Sig. But he didn't toss it through the air like he had for us. No, he headed toward her, holding the weapon grip forward. "You're not going to need to use this, I'm just letting you know now. But if you do...don't shoot me."

Her brow creased as the roar of that car's engine grew louder and was joined by another.

"How about I clock you upside the head with it instead?" she snapped.

"How about, when we're out of here, I fuck you in the back seat of Ben Rossi's car?" he countered. "You can clock me all you want then."

Headlights shone in the distance.

"T," I warned as I stepped backwards.

He followed my stare. "Back in the warehouse, little mouse...*now*."

He lunged for the bag, tossed some of the guns to Caleb, and swung the rear door closed with a *thud*.

We were already running when the racing engines grew louder and the faint *crack...crack...crack* of shots rang out. Glass shattered from the rear of the four-wheel drive.

"Hurry the fuck up!" Ben roared from beside the door of the warehouse.

I gripped the automatic rifle, then slowed just enough for T to catch up and for Ryth to get in front before I lifted my weapon, took aim...and fired.

THIRTY-FIVE

Caleb

Gunfire cracked out beside me as Nick opened fire. "*The warehouse, Ryth!*" I screamed and turned, drew my weapon up, and slipped my finger around the trigger.

She ran...that's all I cared about.

"Motherfuckers!" T screamed as he took aim and fired at the mammoth black Expedition as it hurtled toward us. Bullets pinged against the grille, sparking in the night.

I leveled my sight and jerked the trigger, sending the spray of bullets wide, peppering the side of the damn car instead. The side mirror shattered, sending the four-wheel drive skidding sideways as it mounted the curb and became airborne. I lunged to the side, almost tripping as the car crashed into the gate with a resounding *smash!*

Tobias stumbled sideways, his eyes wide as he searched for Nick first, then me. One slow nod, and he turned and ran. "Nice shot, dickhead," he chided as he tore past.

I wasn't like Nick or T. Words were my weapons, not guns. Still, I spun and took aim at the gleaming black beast as the engine hissed and spat, shooting plumes of steam into the air, and loosed another spray of bullets before I whirled and raced for the open door.

"You *idiot!*" Ben snapped at Tobias as he yanked the heavy chain and closed the heavy steel roller door. "You could've been killed."

"Yeah, well, I wasn't, was I?" T snapped back.

"Only for sheer dumb luck," Ben growled, cutting a glare at T, then Nick, and finally, to me.

I saw then just how close Tobias had been to the head of the Stidda Mafia and it made me sad for the loss of that with our own father.

"In the back, *now.*" Ben gave a jerk of his head.

Ping!

Ping!

Bullets hit the steel door in front of us. We turned and jogged to the rear of the warehouse, skirting around forgotten cutting tables and fixed sewing machines that were rusted and ruined.

"They didn't follow me." Jack shook his head. "I *know* that for a fact."

"Why, because your *buddy* King made sure of it?" Tobias snapped, giving him a savage glare.

Jack gave him a glare of his own.

"Jack's right." Ben twisted the handle on a locked office door. "First, they attacked you tonight at my home, then they followed us here." He stepped back, dropped his shoulder, and charged.

The lock snapped and the door flew inwards, hitting the wall with a *thud*. The hammering sound of bullets peppered the garage door, making Ryth flinch and look toward the sound.

"And I'm pretty certain they were watching you before we met." Ben stepped into the office and moved to a small locked box nailed to the wall. He tried to open it, then stepped backwards, aimed his gun, and fired.

Boom!

Ben moved fast, yanked open the box, and snatched a set of keys from inside. "So, if they tracked you from there to here." Ben moved past us and back out the door. "Then it has to be one of you."

"One of us, what?" T snapped, following him.

We all followed him, moving along a corridor to the rear of the building as the sound of gunfire grew louder from the front.

"That's being tracked," he finished, glancing at us over his shoulder.

Tracked?

I flinched as panicked thoughts pushed in as I turned my focus internally. I tried to remember what had happened in that place. Did they...did they do something to me? Ben yanked open a lock, reached around, and flicked on a light.

"Thank fuck I kept the damn power connected," he muttered as he stepped around the chaos of discarded sewing and dyeing machines.

We all followed, leaving Tobias to close and lock the door behind us...until I sensed something and stopped, then turned around.

Ryth...

Ryth stood just inside the door behind us.

Ryth with her gray-blue eyes impossibly wide.

And that darkness in her stare.

The kind of darkness I took care of for her.

The kind of darkness where I kept her safe.

"Princess?" I murmured and stepped toward her.

"It's me," she whimpered.

Tobias snapped his head toward her, then so did Nick. Everyone else faded from our thoughts. It didn't matter about them anymore. Not her dad or the man who was trying to keep us alive. There was only us, only *her*.

"What are you saying?" T snarled.

She just shook her head. "You know. You all know. It's me they're tracking. Me they...branded. They put something inside me." She wrapped her arms around herself. "I'm the one putting you all in danger."

The way she spoke sent chills along my spine. Shots cracked out, sounding closer now—sounding like they'd broken through the door. I held out my hand. "We have to kept moving, baby. You need to trust us on this. You have to *move*."

"We don't have time for this," Ben snapped.

I flinched with anger and wrenched my gaze to his. "Then we *goddamn* make time."

Boom.

Boom.

Boom.

I shoved the panic aside, listening to the shots ring out in the warehouse behind us and stepped closer again. "We stay together, right?" I licked my lips, trying desperately to bring her back from that place. I couldn't do it with sex, not this time. So I had to try any other way I could. "You know what we went through. We're not doing that again."

"No," she whispered, those eyes shifting back into focus. "We're not."

"So we stay together," Tobias added.

"Just as we promised," Nick finished.

One more step. I held my hand out to her as the echo of boots thundered in the warehouse. "With us, princess."

She took my hand and it was all I could do not to sag with relief. I pulled her with me as we raced back to a gate that led out to some kind of alley.

Ben never said anything, neither did her father. He just looked at her with a sad fucking stare. He pitied her. She sure as *hell* didn't need that.

The hinges of the gate howled as shots rang out, blasting the door behind us. I blocked out the screams of the gunmen, gripped Ryth's hand instead, and pulled her with me through the exit until we were out the other side.

Cold night air hit me like a slap. I exhaled hard as the door behind us flew open. But T was there, taking aim and firing. *Crack! Crack! Crack!*

I jerked at the sounds, wrenched her hard against me, and shoved her forward. "Run!" Nick was there, grabbing her hand, pulling her away as Tobias unleashed a savage roar. *"FUCK YOU!"*

Our movements were a blur of terror. Flashes ignited as we raced along that small alley and out into an empty street.

"*Where?*" Nick barked at Ben as he spun around, lifted his gun, and took aim.

"Wait!" The deep snarl came from the darkness. *"It's me!"*

"Neon?" Ben gasped, then exhaled with relief. "Fuck, I'm glad to see you."

Three of Rossi's men ran toward us, coming from an alley next to a building across the street. The one he called Neon scanned us, sucking in hard breaths. All three looked like they'd been sprinting for their damn lives. But as he stepped closer and slapped Ben's hand with his, I knew it wasn't his life he was trying to save—it was his boss'.

"There's more coming," Neon gasped as a shot rang out with a *crack* behind him.

The guy next to him opened fire, leaving us to focus on the swarm of men dressed in black that rounded the corner at the end of the empty street.

There was no one out here to help us, no cops to serve and protect. There was just us...and a block of empty buildings to be cornered in. They'd never find the bodies—*crack...crack...crack crack crack*—maybe that was their plan all along?

Thud.

The faint sound of a car door slammed behind me. I barely caught the sound, spinning to find nothing but the dull wash of streetlights fighting away the dark. But the others missed it. They missed it while they searched for a way out of here.

"The car's parked on the street behind," Neon muttered. "It's all shot to hell, but it's driveable."

"We can't go back for ours," Ben snarled, flinching as the *crack crack crack* came louder.

The sound of a car's engine came behind the gunmen. There were more coming. More from The Order, to close us in like rats. This was bad...this was really bad...

I turned to Nick.

Crack!

"Fuck!" Tobias barked as he stumbled sideways.

There was a tear in the side of his shirt and behind it, blood.

"Oh, shit," Nick mumbled. *"Oh, shit."*

THIRTY-SIX

Tobias

"Oh, shit," Caleb muttered, staring at my side.

But I didn't stop to look, didn't even swipe at the searing agony that spread outwards. I just lifted my gun, took aim, and fired, hitting him in the leg.

The asshole in black unleashed a cry and went down onto one knee. He lifted his head, and his eyes widened, knowing this was over as I centered my sight and squeezed the trigger. *Boom!* Adrenaline rushed before I was taking aim again.

BOOM!

Gunshots cracked in rapid succession, too loud and too damn close. I lunged for the building as Ben was slammed backwards.

"What the fuck!" Nick roared.

I didn't have time to think—just to *react*.

BOOM!

BOOM!

BOOM!

I swung my gun, but it was too late. One look at Ben and I knew he was in trouble. Blood spread out from his shoulder. Neon jerked beside him and went down. Jack stepped forward, protecting them as much as he could as he fired again and again and again. But it was no use. There were too many rushing at us from around the corner of the fence line.

"We need to run!" Nick roared, stepping forward, taking out as many as he could.

Crack!

Crack!

Ryth was right beside him. Her hands were shaking and her eyes were wide as she fired her gun again and again. Neon shoved upwards and grabbed Ben as he jerked his gaze my way. "We split up. It's the only way we get out of this alive."

"No," Ben growled, shaking his head. But the man was pale, growing more ashen by the second.

"Lucky it's not up to you." Neon heaved his boss upwards, took one look around, and raced for the building across the alley, with Jack close behind.

"Wait!" Ben roared, jerking his gaze over his shoulder.

There was something panicked in his stare, like somehow he knew this was the end...for us. But I was already grabbing Ryth and dragging her backwards.

The man who was a father to me gave a slow nod and let his bodyguard drag him away. But he didn't go quietly, unleashing one more savage roar and opened fire, downing as many of those fuckers as he could.

They scurried like cockroaches, splitting off to race across the alley. I scanned the buildings, lifting my gaze to the towering building in the distance that loomed over us behind the gunmen.

"Let's go!" Nick grabbed Caleb by the shirt and dragged him.

Then we were moving, ducking and weaving as bullets hit the building beside us. I turned, firing over my shoulder, trying my best to cover my family as much as I could. But my gaze went to the empty building across the street where Ben Rossi had disappeared. A pang cut across my chest and this time it wasn't a bullet wound.

Although it might well have been.

Movement came from the murky gloom beside that building. My heart lunged at the sight as a man stepped out. For a second, I thought it was Ben...for a second, I thought it was the father I'd always wanted, protecting me, caring for me, caring...*for...me...*

But it wasn't.

"Dad?" Ryth jerked her gaze his way as we stumbled along. "What the fuck are you doing? *You need to run!*"

"Not without you, sweetheart," he snarled as he lifted his gun and fired, taking out another one of The Order's men.

"*Fuck!*" Nick jerked as a bullet narrowly missed his face. "We need to get out of here, T... *now.*"

We turned and ran, hauling ass toward the empty building in the distance until headlights cut through the night, blinding us.

"*Jesus!*" Nick snarled as a car skidded sideways and came to a stop.

And more of The Order spilled out.

"Oh, fuck," I whispered. "*Oh, fuck...*"

THIRTY-SEVEN

Vivienne

My mind was reeling when I slipped back into my room and closed the door. I flicked off the lights and went to the bed. But I didn't climb in between the sheets. Instead, I sat on the edge and stared into the darkness. "What the fuck was that?" I whispered to the empty room. "What the *actual* fuck *was* that?"

I tried to think, tried to come up with some reasonable explanation as to why London St. James might have a journal full of entries...*about me.*

They weren't just handwritten, rage-filled entries, either. They were pages and pages of personal details filled with dates, photos, and details from the moment I'd been dragged into that place by my shitty foster parents, all the way to the day he'd brought me here. Some entries I found toward the back were even before that, from when the robots allowed me to attend my last years at Harlington Prep. *Jesus, he even* had an image of me with my face buried in a book while I hid in the school library.

How the fuck did he even get that?

A shudder ripped through me, then it was followed by the icy grip of panic as the *thud thud thud* of heavy steps echoed along the hallway, heading for my room. I jumped up and took a step backwards toward the wall. I shouldn't have found that journal. Panic took hold. I shouldn't have looked, shouldn't have read. Shouldn't have...

He was going to take me back.

My breath seized. I fixed my gaze on the murky blur of my bedroom door. He was going to take me back to The Principal and The Teacher and The Priest. I lowered my head, my shoulders curling as shudders raced through me. *Oh, Jesus...no... no...I'm sorry, I didn't mean to look. I didn't mean to find that jou—*the words rose THUD THUD THUD thud thud *thud...* as the steps faded, then were gone, thundering down the stairs, leaving me behind.

He was leaving me?

I hated the pang that tore across my chest. Hated the way in those fleeting seconds I felt...*desperate.* Like I didn't want him to leave me *at all.* But then the feeling was gone, just like the booming of his boots, and slowly the realization slipped in. *Something was wrong.*

I took a step toward the door as that thought took hold. Something wasn't just wrong...*it'd gone to shit.* There was no way Mr. Stone Cold Asshole would run for anything less. I didn't have to think too hard as the memory of what I'd witnessed on that monitor came rushing back to me.

Ryth...

And men who had to be her brothers.

Torturing Killion before they killed him.

She'd stabbed him...stabbed him before her brother...shot him in the head.

"Jesus," I wrapped my arms around my body, desperately wanting to unsee that shit.

But no matter how much I wanted to, I refused to block it out. I needed to remember. I needed to *understand*. Why the hell would London have something like that? More importantly, *how the fuck did he get it?*

The how bugged me more than it should.

I mean, it was a damn CCTV camera, in a man like Killion's home. He wasn't just any man. He was one of The Order's biggest clients. A reputation like that meant he had money and power and a fuck load of both. A shiver raced along my spine...I suddenly grew still. If London could invade a man like Killion's home, then he could pretty well invade anywhere, couldn't he?

I closed my eyes. "Jesus, who the fuck *is* that man?"

My breath stilled as the memory of those journal entries came rushing back.

And what the fuck did he want with me?

I sank back onto the bed, this time sitting on the damn pillow. But I didn't care, because right now, my life hung in the balance —by one very fucking thin thread. No matter how hard I tried, I couldn't work it out. I sat there staring into the dark until my eyes burned, and slowly I realized he wasn't coming back. Not for a while, at least.

I leaned backwards, curled my feet underneath me, and slipped lower in the bed, still dressed in the clothes he'd laid out for me, but then I realized. *He wouldn't like that...no, he wouldn't like that at all.*

A low snarl, and I shoved upwards and made my way to the bathroom, flicking the light on with a slap. "Goddamn motherfucker, now I'm his puppet on a string, aren't I?" I winced, worked the top buttons on my blouse, then yanked it over my head. "I'll wrap that fucking string around his throat if he's not careful."

I undressed and glanced at the camera before I stepped into the shower. I didn't waste time as I scrubbed myself, then stepped out and dried myself. Then I dressed in the goddamn lace negligee he'd had waiting for me on the bathroom counter, peach colored this time. I picked it up, slipped it over my head, and tugged a brush through my hair before climbing back into bed.

London St. James was ruthless and possessive. Still, he hadn't lifted a damn hand to hurt me. I needed to understand why. I closed my eyes. It wasn't because of sex, that was for sure. No matter the hunger I saw in his eyes, he couldn't do a damn thing to me...

Him or his goddamn sons.

I was protected by one flimsy piece of paper...and his signature.

The contract he'd signed was as powerful as his need for me. One broken rule and they'd come and take me back. I scanned the opulent room in the dark. As much as I hated being here, I hated that place more.

That thought carried me down. I drifted, losing time, until the booming of my pulse dragged me back to the surface. *Click.* My eyes snapped open with the sound of the lock on my bedroom door. That heavy thud carried, moving closer to the bed.

"Get dressed," London snarled in the dark. "You have five minutes."

I shoved upwards. "What?"

But he didn't answer, just stood there…*waiting.*

Cold air slipped in to chill me to the bone. I slowly pushed the comforter aside. "London…"

"Four minutes."

I flinched at the cruel tone. He was sending me back there… sending me back to *that place.* "No," I whispered.

"No?"

I lifted my gaze. Moonlight spilled through my bedroom window, catching the glint in those dark eyes. "I'm not going."

He lunged, grabbed my ankle, and dragged me toward him. "You *will* do what I goddamn tell you. *Do I make myself clear?*"

Fear filled me. The kind of fear I hadn't felt in a long time, not since they'd shoved me in that prison cell at The Order and slammed the door closed behind me. I kicked out, throwing off his hold, and scrambled for the other side of the bed. He was on me in an instant, lunging to drive his body against mine, smashing my face into the soft comforter.

"Get off me!" I bucked, kicking and thrashing.

Until he grabbed my wrists, pinning them to the bed above my head. "Stop *fucking fighting me!*"

"I *won't go back!*" I roared, thrashing my body from side to side in an attempt to dislodge him. *"I won't go back to that place. I'D RATHER DIE!"*

He fought me, gripping my wrists. There was no way I could fight him, *no way I could win.*

"I'M NOT TAKING YOU BACK TO THE ORDER!"

I froze, heavy breaths sawing through my chest until they burned. "You're not?"

He released his hold and lifted his weight from me. "*No, I'm not.*"

I turned, looking at him over my shoulder, and taking in lungfuls of air. "Then where...the fuck...are you taking me?"

A savage growl filled the room. "I'm taking you to Ryth."

I spun around, sat in the middle of the bed, and stared at him. "*Ryth?* You're taking me to see *Ryth?*"

He just stared down at me with that stony glare, brushing back the stray strands of his hair with a swipe of his hand. "You now have two minutes, Vivienne. I suggest you hurry."

He was taking me to see Ryth? I'd never moved so fast in my life. I didn't care that I'd just watched her and her brothers attack a man like a pack of wild beasts. Killion deserved to die a painful death after what he'd done to her. I only wished I'd been there to help.

I raced to the closet, yanking the lace nightgown over my head. "I need the light, London!" I snapped, not caring that I was naked.

Click.

The soft white glow illuminated the room. He stood there watching as I yanked on panties and a bra, my hands shaking as I fumbled with the hooks at my back. I didn't care anymore that he watched me. There was no privacy when it came to London. I was starting to learn that the hard way. I pulled on a soft caramel cashmere sweater and cream-colored slacks, then slipped into heels because that's all he fucking gave me. "Okay." I jerked my frantic gaze to him. "Okay. *I'm done.*"

One brow rose. "All that in less than a minute. I'm impressed." He stepped away from the wall and motioned toward the door. "You run from me and I'll—"

"I'm not going to run, London." I held his stare, lowering my voice. *"You know that."*

He gave a nod, then turned and strode out of my bedroom with long, commanding strides, making me hurry to catch up. We were down the stairs in an instant, heading through the house to the garage. My stomach clenched when I scanned the garage and saw the black Mercedes he'd abducted me in.

But he didn't head to that. Instead, he lifted his hand and aimed the remote at a sleek black Audi parked next to it. "Get in," he commanded...

And I didn't have to be told twice.

I climbed in and yanked the seatbelt across, clasping it as London started the engine and hit the button for the garage door. We tore away from the house in an instant, hit the bottom of the driveway, and accelerated hard as we raced through the night.

My mind was a mess, trying to put it all together. Had I misjudged London somehow? Was he actually...*the good guy in all this and not the asshole I thought he was?* My stomach sank at the thought. Maybe I had him all wrong? *Shit...shit shit shit.* What an idiot. I'd been fighting him this entire time and he'd been *what? Spying. Scheming. Finding a way for me to escape with Ryth?*

Excitement took hold.

"London..." I turned to him in the soft wash of the dashboard lights.

But that's all that came out. The words froze in the back of my throat, lodged there with the memory of his hands...and the way he looked at me. He was the good guy here. Still, I couldn't stop a ripple of fear from shaking me as I turned my head. My pussy clenched as my gaze traveled from the rolled sleeves of his black shirt to the faint silvering of hair at the edge of his temple. The man was old enough to be my father and savage enough to be my tormentor.

"Keep looking at me like that, Vivienne, and I might just pull this damn car over to the side of the road and make use of that perfect mouth of yours."

Heat burned in my cheeks. I swallowed the burn, refusing to let him see how much he'd rattled me. "Do that and I might just fight you every step of the fucking way."

He just smirked and changed gears in a seamless transition. "Defiant just enough to keep things interesting and yet aching to be submissive," he murmured as he glanced my way, then said with utmost certainty. "One day, Vivienne, you will choke on my goddamn cock...*and you'll fucking love it*."

That heat seared in my cheeks. I jerked my gaze away and turned to the darkened city streets as I fought the need to lick my lips. I swallowed as I wondered what he might taste like... and how he'd look as he loomed over me, those chilling, empty eyes pinning me in place while he fucked good and hard.

Oh God...oh God. I clamped my hand between my thighs. He noticed, then turned back with a smirk. *Fucking asshole.* How the fuck had I ever thought he was a *nice guy*? He wasn't a nice guy, even if he was turning me loose to run with Ryth. London was a goddamn snake.

He turned, accelerated hard, and turned again. I scanned the buildings around us. It didn't matter how many streets I tried to memorize, I didn't know this city at all. I didn't know how long we drove for, but we seemed to find our way to some back street behind an old apartment building.

London slowed the Audi, then pulled into a gated underground parking garage. One that was locked, except for one section that seemed like it had been left open for us alone. I gripped the armrest, then flinched as he turned sharply and braked hard, swung in the pitch-black gloom, and parked.

The engine died in an instant, leaving a *tick, tick, tick* behind. London didn't speak as he climbed out and closed the door behind him. Then he was gone, leaving me to release my seatbelt and reach for the door handle. But it opened before I had a chance to pull the lever.

"Vivienne," he murmured.

My pulse thrummed as I climbed out, unable to take my gaze from him.

"Stay close," he ordered as he closed the door behind me and reached into his pocket for a small flashlight. "This place hasn't been used in a while."

The bright light was instant, illuminating the empty parking area. I opened my mouth to say *what?* But he was already moving, striding out into the dark, leaving me to scramble after him once more. All I thought about was Ryth as I ran. Ryth, who'd promised to take me with her. Ryth that had felt the closest I'd ever had to family. We'd run together, her, me, and her stepbrothers. We'd leave this place and never look back.

London stopped at a set of chained glass doors, but the chain hung free. The lock was snapped and lay on the ground, the shorn bolt glinting under the wash of the bright light. Hinges howled and grated as London opened the door and motioned me inside.

"We'll need to take the stairs," he said. "The elevator is inoperable."

"Is Ryth up there?" I asked. "Is she up on the roof?"

But he didn't answer, just strode past heading for a door. I focused on my steps, wincing at the filthy floor. The place didn't just look unused. It looked *abandoned*. London climbed and I followed, clenching my hands into fists to not touch the peeling paint on the railing...

That lasted until I hit the third floor. My breaths had turned heavier and hotter, leaving me to ignore the filth and grab the damn thing instead. By the fifth floor, I was gasping and out of breath. London barely seemed to be breathing heavy, his steps strong and sure, and I hated that.

"London..." I gasped, losing count of exactly what floor this was. He stopped and turned. His face was flushed in the glow of the flashlight. "Ryth...is she..."

"Three more flights to go, Vivienne, then you get to see her. You want to see her, right?" His gaze bored into mine

I gave a nod, straightened, then kept going...*three more...just three more...two now*. I lifted my gaze as we rounded the landing, and kept pushing. My stomach clenched, that burn now a searing rasp in my chest. Higher and higher. By the time London slowed, grasped a door and yanked it open, I felt like my soul was leaving my body.

Cold air rushed at us, carrying with it a faint *crack... crack...crack!*

"What the hell?" I gasped, following London out onto the roof of the building. The further I came, the louder the sound got.

Crack!

Crack!

CRACK!

I flinched, yet drawn by the sound as London moved closer to the edge. Sparks flared in the street below, bright against the dark. It took me a second to realize what I was looking at. "Is this some kind of training exercise?"

CRACK.

CRACK.

CRACK!

I jerked, sucking in hard breaths, unable to know where to look as men dressed in black raced around the corner of a building and opened fire.

"No training exercise, Vivienne," London answered, taking a step closer as movement peeked out from the edge of the building. I barely saw them as four figures stepped backwards and fired back.

An icy grip of terror moved through me as I whispered. "What is this?"

Those figures moved further out into the empty street, desperately firing back as their attackers advanced, and as they did, they became clearer...it was a woman...*a familiar woman...*

"You wanted to see her." London snarled. "So see her."

A moan tore free as I narrowed in on Ryth as she unleashed a guttural scream of desperation and fired the gun in her hand.

I jerked my gaze to his. *"What the hell are you doing?"* I stepped closer to the edge, flinching with every *pop* of gunfire that reached me. *"They're firing at them!"*

"They are."

I tore my focus away, searching the empty streets as my pulse boomed in my ears. Movement came from further behind them with the shine of headlights as they splashed against a building, and a dark SUV skidded to a stop.

They were boxed in. No way forward...and no way back. The sudden realization dawned on me. Blood drained from my face. "You bastard." I turned my gaze to those unflinching eyes. "You cold, *ruthless, fucking bastard.* You meant for me to see this all along? You dragged me up here for *what? To watch her brothers die and her to be taken back* THERE?"

He didn't look away, just stared down my fear and murmured. "If you want Ryth and her brothers to survive this, then you will tell The Order what they need to know to sign you over to me. You *will* not cause me problems, do you hear me?"

He turned toward me and took a step closer. Seamless. Smooth. Sliding close like a snake in the water. He moved against me, that punishing stare seized mine as the *crack...crack...crack* of gunfire sounded. "You *will* obey my commands. You *will* belong to me, in any way I see fit. You do that, and I'll get them out."

Sawing breaths cut me to the core.

"You do that, and I'll save her. You *do that,* and I'll allow her to live. But you *will* obey me, Vivienne. I will have no more disobedience. Do I make myself clear?"

I didn't think, I just acted, lifted my hand, cocked it backwards, and lashed out.

SLAP!

His head jerked to the side as I felt the sting in the palm of my hand. "You *bastard...you fucking...bastard.*"

He slowly turned his gaze back to me, rage glinting in that pitiless stare as his phone started to ring. Jaw muscles clenched, nostrils flared, he wanted to hurt me in that moment. I could see that. As he swiped the icon and answered the call, I realized that he could...*with just one command.*

Dread moved through me as he answered. "Are you in position?" His voice was husky, his question raw.

I shook my head, unable to speak. Fists clenched at my sides, I held onto that sting in my palm as my entire body started to shake. Not once did he look away, not to the attack below, nor to the stars sparkling in the sky above. All he looked at was me.

"Wait," I whispered, shaking my head. "Please don't do this."

Something moved between us. A chilling clarity.

He stopped speaking, his gaze fixed as I lowered my head. *Defiant just enough to keep things interesting and yet aching to be submissive.* My fate foretold. He knew with one look...he knew he'd won. In a low, careful tone, he gave the command. "Engage."

THIRTY-EIGHT

Ryth

W E WEREN'T GOING TO MAKE IT...I KNEW THAT WITH ONE look in Nick's eyes as he unleashed a savage roar and kept shooting. *Crack...crack...crackcrackcrack...*

I didn't flinch at the sounds, just kept pulling the trigger until a resounding empty *click* came. Tobias jerked his gaze to mine and handed me another magazine...

I lowered my gaze to his belt, to the last magazine tucked in the waistband of his pants, and shook my head. "Save it." I looked at him. "You'll hit more."

Crack!

Crack.

He kept firing...

Click.

Desperation gleamed in his eyes as he replaced his own spent clip, tossing the empty magazine to the ground. My ears were ringing so loud I didn't even hear the steel hit the asphalt.

"I'm almost out, T," Caleb groaned. *Crack! Crack! Crack...click.*

Caleb stepped backwards as three of The Order's men hiding behind the corner of the building returned fire.

Crack!

Shots came behind us. I stumbled to the side and pressed my spine against the side of an empty building. I scanned the others, searching, desperately thinking. If we went in there, we'd be cornered in an instant. But if we stayed here, we'd be dead in the street—*not me, though, right?* Not me.

I turned to Nick as he snarled and trained his sight on movement before he pulled the trigger.

All The Order had to do was wait.

Wait for us to run out of bullets.

Wait for us to fall.

My stomach clenched tight.

We...weren't...going...to...make...it.

"Tobias," I whispered. I'd never spoken his name like that, not with so much desperation.

He shook his head. "No, little mouse." His jaw clenched with savage ferocity as he aimed and squeezed the trigger. "Not... gonna...fucking...happen."

But it had to.

There was no way out.

And a life locked away in Hell, knowing they still drew breath, was better than a world without them. My tears blurred the gray concrete buildings across the road.

I'd give myself up, knowing they were still out there, knowing that while they drew breath, there was still a chance we'd all be together.

"I have to." Didn't he see that? I took a step out from the side of the building, but with a brutal growl, he lunged, slammed his arm across my body, and flattened me to the wall beside him once more.

"That's not going to happen. DO YOU HEAR ME?" His eyes were wild with fear, that quickly turned to desperation as his roar softened. *"I'd rather die."*

I shook my head, tears flowing silently down my cheeks. I turned to my father. "Can't you do something? *ANYTHING!*"

He just shook his head. "I can't. King is too far away and more of The Order are coming."

There were more *coming?*

So we were trapped.

Like rats.

I spun and unleashed a scream that burned like acid in the back of my throat. There had to be away. There had to be *something*. But I knew. I knew that was a lie.

Click.

Movement came from the corner of my eye as the door next to Nick opened...and two men stepped out.

"What the fuck?" Nick growled, freezing for a second before he realized they weren't with us.

Then he flung back his fist and lunged. Until one of them lifted a gun and aimed it point blank at his head. "Try it and none of you will get out of this alive."

Nick froze. I looked from one to the other. They were identical, except for stark white bleached hair on one of them. It was the white-haired guy who spoke, still aiming his gun at Nick's head. "You want a way out of this, then follow us, or you can stay out here and die." He lowered his gun and took a step back in the darker doorway as the dark-haired twin turned and disappeared into the building.

Nick glanced at Caleb, then Tobias, and me before he stepped forward, grabbed me by the arm, and dragged me with him. We plunged into the darkness of the building, leaving the crack of gunfire behind.

"We have to hurry," Blondie growled, and lifted his phone. He pressed an icon and said one word. "Now."

There was a second…

A second where Tobias, dad, and Caleb rushed in behind us. *BOOM!* I jerked, then spun, staring at the now closed door behind us.

"Don't worry, it's one of ours," he announced, then kept walking, leaving us behind.

"Ours?" Nick barked. *"Who the fuck is 'ours'?"*

The blonde man came to stop in the middle of the warehouse in front of a dark tarpaulin. "Those who are here to save your asses."

I sucked in hard breaths, looking at one twin, then the other, as Caleb strode forward. "Who the fuck do you work for?"

"I know you," Dad murmured. "I've seen you before."

"Impossible," the blonde warned. "Now do you want to talk, or get out of this alive?"

"How?" Nick swung his hand in an arc. "We're fucking surrounded."

BOOM! I flinched as another explosion rocked the air. The blonde asshole didn't even blink, instead he answered, "That's how. So, are we going to do this, or what?"

"Do what, exactly?" Caleb growled.

Blondie bent down, grabbed one corner of the tarpaulin, and yanked it backwards. I flinched and sucked in hard breaths as I stared at the pile of dead bodies, three men and a woman.

"What the fuck is this?" Nick barked, jerking his gaze to the pale-haired twin standing in front of us.

"Let's call this a contract, shall we?" A deep, resounding voice came from behind us.

I spun, then froze as I saw the same man who'd had Vivienne pressed against the wall the last time I saw her, striding toward us, and behind him was... *"Vivienne?"*

She was pale, and strange, giving me just a ghost of a smile as she followed him. I lunged across the warehouse, scrambling toward her.

"Ryth, NO!" my father roared.

But he was too late. I was already opening my arms as she broke away from the man's side to grab me and pull me close.

"Jesus, *Ryth*." She wrapped her arms around me, then pushed me back, scanning my body. "Are you hurt? *Did they hit you?"*

"No, they didn't fucking hit her," Tobias snarled. "Who the fuck are you?"

I just couldn't stop looking at her, at the desperation in her eyes or her beautiful clothes. "Are you okay?" I gripped her arm, feeling the warmth of her flesh. "I thought I'd never see you again."

"Me, too," she smiled, then pulled me close again to whisper in my ear. *"You need to be careful."*

Need to be careful? I pulled back, searching her eyes.

"London St. James," my father stated coldly.

"Jack Castlemaine," the man responded.

The deep snarl in my father's tone made me turn and look at the bodies again, then the rest of them.

"What the fuck is this?" Nick snapped.

"Let's call this an agreement." London started looking over his shoulder at me, then Vivienne. "One that needs to be made rather quickly, I'm afraid. I'm sure you already know there are more of The Order coming. They'll be here in a matter of minutes to capture their asset and return to the compound."

*Capture their asset...*he meant me. Me, I'm their *asset.*

"That's never going to happen," Dad growled as he shook his head.

"I'm glad you agree," St. James answered. "My men will keep them at bay while we assist with the escape." He turned to Tobias and Nick when he said that.

Nick scowled. "You'll help us get out?"

"I will," he nodded, meeting Nick's glare. "For a price."

Caleb grew still. Under the cracks of gunfire that still sounded outside the building, he asked quietly. "And what price is that?"

"I think a fair one is *a life for a life."*

I grew cold, then stepped closer until I stopped in front of those bodies. I couldn't look away. Three men that looked nothing like my stepbrothers, and a woman who was supposed to be me. But there were only three men—I glanced at dad—there were five of us.

"A life for a life," London repeated as he looked at my father. "Is a fair price."

Dad shook his head, his face turning ashen.

"You didn't think you'd just be able to walk away, Jack. Not with everything you know."

Dad shot me a panicked look. *You need to be careful...not with everything you know.* "What do you know, Dad?"

He looked sickened.

"A life for a life," London continued. "I get Ryth and her brothers out of the city, and in return, you'll stay with me."

"Locked away, you mean?" dad met the bastard's gaze.

Crack...crack...crack! Gunfire intruded again from outside.

"Time's running out," London said coldly. "In a minute, not even I will be able to help."

"Do they know?" Dad's tone was unsteady. "Do they know you plot and scheme behind their backs?"

London's answer was a slow, chilling smile.

The blonde twin lifted his phone and answered. "Yeah?" He looked at London.

"Time is up," London declared. "I need an answer, Jack, your life for your daughter's."

I shook my head as my chest tightened and my throat clenched. "No, Dad. No."

We'd already done this before, already traded his life for mine. We couldn't do it again. Not with this man...because I had the terrifying feeling there was no getting out of this, not this time, not with him.

But Dad met my gaze. "My little lioness."

Movement happened so fast all around me.

Like the world, with its brutal orchestra of death and violence and loss, just...carried on.

While a black hole opened up under my feet...and swallowed me whole.

THIRTY-NINE

Ryth

Movement blurred all around me.

The bodies were piled in a corner.

Stacks of debris were set alight.

The roller door to the garage was raised, casting the bitter sting of smoke into my eyes.

My lovers moved with the rest of them, barking orders, firing shots as we moved.

In the middle, stood my father. He stared at me, his dark eyes filled with so much sadness. I swallowed, but not even my saliva would slip around the fist in the back of my throat. "Dad..." I croaked. "Please, no."

He stepped closer. "It has to be this way, Ryth. Better for you, safer for you. They'll never stop coming, otherwise. You understand that, right? They'll never stop." He looked at London, who was on his phone, barking orders and giving commands.

Nick glanced my way as he grabbed a plastic gasoline can from the floor and poured it all over the bodies in the corner.

I shook my head as tears slipped down my cheeks. *"I can't leave you."*

Dad grabbed my hand, dwarfing it with his as he swiped my tears away, and murmured. "You're going to have to, sweetheart. You're going to have to, and you're going to need to carry on. I know—" He swallowed hard, then looked away. "I know you might not carry my blood, but you are my heart." He forced his gaze back to mine. "When a man gives his heart, he gives it wholly and to the end. You are my daughter, my heart, my *life*. I would gladly, in a thousand different ways, hand that over for yours."

Tears flowed and they'd never stop falling.

I couldn't speak.

Could only shudder and weep.

"You need to go now," London commanded.

I sniffled, smearing my tears and mucus with the back of my hand as Dad pulled me against his chest. "I love you. Never stop believing that."

"*Now*, Jack," London snapped.

Dad grabbed my shoulders and gently pushed me back. "Now, I need you to go, my lioness. Become the woman you were always meant to be. Love. Love so fucking hard you feel torn in two." He glanced toward Nick as my stepbrother stepped closer. "They'll protect you, sweetheart." He met my gaze. "They'll keep you safe."

One small shove and I stumbled backwards.

"Princess..." strong arms wrapped around my waist and pulled me toward a car.

"No," I shook my head. "No, Dad. *Please...*"

But Dad didn't move, just stared at me as his eyes glistened, and finally he turned away. Nick had to all but drag me to the car. Car doors opened and slammed shut. Tobias was a blur behind my tears as he leaned across me in the backseat, yanked my seatbelt into place, and snapped it shut.

"WAIT!" Dad roared. *"Wait a minute!"*

I spun, twisted in my seat, and shoved my door open.

"I need a pen..." Dad barked, rushing toward me. *"Someone give me a goddamn pen!"*

My brothers twisted in their seats. "We don't have time for this," Caleb warned as gunfire echoed all around us.

"Here for *Christ's sake!*" London roared as he reached into his pocket and pulled out a pen.

Dad frantically scanned the floor, then lunged and grabbed up a filthy napkin as he rushed toward the car. "Here," he panted, leaning above me.

I could hear the scratching of the pen on the car roof before dad shoved the napkin at me. "Here. I kept this for you. I figured..." his brow creased. "I figured we might've needed it together. But I want you to have it. Use it to keep you safe. Don't ever come back here." He nodded at Nick as he stepped away and gripped the door. "Don't ever come back."

Bang!

We were already moving as Dad slammed the door and the four-wheel drive lunged forward as The Order's men came rushing into the far side of the building. *Crack...crack...crack...*I didn't flinch, didn't care, just twisted in my seat to watch my father as he passed through the open doorway, ducking for cover.

There were men firing back at The Order. Men I could only assume were London's. They blurred as we raced past, tearing away from the carcasses of forgotten buildings and headed toward the streets...

"Fuck!" Nick slammed on the brakes, throwing me forward.

Then we were reversing hard before skidding to a stop once more. Nick shoved open his door and whistled shrilly, the sharp sound piercing my grief.

"Rebel!" he yelled. *"Here, girl!"*

Rebel?

I jerked my blurred focus to Tobias's window. A blur of black came running, tore around one of the Explorers The Order had left behind, and raced toward us.

"Rebel!" I spluttered as she leaped through Nick's open door and clambered inside.

Bang! He yanked the door closed and punched the accelerator as Caleb grabbed her, patting her head, smoothing her ears. "Easy now." he soothed. "Easy..."

Tobias held me as we sped away. I glanced over my shoulder, to the open door of the warehouse. But Dad was gone, they were all gone, leaving thick plumes of smoke to pour out.

BOOM!

I jerked as an explosion rocked the night and the warehouse we'd left disintegrated. Chunks of concrete and debris flew outwards, and dropped into the street. Then we were gone, tearing away from the empty streets littered with the dead.

I felt numb. Cold and empty. Separate from myself. Tobias held onto me, his body shaking just like mine. I didn't remember how we got out of the city, only that we did. Buildings became the highway and cars were traded for trees. We drove and kept on driving, until the sun peeked over the horizon, the bright rays hurting my eyes.

"Ryth," Nick called, making me slowly lift my head to his reflection in the rear-view mirror. "You okay?"

I wanted to say no, that I didn't think I'd ever be okay.

But that's not what dad would've wanted.

He would've told me to be strong, to learn from this. To *grow* from this. To hold onto those who I loved and who loved me in return…and never let go. So, I swallowed and forced myself to speak. "I will be."

Caleb turned around and reached for my hand. "You will. We all will. We'll do it together."

I gripped his hand as he smiled awkwardly at me.

"There's a truck stop ahead. We can stop, shower, grab some food, then keep driving," Nick suggested.

So we did, and pulled into the parking lot. In the back of the four-wheel drive, we found a small case filled with money, fake passports, and IDs. *Stevie Jacobs.* I stared at the name and my face on the card, then looked at Nick.

"Hunter." He lifted his.

"Adrian." Caleb winced.

"Jesus…" Tobias stared at his, his lips curling. "What kind of fucking name is Samuel?"

"A safe name." I stepped closer, pushed his hand with the ID down, and caressed his cheek. "A careful name. A name I'll call you for the rest of our lives."

He flinched as though he finally understood. "For the rest of our lives?"

I drew in the stench of smoke that clung to our clothes, and answered. "I'll call you anything. A name doesn't matter. To me you'll always be Tobias." I turned my head. "And you'll always be Nick and Caleb." I met C's gaze. "You'll always be the men I fell in love with. The ones who protected me, who fought for me...who *bled for me.* You'll always be..."

"Mine," T finished, pulling me closer. "You'll always be mine."

"The napkin," Nick spoke. "The one your dad gave you. What did it say?"

I hugged T tight, then pulled away. "Nothing, just a bunch of numbers."

"Let me see." Nick held out his hand.

I reached into my pocket, gently retrieved it so it didn't tear, and handed it over. He looked at it for barely a second. "It's a bank account number."

I scowled. "How do you know?"

"The numbers of digits," he answered, and lifted his gaze to mine. "Did he tell you anything else at all?"

I shook my head. "Maybe it was a college fund? We can use whatever is in there, it might keep us going for a month or two."

Nick shook his head and handed the napkin back. "We won't need it. I've got that covered."

"Wait, no. Your money is all tied—" I started.

"It's liquidated," he answered.

Both Tobias and Caleb glanced his way. "Everything?" C asked.

Nick just nodded. "Everything. The buildings, the crypto, the accounts. We have enough to last, as long as we're careful."

The warmth drained from my face. "To last how long?"

He held my stare. "Forever."

Forever? The night seemed to sway. I reached out and grasped Tobias's arm.

"Whoa, little mouse." T gripped me tightly. "You okay?"

It all made sense now. The night in Ben's office when he'd closed himself off from the rest of us, that's what he'd been doing. That's what he was doing when he...the memory of his tongue invaded, making my body tremble.

Nick handed me the napkin. "Keep it. Let it sit and gather interest. That way, you have an out if you want it."

"An out?"

He gave a shrug. "If one day you change your mind."

One day you'll want more...

"No," I snapped as those words came back to haunt me. "I don't want an out. Not now, not ever. So I'm going to put this away for when, or if, we might need it and if we don't, then I'm sure I'll figure out a way to use it."

Nick gave a slow, sad smile as I gently folded the napkin and slipped it into my pocket. In the back of the car was another bag with clothes and guns, ones none of us wanted to touch, not knowing it came from London St. James. But we did, with the clothes under one arm and Tobias' hand in mine, we headed for the truck stop. No one stopped us when we made use of the facilities, washing our hair and drying with paper towels, until we stepped out fresher than we'd gone in.

We grabbed food, drinks, and snacks, filled the four-wheel drive's gas tank, and kept on driving.

We pushed hard. My brothers took turns behind the wheel while the others slept. I tried to, but the sound of gunfire still echoed when I closed my eyes, making me jerk awake with my heart hammering as my whimpers stuck in the back of my throat. Rebel seemed to be exhausted as she drank bottled water and ate some dog food from bowls Nick had surprisingly found on a shelf. But she slept on the floor of the car at my feet.

Until slowly, the day slipped away.

"We're staying at a motel," Caleb muttered, waking Nick in the front passenger seat. "We need a bed and a shower and more than canned food."

He pulled into the parking lot of the next decent-looking motel we saw, parked and climbed out, then disappeared as he headed for the office. He returned a few minutes later with two sets of keys, climbed back behind the wheel, and pulled the four-wheel drive further back from the street, parking it outside two adjoining doors.

"Don't worry." Caleb climbed out, shaking the keys. "I got us connecting rooms."

My back was killing me and my legs felt like jelly. It took me a few minutes to get feeling back into my legs after I climbed out. Then we gathered our things and went inside, me with Tobias, Nick and Caleb in the adjoining room. The first thing I did was open the door between us. Not for one second did I want us apart.

Never again...

Never ever again.

FORTY

Ryth

"Dibs on first shower," Tobias demanded the moment I stepped inside the room.

He grabbed me around the waist, lifted me into the air, and placed me gently out of his way.

Just like that, he was back to the same old obnoxious Tobias.

Not even a gunfight and the fact we were running for our lives had changed him. He flicked on the light in the bathroom as I unloaded the bags of toiletries from the truck stop. When I looked up, Caleb waited for me in the connecting doorway and gave a raised brow at T as the bathroom door closed with a *thud*.

"I bet he never even asked you," C said as he shook his head.

"I did!" T called out. "I called first dibs."

"That's not really asking now, is it?" C shot back. "Want to use ours?"

"God, yes," I sighed gratefully. "I'm about to burst."

Caleb moved out of the way as Nick carried the rest of our things into their room and closed the door. He glanced my way as I hurried into their bathroom, switched on the light and closed the door.

"I'll go and see about finding us some food," Nick murmured behind the door.

I dropped my jeans and sat on the toilet, listening to their voices grow hushed as hard, racking shudders shook me. Tears followed, tears that still stung no matter how many gas stations I'd washed my face in. Tears that seemed to never stop coming.

I tried to focus on peeing, but it seemed my body was set on expelling my moisture through my eyes. I closed my eyes, sighed with the relief. By the time I'd washed my hands and stepped out, Caleb had cracked open a bottle of electrolytes and had it sitting on the small table in front of him.

"Drink," he commanded. "Your body needs to hydrate."

I didn't fight. I was tired of fighting, so I just strode to the table as he sat on the chair with his legs crossed and watched me grab the drink. The hiss of the shower sounded in our bathroom. I drank while Caleb watched me.

"Want to talk about what happened?"

My pulse thundered at the thought. Screams waited. Screams, and Viv's haunted stare. *Be careful.* Gunshots followed and Tobias's desperation as I'd almost...as I'd almost...*as I'd almost.* My hands started to shake, sloshing the drink in the bottle. "I'd rather fuck. Can we do that?" I jerked my gaze to his. "Can we please do that instead?"

He rose from the chair, sleek and soundless, and stepped closer to caress my cheek. "If that's what you want."

I nodded and tore my shirt over my head even as my hands shook. "I don't want to think." I stilled, staring at him. "Please, Caleb, please help me not to think."

He came closer, grabbed the shirt from my hand, and dropped it to the floor before he pulled me against him. "I can do that, princess. I can do that for now. But promise me one thing." He pulled back, searching my gaze with his. "Don't use sex with us to shut yourself away. Feel it, feel everything, the hate and the loss and the suffering. Because that's what keeps you here with us. That's what keeps you the beautiful, caring, perfect sister we know."

"Because we cannot lose you, too," Tobias murmured as he stood in the doorway between our rooms wearing nothing but a towel.

Caleb's thumb stroked my back, then hooked my bra strap as Tobias came closer. I tracked his movement from the corner of my eye, until he gently captured my chin, turning my mouth to his. "You're gonna get me filthy again, aren't you, little mouse?" he murmured next to my lips.

God, yes...

The motel room door opened then closed as Tobias kissed me.

"Figured we'd all be hun—" Nick started and stopped. I broke the kiss and turned my head to watch him as he set a plastic bag filled with fast food on the small table and finished with a mutter, "—gry."

The food was forgotten as Nick stepped away from the table, kicked off his boots, and dragged his shirt over his head. There were no words needed. We all needed this. Clothes were flung all over as we climbed onto the bed.

Nick slid his hand along my arm, staring into my eyes. "Christ, I never thought we'd—"

I hushed him, crawled forward to kiss the words from his mouth, then speared my fingers through his hair. I climbed on top of him and reached for the button of his jeans as Caleb tugged my boots off and peeled my socks from my feet.

"No more talking," I whispered, arching my back as Caleb cupped my breasts. "No more thinking, no more fighting. Just this..." Nick rose from the pillow, gripped my waist, and licked my nipple.

I closed my eyes, shuddering at the feel of his mouth...*I never thought we'd*...the words rose and I pushed them away, smothering them with the feel of Nick's beautiful mouth. "God, I want this," I groaned as I opened my eyes to look down. He looked up and our gazes collided.

"As do we, princess." Caleb brushed my hair to the side and kissed my neck. "Forever."

I shuddered at the word...*forever*.

Nick pushed my jeans low. "Tell us how you want it, baby," he growled, then shifted his gaze to Caleb.

"However you need it." Caleb gripped the back of my neck and turned my gaze to his. "We want you to take from us."

"All of us." Tobias tugged the towel from around his waist, leaving it to drop on the floor. "For as long as you need it."

I did, rising up to kiss Caleb. I shoved my jeans and my panties all the way down, and eased Nick's cock inside, riding him nice and slow while I stared into Caleb's dark eyes. I drank his darkness down, swallowed it whole as Nick held me steady against him and kissed my breasts.

This was more than sex tonight, more than desire.

This was the kind of comfort I could only find with them.

The three of them.

I rolled my hips, giving in to the feel of Nick as he stretched me. Caleb's stare didn't waver, searching my eyes until Tobias' gentle lips came at my other shoulder. Then I closed my eyes and lifted my hand, finding the raspy hairs on his cheek, and let the feeling of them take over as Nick grunted, wound his arm tighter around my waist, and picked up the pace.

My bruised, beaten body jolted with his thrusts.

"Oh, *fuck*," Nick growled, driving me down against him as he bucked his hips. I opened my eyes, found his, and that connection howled louder than any scream inside my head. "*Princess*," he groaned, then gave one hard thrust...and came.

I kept rocking, desperately needing the feel of him, but he shifted his body and rolled me over to lie against the pillow, then he slipped free. Caleb lowered his head and kissed my hip, then lifted and worked his way upwards, settling between my thighs. I moaned as he entered me, thrusting harder, taking more.

They would run with me...

All three of them would run, forever if it meant we'd be together.

My heart thundered with the thought of that, swelling and rising as Caleb gripped my hips, then leaned over, braced himself on either side of me, and thrust hard. I gripped his body as my own climax approached. My breaths turned hard, fast, and jagged.

"Jesus...*Ryth*," Caleb groaned against my ear. "I can't..."

I wrapped my legs around his waist and stared into his eyes. There was a spark of fear before that connection took hold. Then all I saw was the love he had for me. The things he'd done, the risks he'd taken, the battle that had scared him just like they'd scared me. His cock drove harder, deeper, as that utter devotion in his stare took hold.

Until he stopped, and his cock twitched inside me as he dropped his head and gave a low, guttural groan against my ear as he came. I sucked in hard breaths, lying there as he slowly pulled away, kissing me on the lips before he slid from the bed.

I lay there, hard pants consuming me...

But I wasn't done.

I wasn't anywhere near done.

The bed dipped, making me lift my head from the pillow.

"Little mouse," Tobias growled.

I lifted my head to him, to the man who'd started this all.

They'd thought it was me who'd crash landed in their world. But it wasn't. I was a ghost on their doorstep. I was *no one*. I knew that now. Knew it by the remnant of my mother's slap on my cheek and by that emptiness that had always engulfed me. I was nothing more than an empty shell when I came into their lives.

They were the ones who had filled me.

They were the ones who'd made me whole.

And it had all started with Tobias.

I rose from the bed, my body aching and throbbing with the need for release. Tobias dragged his gaze along my body and reached out, finding the slick between my legs. "Still needy, little mouse?"

"Always, when it comes to you."

There was a second when the charged energy crackled in the room, then we both lunged and collided. He gripped me hard, then turned, throwing me sideways against the bed.

"Mine." He shoved my thighs wide, winced with a pang of pain as he shifted his weight, and slammed his cock inside. "Ours."

I gripped his shoulders as he thrust. He wasn't gentle, taking me savagely. It was just what I needed. My climax was brutal and raw, taking me by surprise. I clenched my jaw and bared my teeth and, as I came, the bastard grinned.

"That's the way, little sister," he grunted as I moaned and shuddered. "That's the fucking way."

I gasped and clawed at him, pulling him down on top of me. "You. Fucking. Love. Me."

He lifted his head, those intense brown eyes filled with all the answer I needed. "More than anything else in this world."

He gripped my wrists, slid them over my head, and owned me…

Body.

Mind.

Soul.

FORTY-ONE

Ryth

We slept, tangled in each other's arms, drifting into the darkness. Only we didn't stay there, waking every so often to turn to each other. Gentle brushes of lips. The soft stroke of a hand, until the weight settled against me. Sleep wasn't welcome, not when we were so raw.

When I woke in the morning, I was alone. Faint light spilled in between the closed blinds. For a second, fear moved in, making my heart hammer. I jerked my head up from the pillow, to see Caleb sitting on the chair, watching me. "Easy, princess," he reassured. "We thought you could use a sleep-in."

I sucked in hard breaths, trying to quell the pounding of my heart. "What time is it?"

"A little after ten."

"Shit." I kicked out at the blanket. "We need to—"

Caleb rose and crossed the small space between us to caress the mark on my cheek. "The only thing you need to do right now is to breathe and relax."

The door to the next room opened and closed and it took me a second to remember that it was my room next door.

"There she is," Tobias muttered as he stepped through the connecting door and headed for me, bending low to kiss me on the lips. "You sleep okay?"

"Kinda," I answered.

He gave a slow nod, the dark circles under his eyes telling me he'd slept the same. In fact, we all looked the same.

"We ate all the food from last night." T gave a shrug. "So I jogged down to the bakery to get you this."

He lifted a small paper bag in one hand, then a coffee cup in his other. "And this." The smell of the brew made me groan and reach for it. But he just chuckled and pulled away at the last minute. "Easy. Not so fast. What are you going to do for it, first?"

"What?"

"I mean." He gave a shrug. "I had to run for this."

A smile tugged at the corners of my mouth. I scowled and crossed my arms over my bare breasts. "What do you want for it?"

He scowled, squinted, then lunged, dropping the bakery bag onto the end of the bed to push me backwards. "How about you, baby?"

I let out a bark of laughter, glancing at the cup. "Better not have spilled that."

He just smiled, then eased away and handed over the cup. "What do you take me for?"

The outer door to the other room opened and closed, and the familiar thud of Nick's steps echoed through the door.

"Someone's wasting damn time," he growled, looking at the cup in my hand as he came into our room. "Want to eat that on the road, I kind of want to get moving?"

"Sure." I pushed up from the bed. "Can I grab a shower?"

"Absolutely." He gave me a smile. "I'll get our things together."

I took a sip of coffee and headed for our bathroom, shaking my head the moment I stepped inside. Wet towels were dropped in a pile on the floor but there was a fresh set sitting on the counter for me. I closed the door, reached in and turned on the faucets to adjust the temperature, and stepped in. By the time I was done, I felt more alive than I had in a long time.

"Knock, knock," Caleb murmured as he turned the handle and opened the door. "Figured you could do with some clean clothes."

He handed me the same ones I'd worn yesterday, only this time they were freshly washed and dried. "Thanks." I grabbed the clothes and pulled them on.

"Nick's organized a replacement car." Caleb leaned against the doorframe and watched me as I tugged my jeans up and reached for my bra.

"Oh?" I murmured as he stepped closer, slid the straps over my shoulders, and worked the hooks in the back, then slid his finger to adjust the band.

"He said it'll keep us going until we find somewhere to settle."

"Settle?" I turned around.

He met my stare. "For a while at least."

I hadn't thought of what would happen now. I knew The Order were going to look for us until they were given a reason not to.

How long that was, I didn't know. Caleb handed me my shirt and I slipped it on. I guessed our new life started with a new car to go with our new names.

"Promise me you'll never forget me," I pleaded, meeting his stare. "The real me."

"Ryth, you'll always be the real you to me, and to all of us. A name is just a name. Besides," he gave me a wink. "You'll always be our little sister."

I laughed as I followed him out and pulled on my boots. My coffee was barely warm when we piled into London St. James's car and pulled out of the motel parking lot. I ate, shared my bagel with Rebel, and finished my coffee as we pulled into the dealership's parking lot.

I glanced around as I stepped out and found a row of shops across the street, then turned to Nick. "I'm going to be across the road, okay?"

Nick stopped, glanced across the street, and scowled.

"It'll be okay." T gave a shrug. "Buying cars bores the shit out of me anyway, and I could do with some new clothes."

Nick gave a slow nod. "Not out of sight, okay, princess?"

I smiled, he was back to being the big brother. "Deal."

He stood there watching as Tobias and I turned and walked away. T grabbed my hand as we crossed the road and headed for the stores. He was touchy, more than Nick and Caleb. His thumb ran the length of mine as we stepped up onto the sidewalk. "Where first, baby?" He glanced my way.

I scanned the shops and my gaze lingered on the internet cafe. "There."

"You sure?" He cut me a look, one that said, *careful*.

"I'm not going to do anything stupid."

One nod and he motioned me forward. We went inside and he broke away almost instantly and headed to the counter of the small yuppie cafe. He motioned to me, waited for the guy to start the timer for me to log on, and ordered us coffee to go. But I was never out of his sight. I sat down and pulled out the napkin Dad gave me. It kind of felt surreal now. Had that all happened? The gun fight, the terror...Dad handing himself over for the second time to keep me safe.

As I opened up the folded napkin, I knew every brutal second of it had been real.

My pulse thundered as I opened up the browser and punched in the bank ID number. A second later, I had the name Jericho Bank and a phone number for customer service, which I wrote down my own napkin with a pen someone had left behind. Tobias glanced my way as he grabbed the coffees and strode over.

"Do you think I can use your phone?"

"Sure, baby." He handed it over, then glanced at the computer screen before he whispered. "I'm just going to be over there if you need anything."

He took his coffee and headed to a bulletin board to give me a little space. I grabbed his phone, called the number listed, and waited for it to be answered. A few minutes later and a number of personal detail questions, I waited while she verified my answers and retrieved the information about the account.

"Ms. Castlemaine?"

"Yes?"

"Um, sorry for the wait. I had to verify the details of the account were correct."

My stomach sank, *please don't tell me this money is tracked by the goddamn CIA.* "It's fine," I muttered.

"Because there is quite a substantial amount of money in this account and I wanted to make certain you were who you said you were."

Quite a substantial amount? "How much are we talking about here?"

"Fifty million dollars."

My knees trembled. "What!"

"The amount, Ms. Castlemaine. It's just a little over fifty million, three hundred thousand."

"Jesus." I reached out and braced myself on the desk. "Are you sure?"

Tobias glanced my way, scowled, then scanned the cafe.

"Yes, ma'am. Did you need me to repeat that number again?"

Yes. "No," I murmured. "And I can take out that amount whenever I want?"

"Well, there are procedures we'd need to put into place. We only keep a certain amount of funds at the bank at any given time."

But my mind was already drifting, not even processing what she was saying. "That's fine. I appreciate your help." She was still talking when I lowered the phone and ended the call.

Tobias, watching me from across the room, came closer. "Everything okay?"

For a second, I couldn't speak, then I slowly nodded and lifted my gaze to his. "Holy shit, T."

His brow creased deeply, but there was a twitch in the corners of his lips. "I take it that's a good *holy shit?*"

My hands were shaking when I handed his phone back to him. "Let's just say that if Nick has the rest of our lives covered, then I've got the next two, as well."

His brows shot up with a look of surprise. "Jesus."

I gave a laugh, glanced around the empty store, and picked up the coffee he'd bought me, then I took a sip, not that I needed the extra rush. "I guess we need to get back."

"I guess we should." He looked at me strangely, then laughed, grabbed my hand, and hauled me toward the door.

By the time we'd made it across the street, the idiot beside me was beaming. "I think I'm going to start my Christmas list early this year."

I shot him a glare. "Oh, yeah?"

"Yeah, little mouse." He turned that grin to me and my heart fluttered with the look, right before he lowered his gaze to my breasts. "You owe me."

I bit the insides of my cheeks to stop from laughing and turned back to the others as Nick and Caleb strode away from a salesman, Nick with a set of keys to a brand new truck in his hand.

"Our sister has something she wants to tell you." T broke the news first.

I gave him a playful punch to the ribs, one that made him wince. He was covered with bruises. We all were battered and beaten, but still alive...and now, now we had the means and the determination to survive.

"Oh, yeah?" Nick scanned the street behind me then brushed his thumb along my cheek, staring down into my eyes. "You have something to tell us, princess?"

My heart thrummed at his stare. I wasn't just falling in love with my brothers anymore. I was plunging headlong into an abyss that had no bottom.

"Ryth?" Caleb murmured, stepping closer. Concern flared in his voice. "What is it?"

I swallowed and licked my lips. "Dad has left me a substantial amount of money."

"He has?" Nick glanced across the street to the cafe. "That's what you were doing?"

I nodded.

"When you say substantial, how much are we talking here?"

"Fifty million dollars," I whispered.

They said nothing.

I don't think they even breathed.

Even Nick's brows rose at the sum.

"Damn," T muttered. "Now I really am going to need to work on that Christmas list."

But Nick shook his head. "No, you won't. Because we're not touching that money."

Confusion flared and mingled with anger. "Why?"

Nick moved closer, slid his hand around to cup the back of my neck, and tilted my head up to him. "Because that's *your* money, princess.

Your money your father left you. He wanted you to have a way out in case you needed it, so that's what it's going to be, *your* way out."

A pang of pain cut through my chest. All I could hear was his words when he'd told me one day I'd want more. But even though the pain took hold, I saw the desperation in his eyes. He wanted me to be strong, to be careful. He wanted me to be safe…and this was his way of doing that, of making sure that I was never dependent on anyone else again for the rest of my life.

"So you keep that information somewhere safe. I'll get you a new phone at the next stop and we can set you up with a One Password account. How's that sound?"

"Then all we need to do is find a place to live." I stared into his eyes.

"Speaking of…" Tobias muttered as he reached into his pocket and pulled out a brochure he'd somehow stashed away. "I found this."

He handed the folded brochure over to Nick. All I saw was green…and the most stunning mountains I'd ever seen in my life as Nick released my neck and took the paper.

"Apparently, it's a new town and new community. It says *'We pride ourselves on protection and privacy'*. They're calling it—"

"Tutum?" Nick muttered.

"Safe." Caleb's voice made us all turn toward him. He met our stares and motioned his head to the brochure in Nick's hand. "My Latin is a little rusty, but I'm pretty certain it means *safe*."

Tobias grabbed his phone and punched in the details. "Yeah, you're right. So, what do you think?"

The view of the mountains alone was enough to make excitement soar inside me.

"Then it looks like we're heading to Tutum," Nick muttered. "We look, if we don't like it, then we move on, okay?"

I nodded, knowing in my heart we weren't just going to like it...*we were going to love it.*

Epilogue

VIVIENNE

"*Wait!*" I cried, watching Ryth and her brothers drive away.

Agony tore through my chest as they accelerated hard, then braked to a stop. My heart hammered, taking flight for a second as the driver's door opened. But they hadn't stopped for me. A dog came tearing around the corner of the building, limping as she ran, until she leaped through the door and disappeared into the car.

Then they left in a hail of bullets.

But I didn't get to say goodbye. Tears shimmered in my eyes as London grabbed my arm and hauled me backwards, barking orders at his sons as the roller door closed.

"We can't be seen!" London roared, his stare merciless as he glared at his sons. "You understand that?"

The blond asshole lifted his phone, pressed an icon, and started speaking, giving commands as we were pushed toward the back of the building.

"One wrong move," London warned Ryth's father. "And I'll have them killed before they reach the city limits."

There was a flare of anger in Jack Castlemaine's eyes. His hands fisted at his sides. For a second, I thought he was going to lunge and take London to the floor. I didn't know what I'd do if that happened. But I never got a chance to find out. He glanced my way, then leashed that anger inside as the growl of a car's engine sounded close to the door where we stood.

Gunfire cracked out, the sound so loud it was deafening. I lifted my hands to cover my ears, but I didn't have a chance to shield myself before London grabbed my arm, his grip cruel as he pushed me toward the door as it swung inward and a man wearing a black vest and carrying an automatic rifle stepped in and looked at London. "My men are holding them back. We move now."

A quick nod, and London drove me forward, out the door and toward the waiting car. Jack followed closely behind, guiding me to the open car door. Everything happened in a hail of bullets and guttural screams. I was virtually thrown across the seat of the Explorer. Rough hands pushed me forward until I fell to the floor of the car.

He was on top of me in an instant, his arms over my head, his body a heavy weight on mine. "Stay the fuck down, Vivienne," London snarled as the car doors were slammed shut behind us.

I didn't dare move. Tires howled, but I barely shifted as the car hurtled backwards, then spun before surging forward once more.

Oh, God...oh, God...oh, God...oh, God.

The back window shattered. London's guttural roar filled my ears as he crushed me further down, shielding me, then we were gone, leaving the fierce sounds of the battle behind.

Harsh, panting breaths filled my ears, until London suddenly realized we were out of there. He lifted his head and the rush of his breaths faded.

"Are you hurt?" I couldn't move for a second, until London grabbed my chin, forcing my gaze to his. "Are...you...hurt?"

I shook my head, leaving him to glance at Jack, hunkered low in front of the seat and curled against the door.

"I'm fine," Jack answered, driving himself up enough to peek over the rear of the seat and through the shattered window. "Just fucking fine."

"Jesus." London rose, pushing hard against me to climb onto the seat.

But he didn't drag me with him. No, instead he looked down, staring at me like this is where I belonged...*at his feet*.

The red mark of my hand still burned on his face. I couldn't look away, couldn't breathe, just stared at him as the car sped through the city and we turned, braked hard, and came to a stop.

The driver's door opened, and barely a second later, Jack's door followed suit.

"Out," London commanded.

I shoved upwards as Jack was hauled out. "Wait!" I screamed. *"Wait!"*

But London's man didn't even slow, just pulled him toward another car that was waiting. There was panic in Jack's eyes, real, terrified panic. I didn't care what he'd done, didn't care what he represented. All I knew was that he was my one connection to Ryth...other than the bastard who held her life in the balance.

"Vivienne!" London roared as I scurried after him.

"Wait!" I grabbed Jack's arm, trying my best to break the driver's hold.

"Vivienne." Jack shook his head and murmured, "Don't, save yourself. Protect yourself. Do whatever you need to do to stay alive...this is only the beginning."

Then he was ripped away from me and dragged toward one of the two waiting cars. I stood there, watching as they pushed him into the back of the car, then closed the door and drove away... leaving London and me behind. I spun, glaring at him. "What are you going to do with him?"

But London didn't answer. He stalked closer, that savage goddamn stare trapping mine. I stepped backwards as the door to a sleek Lexus opened.

"In the car, Vivienne," London commanded.

Do whatever you need to do to stay alive. Jack's words came back to me as I turned around, defeated, and climbed into the passenger side back seat. The door closed with a *thud.* London spoke to the driver and as I watched the man nod, I realized just how powerful my captor was.

He didn't just own the camera feeds in someone's private home.

He didn't just command an army of hitmen to stop The Order in their tracks.

He didn't just hold Ryth and her brothers' lives in the palm of his hand...

But he did all those things...without a flicker of concern.

As I watched London turn and walk around the front of the car to climb in beside me, I realized how dangerous the man was.

He closed the door, started the engine, and put the car into reverse.

I didn't speak, didn't say a word. Cold fear moved through me as I stared at the crimson mark on his cheek. We drove in silence as he made our way back to the house. It felt like an eternity since we'd left...an eternity of terror. My ears were still ringing when we pulled into the driveway and waited for the garage door to rise before he parked inside.

I waited as he killed the engine and climbed out. In the harsh wash of the garage lights, London waited, standing at the front of the car. Without a command, I slowly climbed out and shoved the door closed behind me, keeping him in my sights I walked toward the door to the house.

I could run...but how far would that get me?

London stalked me like a predator and the heavy thud of his steps incited panic inside. I barely made it inside before his steps quickened.

"Wait!" I spun and shoved my hand outwards, stepping backwards toward the stairs. "I..."

I tried to think of something to stop him...but there was no going back. Not now. Not after what had happened. My heel hit the first stair, pitching me backwards. My nails buckled as I caught my fall, until I slipped, hitting the stairs hard.

I lay there while London loomed over me. "The contract," I pleaded. "The contract."

His lips curled and that bestial gleam sparked in his eyes as he lunged, caged my throat with his grip, and snarled, "Fuck the contract."

Then he kissed me...hard.

. . .

WANT MORE? *I've written a special scene 6 months later with Ryth & the guys just for you* ♥ *here.*

Preorder Owned here

She's one defiant, forbidden, pain in my as*.

One I can't touch.

One I can't train.

But Vivienne is mine. Body. Soul…

And most importantly, her bloodline.

None of them understand how important she is.

But I know.

My sons and I will protect that information - her - to the death to keep it for ourselves.

So, she'll remain here, under my roof...obeying my rules.

Resisting me at every goddamn opportunity.

Playing her defiant little games with our control.

Until I find my resolve slipping.

I'm cold, calculating.

But I'm a man who finds himself becoming obsessed with her.

And I'm not the only one.

I see the hunger in my son's eyes.

See the way they react around her.

She won't be wearing red for us...

Because she won't be wearing anything at all.

I'll take her downstairs...and show her exactly who is in control here.

I'll show her what it's like to be owned...

Printed in the USA
CPSIA information can be obtained
at www.ICGtesting.com
LVHW042319151223
766286LV00056B/92